What Love Sees

A Biographical Novel

Susan Vreeland

Copyright

To

Jean Treadway Holly

Contents

A Wedding Toast

St. John tells how, at Cana's wedding feast,
The water-pots poured wine in such amount
That by his sober count
There were a hundred gallons at the least.

> It made no earthly sense, unless to show
> How whatsoever love elects to bless
> Brims to a sweet excess
> That can without depletion overflow.

Which is to say that what love sees is true;
That the world's fullness is not made but found.
Life hungers to abound
And pour its plenty out for such as you.

> Now, if your loves will lend an ear to mine,
> I toast you both, good son and dear new daughter.
> May you not lack for water,
> And may that water smack of Cana's wine.

—Richard Wilbur

Prologue

I suppose I am in love with sound—loons, cathedral organs, opera arias, mooing cows. Even bickering children have their appeal and the lonely drip of rain from drain pipes that I hear now. It doesn't matter whether sounds are elegant or harsh. I love them all. Sound is not denied me.

Father couldn't understand why I shut him up during his last visit west when a killdeer trilled a holy melody right outside the kitchen window. I think he was just shocked because I told him to be quiet. I didn't used to do that. In the years when I was really his daughter, I would no more have thought to shut him up than to stop the dawn.

I don't remember what he looked like. I think he may have had a high forehead and square jaw, but that doesn't tell much. His voice always told me more, that deep-throated resonance that spoke his disapproval with a grunt. Mother's disapproval was kinder, yet I never felt I knew her as I knew Father. Eventually their faces faded into mistiness. They came to be voices only, that and the scents of pipe smoke and rose cologne. Mother taught me restraint; Father, patience.

I came home to Hickory Hill, to that enormous Georgian brick house where I grew up, to hallow the death of a parent. What I felt was not so much sorrow at Father's death—he lived as he wished to, the manager of the tiny universe of our family—as wonder at my own life. For all your life you have a father, an inexorable tie to home and origins. And then one day he vanishes. All that you have become, because or in spite of those origins, is thrown at you and a deep voice says, "Here, take yourself. Proceed alone. You are free." And then, piece by piece, you put his words to rest.

The house was colder than I remembered it, and footsteps echoed as they do in museums. I walked the whole house, my fingers trailing over the one grand piano left from a pair, and then the cold iron rail of the staircase, not that I needed to feel my way. I leaned out my old bedroom window to breathe the roses from the terrace below but smelled only earth sodden by November rain. I went back downstairs.

If Father had been poor, I'd have grown up faster. Since I couldn't quite decide which of two events lurched me from childhood into adulthood—returning home from Harkness Hospital or leaving home for good—both battled for attention as I stood in Father's wood paneled library utterly empty without his pipe smoke. Here he had taught me to be a stoic, even before I knew the word. Privately I knew how to cry, but not to scream. Too public.

Father, what color was your hair?

Chapter One

1930

"Keep your head still, Jean."

"I am."

That seemed to be the only sentence anybody ever said to her. They didn't know how hard it was. With her eyes bandaged for months, there was nothing to do. Nothing to look at. The door, window, dresser, everything in that blank hospital room swam vaguely in her memory. The sandbags on both sides of her head felt hot and her back hurt from lying in bed all day.

She wished Lucy were here. Back home months before, the day her doctor told her she had to keep her head still, her younger sister Lucy read the Sunday funnies to her all afternoon until they could get her to the hospital. She even described what the characters were doing—Andy Gump, and Orphan Annie with her saucer no-eyes.

Once, years earlier, before she was old enough to read the comics, some older kid laughed at her and said, "Those stupid glasses make you look like Orphan Annie." She had them since she was two and was afraid not to wear them. Both of her brothers wore glasses, too. Later, when she saw Orphan Annie in the comics for the first time, those round white eyes shot off the page at her and she hated Annie and turned the page to Mutt and Jeff so quickly she ripped it. But she was curious and the next Sunday she forced herself look at Annie's eyes for a long time, until she got used to them. Almost anything was bearable if you got used to it, Mother always said, so she looked for Annie each week. She discovered Annie wasn't scared of anything and she did exciting things, maybe because she was an orphan. Eventually, Annie became her favorite. Jean did look a little like her, she guessed, because her hair was curly too, but not red like Annie's. Just plain brown. In bed in the hospital, she wondered what Annie did this week, but Lucy probably wasn't going to come, so she wouldn't know.

Most of the time Lucy didn't visit with Mother and Father. And even they could only come from Connecticut to New York on Sundays. When they were here, she felt a little like she were back home at Hickory Hill. It wasn't anything Mother and Father said or did when they were here. All they could do was sit in the room. Mother talked about Jean's brothers, and Father talked about Babe Ruth and Lou Gehrig. It was Father's pipe smoke that made her feel homey. It smelled like cherries and burning leaves, and for the hour they were there, she didn't breathe the ether of the hospital.

"Did you read the funnies this morning, Father?" she asked the last time they came, but she didn't really think he had.

"No."

"Nurse Williams said that last week Annie sold pencils on the street next to a man who was selling apples. Did you see any real people selling pencils?"

"Where?"

"Outside on the street. Miss Williams said it's true—that men are selling things in the streets and people are standing in lines for soup."

"We didn't see any near here, but there are some." Mother's voice got softer. "Some people are having a hard time."

That last visit was over so fast. Father didn't even touch her when he said goodbye. He just said, "Keep your head still, Jean."

How many times a day did she hear it? Even in the middle of the night she heard it. Last month for her twelfth birthday Father and Mother had brought her a chiming clock, made by the Ingraham Clock Company, the business Mother's family owned. There was a button she could push on the left side and it would chime the hours. The button on the right side chimed the minutes. It sounded musical and the last note always echoed. Once she woke up in the middle of the night and wondered what time it was. Still lying on her back, she slithered her hand sideways out of the covers and found the left button. Three chimes sounded, but before she could find the other button, she heard, "Jean, keep your head still." Right in the middle of the night! Sometimes she wanted just to tell everybody never to say it again, that she was trying as hard as she could.

One other sentence echoed with it in her mind every so often, but that was her own: if it doesn't work. That sentence, she never knew how to end. Keep your head still…but if it doesn't work. The words battered at her in a nightmare that never ended. She'd already lost sight in one eye, two years earlier, from inherited causes, Dr. Wheeler had said. This would be different. She tried not to think about it, but couldn't help it. There was nothing else to do.

If it didn't work, and she'd never see again, what would it be like? Would her friends still want to be with her? What about Sybil? Would they ever go out to that secret place behind the mulberry tree in Sybil's back yard to smoke? She remembered and it made her happy, but she wasn't even supposed to smile. It might disturb her eyes. She and Sybil used to find horse chestnuts and dig out the insides with a knife in order to stuff them with withered grape leaves. Then they'd poke a hole in the side and wedge in a thick, hollow spaghetti. If they were careful and the spaghetti didn't break, they'd light it. It tasted terrible, but it made a lot of great smoke. It was better than smoking corn silk wrapped in *The Bristol Press* with her brother Bill. That just tasted like burning paper.

She could still do that even if, well, if she couldn't do other things. And if the operation didn't work, she could still go to dancing school. Maybe. But would Don or Bobby ask her to dance? The thought jabbed at her. What would happen when they played Truth, Dare or Consequences? Would they kiss her behind the pillow like they'd done before, both of them? She liked Bobby. Once he brought wild pink arbutus to her from the woods on the Hill—they smelled like spring—and he was the first one to write in the scrapbook her class sent her on her twelfth birthday. She remembered part of his poem:

If wishes were horses

I'd take a long ride

Down to New York

To be by your side.

That was nice. There was more of it, too, which she couldn't remember no matter how hard she tried, and the nurses were too busy to read it to her again. Bobby seemed older than the others to write that. Well, she could still climb the apple tree with him if he dared her to.

But if it didn't work, that is, if she couldn't see, she wasn't sure about climbing onto the roof. It was three stories up. She hadn't been afraid at all before. She'd done it lots of times. It was exciting. "I dare you to touch the lightning rod," she'd whisper to Bill at breakfast. He was a year older.

"Dares go first."

Just what she was waiting for. They'd climb out Bill and Mort Junior's bedroom window to the second floor terrace roof. That was gravel and flat—easy. Then they'd hoist themselves onto the steep slate part and go up higher, to the third floor dormer windows. She remembered how the soles of her feet throbbed when she sidestepped across the pointy peak of the roof out to the edge to reach the lightning rod, but that didn't matter. She would do it anyway, usually even before Bill would. Mort was too old. It wasn't any fun to dare him. If Father ever found out, they'd get a tongue-lashing. Now, even Bill probably wouldn't dare her any more. She took a deep breath and let it out slowly.

She remembered how free it felt way up there, level with the top branches of the hickory trees in the woods. Hickory Hill, their house, was almost at the top of Federal Hill which everyone in the neighborhood simply called "the Hill." From the roof she could see the grass triangle of Federal Hill Green where she went to school. She could see into the town of Bristol, to Father's gray stone bank and the high school, but she couldn't quite see the industrial part of town by the river or Horton Manufacturing Company, the factory Father owned. When she was up on the roof, she felt like a bird, or at least like she wanted to be a bird. Not forever, just for a while. It would be nice now, she thought. Birds could move their heads. They could go anywhere.

Except Chanteur couldn't. Poor Chanteur was in a cage next to her, the only thing in the room that seemed real. She knew everything the canary could sing, the short little chirps that sounded like he was practicing scales. Then there were lyrical passages that reminded her of "Greensleeves." She wondered what Chanteur looked like. Maybe she'd never see him. She had to find out. That was all, she just had to.

The hospital seemed quieter than usual. No one had walked by in the hall for a long time. If she were quiet, maybe no one would discover her moving around. She lifted the covers and slowly swung her legs out over the edge of the bed. Her heart beat so hard it made her chest and throat bounce. She slid down carefully until her toes touched the floor. It felt like cold stone. With her hands in front of her, she edged toward the bird's song, trying to keep her head very still. The room was smaller than she remembered so her foot rammed into the table leg and shook the cage. The bird stopped singing.

"It's okay, Chanteur," she whispered. "I won't hurt you." Her hands sought the door of the wire cage and opened it. She reached inside and he started flapping around. Feathers brushed by. Probably his tail. Not very soft at all. His body would be softer. She moved her hand to the left. Wings flapped. Tiny claws scraped across the back of her hand to the right. She went right. The bird let out a screech. She drew in her breath. "I won't hurt," she cooed again. She kept her hand still. Maybe he would calm down and stand on her finger. Nothing happened. She closed the cage door and picked her way back to bed, her heart thumping.

"What's all that racket?" Nurse Williams asked at the doorway. "You've been out of bed again, Jean Treadway, I just know it."

"Who, me?"

"You've been moving your head, bothering that bird again, haven't you?"

"No, I wouldn't hurt him. He's my yellow music box."

"Yellow? That bird's not yellow."

"I thought all canaries were. What color is he?"

"Kind of a blue-gray."

It wasn't an important thing, but it shocked her. She couldn't assume anything anymore.

Another patient, Mrs. Whitelaw-Reid, whose husband owned some big New York newspaper, gave her the canary. It didn't occur to her then to ask what color it was, but later when Mrs. Whitelaw-Reid gave her a fluffy comforter for her birthday, she asked what that looked like. Comforters could be any color. "It has yellow flowers on a white background," Mrs. Whitelaw-Reid said in a voice that reminded her of a clarinet. Now Jean wondered whether this lady looked as soft as she sounded. Or maybe she was big and mean-looking and only sounded sweet. How was she to be sure of anything?

A few weeks earlier, after Jean's second operation, Mrs. Whitelaw-Reid bought her a typewriter. It was such a big gift she didn't know how to respond. What did Mrs. Whitelaw-Reid know that would make her give her a typewriter? It made a hollow feeling in her stomach.

After four months in Harkness Hospital, Dr. Wheeler told her it was time to take the bandages off again. The first time hadn't worked. In fact, it was worse. Everything looked all slanty and it made her dizzy, so they had to do it over.

"Finally," she said. "Now can I sit up and move my head?"

Dr. Wheeler chuckled. "Yes, Jean, that's what it means."

That was the last time he chuckled that day. All during the tests he kept asking her, "How many fingers can you see?" Then he just asked, "Can you see my fingers?" Then, "What can you see?"

"Just light and dark. Shadows moving."

He was quiet for a long time. She felt her breathing come in waves. It seemed the only thing she was sure of. "What are you doing?" she asked.

"Writing." He sat down on her bed and took her hand. "Jean, I don't like having to tell you this, but I don't think we can do any better. I'm sorry. The retina wasn't just detached. It was torn, too. That probably happened when you fell off that horse. It just made things worse. Right now we just don't know enough yet about retinas to repair it."

Her throat clamped shut so that she couldn't speak. She felt numb.

"If you could have waited a few more years to have your trouble, I might have been able to do more for you." His voice sounded tired, kinder than father's, and the words hung in the air in front of her, strange and hollow, like the echo of a great bell.

"You mean I won't be able to see, not ever?"

"I don't think so."

She had wondered how he might say it to her and now here it was, just like that: "I don't think we can do any better. I'm sorry." So it happened? It's over? That's it? Me? Me. He's talking to me. She couldn't swallow.

What if she hadn't moved her head? Or gotten out of bed? Would it have made a difference? She had to know. Her lips felt dry and she moistened them but she still couldn't ask. She didn't want him angry with her.

He just sat there without moving, his weight making her bed dip down. Her hand grew hot and sticky in his and she pulled it away. In the quiet she felt his helplessness cross the space between them, a feeling entirely new to her, and she understood that he was genuinely sad. For an instant everything else slid away and she felt sorry for him because he had to tell her he had failed.

"I've seen a lot already. Twelve years." Then it all rushed at her. She felt her bottom lip quiver, her eyes water, and she turned away. Why wouldn't he just go away so she could cry or scream or do something—she didn't know what. She held tight onto herself until she felt him get up from the bed.

How was she to know when she was actually alone? Anybody could be walking by the doorway. She didn't always hear their footsteps. It was like she still had the bandages on. Nothing seemed real. Not even this.

After a while there were muffled voices in the corridor. She strained to listen.

"I can't believe it. She didn't cry or anything when he told her. Just sat there like a stone statue."

"What did you expect?" That was Nurse Williams. "You don't really know her defeat just because she doesn't scream it. Let her be discreet about her grief. It's the New England way."

She felt watched. She slumped down in bed and pulled the covers over her head.

What did they expect? Screaming? Father would expect self-control. Just like his own. And Mother? Mother always said there was a reason for not expressing things that hurt. There might be less to feel. Maybe she could crowd it out by knowing she had behaved well.

What this would do to her life, she was afraid to guess. She could still go to dancing school. But why? Bobby and Don wouldn't ask her to dance, now. She felt stifled and shoved down the covers. Well, she could still go skating on the pond. You don't need a partner to skate. And if somebody helped her, she could still climb the apple tree. But she was never going down Kelly's Hill on a ripper again, or even on a sled. That was too scary even when she could see.

Some things wouldn't change. She still wanted to smoke in secret, that was sure, but with real cigarettes. She would ask Tready. Cousin Tready was a year older and she smoked Old Golds that she snitched from her father. She would ask her. Play cigarettes were kid things anyway, and kid things seemed foolish to her now.

That night, Nurse Williams kissed her goodnight and it shocked her. Miss Williams' fuzz on her lip tickled. She must have a moustache. The thought made her cry a little there, right in front of her.

"Now you try to go right to sleep, Jean."

"Was it sunny or cloudy today?"

"A little cloudy. Why?"

"Oh, nothing." She pulled the covers up under her chin. "Good night."

She wondered if the last day she had seen was sunny or cloudy. She wished she knew, but she couldn't remember. It was horrible that she couldn't remember.

When Father and Mother brought her to Harkness in the cushiony back seat of the Packard limousine five months earlier, it was fall. Then she could still see enough to know that Connecticut was blazing with orange and gold. Mother kept saying, "Look at the trees, Jean. Just look at those trees." She wished she had.

Now, a month after Dr. Wheeler took the bandages off, she rode home with her canary and cage wrapped in blankets on her right and her typewriter in its bulky case on her left. "It's snowing a little," Mother said. She heard her mother's voice as if for the first time. The words fell delicately, just like the downy whiteness she imagined falling along the roadside. She didn't answer. She was studying a new alphabet. Her fingers inched across a stiff, perforated page.

Bobby still brought her flowers and she tried to do things with Sybil but she felt awkward, young and old at the same time. It was embarrassing to ask to be with her, like she was asking for a favor. Instead, she spent her time learning to type and to read the six-dot Braille cell. In a way she had not expected, the world was new again. Home was still cozy, but different. The terrace roses below her bedroom window smelled sharper. The Ingraham family clocks chimed louder and reverberated longer. A bronze statue of Nathan Hale stood on a pedestal in the library. That first winter she noticed how cold the bronze was. When summer came the figure attracted the heat from the bay window and she could barely touch him.

But the world was smaller than ever before. It consisted almost entirely of Hickory Hill. From the moment she arrived home, not a piece of furniture was ever moved. Her first need, Nurse Williams told her, was to relearn home, to sense the length of the staircases, the route from her bed to the bathroom, the distance from the twin grand pianos at one end of the living room to the fireplace at the other. It was forty feet, but how much did forty feet feel like? She paced it off. The polished wood of her piano felt smooth and cool. She held her hands in front of her and walked until her toes touched something hard. She smelled ashes and reached forward and felt the wood paneling of the fireplace.

She remembered the first time Father had shown them the new house six years earlier. On moving day she and Lucy raced their brothers across that room and screamed when they beat the boys. Since then the living room had lost that spirit. Now it contained gentle conversation of Mother's reading club, teacups placed carefully in saucers, her own piano practice. No more races. No more screaming. Now the only laughter in the living room tinkled as in crystal goblets. It didn't roar. The sounds felt comfortable to her now.

The dining room, too, gave her a feeling of warmth. Whenever she walked in, she smelled flowers. Her place was at Mother's right so Mother could butter the toast and set it on her butter plate at breakfast. It would always be there. She could count on that. If something were missing, Mother would step on the buzzer under the Persian rug. Mary, chattering like a blue jay with Delia in the kitchen, would cut off the gossip mid-sentence when she slid around the Oriental screen into the room. It often amused Jean. She remembered how proper and serious Mary tried to look in her gray moire dress and white apron, and wished she knew what she had been talking about.

Father, always in a suit and tie, read the paper at breakfast. "You know that's discourteous, dear," Mother would say, but he read anyway, except when he was making announcements. Father always made announcements. "This summer we'll visit Aunt Anna in Switzerland," he'd say. Or, "I bought a farm yesterday, children. Now we'll always have fresh milk." Or, "Bill will apply to Yale next year." And then he'd go back to reading without saying another word.

Once, several months after coming back from Harkness, Jean reached for her milk but moved too quickly. Her glass tipped away from her and spilled before she could catch it. She gasped. Father's paper crackled and Mother sounded the kitchen buzzer.

"Why don't you watch what you're doing?" Father said.

"Mary, get something to wipe this up," Mother said, her voice calm. "She will. She'll be more careful next time."

"I'm sorry," Jean mumbled. How could he have said that? She knew why. It was nothing new. He wanted to treat her just like everyone else. Eventually, she learned to reach for her glass slowly, not quite walking her fingers across the table, more like gliding them while touching the tablecloth lightly.

One morning more than a year later, Chanteur was singing loudly right behind Father. "Can't even concentrate to read in here with that bird screeching."

She couldn't tell if he was serious or joking. "He sounds pretty, Father." She swallowed. She wasn't used to contradicting him.

"You like birds, don't you, Jean?" he said, less a question than an observation. "I think you'll like the camp we've chosen for you this summer. It's in Vermont and there'll be plenty of birds in the woods."

"Is it a camp for blind kids?"

"No. Just a girls' camp."

"Will Lucy go too?"

"No, she's going to Cape Cod."

"But how can I?"

"You will."

Then she heard him turn the page.

Camp? He hadn't even asked her.

Chapter Two

"I like to walk behind you, Jean," Icy said.

"Why?"

"I like to watch your feet pick out the path."

"Must look pretty silly."

"No. I just like to watch it. You've got small feet. They look like hands in mittens."

"Trying to find a pea." Her hand rested on Ellen's shoulder in front of her as the line of girls hiked through the woods. She felt the earth harden beneath her feet. That meant rocky ground might lie ahead. Time to concentrate more. She didn't think she walked much slower than the other girls, only more carefully and probably less gracefully. Walking was a matter of trust, different from the trust she felt toward people. It was more a dependence on herself, a trust in her own new awareness. If she didn't concentrate all the time to pick up the clues, she stumbled. And that, of course, was different than the others.

She heard twigs cracking under foot and the sound of dry branches scraping against someone's jacket. "Hold them out for that blind girl," someone up ahead told Ellen. It sounded awful, "that blind girl," as if she was something to stay away from, something that didn't have a name, as if just because she couldn't see that meant she couldn't hear either. A breeze made the skin on her arms tingle and she shivered. Birds chirped in the trees. "What kind of birds are those?" she asked.

"Robins and maybe wrens," Icy said. "Finches, too, I think. They make that high little chirp, fast, like old women gossiping."

"They sound like piccolos to me," said Jean. Suddenly, like a whip, a twig snapped across her face. "Ouch!" she cried. It stung and made her eye water. She gulped air and lost her footing, but stumbled ahead quickly in order to keep her hand on Ellen's shoulder.

"Sorry." Ellen's voice was breezy.

That word, so casual, stung her, too. She blinked her eyes and wiped away the wetness. This was the third time today. Why couldn't Ellen—or anybody—remember? Unless, of course, she let it happen on purpose. That was too awful to think—that people could be like that. Just let Ellen try walking through the woods blind and let's see what she does. It hurt to swallow. She tried to think about something else—about how the woods smelled fresh and piney. When Icy walked ahead of her, though, it never happened. She could relax more then. If only they were walking in a different order.

Off to the left she heard other voices. "Hi-lo inni minni kaka, um chow chow, oo pee wawa, ay-dee, ai-dee, oo-dee, you whooo?" The Camp Hanoum call. It sounded pretty silly, she had to admit, but kind of musical, too. She joined in when the girls in the line chorused back. The chattering up ahead increased, sign that two pathways merged.

"We'd better hurry," someone said, "or Luddy will be upset."

Mrs. Luddington gave a piano concert once a week and she didn't tolerate latecomers. Secretly, the girls looked forward to the big cry. Every week Miss Throstle, the singing teacher, sang the same soppy love song. They all mopped their eyes appreciatively each time and joined in on the chorus. By the last verse everyone was sobbing with their arms around each other. Not to miss this week's tears, they stepped up their pace.

"Jean, stop," said Icy from behind, grabbing her forearm to make her. "Listen." Arm in arm they stood immobile while the others went on ahead. A loon called far out on the lake. They both sucked in their breath and didn't move until they were sure it had finished.

"Doesn't it just give you the creepies?" Jean asked.

"Yeah, wonderful."

"Mysterious."

"Eerie."

"Spooky."

"Lonely," said Icy, stretching out the "o."

"He only knows a minor key. That's why he sounds so—haunting." Jean made her voice quaver on the last word. The air moved coolly through her hair and they stood together breathing-in the natural world.

"You know, Jeanie, when the wind blows, the under parts of the leaves turn up and they look all silvery."

"Which leaves?"

"Poplar, I think," Icy said, pulling her along.

To Jean, the concerts were the highlight of the week. On the way out to the barn she felt the last faint afternoon sunlight on her face and the spongy earth softening her footsteps. That told her they were in the clearing. Icy helped her over the stile and across the meadow. She stepped in a squishy spot and took a huge step afterward to avoid it with her other foot. Soon she heard girls talking. "We're at a big old barn," Icy told her the first time they'd come there. "It has wide double doors that open onto the meadow. It's kind of like a stage." Icy was good about describing things. They bunched up a mound of crunchy pine needles and settled in, smelling the woodsy, humid earth. A needle stuck Jean sharply and she sucked her finger.

Girls nearby burst into laughter, even though no one said anything. "What's so funny?" Jean asked.

The laughter died. "Oh, nothing."

She knew, though. Probably somebody did something funny or made a face, and explaining it was too much trouble. It wouldn't be funny anymore. That happened often. She let out a breath, drew her knees up under her chin and waited for the music.

That blind girl, she thought again.

She was glad to sit next to Icy. It felt as though she'd known her a long time.

Luddy announced she would begin with Brahms. Each week was a different composer. Luddy told the girls about the composers' lives so that Jean began to link the names with the music. There was something thrilling about hearing a piano outdoors, the notes mixing with the breeze and insect sounds.

That night in the musty canvas tent, the melody of Brahms' Lullaby played in her mind and mingled with the crickets. She thought of all the things they'd done this summer, how they stretched their days long into late northern sunsets to fit in so much—singing lessons, hikes in the woods, bird and plant identification, storytelling, swimming, boating, quiet afternoons weaving in the crafts center when the others were playing tennis. Weaving she could do. While she sat high at the big loom, the aroma of wool made heavy by the humid forest, her fingers moved over the tightly drawn warp and threw the shuttle. She could feel the patterns made by threads of different thicknesses. The weaving room was peaceful. She could relax for a while by herself and she didn't have to keep up with the others. She liked being with other girls, but sometimes it was nice to be alone. Tennis was a silly old game anyhow. Running around after a ball for a while and then what do you get? Nothing. But in the weaving room she was producing something, making a scarf for her dresser back home.

She rolled onto her side and her cot creaked. Her sleeping bag scraped against her sunburned knees. The scratchy tingle reminded her of how the sun beat down for three solid days on the river. Small price for the chance to be out in a canoe with the others. She had done her share of paddling, too. Her aching arms told her that. She liked the rhythmic sound of the paddle against water and the little forward thrust each time the water gurgled. For those nights on the trip they slept with their bedrolls right on the ground, the scent of night and leaves so clean it made her nostrils open enough to imagine she smelled the cold purity of the stars. It felt free and new and even a little wild. Probably wilder than Father thought she'd be. That pleased her oddly, and she relished the new sensation.

Near her, a cricket cried out urgently against the background of frogs. She heard Icy shift positions on the other cot.

"Icy, are you still awake?"

"A little."

"I can't sleep." She sighed. A breeze came through the open tent flap. "That cricket must be right in our tent."

"The frogs are having a competition," Icy mumbled. "Too many frogs to sleep."

"No. Too many thoughts." She lay still for a few moments listening to Icy breathe. "I can't believe I didn't want to come."

"Why didn't you? I couldn't think of anything else since last summer."

"Afraid." The word stood out alone against the night sounds and surprised her. She knew now she had been ready for what

the summer held. Father had been right. Camp Hanoum taught
her many things. Here she learned to love the natural world
however she could—through the feel of the rough bark of a
hickory, the smell of certain leaves crushed in her hand, the
honk of the last Canada geese heading north, the coolness of
lake water passing between her fingers. She had done most of
what the other girls did. She was even bitten by mosquitoes just
like everyone else.

"Did you get any new bites today?" she asked Icy.

"Yeah. Two or three."

"Me, too." Lake water lapped rhythmically against the shore
outside their tent. "Why do you think those girls still don't know
my name?"

Icy didn't say anything. Then she wiggled around on her cot.
"Do you really want to know?"

"Yes."

"Maybe it's because you don't look at them when they're
talking."

"What's that got to do with it?"

"You've got to turn your head toward anyone speaking. Let
people see on your face what you're thinking. That's what
everyone else does. Otherwise you look dull and uninterested
and nobody will want to talk to you."

It stunned her. No one in the last two years, not even Mother
or Lucy, her own sister, had thought to tell her that. She
wondered how she looked. She could remember her face a little,
kind of round with thin lips and brown eyes, but she couldn't
remember any expressions. She moved her face around, opened
her eyes wide, narrowed them to slits, smiled a little, then a lot,
drew her eyebrows together in what felt like a frown, stuck out
her lips in a pout, pulled them inward and tried to imagine what
she looked like.

Nobody else had to think about what their face looked like. This was just one more thing. Loons didn't know the difference between people. They sang just to sing. Sun and breezes touched them all. But people, they knew the difference, and not very many would she ever find, like Icy, who would get beyond that difference. So that was it. All her life, all the summers ahead, and the winters, she would have to work harder at just plain living.

Chapter Three

Jean opened her bedroom window wide. A slight breeze brushed the lace curtains against her bare arm. The sound of katydids meant the end of summer at Hickory Hill. It felt good to be home.

She gathered a monstrous pile of dirty clothes, almost everything from her suitcase, walked into the hallway and dumped it down the laundry chute. In the next room she heard Lucy laughing with Mary, one of the maids, a hefty Irish girl who Jean thought could scare an army. She knew Father and Mother didn't approve of their daughters getting friendly with the maids, but they did it anyway when Mother was away at the DAR, the Red Cross, or the Colonial Dames. The maids were fun. There was something real about them that made them different from Mother's friends.

"What's going on in there?" she asked.

"Oh Jean, you've got to hear this. It's a scream," Lucy said. "Tell her, Mary."

"Last weekend I went home to Hartford for a night," she began again in her husky voice. "It was raining hard, not a night for strolling. A man followed me when I went to the station and got on the same train as I did. When I got off, he did too. When I got on the bus, he got on and sat behind me again. I didn't dare look around, but I knew he was there. Then he got off at the same stop I did and walked behind me on the same streets."

"Weren't you scared?" Jean asked. "I'd be petrified." She faced in the direction of Mary's voice and tried to make her face show concern, as Icy had said.

"Of course, but by the time I got to my corner, I was just angry. I was going to teach this hooligan a lesson."

"How?" Consciously, she raised her eyebrows. It felt silly, but she had to do it.

"I folded up my umbrella and gave him a couple of whacks over the head that sent him sprawling. The next morning my neighbor Katy called in a tizzy and told me never to walk home from the bus alone at night again. She said her brother hadn't come home the night before. Some thug had walloped him and they found him passed out in the gutter on the corner."

They all laughed again, and Jean felt a smile come naturally. "Your life is one big adventure," she said.

She walked dreamily back to her room. The maids really lived. They were out there rubbing elbows with the world. If the universe consisted of Hickory Hill, Camp Hanoum and nothing else, she'd be supremely happy. But what about the rest of life? In a few weeks school would start and that meant struggle. She remembered what Bristol High looked like—dull gray stone with wide steps up to heavy double doors, like a prison or some dead museum. Absolutely forbidding. The old gray castle, everybody called it. It seemed like a fortress to her even when she could see it. Now it would be worse. Now she would have to go there. How could she ever be a part of it? If only Icy lived in Bristol.

One noon months later, the wooden-sided station wagon chugged up the hill from Bristol High. Girls packed inside crooned "Smoke Gets In Your Eyes."

"Everybody but you thinks Rudy Vallee's a lot better than Lanny Ross, Jean," said Louise Barnes, sitting next to her in the front seat.

"But have you ever heard Lanny Ross sing 'Moonlight and Roses?' I just swoon."

"You just have a crush on him."

"That's not true. His voice is divine."

"But that's all he's got. Rudy Vallee was a Yale man."

"So what?" Jean heard Henry stifle a laugh and it gave her courage. "That doesn't make any difference, does it, Henry?"

"Leave me out of this, girls. I'm just driving."

Father had taught Henry, their gardener, how to drive just so he could go down the long hill and across the Pequabuck River every day to bring Jean home for lunch. For Jean, walking both ways would have used up the whole lunch break. No one else at Bristol High got such service, so even the ritzy gang from the Hill all wanted a ride. Boys climbed in back, hung on to the running boards and jumped off when Henry got to their street. It was one time every day she could depend on for camaraderie.

The trip back to Bristol High after lunch would be another matter. Since Father had decided that she could walk that, she needed someone to walk with her. Every day she dreaded the pressure of finding someone to guide her back after lunch. Louise, the richest girl on the Hill, lived closest. "Will you walk back with me after lunch?" Jean asked her in a low voice.

"Oh, I can't today, Jean. Ken wants to walk me back."

It had been the same yesterday and the day before. Not just with Louise, but with all the Hill girls. Even Lucy had her own crowd. She wasn't just asking for someone to walk with. It was as though once a day she was asking for friendship. But friendship wasn't something you should have to ask for.

"I'll walk with you," a soft voice from the back seat offered. It was someone she didn't even know, a girl named Lorraine Dion who was eating lunch at her boyfriend's house on the Hill that day. The offer caught her off guard.

"Thanks." She couldn't figure it out. She'd heard that Lorraine lived across town, near the Irish section. Why wouldn't she want to walk back with her boyfriend, like Louise did? Jean felt odd, like she was being used for something. Maybe it made Lorraine feel important to be needed by someone on the Hill. Well, at least it took care of today.

The next morning before school Lorraine appeared at the front door. "I've come to walk Jean, I mean to walk with Jean to school," she said to Mary at the door. Jean couldn't understand it. Yesterday Lorraine hadn't mentioned she would come this morning. She wondered how far she'd walked already.

It was always awkward to walk with a new person the first few times. Lorraine cupped her hand under Jean's elbow, trying to steer her. Anybody could tell it wasn't working. It only made Jean's shoulder cramp up.

"It's better if you just bend your arm and I take hold," Jean said. At every curb Lorraine stopped abruptly and said, "Step down." Embarrassing. Why couldn't she be more subtle?

"You don't have to announce it. I can tell if you just slow down." After a while she added, "I know it's not easy walking with me. It's better when I don't have to carry this stupid case."

"What is it?"

"A typewriter."

"Why do you have to?"

"I need it both places, to take tests and do homework. The one I keep at home is being repaired." It banged against her knee when she stepped up onto a curb. She tried to keep it higher by bending her elbow, but it was heavy and her arm began to ache.

"Do you use it in class?"

"Uh-huh." Jean stopped and shifted it from one hand to the other and Lorraine walked around to take her other arm. "For tests. Oral ones. I have to type "y-e-s" if the statement's true, "n-o-period" if it's false."

"Why the period?"

"Three keys for every answer. The principal told me to. 'To prevent cheating by listening,' he said." Jean smirked. "He didn't have to worry. The poor guy who cheats off me will fail for sure."

"How do you study?"

"Oh, Mother reads the chapters to me and I just try to remember. Sometimes she hires people to read to me. There aren't any Braille textbooks. It doesn't work very well. I'm no sparkling student."

They talked in spurts with awkward pauses in between. They only had a few mutual friends. Finally, Jean asked what she'd been wondering. "How far did you walk this morning already?"

"From across the river."

"But that's near school. Why did you come way over here?"

"Just felt like it."

It didn't make any sense. Why couldn't someone she cared about walk with her instead of this person she didn't even know? It made her uncomfortable. If she had to feel dependent, it would be easier to feel dependent on someone she liked being with. Like Tready.

"Do you know my cousin, Mary Treadway?"

"No."

"I didn't think so. She's actually a year older but we're still in the same grade. They put two grades together in elementary school, so I skipped third. Anyway, she only lives a few blocks away. She can walk with me from now on."

Lorraine was quiet the rest of the way to the high school. Jean didn't talk either. She knew what she did was rude, cutting her off like that, but she didn't want Lorraine thinking she could be with her all the time. Lorraine wouldn't fit in with her friends. Too blah. None of the Hill crowd knew her.

Jean didn't hear much about her any more that year. If Lorraine rode in the station wagon with her boyfriend at lunch again, she didn't speak, so Jean didn't know if she was there.

Every day at lunch Jean switched off from one girl to another, making sure not to ask the same one twice in a row. When she couldn't get anyone else, Lucy or Tready walked with her. It'd be easier if she could always walk with Lucy. "Can't you just make Lucy do it?" Jean pleaded to Mother one day.

"That wouldn't be very fair," Mother said. "She has her own friends her age that she wants to be with."

"Can't Henry drive me back?"

"Well, Jean, he's got other work to do, and that's his lunch time."

Jean knew that wasn't the real reason. It was part of Mother's plan to help by not helping. "It will be good for you," Mother had said when high school started, "to talk to different girls while you're walking." Easy enough for her to talk to people, even strangers. But she wasn't asking them for any favors. She didn't know how embarrassing it was to have to ask every day for the same thing. Even Lucy couldn't possibly understand. Maybe Icy could, but Icy lived in Litchfield, and for the time being, they had to make their friendship survive on letters alone.

Each day had its share of problems at school, too. One student from each class was assigned to walk her to her seat in the next classroom. Sometimes the pull on her arm felt grudging and she wondered if the person's face showed it. By scattered dependencies she stumbled through her first two years. She did poorly in Latin her first year, switched to French her second and still didn't do well. Her third year she signed up for German.

Agnes Jennings taught German. She may have been American, she may have been Irish, but one thing was sure. She wasn't German. The German Jean heard sounded American. Miss Jennings held Jean after class the first day. "In a week or so, after I get to know the class, I'm going to pick someone to tutor you during study hall. You can go into the teacher's room and have the lesson read to you."

"Thank you. I'm sorry to cause a problem."

"It's not a problem. If I pick carefully, I think it will work."

Miss Jennings picked Lorraine Dion. Jean felt her cheeks flush hot when Miss Jennings told her. If Lorraine noticed, she didn't say anything. When Miss Jennings sent them out of the room to study together, Jean felt Lorraine's elbow touch her hand so she could hold on, instead of the awkward way she'd done it before. She had remembered all this time.

In their nervousness, they dug into the lesson as a safe relief. When they finished, there was still some of the hour left. "What made you decide to take German?" Lorraine asked.

Jean groaned. "I've already tried French but couldn't spell it. Those phoney old Frenchmen made up their language just to trap anyone who's never seen the endings of the words."

"Oh, I guess that would be hard."

"I could have just as well learned Chinese or even Egyptian with all those funny scratches."

"Yeah, at least German is spelled the way it sounds."

"I had the same trouble my first year in Latin."

"Anybody would with Klimke. He's a terror."

"Some people like him, though."

"They're the ones who are getting A's."

"He sounds so gruff. What's he look like?"

"Kind of chunky with a wild mop of white hair. Wears vests. Looks like a grandfather, or a college professor."

"Once he passed back a quiz, and I guess I did better than usual. He shouted in his big voice, right next to my desk, 'For heaven's sake, Jean. What did you eat for lunch yesterday? You got a 'B!' I nearly died. I probably got all red, and I didn't know whether to smile or scowl."

"What'd you do?"

"Just sort of folded up the paper. He didn't have to make a joke of it. Then when he handed out the grades at the end of the term, even though I passed, he said, loud, so everybody could hear, 'It would be better if you felt you didn't have to take Latin next year.' You can bet I didn't."

Jean was a little surprised at how comfortable she felt with Lorraine in spite of that awkwardness two years earlier. The voice coming across the table seemed so plain and natural. They worked through the lessons quickly and they both scored high on the tests.

One day late that fall when they got to the teachers' room, Lorraine asked, "What's wrong, Jean? You look upset."

Just what she hoped Lorraine wouldn't ask. She'd tried to hold her head down so no one would see. Her eyes were probably red and puffy. Lorraine's voice sounded kind. Maybe it was okay to tell her. "Is anybody else here?"

"No."

"The principal sent his secretary out to get me from my first class this morning."

"What did old pudding-face want?"

She laughed even though a moment earlier she was afraid she'd cry. "I'm excused from science and math."

"Lucky you! What's wrong with that?"

"Nothing, I guess, only the way it happened. Mr. Collins is my math teacher and he said, right in front of me, like I was a piece of furniture, 'Frankly, I can't see how she can ever learn math.' Only I was sitting right there. He could have at least talked *to* me instead of *about* me. I felt like telling him I'm not deaf or dead. Only blind."

"Did you?"

"No."

"You should have. Just because he's a teacher doesn't mean he knows everything. He's really the one that's blind."

Jean dipped her head. She wasn't sure whether the hard lump in her throat was because Mr. Collins was insensitive or because Lorraine was the opposite. She tried to think of something else to talk about. "Today in English Miss Fitzsimmons read another poem. We knew it was coming. She started like she always does, squeaking out, 'Here's yet another treasure from the literary giants of New England.'" Jean tried to mimic her. "It didn't make any difference. I still heard George Jameson snore behind me."

"He doesn't snore in German class."

"Of course not. There's more to Miss Jennings than Miss Fitzsimmons. Who can be afraid of a squeak? What's Miss Fitz look like, anyway?"

"Like a pencil. Her face is as tall as she is and her hair's turning gray. She's not very pretty."

"Too bad. I wonder if she'll always be Miss Fitzsimmons."

"Always? She's already an old maid, Jean."

"But she doesn't sound old. She just sounds small." It was another shocker, like her blue canary.

That winter Lorraine told her, "I'm going to learn how to write Braille."

"You are? Whatever for?"

"So I can Braille the German lit book for you. I got a punch and the right kind of paper and I signed up for lessons downtown."

Jean's mouth opened, but no words came out for a moment. She shook her head slightly and her eyebrows drew together. "But, Lorraine, it'll take you forever. You don't have to do that. Miss Jennings never expected that, and I don't."

"I know." Lorraine's voice sounded like a bird, so simple, as if what she was saying was as commonplace as saying "I caught a worm this morning."

Jean went home that day in a daze. No one had ever done anything that took so much time, just for her. Lorraine seemed suddenly older, even older than Tready. Maybe her plain home life had done it. Jean remembered Father talking about the Depression one evening and she wondered out loud how it would affect Lorraine.

"Destined to work on the line at the parts factory," he said. "Soon she'll be happy to spend days rolling ball bearings around on mirrors to detect flaws."

"Father!" she started, but as usual, didn't know how to counter him. He obviously knew more of the world than she did. "That's a horrible thing for Lorraine to have ahead of her."

"Why?"

"Because..." She felt her insides wither, felt his indifference, his superiority cross the dinner table between them. "Because she doesn't deserve that."

"The world doesn't hand out just what people deserve, Jean. You ought to know that."

She ought to know that. She ought to know that. That didn't make it right. Didn't make it so you couldn't care. But her throat dried and she couldn't say any more. Not to him.

Chapter Four

In the spring of 1934 Jean invited Lorraine to Hickory Hill for a Saturday. When she told her parents ahead of time, Mother said, "Well, I suppose that would be all right. She's done a lot to help you in class."

It was a comment with an edge sharp as Mother's cut crystal. Mother wouldn't have said it if she'd asked to have Louise Barnes visit.

As soon as Lorraine stepped in the front door, Jean could tell she was uneasy. "Two matching pianos! You didn't tell me you had two," Lorraine said, trailing close behind her through the house. "You have to walk a mile to get around anywhere in here. There could be lots of people in here and no one would know what anyone else was doing."

"Certainly not me," Jean said. "I always have to ask.

After Lorraine had gotten over her surprise and they had a snack, Lorraine played "Claire de Lune," the new piece she was studying. Jean loved it, a new person playing in her home.

On their way to the verandah and the pool, Jean smelled Father's pipe in the library and stopped at the doorway to introduce her. "You play beautifully," Father said.

"Thank you." Then she added in a breathy whisper, "Walls of books." Two walls, floor-to-ceiling, held leather-bound volumes. Lorraine's voice trailed off, reading. "Browning, Bronte, Cather, Dickens." She took a few steps further. "Stevenson, Thackeray, Turgenev. Just like a real library. Has anybody ever read them all?" Father chuckled.

"Mother reads aloud to me on Sunday afternoons and sometimes in the evenings," Jean said.

"That would take forever. I can't believe it. A whole room just for books."

"Oh, we do other things here, too." It pleased her that Lorraine liked the room, though she didn't have to make such a big deal of it. She thought of the evening cocktail hours with Father talking from his great cushy leather chair and Mother doing needlepoint by the fire. "We just live in here," she said. The chairs, lamps, Father's giant desk nestled in the bay window, they seemed to have taken root, just as the family traditions had, within the library's paneled walls. Because of that, the library was a holy place—the most private part, the core of the big house. She had grown up in its warming shelter. "It's cozy," she said simply, and shrugged. "Come on."

Jean walked ahead of Lorraine out to the verandah. The boxwood hedge surrounding the pool sent its fragrance across the water. It told her she was close to the edge. She took off her wrap, sat down on the coping and lowered herself in. It felt refreshing. Swimming was the ultimate in freedom, she thought, as she stretched and kicked and then began a lap. On the way back she asked, "Aren't you going to swim?"

"Oh, I don't know how. I'll just stand here in the water."

"You mean you never learned?"

"No, I guess not. I like watching you, though. Go ahead."

Jean did vigorous laps, reaching out for the pool wall just in time again and again. It was good to move so fast and energetically. The pool was the only place she could. In the water she was equal. Camp Hanoum had taught her that.

"How do you know when you're at the end?" Lorraine asked after she stopped. "You never bump yourself."

"Oh, sometimes I do. It's like the stairs. After a while, I just know."

In the evening they listened to music in Jean's bedroom and talked of Lorraine's two boyfriends.

"Which one do you like better?"

"Don, I guess."

"How come?"

"Mm, I guess it's because I talk to him more. It's just easier to be with him."

"I can't imagine what it would be like to have one boyfriend, much less two. I'd probably forget which one I'd said things to."

Lorraine let out a quick, two-note laugh. "That has happened. Sometimes I catch myself just in time."

Jean sighed. "That must be heavenly. Just so you don't forget which one you've done certain things with. Don't feel badly about this, but you sort of remind me of the maids. I mean, they really live, have men and adventures instead of, well, like me."

"But what about Andy?"

"That's nothing. I hardly know him."

"I heard he's taking you to the dance next week."

"Doesn't count. Someone arranged that."

"Who?"

"I don't know. Mother mentioned something once about his mother going to DAR, too, so I think it was the two of them. I could tell the moment he asked me. He sounded so formal and he cleared his throat first. What's he look like anyhow?"

"He's a dreamboat. He must be over six feet tall."

"I can tell that. His voice comes down from the ceiling."

"And he's blond. And he smiles. Well, the way he smiles is sort of like he knows you like to look at his smile, so he does it, just to make you happy."

"Won't move me."

"You'd know he was smiling. It's so warm it'd burn you if you stood close. He's everybody's dream hero, Jean. Just enjoy it."

Jean gave a sharp little grunt. "Let's go have some cocoa." She stood up and Lorraine followed her down the stairway. "The cook's upstairs, so we'll have the kitchen to ourselves. I really can't cook, but I can make cocoa. Delia taught me." She led Lorraine into the kitchen.

"Have you always had a cook?"

"As long as I can remember. Oh, sometimes Mother cooks on Delia's day off. Or on Sunday."

"And always a maid, too?"

"Usually we have an upstairs and a downstairs maid. Most of the help we've had are Irish. Mother gets them fresh from Europe and trains them. The first cook I can remember was Swedish. Amanda. She always wore a white cloth wound around her head, I don't know why, and she swore in Swedish whenever it came undone. I wish I could remember the words. They sounded cute, not bad or ugly at all. Then I could say them and nobody would know."

"Did you like her?"

"Yes, but I felt awful once."

"Why?"

"Lucy and I came in here one night for a snack and I smelled something rotting. Vegetables, I thought. I held my nose and burst out, 'What's that awful smell?' But it wasn't food at all. It was her feet. Lucy said she only had one pair of shoes and they were too small. She'd cut out the canvas tops, and her toes were lapping over the front edge. I just felt sick. I went back upstairs and didn't even eat what she gave me."

Jean felt along the edge of the counter for the row of ice box doors, opened the third one and stood in the coolness a long time before she found a milk bottle. She edged her way to the rack where pots and pans hung, holding her hands high as she sidestepped in front of them, then felt for the right sized pan and unhooked it.

"We've had Delia for years. Her pans are always greasy, but I like her. She scuffs around in some kind of felt slippers. See that dinner gong in the passageway?"

"Yes."

"You can make little melodies on it, like chimes on a pipe organ. When we got Delia, I showed her how to play a tune. It sounded lovely, but it only lasted a few days. After she stayed a while, she just gonged us to dinner. I think she must be 110 years old."

Jean poured in the milk. Then she felt her way to the pantry. "She's good, though. She always puts the cocoa and sugar right here on this shelf, level with my waist." Jean reached right for the two containers and set them on the counter. She felt for a spoon from the spoon drawer, found the cocoa tin again and dipped in the spoon, then touched the hollow of the spoon to make sure it was full. She dipped and touched four times, dropping the cocoa into the saucepan each time. Then she did the same with sugar. She stirred it tentatively and carried the saucepan to the stove. The task absorbed all her attention and for a moment, she didn't talk. She turned a knob and the far right burner ignited. She lost the pan a moment and had to sidestep along the counter until she found it. Then she put it on the burner. Odd, she didn't feel any heat yet.

She made her way to the cupboard, brought back two cups and saucers, then sat down at the kitchen table to wait for the cocoa to heat. Lorraine stopped talking. Jean heard her shift her weight in her chair. She scooted it back, then scooted it forward again.

"What's wrong?"

"I think you put the pan on the wrong burner."

A cloud descended, black as ever. "Oh." She moved haltingly when she stood up to change it. "No wonder I didn't feel the heat yet." She couldn't help her voice cracking.

They were quiet while the cocoa was heating. She heard Lorraine move in her chair again and wished she would say something. When the cocoa was ready, Jean brought it over to the kitchen table slowly. "It's good," said Lorraine. Jean's mouth made nervous little movements she couldn't control. She felt public, naked. It was as if she were a cripple and Lorraine had stepped into her bedroom uninvited when she was wrestling to get upright and out of bed.

"Don't feel bad, Jean. It's not so important. You always handle everything else so well." Jean warmed her hands around her cup and tipped her head down, as though she was looking at her cocoa. "In fact," Lorraine added, "I don't see how you do what you do."

Her voice sounded so earnest that Jean thought she had aged in the space of a few minutes. She didn't know what to say but wanted to talk more and about something else. "Lorraine."

"Yes."

"Why do you think Miss Jennings chose you to tutor me?"

"I'm not sure, but she lives near my aunt over on the other side of town, you know, by the river. I guess because of that, she knows my background a little. Maybe she thought it would be good for me, build up my confidence."

"I can't believe you need to feel better about yourself. You already have two boyfriends."

"That doesn't mean anything, really. I don't have the things I—the things you have, here. Not things exactly, but advantages. My family isn't like yours, Jean."

Jean took a sip of cocoa and felt it warm going down, felt its comfort. "You know, at the beginning of high school when you walked me to school, I didn't quite trust you. That was stupid of me. I mean, I didn't know why you were—"

"I know. It's okay."

"But why did you come all the way over here to walk with me?"

"I was curious, I guess. About how you did things. How you got along. It was just interesting to me. I thought it would be nice to have a friend who was different." Her voice became softer. "At the time I thought maybe you could come to need me. But actually, I guess I needed you." It was a courageous thing to say.

"Funny. I always felt I was the one who constantly needed someone else."

Jean felt Lorraine's arms around her. Something turned liquid inside her. She hadn't been hugged by anyone for a long time.

After a few moments Lorraine tapped her cup gently against the saucer. "Can I have some more cocoa?"

Chapter Five

Jean went to bed that night feeling a rare contentment, as if for those hours, in spite of the trouble with the cocoa, some burden had been temporarily lifted. She had grown to like Lorraine even though she wasn't part of the Hill. In fact, she felt more comfortable with her than with Louise Barnes or any of the Hill crowd except Tready.

It was puzzling. Cousin Tready had style, sophistication, and Lorraine obviously didn't. It occurred to her that she never really knew how Lorraine dressed. It probably wasn't stylish, like Tready. If it weren't for other people, she would enjoy being with Lorraine just as much, but Lorraine wasn't popular. Tready was. And fun, too. Anyone on the Hill could be sure a party would be lively if Tready would be there. And if Tready were invited, Jean probably would be, too.

It wasn't that Jean wasn't invited to Hill parties on her own. She was, sometimes, but she knew why. The girls' mothers made them ask her. She could tell when a voice carried the barely discernable off-key tone of obligation. She felt it as the sour taste of insincerity. What was worse, Mother made her go regardless of how the invitation was delivered. "It will be good for you, Jean." Good to feel like a wallflower, she often muttered to herself.

With Tready, though, she felt lighthearted acceptance. She could ask her anything, silly things that she'd never ask Lorraine. Lorraine would take them too seriously.

"Will you teach me how to put lipstick on?" she had asked Tready when she was fifteen. And Tready stood behind her in front of a mirror and pretended Jean's lips were her own.

"Tell me what I look like," she said when they were finished. "I mean compared to others."

"Well, your skin's clearer than a lot of other girls. And you're shorter than most, smaller too. Petite."

"Tell me honestly, Tready. Do I look like a goon in the clothes I wear?"

"Oh no, Jean. I'd tell you if you did."

"Am I, am I—?" Maybe her eyes made her awful looking.

"Are you what?"

"Am I average?"

"Better than that, silly. Stop worrying."

It had satisfied her some then, but now, two years later, she still wondered. Maybe she always would. Maybe that was just part of being a blind woman.

One Saturday toward the end of high school, Jean asked Tready to teach her how to iron a dress. "I'm almost eighteen years old and nearly out of high school and I still don't know. Every time I ask Mother, she just says, 'Oh, Jean, just let Mary do it. It's simpler.' So Mary gets more work and I can't practice. Will you?"

Tready let out a sigh. "It isn't hard. Even a dunce can do it. Okay. Someday."

"Let's do it now. It's Mary's day off." Armed with a dress already worn once, Jean led Tready to the laundry room.

"Well, let's see. The flat skirt part is the easiest. You just start there."

"In the middle?"

"No, I guess not. You start at the hemline. You can find that." Tready laid the dress on the ironing board and Jean explored it with her hands and found it two layers thick.

"I think I remember seeing something hanging down."

"Uh, I guess so. Sleeves or something. Then you work your way to the top, up to the collar. Then you go out and do the sleeves and end with the cuffs."

"Sounds wrong to me. Come on Tready, tell me. Have you ever ironed anything in your whole life?"

"Not a scrap."

"You ninny. Why didn't you say so? Move over. I think you start at the top."

Jean couldn't wait for an occasion to surprise everyone. On Mary's next day off, Jean picked a cotton shirtwaist from the pile of clean clothes and tried again, this time beginning at the collar. It was hot work, but her zeal was hotter. She burned herself twice trying to find the iron after she'd set it down. She wrestled with it for half an hour and when Delia gonged for dinner, Jean put it on and went downstairs.

"How do I look?"

"Fine," Mother said absently. A match struck against a matchbox.

She's lighting candles, Jean thought. She isn't even looking. "I ironed this dress myself," Jean announced in a voice bigger than normal.

"You what?" Lucy squawked.

"It looks lovely." Mother's voice was more direct.

Lucy didn't say another word. No one said anything for a few seconds. Even Mort stopped talking to Father about the stock market. Mother must be shooting everyone one of those don't-you-dare-say-a-word looks that she remembered from childhood. She tried to smooth out the skirt with her hands. It must look awful, but they aren't telling me. She sat down quickly next to Mort. After a few minutes he leaned over and whispered, "I'd be proud to have you as my date."

Eventually, Jean asked Tready the big question. "Will you teach me how to smoke? I don't mean just for play, like when we were kids, but smoothly." Learning to smoke, to hold a cigarette with utter casualness and still be careful—surely that would make her one of the Hill girls.

Her enthusiasm was tinged with nervousness. In the upstairs bathroom with the door closed, they sat down on the floor. They'd never done it in the house before. Tready lit a cigarette and put it between Jean's index and third fingers. "Hold your fingers straight and crook your wrist back, like this." Tready moved Jean's hand into position.

"Ouch. Why?"

"It looks better that way. More sophisticated."

Jean dragged on the cigarette and choked. "It still tastes brown."

"Brown?"

"Like dirt," she sputtered. "Awful."

"Don't inhale. I never inhale. Just take a little draw and blow it out."

"Jean drew in another time, cautiously, and blew out the smoke.

"Hey, don't aim for me, Jean. Blow the smoke up, not out."

"Sorry."

"People sometimes do it in a puff just before they're going to say something. It looks intellectual."

Jean tried it. "Like that?"

"Yeah. I don't know how you're going to know when to flick the ashes, though."

"I can remember every few minutes. How do I do that?"

"Tap it with your index finger after you've found the ashtray."

When they finished most of the cigarette, Jean put the butt in the toilet, opened the window and tried to wave out the smoke. They arrived late for cocktail hour in the library, a trail of cigarette smell following them.

"What have you two been doing?"

Father must know already. The tone in his voice told her that. "Smoking, Father," she said cheerily. Maybe he'd be impressed with simple honesty. His glare burned through the darkness. How did he find out so soon?

"I don't ever want you to smoke again until you're eighteen."

"Yes, Father."

But she did anyway, and swore Tready to secrecy.

Just before the end of the school year, after a session studying German in the teachers' room, Jean asked Lorraine if she smoked.

"I did once, with Don. But I didn't like it. Besides, I don't want to start an expensive habit."

It was an odd remark. Jean had never thought of smoking as something to do or not do because of money. Then Lorraine asked Jean to her home for a Sunday afternoon dinner to celebrate the end of high school. Lorraine had never invited her there before. In fact, she never even talked about her house. Maybe it wasn't an easy thing for her to do. Still, she said no.

There was a lawn party at Farmington Country Club the same Sunday and Tready was going. If Jean went with her, she could show the others that she was smoking now, too.

As soon as she and Tready got to the party, Louise Barnes drove up the sweeping driveway in her new Chevy roadster. "Graduation present from Pops," she said. "I had to have *some* way to get to Bryn Mawr."

"But it's too small," Tready teased. "After you pile all your clothes in there, you won't have any space for your golf clubs."

The boys swarmed around the car and lifted the hood to look at the engine, and no one noticed that Jean was smoking. Conversation swirled around her but nobody talked to her.

"Do you know where you're going yet, Cookie?" Tready asked.

"Skidmore. To study art. It'll be heavenly. Have you heard yet?"

"Yes, Sweetbriar."

"Where's that?"

"In Virginia."

"You'll come home talking like a southern belle on the arm of some handsome, slow-talking great-grandson of a confederate general, and poor Jack will be forgotten."

"Oh, don't worry about poor Jack. Poor Jack's headed for Harvard."

"Did you hear that Mavis got accepted at Knox? Her first choice. Because of the riding program."

Jean wished she could sink into the grass. She prayed she wouldn't have to say she hadn't been accepted anywhere. In fact, it looked like she didn't even have enough credits to graduate. The afternoon stretched long and her feet hurt, but she didn't know where a chair was and didn't want to call attention to herself by asking. High school ended with a fizzle.

That summer the Hill girls visiting the Treadway pool talked incessantly about college. Jean swam laps, climbed out at the far end of the pool and lay down out of earshot on the narrow strip of coping between the pool and the grass. The hot cement warmed her stomach and the sun dried her back. It was comforting. More than the water separated her from them. She'd never really be one of them, no matter what Father or Mother would do. She knew why Father had the pool built, so friends would come to visit her on her own home territory, where she could move freely. No other Hill family had a pool. Oh yes, Father could do a lot to build a nice little world for her here, but he couldn't get her admitted to a school.

It would be wonderful to be going away to school, to live with other girls, go to mixers at boys' schools, be out in the world, dance. She was a good dancer. Following somebody's lead was easy. A cloud went by and she felt gooseflesh on the back of her legs. Of course she'd have to study there, but that was okay. She could get along.

From across the water someone must have said something funny—she didn't know what—and the girls laughed. All their lives were expanding. Hers wasn't. Maybe never would. She turned her face in the opposite direction.

The next day a letter came from the Masters School in Dobbs Ferry. Mother had been writing to prep schools, finishing schools, universities, anywhere that might take her. Mother's voice fell when she read the response. "Although we realize that Jean Treadway would be an able candidate for our school, we regret that we are unable to accommodate a young lady in her position."

Why don't they just say it? Blind. She heard Mother fold up the letter and put it back in the envelope.

"Well, at least they were polite," Mother said flatly.

"Careful, I'd call it," Jean said. "Was that the last one?"

"The last I wrote to, but maybe an education editor of some magazine, *Vogue* maybe, would know of some smaller school that might be more flexible. I'll keep writing."

Jean wandered through the house and out to the verandah. The humidity hung heavy. Like time, she thought. She lifted her hair from the nape of her neck where it felt sticky. Then she let it flop down again and her shoulders sagged. She knew she was a problem now that high school was over. Of course she probably could go back to Bristol High. They hadn't given her a diploma so she hadn't officially graduated. No, that would be too humiliating. And she still wouldn't be able to do math and science. So here it was, the great family dilemma—what to do with Jean. She came back inside and sat at the piano. Her fingers touched the keys without purpose. She wondered what Lorraine was doing. Working, probably. And Icy. She hadn't seen her for ages.

Summer inched along. One evening she overheard the family in the library.

"Her life should be altered as little as possible."

"Father, you don't always have to make her life so normal," Lucy said. "I wish she could do something special."

A lump exploded in her throat. It was a brave thing to say to Father.

Toward the end of summer, Mother's voice was urgent when she read the return address, "Andrebrook, Tarrytown-on-Hudson, New York."

"What is it?"

"A small, very small, academic finishing school. 'Certainly, we are delighted to accept Miss Jean Treadway and expect her to arrive Thursday, September 10, between the hours of two and four in the afternoon. Cordially, Miss Lillian Clark Weaver, Headmistress.'"

Chapter Six

On September 10, Father directed Vincent, the new chauffeur, to turn the car left into a driveway. Instinctively Jean put out her right hand to brace for the turn. It seemed a long time before the car slowed down.

"It must be a big place," she said.

"Big for a house. Small for a school. It's set back from the street a long way. Two story, a white colonial," Father said.

"I think it's Greek revival, dear," Mother said.

"Yes, indeed. It has Corinthian columns."

"They're Doric, dear."

The Packard limousine pulled up to the porte-cochere behind a row of tulip trees.

"Do you see anybody?"

"Some lanky woman who looks like a giraffe is walking over here," Father said.

"Good afternoon. I'm Miss Reynolds, the secretary. Won't you please come in? Miss Weaver will see you in the drawing room."

Lillian Clark Weaver greeted them with a low, gruff voice, but her words were kind enough. She was quick, even brusque, as if she'd always be in control. Just Father's type. It sounded like she wore clumpy, old lady shoes, too. When Jean groped for a chair, Miss Weaver smoothly moved one right within reach, without losing a beat in her explanation of the rules of the school.

"All girls are to speak French exclusively until after one o'clock lunch every day, except during classes. Demerits shall be given for disobedience of this practice."

Criminee, Jean thought. At least I don't have to spell it.

"Accumulated demerits will prevent girls from going on outings."

Like what, she wondered. Anything I could do too?

"Girls will dress for dinner. On Sundays their dinner attire shall be a floor-length gown."

Tready would fit right in here, she thought. "How many girls are there?" she asked.

"Thirteen this year. At Andrebrook, education isn't a mass process. We give a thorough, adult background in the liberal arts. Do you know what field of study you would like to pursue?"

"Physiology."

"Oh, I don't think so." She cleared her throat and sat down at a large antique desk. "Let's keep thinking." Deftly Miss Weaver steered her to a course of study heavy in literature and languages. "I think this is adequate, don't you, Mr. Treadway? French, German, world literature, music history, piano, and western civilization." Miss Weaver stood up without pausing for his response. "Now I'll show you the buildings and grounds."

She led them through the first-floor rooms. "We use these sitting rooms as classrooms, since classes are sometimes only three or four students. Larger classes are held in the library."

"What's this room?" Jean asked.

"The dining room."

"It smells like sweet peas."

"It has French doors opening onto a terrace," Mother explained. "How light and airy."

Miss Weaver led them outside. "We often eat lunch out here in good weather."

"What a lovely garden. Jean, there's a rose arbor around a sun dial," Mother said. "And a wide lawn with Italian cedars at the edges. You remember what they look like, don't you? What's that behind those wisteria vines?"

"Tennis courts."

"It looks like a stable out there beyond the grass, too."

"Yes, and around to the right there's a riding ring," Miss Weaver added. "Girls will ride every day after classes at two o'clock, except on the groom's day off. Andrebrook girls are permitted to ride on the Rockefeller estate bridle paths through the Pocantico Hills. They can pick up the trails right across the street. Girls will also be instructed in polo by our riding master, Herr Frederich."

"Jean's doctor has not permitted her to ride," Mr. Treadway interjected. "He fears more damage because of the jolts."

"Unfortunate. See what can be done to get permission for her. We don't want her to be left out. Certainly she can learn to ride."

Jean tried not to smile. Nobody had ever talked to Father that way.

"Life is to be lived, not merely observed," she went on. Jean was bowled over. She'd give anything to have seen Father's expression. Saying goodbye to him, she felt breezy and lightheaded.

Two days later they had an orientation week at Mohonk, a private lake where they stayed at an old fashioned hotel, "just like in Switzerland," Miss Weaver said. They left the cars five miles below the lake and arrived by horse and buggy in time for afternoon tea. It was fun, but the bounces hurt her rear end.

"I've taken my girls to Mohonk to begin every fall term since I started Andrebrook in 1920," Miss Weaver said. "You'll get acquainted more quickly here."

They soon learned the real reason: Miss Weaver loved to hike.

"What's she look like?" Jean whispered to another girl as they gathered the next morning for a hike.

"Silly, actually," said a girl named Sally Anne. "She's got on heavy hiking boots, knickers, long wool stockings, and a sweater tied around her middle."

"And white frizzy hair and a funny wool hat," said another.

"She walks like a man, with huge steps."

"Must be the picture of outdoor vigor," Jean said.

Miss Weaver paired Jean with a girl named Dody Rollins and set off along the lakeside at a good clip, talking as fast as she was walking. She told them wonderful tales of former Andrebrook girls, of going to opera in New York and of traveling in Europe during the summer, of skiing Cortina and mountain climbing in the Dolomites, of producing Shakespearean comedies and of going to dances at military academies. Jean wondered how she could ever fit in. Icy would love it. It surprised her that she thought of Icy again. Maybe because she was hiking in the woods with a group of girls again. Maybe because being here without Icy, or anyone she knew, she felt alone, far more alone than she ever felt the first days at Camp Hanoum. She wished she wouldn't be so shy, but she didn't know how not to be.

The thirteen girls marched along surrounding Miss Weaver. Holding onto Dody's arm with an iron grip, Jean scrambled to keep up so she wouldn't miss hearing anything, and so she wouldn't call attention to herself. At the end of the hike everybody was breathing heavily, but Miss Weaver was still talking, with complete composure.

"Tomorrow afternoon you are to explore the trails by yourself, all together. Certainly you will go with them, Jean," she said, as if reading her mind.

The next afternoon came before Jean was ready for it.

At first the trails up hill were wide and smooth, easy enough to negotiate. Trooping along with others at Camp Hanoum had taught her how. She didn't want to be a nuisance to the others so soon. But she felt the spirit of the girls' new independence grow, and it made her apprehensive. Who knows where they would go? The trail became steeper and more uneven. It must have narrowed, too, because branches were closer on both sides. "Are we still on the main path?"

"No," someone answered.

Then she felt a rock wall on one side. "Where are we?"

"In some kind of a ravine."

"Where does it go?"

"We can't tell yet. Up."

She was determined not to cause them difficulty. Even though she stumbled every few steps, she tried to walk as close as she could to Dody ahead of her, one hand on Dody's shoulder, the other feeling for the rock wall. Soon she discovered rock on both sides of her.

She heard a weak, squeaky cry up ahead. "I'm stuck. I can't move," someone said. The others had to pull fat Mimi from the top and push her from the bottom to get her through the crevice. At least I won't cause them that problem, Jean thought. Miss Weaver was right. They got acquainted fast.

By keeping her hand out to the side and by putting one foot in front of the other, Jean made it through the narrow part. Eventually, they came to a wooden gazebo at the top of the hill and collapsed on the benches lining the perimeter.

"We're supposed to be able to see into four states from here," said Dody, breathing hard, "but I can't tell what I'm looking at."

"Look at that crooked little trail down there," said another girl with a high voice. It sounded like Sally Anne. "Let's see where it leads."

"Are you crazy?" someone shouted back.

"Come on," she insisted. "Just for a ways."

"What does it look like?" asked Jean.

"It's pretty precarious. Just wait here."

Jean did as she was told. The way they dismissed her so quickly hurt, but what was she to do? She wasn't even sure who was talking.

She followed the railing around the inside of the gazebo and sighed as she sat down on the bench to wait. Their voices got fainter and more indistinct until she couldn't hear them at all. She had no sense of how much time was passing. It seemed long. She listened for birds, but there were no sounds except a breeze whooshing through trees. She didn't even know what kind of trees. Even that would give her something to think about. She'd been afraid to ask too many questions. Icy would have told her without being asked. She stepped out of the gazebo under the sky to try to smell what kind. Nothing. She couldn't tell. No warmth fell on her face or shoulders. The sun must be low.

These were new friends. She knew none of them two days earlier. Maybe they had forgotten her. If they did, Miss Weaver would be furious, that much she knew. And then they'd resent her, and would have to drag her along just because they were told to.

She'd have to earn their friendship, that was all. Her resolve solidified. She sure wasn't going to spoil it right off by being a baby. Was friendship something everyone else had to work so hard for? She sat on the bench and waited. A lone bird sang but she couldn't identify what kind. If Icy were here, she'd look it up in her bird book. For some time she listened to its chirpy melody. It reminded her of a passage in a Chopin etude Mother had taught her.

A twig broke. When she heard voices, her breath came in a surge of relief. She stood up and wiped her damp palms on her hips. Someone said her name. Her name. At least that was something. "Boy, am I glad you came back," was all she said. She made it a point to smile and look in the direction from which she heard her name.

Chapter Seven

The single chime signaled one o'clock. "Halleluia. No more French until tomorrow morning." Jean heaved an exaggerated sigh of relief. "I've got to admit it is getting easier." She remembered Miss Weaver's standard, all-occasion line, "Of course you can. Just set your mind to it."

Elsa Flagstad slammed the book shut. "I'm never going to learn that frilly language. English is hard enough and I already speak good enough German." Jean had been translating orally the French lessons into German for her. It gave her a sense of acceptance with at least one of the girls, but Elsa was different from the others, too. She was foreign. Maybe that was why Miss Weaver had them room together.

"Is German anything like Norwegian?"

"No, but all Norwegian children study German."

As with the study sessions with Lorraine back at Bristol High, Jean and Elsa couldn't stick to the subject and fell into talk about other things, usually Elsa's mother, Kirsten Flagstad, the Wagnerian soprano making her debut at the Met that season. The world of music and opera librettos was far more interesting to both of them than conjugating French verbs in the pluperfect.

Jean gathered up her music and made her way to the piano in the parlor. The room smelled of roses. Eventually, the other girls thumped down the stairway in their riding boots, heading for the stables and riding ring. "See ya later, Jean," Dody called into the room. Dody always did. Most of the others just walked right by every day.

For a moment after they passed, the room echoed with their footsteps. Then, alone again. She took a deep breath and started in on "Liebestraum." It was a comforting melody but the awkward Braille music was slow going. She had to stop every few measures to read with her fingers. Maybe the Chopin etude Mother taught her last summer would be easier. She played the Chopin four times up to a point and each time the notes trailed off to nothing. Her hands dropped to her lap and she sat still for a long time. Always there was struggle. Always something separated her from the others. She drew her mouth inward.

"What's wrong, Jean?"

It startled her even though Miss Weaver's voice had a rare softness. She hadn't known anyone was in the room. "I can't remember. Mother taught me the whole thing. It took most of the summer. And now I can't get beyond that measure." She tried to make her voice sound casual.

"I'll investigate a professional teacher. I think I know of one in Manhattan who will take you. Maybe she can come once a week."

Miss Weaver's thick heels clomped down the hall. "Thank you," Jean said after her. But her words sounded weak. Just a fumbling thank you wasn't enough. She knew Miss Weaver would find someone, too. When that woman made a decision, she always got results.

At dinner the girls made up for what they didn't say in French at lunch. Miss Reynolds—the girls called her Rene—sat at one table, Miss Weaver at the other.

"LCW will start another book tonight, don't you think?" Dody said to Rene. They had fallen into the habit of calling Miss Weaver by her initials. She didn't seem to mind.

"What a bore," Sally Anne whispered. "Pinch me if I fall asleep."

"It's not a bore," Jean answered, keeping her voice low. "I love it." After dinner in the library, Francisco, the Filipino butler, served coffee in demitasse cups on a silver tray and they all listened to Miss Weaver read novels or plays in her throaty voice. It was a warm, animated time. The room seemed peopled by characters living out their triumphs and defeats, with Miss Weaver's raspy voice unraveling the struggles of all humanity. Through language alone, she could see a boy selling newspapers on a bridge in the rain, a mother sitting by the roadside weeping over a sick child, an immigrant's chest heaving in anxiety and excitement as he stepped off a train in a strange city. She always imagined herself the female lead and felt anguish at her fictional choices. Through stories she could, momentarily, live more broadly.

"I don't care if you think I'm silly. I don't ever want her to stop."

"Well, she will tonight," Rene said, "because I'm reading!"

"You?" Sally Anne's spoon clanked on her plate.

Served her right to be embarrassed.

"What'll you read?" Jean raised her spoon to her mouth. The beef broth dribbled off and splashed into the bowl. Her cheeks flushed hot. Rats. Just when they were probably looking at her. She dipped in again and concentrated on holding her spoon flat. When she touched it to her lips the spoon was empty. The thin, clear soup didn't weigh enough for her to tell if she'd gotten any. Beef broth nights were always humiliating.

"Ibsen's *The Doll's House*. It's a play."

"Sounds like a nursery. What's it about?"

"A young wife who's unhappy with her perfect, narrow, protected married life. It brought a storm of protest when it came out about fifty years ago in Norway and now a new production of it is opening on Broadway."

Every night that week Jean listened intently, her eyes watering in empathy for Nora. When Rene got to the end of Act III, the room was quiet for a few minutes. Jean heard people shift their positions in the tall wingback chairs. "I feel for her," she said. "She wanted a real life so desperately, not some phoney, prepared little world." No one else said anything. "I can hardly believe she did it, though. Left just like that, walked right out the door." Jean's voice dropped. "I wonder if any of our lives will be that narrow."

"Not mine," Polly declared.

"Of course not yours, but you're a westerner. For us in New England, it's different."

"How?"

"More stuffy. More controlled."

At the end of that week, they all went to see the Ibsen opening on Broadway. Jean cried in the darkness during the third act.

Most of their evening reading was related to theater they saw: Katherine Cornell as Shaw's *St. Joan* at the Martin Beck Theater, Helen Hayes in *Victoria Regina* at the Broadhurst, the Lunts in *Taming of the Shrew*. And then there was opera. Miss Weaver always made them read the librettos first. "We're going to do it right," she said.

The girls went in style. They wore long gowns and black velvet capes and were driven in a pair of black limousines. They often went to dinner first, usually at some little restaurant in Greenwich Village. Once it was Spanish. Jean could feel the flamenco dancers and tambourines pounding out their heated rhythms right near their table. She felt her heartbeat quicken, and she leaned forward in her chair during the whole meal.

More than anything else the girls did together, Jean loved going to the opera. She didn't need to have everything explained to her. Strong emotions shot out from the stage in sound. With opera, nothing was denied her. At the Met that season the girls cried at *Madama Butterfly* and thrilled at *Lakme* with Lily Pons. But Madame Flagstad's performances enthralled them most, for she was theirs. When she sang Brunhilde in *Die Walkure* the girls cheered. When she sang Isolde, they wept. After every opening the girls trooped backstage to see the grand diva, object of their worship.

Elsa and Jean went alone by taxi to Beethoven's *Fidelio*. They had been invited to Madame's hotel afterwards. Back of the Met after the show a crowd of people still shouted "Brava, brava." They thronged Madame for autographs, overpowering her and the two girls. Jean was shoved. For a moment she lost Elsa's arm and stood alone among shouting, shoving people, trying to keep her balance. Shoulders, backs and elbows jabbed at her from all sides. She felt like a thin reed sucked in a spiraling eddy. The world swirled in terror. An arm grabbed hers and yanked her through the crowd and into a car.

"Oh, Yeanie," Madame said in heavily accented English, "I'm so sorry it frightened you."

"It's all right. Nothing happened."

But her eyes watered and she was quiet for a while in the back seat of the taxi. This was what she had wanted, though, to be out in the world. This was adventure. She took a deep breath and tried to settle herself.

"Madame Flagstad, what's your favorite role?" she asked.

"That's a hard question, Yeanie. There are too many. Isolde, I think. I love the *Liebestod* aria in the end."

"I was hoping you'd say that. It's so tragic."

Trips through New York crowds made Jean feel more mobile even though she always walked holding someone's arm. Once they went to Madison Square Garden to see the National

Horse Show. Dody sat next to her and described the equestrian moves in terminology she had just learned from their riding master. "It must be impressive," Jean said wistfully.

She wrote home every week afterward to find out whether Father had asked Dr. Wheeler if she could ride. Maybe riding was something she could do. All the other sports the girls did— tennis, squash, skiing—were beyond her, but riding might not be. It's true, she did the ski joring, being pulled on skis by a horse on flat ground, but the girls didn't do that often. Riding they did every day. If she could ride, she wouldn't have to be alone in the afternoons. She'd be one of them.

Finally, a letter came from Mother. Jean had Dody read it. "The reading club was here yesterday. We discussed Balzac. Father was appalled. He said the ladies are titillated by the vicarious living they do at the reading club meetings. Bill is doing well at Yale and Lucy is planning a party for next month. Mort's learning how to punch a time clock at Babson. Dr. Wheeler called yesterday and said he would see no further harm in your riding."

Jean grabbed the letter and headed for the landing, felt for the handrail and scrambled down, counting the stairs.

"What's your hurry, Jean?"

"Where's LCW?"

"In her room, I think."

She turned on her heel back up the stairs. One, two…thirteen. To the left she heard bath water being drawn in LCW's suite. She knocked on the door anyway.

"Yes?"

"Miss Weaver, I can ride. Father asked my doctor, and he said it's okay."

"Of course you can ride, Jean. I knew you could all along," she said through the door.

"When can I start?"

"Tomorrow. I'll tell Herr Frederich and we'll measure you for breeches."

Andrebrook horsewomen wore khaki gabardine jodhpurs with leathers, black wool blazers, polished black boots, white silk shirts and stocks, white gloves and black derbies. Custom. The bill was sent to Father. Miss Weaver wasn't going to have her girls wandering through the Rockefeller estate looking like a bunch of ragtaggles.

Frederich, the riding master, lived above the stables, a respectable distance across the sloping lawn from the main building and the girls. English saddle was his specialty, so all the girls rode English. He gave Jean Glory Girl, a white nag, gentle and safe enough for her, he promised Miss Weaver. "She's an old poke," Jean grumped the first day. "Can't she go faster?"

When Herr Frederich announced a moonlight ride through the Pocantico Hills, the girls tittered in excitement.

"Oh, Jean, he looks so handsome and he rides so tall and straight. He rides ahead of us and we can see his silhouette on his horse up ahead. It's divine."

"You mean he's divine, Sally Anne. Don't quibble. We know you're in love with him." Dody's was the voice of reason.

"I am not. It's just that he looks so—hm—in the moonlight. It's the moonlight, Jean, that makes it all so dreamy."

"Doesn't matter to me if it's moonlight. I'm just glad I get to go."

"He'll make you ride on a lead line, though," Dody reminded her.

"So what?"

"Just imagine. *He'll* be holding the other end." Sally Anne fabricated a swoon.

"I don't care."

"Listen to you," Sally Anne teased. "You do, too. It makes you special."

"You're just jealous because I get to ride closest to him."

"Did you know Frederich watches you all the time?" Dody asked.

"I don't believe you."

"He does, Jean," Sally Anne agreed.

"He just feels protective. He doesn't need to, though."

"Don't tell him that. He might stop."

She did anyway. Not being singled out was far more important than Frederich. Eventually, in preparation for the yearly Andrebrook Horse Show, Herr Frederich allowed her to ride without the lead. He still rode right ahead of her in order to give her warnings like "turning right" just in time for her to adjust her weight.

One day something spooked Glory Girl and she shot off in front of Frederich and everyone. He took after her at a gallop. "Low branch, Jeanie," he shouted.

Jean bent down next to Glory Girl's mane. Her derby flew off and she felt twigs scrape across her shoulders. She raised up again and held on.

"Duck!"

This time she stayed down, close to Glory Girl's mane. It seemed to her a perfect position, just like a jockey. The movement felt different. She'd been afraid to lean that far forward before. Eventually, Frederich caught up and Glory Girl stopped. "Are you all right?"

"Of course, I am." She smirked even though she was breathing hard. That's what Miss Weaver would say. "It was terribly exciting. How far did I go?"

"Maybe half a mile."

"It never felt like that before. In fact, it felt wonderful."

"Well, it's not supposed to hurt." He chuckled. "You did fine, Jeanie. Do you think you can stay still while I go back and find your hat?"

"Only if I have to." She grinned. Miss Weaver was right again. Here was something she could do.

Her piano was often silent in the afternoon now. She had to train for the horse show. Most afternoons she was dressed early. "Who's ready?" she'd call out her door, anxious to drag the first one down to the riding ring. They were learning drills and formations just as they had seen at Madison Square Garden. Herr Frederich would call out commands and Jean had to memorize how many strides for each command in order to know where she was.

On a horse, away from the security of the earth and in an open ring with no walls to bounce back sound, all sense of space and dimension vanished. On the ground her own legs and the length of her stride told her how far she had gone. Now she didn't have that guide. She could only guess about the stride of the horse. At one point in the routine her position was on the outside of a pinwheel. She had to sense her distance to the horse next to her on the inside so she wouldn't stray off, away from the line. Sometimes Dody had to tell her, "Move in a few feet, Jean." Worse than that, sometimes she got confused and had to ask where she was. She had to stay alert to move in rhythm and still perceive constantly changing spatial relationships. After every practice her shoulders ached from tenseness, but that didn't matter. The ring, even more than the classroom, was a new arena for learning. Of course, she could do it. Miss Weaver had said so.

Though learning to ride was exciting, the closeness it brought with the other girls was far more satisfying. She sensed they thought her more self-sufficient than before so they pampered her less. It made her relax. She was aware of their move from pity to friendship but doubted if they were conscious of it.

Jean felt even more accepted when Sally Anne showed her how to pin up her hair. One Saturday before an opera trip, Jean sat on her bed with a dish of bobby pins and a half cup of water. She was in a hurry and every curl was a battle. Sally Anne saw her struggling and deftly took over without a word. "There now, I'm finished," she said. "But I didn't tell you. I spit on every curl. Ran out of water."

At last Jean felt she wasn't being crushed by kindness.

The events of one night made her feel drawn into their circle permanently. Late in the evening the girls on her floor were noisier than usual. When Jean pulled back the covers and climbed into bed, her foot jabbed at a fold in the sheet and she couldn't get in. "What's the ma—Who short-sheeted my bed? Dody, did you?" she called out into the hallway where she heard laughter.

"Who, me?"

"Sally Anne, you did!" Jean lunged toward Sally Anne's giggle.

"Not I," Sally Anne said innocently, turning Jean around.

"Said the little red hen," Elsa mimicked.

Sally Anne gave Jean a gentle push in Elsa's direction.

"You did, Elsa! Then I'm just going to sleep in your bed!" Jean scrambled toward Elsa's bed and heard a funny kazoo noise.

"What's that?' Jean asked, climbing in.

"Just some toilet paper on a comb. Try it." Elsa handed it to her and got another. Sitting up in bed together, the two girls went through a child's repertoire, from "Yankee Doodle" to "I've Been Working on the Railroad."

"We're not kids, Elsa. We've got to do something more cultured. What about that "*du du*" German song?"

"*Du, du liegst mir im Herzen*," Elsa sang, and they started in industriously on their combs.

Miss Weaver's clompy shoes echoed at the base of the stairs. "Girls, lights out."

"But we're playing in German," Jean protested, eliciting giggles from the open doorways down the hall.

"*Geht ins Bett!*"

"Yes, Miss Weaver," Elsa said in a singsongy voice.

"*Seid ruhig!*"

"Good night, *Fraulein* Weaver," Jean chorused, placating her and generating more titters down the hall.

Willingly she made her way over to her own bed and snickered as she wrestled to remake it. At last she was one of them, chastised in front of the group. She knew that even though the others thought she was a goody-goody, they valued her loyalty. There was an unspoken arrangement, sacred as any ancient rite. The girls on her floor wouldn't tell LCW that she read her Braille novels after lights-out, and she wouldn't tell the crazy things they did, like Sally Anne climbing onto the roof in her slip to look into the boys' school beyond the stone wall. She never breathed a word about the Polly Gillespie orange escapade.

Polly was a platinum blond from out west, "probably some sprawling ranch," Dody told her once. Polly had a voice that clattered like cold emeralds tumbling out of a treasure chest, her words loud and older than her years. She'd been everywhere already even though she was youngest. Jean didn't doubt that she'd done just about everything, too. She imagined her as gaudy butterfly fluttering her eyelashes and waving long, red-tipped fingers. Without fail, she always came back late from holidays because of an asthma attack. "How does she always plan it so well?" Jean asked Dody. Once after semester break Polly arrived a few days late with a basket of oranges.

"For the girls," she told LCW.

"How thoughtful of you," Miss Weaver had said. That was before the laughter got louder and louder on the floor above.

Upstairs Polly drew the girls together in her room. "I've got something for everyone. Western oranges."

"What's so different about western oranges?" asked Sally Anne.

"Try one."

Sally Anne took the largest one and peeled back the skin. She separated the sections and popped a fat one into her mouth. "Ooh, juicy." She let out a knowing squeal. "Pass 'em around."

Most of the girls grabbed, but a few held back. Jean slurped up the juice with the rest of them. "Why are they so juicy?" she asked.

"I injected them."

"With what?"

"Gin."

Amid the squeals of laughter, one girl quietly moved toward the door. "Oh, Cathy, stay," urged Polly.

"No, I've got to study."

A few moments later Jean heard her close the door to her room down the hall.

"Lame excuse. She's so dull. She's got no personality. No sex appeal either."

Polly's remark stunned Jean. The sex appeal wasn't what bothered her. Admittedly, she had no notion of what that consisted of, but she had never considered Cathy dull, just quieter than the others. Did that make her dull too? She couldn't stop wondering. The next day after lunch, Jean followed Dody into her room.

"Is anybody else here?"

"No."

"Close the door."

"What's wrong?"

"I feel stupid asking this. Is Cathy really dull? Do you think so, Dody?"

Dody didn't answer right away. "Sit down, here, on the bed." She touched Jean's hand to the bedspread. "I guess maybe you don't see the way we do. Yes. She is. Polly was right. But that doesn't mean you can't be friends with her."

"How could she say it, though? Right out there like that?"

"Saying it doesn't matter. We all know it anyway."

That night Jean didn't read after lights-out. She sat up in bed for a long time. Here was someone else who probably felt on the outside of things. Jean imagined the hollow feeling Cathy must have had, sitting in her empty room the night before when the others were having fun, like swallowing a hard candy too soon and having it ache in your chest until it dissolved. But Cathy seemed happy enough. Maybe it didn't matter to Cathy. Maybe it shouldn't matter so much to her either. Andrebrook wasn't all that the world consisted of, and school was ending soon anyway. And then what? That made her slide down and pull the covers up.

A few days later, Jean attempted doing her hair herself again. When she went down to the dining room for dinner, Sally Anne said, "Oh, Jeanie, you look lovely."

But she knew she didn't. Sally Anne's sugary voice sounded just like Mother's had in the dining room when she had ironed that dress herself.

"Tell me the truth."

"I am, Jean. Don't you believe me?"

"No."

In June, 1936, after two years at Andrebrook, Jean was officially "finished." There was a small ceremony out in the garden for the girls leaving, and Miss Weaver gave a speech about the value of culture and the need to stay alive by continuing to learn and to experience all they possibly could.

Jean listened intently, feeling as though Miss Weaver was speaking especially to her. At the first cocktail hour back home, she repeated it to Father. In the same breath she added, "and Miss Weaver has more space this summer. She always takes five girls to Europe and she only has two so far. It's an educational experience."

She heard him light his pipe. "Europe. Well. What countries?"

"Mainly Germany. Austria and Italy, too, and maybe France. But Miss Weaver likes Germany best. She always says 'The roots of western civilization penetrate deep in the Teutonic world.'" Jean pulled in her chin and mimicked Miss Weaver's deep voice, stretching out the "o" in roots and trilling the "r."

"Seems a suitable finishing off. You worked hard. We'll see."

"There's only one thing."

"What's that?"

"I'd be a bother to the other girls. And if I'm alone, Miss Weaver will drag me through every museum and explain every painting inch by inch."

It was a little easier speaking to Father now. She heard him pouring another drink. Evidently, he was thinking. Time to be quiet and wait. Things had to settle with Father on his own terms.

Two days later at breakfast he asked, "Who was that girl with you at Camp Hanoum, the one you liked so much?"

"Do you mean Icy Eastman?"

"Is that the one who always described everything for you?"

"Yes."

"Have you kept in contact with her?"

"Oh yes. We write letters, and she came to my birthday party last year."

"What's she doing now?"

"Working at a bank. She lives in Litchfield."

"Why don't you call her up today? If she can take off from work, I'll send you both to Europe."

"Oh, Father, do you really mean it?"

"Wouldn't say it otherwise. And Lucy too, if she wants to."

"Oh, thank you, Father," both girls chorused in their rush around the table to hug him.

"Don't ambush me from both sides." He chuckled. "Can't a man eat his breakfast in peace?"

Mother cleared her throat. "What about the trouble there?" she asked. "You know on the radio they say there were civilians murdered in Madrid, nuns and children and—"

"Irrelevant," Father declared. "Weaver isn't taking them to Spain. That's just a rumor anyway."

"I hope you're right. But in Germany there were troop parades."

"Those bluffs strutting around Europe are only putting their manhood back together after losing the war. Let them," Father said. "Why shouldn't they go?"

Chapter Eight

Miss Weaver and five girls walked the cool, dim passages of Cologne cathedral.

"Our footsteps echo." Arm in arm with Icy, Jean knew she didn't need to say it. Undoubtedly Icy was aware of it, too.

"Can you feel how big it is in here?" Icy asked.

"Not exactly, but sounds come from a long way off."

"The ceiling seems a mile away. It has stone arches, kind of pointy, and they cross."

"The stone even smells damp. Are we passing a window?"

"Yes. A tall one. The stained glass glows like jewels. How'd you know?"

"I just had an eerie feeling of light or something."

Suddenly, the organ began, a sustained full chord. Instantly, Icy and Jean stopped. Sound filled all space. Jean turned around. "Where are the pipes? I can't tell."

"Behind us."

The resonant chords and ranks of voices bounced off the vaulted ceiling so that the music, overlapping measure upon measure, lost its distinctness.

"Don't you feel small?" Lucy asked, catching up behind them.

"That's by design," Miss Weaver said. "Gothic church architecture was calculated to minimize the individual and maximize the loftiness of orthodoxy. Easier to mold the illiterate into obedience."

LCW had something to say about everything. To Jean, it all seemed so absolute, so logical. She was an authority on all matters.

The last chords from the organ lingered. Jean still didn't move. A startling quiet sucked up the echo and it seemed as if she'd forgotten how silence felt. She wanted to absorb the hushed stillness and the sense of space. Too soon the mood was broken by people talking and moving around. The girls and Miss Weaver passed through the heavy doors into the brightness of the cathedral square. Jean's eyes watered. She waited while the others adjusted to daylight.

"Four months ago Hitler's troops marched here to show his presence in the Rhineland," Miss Weaver said.

"What's so important about that?" Lucy asked.

"My dear, he violated the Treaty of Versailles, arming the country in outright defiance of an arms limitations agreement. That's what's important about that."

"I'm hungry," Jean said. "That's what's important about me. Can't we eat soon?"

Down river at Koblenz they stayed at the Hotel Fürstenhof. LCW had always stayed there. It had a broad balcony overlooking the wide boulevard. This Sunday morning it was a popular place because breakfast was served outside in the sun. All the tables were crowded, and Jean bumped into several chairs before she got situated. Miss Weaver insisted that at every meal a different girl would order for the group. This time was Jean's turn. The girls told her what they wanted and she stumbled through with her Agnes Jennings pronunciation of German. "Adequate but not brilliant," Miss Weaver remarked. They were served. That was all Jean cared about.

A clock tower struck ten, unleashing chimes from churches all over the city. The resounding clangor was so deafening the girls couldn't hear Miss Weaver's lecture about the surrounding architecture. Chimes rolled layer upon layer, like an ocean wave rolling on top of another wave. Eventually, the wild disorder of noise took on a low, heavy, staccato movement, dull and thudding, coming from one direction. The throbbing became more distinct, reducing the chiming bells to tinny decoration in comparison with the reverberating base rhythm.

"What is it?" Jean raised her voice.

"Soldiers," Lucy shouted in her ear.

They came closer, a million lead weights pounding the boulevard below. Jean felt the balcony vibrate in response to the measured thud, thud, thud. She held onto the edge of the table in front of her. It vibrated, too. Quick, hard, sharp, the beats thundered in her head. She barely took a breath until, gradually, the pulsing retreated.

"They walk so funny," Lucy said after they passed. "They keep their legs straight in front of them and march like wooden soldiers or stick figures."

"The goose step," said Miss Weaver.

"What did they look like?"

"They were just boys, but they looked so stern," Icy said. "They all wore brown shirts and black boots."

"And red arm bands with some kind of emblem," Lucy added.

"It's a swastika," said Miss Weaver, "and when it's on a flag it's called *die Blutfahne*, blood flag. It's the Nazi party symbol."

"The whole thing gives me the creeps," Jean said.

The girls described the emblem when they saw it again, a black twisted cross in a white circle on a field of red. In

Heidelberg, two-story banners hung along the streets. Each time Jean heard them flapping in the breeze every thirty paces, her stomach felt unsettled. "How many are there, anyway?"

"I stopped counting," Lucy said.

"What are you doing—counting the men in uniform instead?" Jean chided.

Heidelberg was honoring the 500th anniversary of its university. The ancient town went wild. There were music festivals, sword dances, boisterous speeches in squares. Rowdy singing poured out of beer halls into the streets. It all gave Jean an uneasy feeling of dread that the world had become so loud and strident. In order to get something to eat, Miss Weaver and the girls joined the shouting throngs of students shoving their way across a stone bridge. Lucy and Jean got separated from the others in the narrow passageway. People couldn't move ahead. They were stuck, stomach to back to stomach.

"Can you see the others?"

"No, but they must be up there," Lucy shouted.

They braced themselves against the crowd and plowed ahead. Jean held onto Lucy's elbow with both hands. There were bodies touching all sides of her. Everyone inched his way across the bridge. Her clothes felt tight and the air was stifling. Here was that terror again, feeling like a newborn calf being shoved ahead in a stampede.

"Aren't we near the end yet?"

"I can't tell."

A sudden heave of toppling people threatened to push them against the passageway wall, but a man behind them quickly interfered, cushioning them when they were pushed. Jean felt his chest against her shoulder struggling to push back the other way. "*Bleibt zuruck*," he muttered sharply in the opposite direction. She didn't know whether to be thankful to him, or to be afraid.

She'd come to trust people, but maybe he was a Nazi. She held on more firmly to Lucy's elbow.

"Ouch!" Lucy cried. "Don't pinch."

"Do you see Icy?"

"No, I told you that."

Even the New York crowds coming out of Madison Square Garden didn't have this frenzy. A long half-hour later, they met the others at the restaurant, but Jean didn't breathe normally until she was back in the pension that night.

Germany swelled with nervous motion that summer, and it seemed to Jean that Nazism was in a great hurry. In Dinkelsbühl in northern Bavaria a Youth Day parade took over the annual Kinderfest.

"They're only kids," said Icy. "So young they're still in short pants and knee socks. Some are carrying swastika flags."

"Is it the children beating on the drums?" Jean asked.

"Yes."

"Sounds like little toy drums." Ranks of children sang *"Deutschland, Deutschland uber alles."* "It's a thrilling song, isn't it? So spirited."

"They look kind of menacing to me," Lucy said. "Puffed up and too serious to be kids."

"They should be riding bikes and fishing during the summer, not out marching," LCW said. "Something's awfully wrong."

The remark made Jean feel ignorant. Miss Weaver's voice lacked its usual husky authority. That, in itself, made Jean uneasy. The next day they left Dinkelsbühl by train. As they neared Munich, Jean sensed Miss Weaver's spirit rally. "We're going to have a marvelous time in Bavaria," Miss Weaver declared. "In the Teutonic world lie the roots of Anglo-Saxon culture, much deeper than any boys marching around for a summer, and Bavaria, Munich especially, is the center of the Teutonic world. It's the seat of schmaltz and students, high art and oompah. So for the next three weeks I expect you to absorb its spirit."

They did. Jean and Lucy bought quilted jackets, dirndls, long aprons and black velour hats in the style of Tyrolean mountain climbers. They all ordered beer in the Hofbrauhaus. They took side trips out of Munich to see the opera *Jederman* in Salzburg and a medieval street pageant in Innsbruck. The longest side trip was to the Wagner opera festival, the *Bayreuther Festspiele.*

On day trips Miss Weaver never let the girls stop to go to the bathroom. While trooping through museums or riding in hired cars, she never stopped. She was Iron Lady. "You must learn control," she'd say. "In all aspects of life, even this. Master your bodies with self discipline and it will elevate your character." They didn't stop from Munich to Bayreuth.

The little troop checked into a third-floor room at a second-class inn. They rarely stayed in first-class hotels. Miss Weaver was firm on that. "We're going to mix with the people," she declared. By the time they got to the inn, the girls were squirming, concentrating on keeping their muscles tight, not on mixing with any people. As soon as the innkeeper gave them directions, they rushed upstairs to the single bathroom.

"I don't know how waiting forever to go to the bathroom will improve my character," Lucy snapped, holding onto her arm at the elbow. Jean felt Lucy stop suddenly at the top of the stairs.

"Don't stop, Lucy. I can't wait."

"Ssh."

Jean felt Lucy shift her weight back and forth. Jean did the same. Lucy fidgeted in silence. "Where's Icy?" Jean whispered. Lucy's arm muscles tightened and told her not to ask questions. She heard a toilet flush, heard a door open and shut, heard it flush again and heard heavy boots walk away down the wooden corridor.

"What's the matter?" she whispered.

"There was a man ahead of us in a Nazi uniform." Lucy darted for the toilet, leaving her with Icy.

"So? Why did you shut me up?"

"He was scary looking," she said through the door. "He stood like he had a board in his back. No expression to his face. Didn't even smile at us."

"And didn't offer to let us go ahead, either," Jean remarked.

Icy giggled. "Even with his uniform he had to wait in line like anyone else."

"He was sort of handsome," Lucy said through the door. "Too bad he's a Nazi."

On their last trip to the bathroom that night they found rows of boots lined up down the hall. "There's an army of Nazi officers on our floor," squealed Icy. "They all must be over six feet tall to have boots that big."

"And all of them blond Adonises," Lucy added.

First thing the next morning Lucy gave her the hallway report. The row of tall boots gleamed.

"Probably the job of the innkeeper's wife to polish them during the night," said Miss Weaver, none too cheerfully.

The festival opera was *Der Meistersinger*. They had fine seats in the orchestra, right under and slightly in front of the imperial box. "Wagner's daughter-in-law, Frau Siegfried

Wagner, is supposed to make an appearance tonight, so watch that draped box," she said.

The opera house was packed. At an unseen signal, a hush settled through the audience. Three figures stepped from behind heavy velvet drapery into the imperial box. Immediately, everyone rose in silence and faced them. Jean heard sharp footsteps come out to the edge of the box, and the others craned their necks to see. Icy gasped. "Turn around, Jean. I think it's Hitler."

"Quit teasing," Jean whispered.

"No, I mean it. I think it's him."

"What's he look like?"

"He's just standing there scowling with his chest puffed out and his lips tight." From somewhere in the orchestra a voice shouted, "*Heil* Hitler." Then the thunderous response, "*Heil* Hitler."

Above them, the man clicked his heels and his right hand shot out over the balcony. "*Sieg Heil*," he bellowed, more a command than an acknowledgment.

The audience thundered back, "*Heil* Hitler! *Heil* Hitler! *Heil* Hitler!"

The passions rose in the close, oppressive air of the opera house. Jean felt suddenly hot in her heavy quilted jacket.

"We don't have to do this. We're Americans," Miss Weaver muttered.

Below the *Führer*, the six stood silent, arms at their sides. The *Führer* noticed and his scowl lines deepened. When the chanting stopped, he pursed his lips together, scowled down at the frozen American schoolgirls and their white-haired leader, muttered something and clamped his mouth shut just as the orchestra swung into the overture.

Soon they were lost in the opera and its wealth of characters. The stage was alive with color, movement and song. Jean was swept away from the politically charged present. What did it matter to her, anyway? She thought of Madame Flagstad and surrendered herself to sound.

After the performance they walked to a nearby restaurant. Seated by the window, the others could see the surge of life in the street. Against the hum of traffic, Icy described the river of people rushing by. "There's a short woman with a paisley scarf tied under her chin. She's being pulled by a dog on a leash. An errand boy carrying a package wrapped in brown paper and twine is trotting down the street. A thin woman is selling flowers at the corner. I can't tell how old she is. Young, sort of, but already old. Drawn cheeks and sad eyes. A man with knife-sharp creases in his trouser legs is hailing a taxi for a lady. He's leaning in, saying something to the driver. Oh, he just spotted the flower seller. She's coming toward him. Looks like he'll buy. Yes, he's handing a spray of violets through the cab window. The taxi is moving out into the traffic and he's just standing there at the curb."

"Can you see his face?"

"No, just his back. He's walking away now."

A wistful smile played over Jean's face. She was there. She was part of it. The world was full and alive and spirited.

A Nazi officer stepped abruptly into the restaurant doorway. Silver and glasses fell silent and all conversation stopped. In mimicry of his *Führer*, he clicked his heels and shot out his arm. Again, "*Sieg heil*."

Jean stopped chewing the bite of sauerbraten in her mouth and swallowed it whole. She heard Miss Weaver and the other girls put down their forks. The whole restaurant responded in unison—"*Heil* Hitler!" Jean heard the boots come closer. Standing tall over their table, the officer waited for a response.

The restaurant was silent. Her heart pounded like a tom-tom. She felt the stares of everyone in the restaurant riveted on the back of her neck. She held her breath, confused, waiting for some direction.

"*Sieg heil.*" The voice above their table was deep, commanding, impatient. Her chest ached where her bite of food lodged. Slowly, Miss Weaver mumbled the hated response. The girls followed in flat voices. Then Jean did, too. Her mouth tasted sour and her chest throbbed. The boots stomped out the door and down the street.

"Mindless," Miss Weaver muttered.

The word stabbed at her. The other girls spoke only in undertones during the rest of the meal, about anything but what had happened. Jean didn't follow the conversation. Something had collapsed inside her. Miss Weaver, the invincible Miss Weaver, had revealed a crack. A Nazi, nothing more than boots and a gruff voice, had bullied her and for one moment, control wasn't within her grasp. A bigger authority, hard, cold and foreign, shrank her. Jean wished that just for this moment she could see. Miss Weaver's face might tell her things, how the ordered world that she always explained so logically had become jangling. How something wasn't right in her beloved Teutonic civilization. But looking at Miss Weaver now might be like Lorraine looking at her over the cups of cocoa, a violation of the privacy politely given at moments of failure. For the first time, Miss Weaver seemed vulnerable to something, more like her own unsure self. For those moments in the restaurant, with the hum of traffic and the tramp of human feet outside, she felt unutterably close to her, though she doubted if Miss Weaver would ever guess.

Afterwards, back in Munich, the girls avoided walking under the arch that led into Marienplatz where the glockenspiel on the town hall chimed at noon. A Nazi officer was always stationed there and gave the *Heil* to everyone who walked through the passageway into the square. He expected the proper response. The girls learned a little cutoff to get to the square by another route. "You know, other people are taking this route too," Icy remarked. "And they're German."

The security of Hickory Hill seemed a long way off. Although Jean knew she didn't understand the political situation, privately she felt thrilled to be where big things were happening. Still, better not to tell such things back home. She wanted Father to let her travel more. He didn't have to know everything. She borrowed a typewriter at the pension and wrote:

August 19, 1936

Dear Mother and Father,

I'm getting enough of culture. Yesterday we went to the Hofbrauhaus and had some beer. I can drink a mug of it now without making a face, and so can Lucy.

Our few days in Italy went by too fast. LCW insisted that everyone except me climb Cinque Torre in Cortina. It must have been dreadful. Lucy collapsed on the floor in our hotel room the second she came in. But they did sign the roster at the top and Angelo, our Italian guide, yodeled.

In Verona I finally learned what Italianate Renaissance architecture is. There was a balustrade along a staircase in the palace, and I could feel the stonework. We heard a Bach Missa in the Piazza San Marco in Venice, but the pigeons kept up a racket flapping their wings. Suddenly, they'd fly at us out of nowhere. Terrifying to me. Otherwise, *alles ist in Ordnung*. We hate to leave.

Jean

Chapter Nine

She heard him humming up ahead. It wasn't like him to hum so gaily.

"You sure seem happy today, Father."

"Why shouldn't I be? I'm on vacation and it's a gorgeous day. The water is deep turquoise, so bright I'm squinting."

"Do you mean to say you'd rather do this than work?"

"Yes, indeedy. Give me a bicycle ride in Bermuda any day over a stuffy office. Besides, it's good for you. Gets you out a little."

"You're just using me as an excuse. You wanted to come anyway. I wasn't born yesterday, you know."

She heard him breathing hard. He didn't answer. Every morning since they'd arrived, she and Father took a ride along the waterfront on a rented tandem.

"Oh, do you feel that breeze, Father? Isn't it wonderful? Smells like the sea."

He shouted back to her, "Pump hard, Jean. Hill up ahead." The pull on the pedals grew harder and she bent into it. Her stomach contracted. She felt perspiration form at her temples and she took in great gulps of humid air. Her cotton blouse stuck to her back. It was a long time before she could pedal more easily. Then, suddenly it was over.

"Thanks for the ride, Jean. I needed that rest."

"Father, you coasted! There wasn't any hill at all, was there?"

Father hummed some more. "You didn't remember it from yesterday did you?"

"Father!" She was surprised at his playfulness. He hadn't teased her so lightheartedly since she was a child. Pedaling behind him, she smiled at nothing in particular all the way back to the hotel.

Pleasant moments didn't make her feel less a wallflower daughter, though. Being toted off to an island vacation by her parents wasn't her idea of adulthood. She was grateful, but she had no freedom to explore on her own. Europe with Miss Weaver had been more exciting.

That night after dinner she stayed up alone in the hotel lobby. The breeze drifting in through an open window felt refreshing after the sultry day. A trio in the lounge played "Begin the Beguine." Men and women talked together and laughed. She wanted to be a part of the jovial sounds surrounding her. She groped in her handbag for a cigarette. It took four matches before she got it lit. She blew the smoke upwards the way Tready had said was sophisticated. Some time when she was alone, she'd have to practice aiming the match for the end of the cigarette in her mouth. It was hard to make it look smooth. She reached for an ash tray on the table next to her and hoped someone would come up to talk.

No, not just anyone. A man. It was natural for a girl of twenty, she told herself. Why not recognize it? She listened to the music, the light evening talk and the clink of ice in glasses. A couple came from behind her, headed toward the lounge, the woman's high heels on the bare wood floor a high tap, tap; his, slightly less frequent, a solid, deeper sound. In the lounge the trio swung into a foxtrot. The sound of solid heels came toward her. Man's footsteps. She tried to make her face animated the way Icy had taught her.

"Hello," a voice said.

"Hi."

For a sliver of a second the rhythm of his footsteps broke. Was that an invitation? She didn't breathe and tried to think of something clever to say. Then he walked on. She knew he could tell. Why was it that a blind person always makes others ill at ease even if *she* is perfectly comfortable? Stupid, but true. So it was up to her to have the social finesse not only to initiate contact but to put everyone else at ease. Her shoulders slumped. She hated her weakness, her inexperience and timidity, and wondered if she would still be shackled by them if she could see.

A man, yes. But not just any man. One who would be natural with her and not treat her like a china teacup. She sighed quietly and a little scowl came over her face. It would be wonderful, but not likely. She had to be realistic. A longing pulsed in her, that was sure, but a longing for what? Her parents gave her all they could. It was just that riding in tandem with Father wasn't enough. Maybe I don't understand myself, she thought. Maybe I want something different from what the world thinks poor little rich blind girls should have. Or do. Or be. The want had ached intermittently for over a year, like a headache or toothache that comes and goes, and when it returned, like tonight, she found she'd forgotten to be grateful for the time it wasn't there. She ground the cigarette out in the ash tray.

She imagined herself years from now, a spinster with an afghan over her knees, wondering out loud in a thin voice about the world. Only a paid companion would be there to answer. She would have passed years in solitary reading. And when Mother or Lucy could no longer take care of her, what then? Her brothers would kindly file her away in some private and expensive institute. Until all her senses vanished. A knot formed in her stomach.

She listened until the trio finished the set, her hands restless in her lap. Mother came into the lobby. With her smiling voice, she walked her back to their rooms. How could Mother always be so cheerful? Well, she had no worries. A little like Ibsen's Nora but without the rebelliousness.

The next summer the family took a cruise. Towns and coastlines glided by in an invisible panorama. In Madeira in the Azores Jean and Lucy braved the famous basket ride down steep stone streets into the town. No doubt about it. It was fast. It was frightening. Jean loved it. Miss Weaver's trip had taught her the courage to enjoy. At a resort hotel in Lisbon the band played "Tiger Rag." It made the world seem small. At Mont St. Michel Lucy described the spires and towers, but the ancient abbey was just steps to Jean. Madame Poulard's omelettes made more sense. At Oban in Scotland, she heard bagpipes on the dock. At Bergen, she felt the water smooth out as they entered the fjords. She stood out on the deck and held her face to the quiet, cold air and knew she was looking at a glacier.

Cold or warm, noisy or quiet, the ports floated by and Jean wondered what she would do next. Not in the next town, but next in her life, when she got home. There was always that to figure out. What to do next. She couldn't just spend her life chitchatting with women. Restlessness and doubt tugged at her like an anchor all the way back across the Atlantic. Every evening at twilight Jean and Lucy walked the upper deck, their faces to the wind.

"So now that we're headed home, what's ahead?"

"Just water."

"You know what I mean. What do I do at home? Everybody else has something. Bill has Yale. Mort has a new wife, and you have Garland."

"You can come visit."

"Dody's going back to Vassar. Sally Anne's forever at a party."

"What's Elsa doing?"

"Going with her mother on a concert tour out west."

"We'll go on another trip soon. Mother wants to go across Canada by train."

"I can't just wait at home until Father decides it's time to entertain Jean again with another trip. I don't think they know what else to do with me." She turned from Lucy toward the railing and the sea. The whole vast world seemed cool and uncertain, with no new light promised. "But what should *I* do with me? I have no goal, and no one to be with." Lucy didn't say anything. That showed that there was no simple answer. "I have no plan." Her voice cracked. "I-I don't know enough to do anything other than just feel one step ahead. I always have to make choices without knowing or seeing enough." She realized she was stuttering. She'd never spoken so openly to Lucy, but here, with the sound of the wind engulfing them, separating them from everyone else, she felt a closeness she hadn't known back home.

"Just because other people can see doesn't make their way more clear," Lucy said softly. "I don't know any more than you what to do with my life. I just go on, that's all."

Wind flapped her jacket sleeve rhythmically and water churned below them against the deep hum of the engines.

"There's always music," Lucy offered.

Yes, there was that. Nothing thrilling, nothing to make a life out of—she would never be good enough—but certainly pleasant. There had always been piano. She could recall as a child seeing the round black notes on sheet music. They weren't round exactly, more like tiny black eggs bouncing along the lines. Something about the way they looked was cheerful.

When they were settled at home, Jean began again to study with Mrs. Sturdivant in New York, the teacher Miss Weaver had hired for her. Between lessons, Mother taught her note by note the work for the next week. "This is your next measure on your right hand," Mother would say. Then she'd play it. "Start on A. Play it as an arpeggio in the tonic chord for two octaves. Run down the scale two octaves. That's the next two measures." Jean copied her, drilling it into her head. Her concentration and memory sharpened.

They gave a two-piano concert and invited a hundred Bristol friends. The living room became Hickory Hill Music Salon. The twin grands were dovetailed together in front of the fireplace and they had printed programs: Mozart's Rondo for Two Pianos, Grieg's Piano Concerto in A Minor with the second piano doing the orchestral part, and Jean's favorite, the Ahrensky waltz. No matter what music she played, though, it all seemed like variations on one theme: What shall I do? What can I do? What am I good for?

She couldn't dominate all Mother's time to teach her everything note by note, but she could do something else with music. She knew enough piano to teach beginners. She asked Vincent, their chauffeur, to take her to the local girls' club. Could they use a beginning music teacher just to teach children the basics? Yes, of course they could. The words shot back at her without a pause. She smiled; they sounded like Miss Weaver's. Vincent drove her there once a week.

Vincent would drive her anywhere, for that matter. She sought out other needs in the community. Surely, some places needed volunteers. At the family welfare center she helped a little girl who had a cleft palate, drilling her on sounds. She served at the Visiting Nurse Association. She joined the Junior League and the Red Cross. Vincent was always available, always accommodating. But she had a nagging feeling she wasn't doing these things simply for themselves. They filled time. And Mother's friends always said, "How wonderful for you to do that, Jean." But was that really her? Maybe it was self-love that actually motivated her, doing praiseworthy things so she'd be loved. A justifiable substitute, she supposed. Still, the pain of limitation pulsed.

Except when she was with Icy. Icy lived in a second-floor flat with her mother and sister in Litchfield, 18 miles away. Once a week after work she picked up Jean and they spent the night together at Icy's.

Icy Eastman didn't have interests. She had passions. They were the same as Jean's—music, opera, books. Icy and her mother talked about politics, too, something Jean never heard about at home. Together Mrs. Eastman and the girls listened to operas on the radio and talked about composers and musicians and authors. "I know everyone says Jeannette Antoine's not as great as Lily Pons," Jean said one night. "I guess they're right, but I still like her."

"Jean, if you think Jeannette Antoine is good, then you think that," Mrs. Eastman said flatly. "It doesn't matter what anyone else thinks. Hold your ground. Your ear is as good as anyone's. Later if you change your mind, that's okay too. Say what you think even if it's different from what others think."

She liked that in Mrs. Eastman, that spunk. After Mrs. Eastman went to bed, Icy and Jean huddled on the floor wrapped in a blanket tent to catch heat through the furnace grating from the family below. "Your mother is so easy to be with. I bet you can talk to her about anything."

"Just about."

"Sex?"

Icy nodded.

"I've never discussed sex with my Mother. It's not just that she's a New Englander. She's always so distant, about everything."

"Your mother's very much a lady."

"Even to Lucy and me. Maybe I'd be too embarrassed to talk to her anyway. I'd be curious about something, but I couldn't bring myself to ask."

"So, ask me. Not that I'm an authority."

Jean's questions poured out: What does making love feel like? What does a man's organ look like? How do you know whether you really love a man? How do you know when you're pregnant? Can you have sex when you're pregnant?

"I feel so naïve not knowing this, but what kind of women have sex appeal? I mean, is it only physical qualities or is it some kind of aura?"

"Both. For some men it's more subtle, how you move, how you look at them, what you say."

"That I know."

"For others, the more simple-minded, it's just the size of your breasts."

"Well?"

"Quite adequate, silly. Especially since you're so petite and have a small waist."

The Eastmans were a liberating influence. Mother and Father didn't take too well to these intimate visits with a family outside their social circle, but Jean went anyway. "I like them," she protested gently. She knew what she really meant, though she would never say it to Mother. The Eastmans filled a need left empty at Hickory Hill.

Few of Jean's other friends were in Bristol. The Hill crowd was in college or already married. Occasionally she spent a Saturday with Lorraine, playing piano together at Hickory Hill, but that wasn't often because Lorraine was busy with two jobs, saving to get married. Once they went to a Saturday matinee of *Gone With The Wind*. They sat in the last row and Lorraine described the action to Jean in whispers. By the end of the movie, Lorraine was hoarse and both girls were shaken.

"You look pretty bleary-eyed," Bill said when he picked them up.

Jean groaned. "We feel like we've been though the war."

"The burning of Atlanta, all those war casualties, birthin' babies. No wonder our eyes are red," Lorraine said.

"Here, ladies, hand over your hankies. Let me ring them out."

"Quit teasing, Bill. Ginny would have cried, too," Jean protested, referring to Bill's fiancée.

"But wasn't Clark Gable divine?" he said, mimicking her.

"No!" they wailed. "He left her!"

"You mean you didn't like it, all that passion and sugar-coated history?"

"No. We loved it," they said, laughing at themselves.

Occasionally Dody spent a weekend at Hickory Hill. Vassar wasn't too far away. Sometimes Dody got dates for Jean with men she met at West Point mixers. Once after Dody had been home in California for the summer, she burst into Jean's room and sat on her bed.

"Jean, I met this man at home."

"So, what else is new?"

"Listen a minute. He lives in a little town east of San Diego called Ramona, or something like that. I think he lives on a ranch."

"A cattle ranch?" Jean took out a file from the vanity to do her nails.

"I'm not sure. Turkeys maybe."

"You can't be serious." Already it sounded foolish.

"That's not the point. The point is that he lost his sight too. Something about a high school football accident. I didn't ask. He went away to college to study dairying or some farm thing, but had to quit when he lost his sight completely. He's back at home now and he thinks his life's a ruin. He's over the worst of it, but still." Dody paused. "Would you write to him?"

"Me? Why me?" She hadn't anticipated the question.

"Oh, Jean, you know. You've been through it all and you know what it's like. You can read Braille and type and play the piano. Your life hasn't stopped. He needs to hear about that, that a normal life can be possible. Will you write to him?"

Jean got up from the bed and turned on the radio on the round table by the window. Benny Goodman was playing. She fingered the tassel on the drapery pull and stood as though she were looking out across the terrace. So Dody thought her life hadn't stopped. And all this time she felt like she was waiting for it to begin.

"What would I say to him?"

"Just what you're doing. Music. The Red Cross. You know, teaching that girl to speak."

Jean moved to the closet and felt through her dresses. She pulled out a short-sleeved blue shirtwaist with a peter pan collar to wear to dinner.

"What's his name?"

"Forrest Holly."

"Sounds like some kind of plant."

"Jean, just do it. How can it hurt you?"

Dody was a good friend. Jean didn't want her disappointed or annoyed with her. Friends were too valuable. She remembered how, right after she lost her sight, she was so afraid she'd never have friends again. "Leave his address on my desk."

Jean still saw Sally Anne, too. Ever since Andrebrook days Sally Anne invited her to dances in Jersey and talked continually about men. "You've got to live a little," she kept telling her. Sally's boyfriend Don had a friend, Jaime, and the four often went out together. Vincent would put Jean on the train near Bristol and she'd get off at Grand Central. Sally Anne would be right there at the platform. Sometimes Don was with her. Sometimes Jaime. One day it was Jaime alone.

Jaime was Spanish, born in the Philippines, and he lived at the YMCA in Summit, New Jersey. One thing could be said for Jaime—he was attentive. When Jean was at Harkness again for a cataract operation, Jaime visited her every night. She'd never had attention like that before. It made her feel buoyant. At least she had Jaime to think about. "When you get out of here, Jean, I'm going to take you dancing," he said. "We're going to dinner first and then to the Chanticleer and they're going to play 'I'm in the Mood for Love.'" She wasn't sure whether his attentiveness softened the negligible results of the surgery, or whether she was so used to disappointment that it just didn't penetrate. Instead, her mind was on their next date, an evening at Rockefeller Center with Fred Astaire and Ginger Rogers in *Top Hat*. They often went dancing, and since Jaime was Latin he really knew how to lead. And since Jean was so sensitive to touch, she knew how to follow. They danced well together.

Eventually, Jaime visited Hickory Hill. "Father isn't entirely thrilled about any man named Jaime," Jean told Icy after his first visit. "To him, appropriate men are not named Jaime or Rudolfo, but George or Stanley or Robert, or anything you can say without having to roll your 'r's' or clear your throat." She began to call him Jimmy at home, but when they visited the Eastmans, he was Jaime again. Jean knew her parents didn't wholly approve because he was Catholic.

"It's not that we have any prejudice against the religion," Mother explained. "It's just that the serving people in Bristol are Catholic."

Mother's attitude made her graciousness to Jimmy false, to Jean at least. Jimmy didn't seem to notice. He loved the Treadway hospitality. He basked in it. Hickory Hill was far different from the YMCA. Still, the Hill was formal. Stuffy even. Jimmy liked the weekends they spent at the Eastmans better. Except for the coupe. Whenever Jimmy came to Hickory Hill, Father let him use the Packard convertible coupe. It was Yale blue.

Once, driving home from a dance at Farmington Country Club, Jimmy sang a song from *Top Hat*. He put his arm around her, pulled the Packard up the circular driveway and gave her a quick, familiar kiss on the forehead before he turned off the engine and got out. He swung around quickly to open the door for her.

"My lady." In an extravagant gesture she could only guess at, he offered her his arm and ushered her to the door, humming all the while. Inside, everyone was asleep. Even though it was early morning, Jean wanted to preserve the mood a little longer. "Let's have some cocoa. I can make some."

They turned to the right, through the maids' sitting room to the kitchen. Jimmy still sang softly that he was putting on his top hat. She was quite sure he didn't own a top hat, but it would be unkind to ask him. Father had several.

Jean felt along the counter for the third ice box door. She found the milk and reached for a saucepan from the rack.

Jimmy executed a few fancy turns with an imaginary dancer, his heels clicking on the kitchen tile.

Jean walked over to the food cupboard and reached right for the cocoa and sugar. Delia hadn't failed her. Then back to the spoon drawer. She poured milk into the saucepan, keeping her finger over the lip to feel how much she'd gotten. She kept pouring and pouring but didn't feel the level of the milk. Surely she had enough. She poured more.

"'I'm steppin' out, my dear, to breathe an atmosphere that simply reeks with class.'" He turned from his imaginary partner. "Jean, stop!" The milk spurted out in little spouts and dribbled down her dress and onto the floor. "That's not a pan. It's a thing with holes."

"A colander? Oh no," she wailed.

Quickly he pulled her away, grabbed the colander, put it in the sink and began to laugh.

Why did something have to happen every time she made cocoa for someone else when she did it fine for just herself?

He toweled off her dress and took her in his arms. "Wee Mouth, don't worry." He chuckled again, tenderly. "It just looked so funny, little squirts of milk coming out in all directions."

"I guess it must have." His kisses took away the pain of inadequacy, and she laughed a little too, settling into his embrace. She knew he was good for her because he treated her naturally and he explained things. And his attentions made her feel womanly. She must surely love him. He was comfortable and fun.

One afternoon Jean was playing "I'm in the Mood for Love" on the piano. Mort brought in the mail. "Letter for Jean," he announced.

"From Jimmy?"

"No. From California. It's typed. Badly." She didn't want to be teased so she just took it without comment. She kept it unopened on her dresser. When Tready visited a few days later, she asked her to read it.

"'Dear Jean Treadway, You probably know that Dody Rollins asked me to write to you. I don't much know what to say. I live in a little town called Ramona in California. It's a ranching town but there aren't any real big ranches around here. Our little 20 acres is called Rancho de los Pimientos because of the pepper trees. My brother Lance raises turkeys. I have one brother, four sisters and some cows.' This is a scream, Jean. Who is this guy?" Tready asked.

"Keep reading."

"'I have a flea bitten old gray gelding, too. I named him Snort because that's how I know where he is. My sister Alice and I ride all over the backcountry on dirt roads to visit cattle ranches and Indian reservations and arroyos. That's a Mexican-style canyon.

"'The Boss, that's my father, raises pea fowl. We used to have a porker named Bessie Belch because she did, until the depression made us slaughter her, bless her heart. Maybe you'd like to write back and tell me about you. Forrest Holly.'"

Tready handed it to her. "The typing's terrible. I could barely read it. Who is he?"

"Just someone in California Dody wants me to write to." She felt for the wastebasket with her foot and dropped it in.

"What do you know about him?"

"Not much."

"You going to write back?"

She shrugged. "What are you going to wear to the dance at the club?"

Weeks later when Jean was bored and no one was home, she sat down to type Forrest a letter. She had promised Dody, so she had to. It would have to be read to him. She wondered who would do it. His horse? Not knowing what to say, she started lamely, telling him about Lucy and her two brothers and Mother and Father. "We're a nice family, and we're happy, but we're not too smart. Don't you read Braille?" It was a short letter.

At least she could tell Dody she did it. When Icy came to pick her up that night to go to Litchfield, Jean took the letter and address and asked Icy to address and mail it.

At Icy's house, Mrs. Eastman hugged her at the door. "We have some great news for you. I made Icy promise she wouldn't tell you until you got here. Did she?"

"No. What is it?"

"We read in the paper last week about a new system for guiding the blind. They use trained dogs on a harness. Have you ever heard of that?"

"No."

"The blind person can feel the slightest hesitation of the dog when there's danger." Icy talked fast. "It's just been brought to this country a few years ago and is being taught at a place called The Seeing Eye in Morristown, New Jersey. You have to go there for a training period of several weeks."

"We couldn't wait to tell you. Why don't you get one?" Mrs. Eastman asked. "It would be just the thing for you. Then you could go around town yourself."

The idea was astounding. Three times Jean asked Mrs. Eastman to read the clipping. "I don't think Father would approve."

"Jean, some day you're going to have to stand up for yourself, for your own opinions and needs."

She knew Mrs. Eastman was right. The next week she had another letter for Icy to address and mail. It was to Morristown.

"What did your father say?"

"He doesn't know. This is just an inquiry, Icy."

"Mom will be proud of you."

Soon Jean learned that there were two things Father didn't want. He didn't want her writing to some poor blind cowboy in California and he didn't want a dog. On both counts she had spoken too much. She knew he acted on some stupid fear that she'd get entangled with people of a lower social class. She'd felt it with Lorraine all along, and now she felt it with Jimmy. Tackling both of Father's objections at once would be too formidable. She chose the one she cared about.

"What's wrong with a guide dog, Father?"

"You don't need a dog walking you all over town. You've got Vincent. He'll take you anywhere you need to go."

"That's not the point." Wasn't it obvious there was a difference?

She had started, but she didn't know how to follow through. Mother had taught her years ago it was best to let some things lie. "Let the idea work on him. Just wait," she always said.

She waited. Two weeks.

"He can't accept the idea that a dog can do something for you that he can't provide." Mother patted her on the arm.

She knew she'd have to use the cocktail system. It had worked before, the first time she went to New Jersey to visit Jimmy. It had worked as a child when she and Lucy wanted to go to the sailing camp on Cape Cod. That's when she discovered it, when she was ten. Getting a dog was important, at least as important as anything else she'd ever done. She would wait until Friday at cocktail hour when Father was relaxing with his manhattan.

Jean was already in the library when Father came in. The air wasn't moving at all and it was stuffy in the closed up room. She stood up to open a window. She knew what she was about to do would mark a turning point in her life, would begin to break the cords of dependency her father still seemed to need. That's what it would be for her, like opening a window.

Timing was everything. She had waited this long. A few minutes more wouldn't matter. She knew the sounds well. She could count the number of times he went over to the sideboard to pour himself a drink and could judge by that, but that wasn't as reliable as listening to his voice. When he was ready, there would be a different tone to his laughter. It would be a little more jovial. And he would talk faster. That told her to go ahead.

"Father, I applied for a dog at The Seeing Eye. I've been accepted if I still want one. And I do."

"I thought we've been through this already."

"It wasn't resolved."

"You don't need to be traipsing all over town with a dog."

"Why?"

"I would worry about you, honey."

"You should worry more if I'm stuck at home forever."

"You don't need to stay home. Vincent will take you wherever you want to go."

"That's different."

"What's the difference?"

Jean swallowed. She'd backed down at this point before. Now she had to go on. She moistened her lips. "Independence."

This time it was he who didn't have an answer. She felt him looking at her. Maybe it was better that she couldn't see his expression. She faced him directly, holding her face up to his. She swallowed, blinked, but didn't turn away. The clock on the mantle ticked loudly, filling the silence. Father tapped his pipe against an ashtray. She heard him scrape the bowl and pack new tobacco in, heard him light a match. But she didn't smell the cherry smoke which always followed the sound of his wooden match. Moments passed. Instead, she heard him get up from his leather chair and walk toward her.

He touched her gently on the shoulder. "If you really want to, Jean, I'm not going to stop you." His voice seemed to come from a long way away. It sounded old and maybe a little tired. His hand rested on her shoulder after he'd finished, as if he wanted to sustain contact. Apparently he could think of nothing else to say.

She heard him walk slowly out of the library and onto the verandah.

Chapter Ten

Mrs. Campbell, the secretary of The Seeing Eye, took Jean into the dining room and sat her between two men. "Jean, on your left is Vic Gulbransen. Vic's a chiropractor from St. Louis. Vic, this is Jean Treadway from Bristol, Connecticut."

"Hello," she said.

"Sit right down here, Jean. Looks like we're going to get fed in a minute."

She was already seated. A rough voice came from her left. "Glad to see we're gonna have some women in this group. I was worried we wouldn't have any skirts to chase."

"Who are you?" she asked.

"The name's Ham Walker."

"You better watch out for him, Jean. A sweet gal like you. I'm Louey."

"And I'm Dale Richardson," a mellow voice drawled from across the table.

"Are you from the South?" she asked.

"Tennessee."

"How many are here?"

"Six men and one other gal, but she's eating up in her room."

"Six?" Jean's voice went high. She'd never eaten with that many men when she was the only woman. "Whew! It's kind of warm in here, don't you think?"

"It'll be plenty hotter tomorrow, you can count on that." She didn't know who responded.

Plates clanked on the bare table. "Potato salad at ten o'clock, roast beef at six and tomatoes at two." It was Mrs. Campbell's voice, not actually unfriendly, but certainly businesslike. The idea was terrific, to treat plates of food just like a clock. Jean picked at the tomatoes but couldn't find a way to manage them. They must be stewed because her fork touched a small dish on her plate. She changed to a spoon but couldn't cut one. They slithered out from under the edge of her spoon each time. She explored her plate.

"Where did she say the meat was?" someone asked.

"Six o'clock," she answered.

She found something that felt like meat, but for the first time, there was no sighted person eating with her to see her dilemma and cut it for her. She ate the potato salad and scraped several times on that part of her plate to get all of it. She was too curious not to know. "Are all of you cutting your meat?"

"No, but I'm eating it anyway. What does it matter?" He had a point, whoever it was.

Next to her Vic Gulbransen stood up and brushed her elbow. "Anybody want another drink? Jean, can I get you anything?"

"No, thanks."

"I'll take another iced tea. A gallon of it." That was a new voice, Ray Johnson. When Vic came back with the drinks, it took the two men awhile to pass it across the table. "Anybody find the salt?"

"What for?" Jean asked.

"My drink. Everything. Been sweating so much I'm dehydrated. Haven't you heard of using salt for that?" Ray asked.

"Never."

"Where've you been all your life?"

No where, she thought. After dinner she still felt hungry. She heard someone light a match. "Who's smoking?"

"Me. Vic. Want a cigarette?"

"Yes, but how did you get it lit so fast? I have the hardest time doing it for myself."

"Here, let me show you." He held a cigarette and a match book toward her until she found his hand. "Hold the match between your thumb and middle finger, not your index finger, when you strike it."

"That's hard to do."

"Wait. First put the cigarette in your mouth. Got it?"

"Uh-huh."

"Okay, now strike the match. Got it lit?"

"Uh-huh."

"Now put your index finger of the hand with the match on top of the cigarette and slide it to the end so you know how far. Then you can aim."

She puffed for a moment. "It worked. I guess I needed a blind person to tell me that."

"Or a gentleman."

The comment stopped her short. It was true. But then she never asked Jimmy for help in learning how to do it herself. She hadn't asked anybody since she and Tready had smoked in the bathroom years ago. Maybe a sighted person wouldn't be of much help anyway. She inhaled deeply.

That night up in her room she wrote a letter home.

Dear Family,

They have typewriters for us to use and a piano in the recreation room. The men all drink beer with dinner. Already I learned how to light my cigarette myself. I know you won' t be pleased with that, Father, but it' s part of independence. We can smoke anywhere except in bed. I' ll have to learn how to cut my own meat. I' m kind of hungry at the moment. Golly, the whole business is so inspiring. The attitude is so natural. There' s no way to avoid bumping into things or each other. No one will help you.

Lillian, my roommate, is an old maid and has been in radio plays. She keeps to herself, but that' s okay. One man in the class, Dale Richardson, has a slow drawl, delicious to listen to, but he doesn' t talk much. He was injured in a hunting accident and is very subdued. I don' t think he' s been blind very long. There' s an Irishman from Indiana, Ray Johnson, who has a refreshment stand in a court building. He' s a screwball who keeps us in stitches and kids us to pieces. Louey Bruner has a newsstand in Worchester. I don' t think I know what Ham Walker does. Mrs. Campbell told me he has a terrible scar on his face. He' s loud and a little crude. And there are others. It' s great to meet so many different kinds of people. Already the world seems larger. Love to all, Jean

The next morning Mr. Lee, the instructor, took Jean aside. "You haven't ever been out on the streets alone, have you?"

"No, I guess not."

"Always had someone to walk with?"

"Yes."

"I can tell. Your biggest problem is that you don't know where you're facing. Do a quarter turn to the left." Jean turned to the left. "Do another." She did it again. "One more." She did it again. "You're facing me again now. It should have taken you four, not three. Follow me over here to this corner. You'll need to practice this before you get your dog. Here, feel this wall. And this one. You can tell where you're facing now, can't you?"

"Yes."

"Practice quarter turns with your arms down at your sides and then feel where you are. Concentrate on how much you're moving your feet. Stay here and work on this until I come back."

Her back became rigid and she felt her teeth grind together. Already she was separated from the others, just when she was beginning to feel comfortable. The night before had been wonderful, all that joking and getting to know each other, with her the only woman. Now here she was, alone again. Mr. Lee, the expert. Well, he didn't know everything. He certainly didn't know how she felt, or else he didn't care. She did four turns and held out her hands. No wall. No wall anywhere. She felt her chin quiver. At least they couldn't see her. Except for him.

The next afternoon she wrote:

July 24, 1941 Dear Family,

Are you in suspense about my dog? Lucy, don' t die. She' s a boxer, a brindle, and her name is Chiang. Everyone else has a German shepherd. There is always one boxer in a string of ten trained dogs. I think I got her because she' s supposed to be less high strung and easier for me to handle. I can love her in spite of it, I hope I hope. Chiang rhymes with fang, and it makes her seem so sinister. They told me her face is fierce looking, a little like a bulldog, but maybe that will be okay. This whole thing is a lot harder than I thought it would be, but maybe I' ll come home a different person. There' s more to all of this than just getting a dog. I want you to be proud of me. Love, Jean

So much happened in one day that the next night she had to share it. Exhausted and with Chiang at her feet, she wrote:

Dearest Icy,

Chiang and I were friends from the first clap of hamburger in her mouth. Can' t wait for you to meet her. I' m thrilled to be here and am so glad you and your mother encouraged me to do this. It' s the most important thing I' ve ever done. Did I type ever twice? I can' t remember sometimes. Well, I meant it. Get this, Icy. For the first time in my life, I' m surrounded by men.

So many things are funny here. The dogs all go to dinner with us. By that I mean that when we, all eight of us in my class, are in the dining hall, eight dogs are under the dining room table at our feet. It' s a scream. Nobody knows where to put his feet. We had ham for dinner tonight and halleluiah I cut it myself. We either find a way to eat it or go hungry.

This morning we took our first training route with
our dogs. Before this we practiced with imaginary dogs.
It was hard because the dogs are so used to Lee, the
trainer, having the harness. Chiang walks fast. That
means I have to walk just as fast to get the tension right
on the harness in order to catch the signals. We learned a
new command, " hop up." It means step it up a bit, get
going. I can' t imagine I' ll ever use it, though. We
walked miles and I was puffing. I haven' t been
unsweaty since I got here. But I' ve got to keep at it and
not let her get away with a thing. She did a swell deed,
though, in keeping me from crossing when a car pulled
up in front of us.

She stopped her slobbering today, and I guess that' s
because she' s not as nervous and excited. I' m a much
drier and cleaner person as a result. But I don' t care.
It' s too important not to put everything into it, so I just
let her slobber on me.

With drools of love, Jean

The next day Jean felt self-conscious out on the street by
herself so she wanted to get the routes over with fast. She
couldn't get Chiang to go fast enough. "Hop up," she pleaded
minute by minute, astonished at herself.

A week later she wrote:

Dearest Family,

We took the afternoon route in pairs and Dale
Richardson and I did pretty well, so we were told. I

don' t mind saying that at one point if I' d given in to where he thought we should go, we would have been lost, but I stuck to my guns. The least of my troubles seems to be memorizing the routes, but that' s a big problem for most of the others. My main trouble is keeping my direction. When I give Chiang the order " forward," my body must be in the exact direction I want her to take me so she' ll know where to go, but sometimes I don' t know what direction that is.

After we finish the route, Mr. Lee (we just call him Lee now) leaves us on a bench at the bus station. Our bus comes along, we listen to where the door opens, then heel our pups into the bus and go to the back seat. The drivers drop us off in front of the institute, and then the dogs lead us right to the door. The drivers are good to us and kid us along.

Last night Chiang joined the Sooner Club. She' s the third member from our class. The motto of the club is " I' d sooner do it in the house than in the park." I had to learn to find it and clean it up. Ick.

Thank you, Lucy, for the cookies. They arrived fine and yummy.

Love to all, Jean and Chiang

She sealed the letter, crawled into bed and relished the feel of cool sheets against her skin. Still, she didn't sleep well. The dogs were supposed to be kept tied to the beds. Chiang was restless and kept flopping over on her other side, and so her chain rattled on the bare floor. Each time Chiang flopped over,

Jean did, too. At least she had a large rug in her bedroom at home.

She relived the struggles of the day. Tending to Chiang was like taking care of a baby. Always there was tension. Jean couldn't let up, even for a minute, just to relax. Too many times Chiang wouldn't do what she wanted. Sometimes when she said, "Forward," nothing happened. It was embarrassing to have to repeat the command again and again. All she could do was stand there like a fool and wait. And when she did get Chiang walking, sometimes she stopped to sniff something. The others' dogs didn't do that. And they didn't let out noisy smells under the dining room table, either.

Chiang breathed a deep, satisfied snore, puffing air out the side of her mouth. And the rest of the dogs don't snore like a doddery grandfather. Getting adjusted to a dog must be something like getting adjusted to a husband, she thought. So what was that supposed to mean?

Idly, she wondered what Vic Gulbransen looked like. He was always so kind to her and had a soft voice. She could tell from the direction of his voice that he must be tall. And he liked music, too. She and Vic were going to buy the *New World Symphony* for Lee. Vic must be good looking to be that nice to everyone. But that was a silly thought. Entirely illogical. Still, she hoped it was so. Then she realized maybe she'd never know. Unless she asked Mrs. Campbell. Vic wasn't married. That she knew. But she also knew that St. Louis was a long way away. After this class, they'd probably never see each other again.

She rolled over. It was too hot even for a sheet. At home, she'd sleep without one, but here, she wasn't sure who might walk into her room by mistake. But if it was a student, what would it matter? She pulled it part way up and turned her pillow over to put her face on the cool side. She kept thinking of the final test. It would be on the downtown streets of Newark with traffic and noise. They would have to use city buses during rush hour. She'd gotten nervous and headachy all day just thinking about it. It was unknown territory to be faced alone. "You're not alone," she remembered Lee saying. "You have your dog." But sometimes that didn't seem enough.

The next day heading out for the routes, Ham bumped into Jean. It wasn't the first time. He did it practically every day. His heavy shoe scraped against her ankle. "Damn it, José," Ham said to his dog. "Get away from Chiang's ass." She heard Ham shake his harness.

The comment stunned her. She just stood there. "Move on ahead, Jean," Lee said.

"Forward," she said quickly to Chiang. Her voice quavered. Chiang turned back toward José. "Forward," Jean pleaded again. Chiang pulled her around backwards right into Ham's sweaty stomach.

"Speak up, Jean," Lee scolded. She panicked and yanked on Chiang's harness.

Ham shouted, "Heel," yanked on his harness, and José obeyed.

"Quarter turn left and forward, Jean," Lee directed and Jean followed.

"Forward," she said with all the voice she could muster. Her heart was racing and she stepped quickly. "Hop up," she said. She wanted to get clear away from wherever Ham and José might be. She felt perspiration slide the harness in her hand.

"Don't be so passive," Lee told her after dinner that night. "No dog will mind you with that timid little voice. You've got to sound like you mean it." Lee sounded like he meant it. She felt like she was being chastised by Mr. Klimke in Latin class.

"Wanting a dog to do something and telling a dog what you want are two different things," he went on. "The difference has got to be your voice and a firm hold on the harness. Those are the only two ways your dog will know she has to obey."

"No matter how many times you tell me, it's the only voice I've got."

"You're wrong." She heard him sit down next to her. "Jean," he said quietly, "I see the blind living under some self-imposed cult of meekness as if, by being blind, they have to be milquetoast, apologizing by the way they stand or speak for the space they're taking up on this planet." She felt like he meant her alone. It made her feel worse. She hoped no one else was around to hear him say this. "But that doesn't have to be. Whether you or your family recognized it or not, you didn't come here just to get a dog. You came here to learn independence. The Seeing Eye intends to shatter that meekness and replace it with self-esteem and self-reliance. So speak up and stand up straight."

Jean blinked away the wetness, stood, and walked toward the doorway to the yard. She bumped into the doorjamb, adjusted, and went outside. She touched her forehead. Already there was a lump forming. Tears came. The early evening air hung heavy and her palms, her underarms, the crease opposite her elbows all felt damp.

She didn't actually want to feel sorry for herself. It wasn't very grown up. All the others were facing challenges as great as her own. New Jersey was sweltering, and training entailed a lot of walking so everyone was losing weight. Ray Johnson sat on a woman in the bus one day. Louey Bruner, who had lost his sense of taste when he lost his sight, ate half his paper plate with his hot dog one night. But still it was worth it. The struggle must have its purpose, or the others wouldn't do it, either. She didn't question that for a moment.

She walked along the side of the building. Her hand traced a row of bricks. She had never wanted anything before as strongly as this, so strongly that it hurt. She squeezed the hurt out of her eyes in warm tears. But she hadn't known what it would be like. She had thought a dog could replace people and could lead her around. Maybe instead, she herself had to replace other people. The dog was only a vehicle. Maybe that was what she had to want, self-direction. If she could just turn the force of that desire into doing the right things, then she could master this dog business. She pursed her lips. The desire for a dog wasn't the same as the will to succeed, though. The will had to come from within, from concentration based on commitment, not just to prove to Father she had made the right decision, but to prove it to herself.

Concentrating, she turned a quarter turn, paused to think, then did another, then two more. She stretched out her hand. The bricks were where they should be.

Chapter Eleven

Two more weeks at The Seeing Eye widened their routes and welded the group closer. Jean rolled a clean sheet into her typewriter and wrote:

Dear Lorraine,

I was so excited when I read your letter. Certainly, I' ll be a bridesmaid at your wedding. I think I could do just about anything now. The dogs have helped us so. I hope you' ll be able to have a real church wedding, no matter how small. I' d get married out in a field at this point, if only to be married.

Your second page of Braille was quite elegant, and I could read the first page, too, even though it was backwards. You keep it up. Tell me anything you want after you' re married because I

Oops. I was interrupted by Lillian, my usually unsociable roommate, and forgot my last word. Anyway, I' ll be coming home Monday. Hooray! I' ve worked hard here and can do so much more on my own now. My parents will have to let me do things they didn' t before. I feel like a new person.

Ever, Jean

"Christ, it's hot," Ham said the next evening in the recreation room.

"Stifling," Jean agreed. "I don't feel a hint of breeze. Are all the windows open, do you think?"

"I checked them twice."

They played cards with Braille cards and called out their plays. The dogs dozed beneath the table.

"I'm glad I'm not a dog," Jean said. "All that hair. Those poor pooches. It must be like wearing blankets. I didn't even want to sleep with a sheet last night."

"Oo-ee. Did you?" Ham's voice reached a rough falsetto.

"Never mind."

"Aw, come on. Tell us," Ray teased.

"Of course she did." It was Vic's voice.

"How do *you* know?" Ham chortled.

"She's from New England, isn't she?"

Jean felt a smile creep over her face. Here she felt more womanly than she ever had before. Vic often came to her rescue when they teased her. It was kind of him, but he didn't need to. She enjoyed it. She wondered for the hundredth time what they all looked like. They were from all walks of life, from different social classes, of all ages. In spite of that, she felt like them. Their one similarity united them in a way she could never feel united with Lucy or the rest of the family—or with any man.

"What does a chiropractor actually do?" she asked Vic.

"Manipulates the joints to get them into alignment."

"How do you know if they're not?"

"Feel. I can tell what needs to be altered by how it feels under the skin."

"Does it hurt?"

"Sometimes. Usually not."

"Mostly for people's necks?"

"Backs, mainly. You mean you've never had someone rub your back?"

"Heavens, no."

"Here. Lean forward." He walked around to the back of her chair. Gently he put his hands on her shoulders. She tightened up. "Relax." He rubbed the back of her neck until her head fell forward naturally.

"Ooh, it feels good."

"Ssh. Just relax."

Relax? His touch made her do anything but relax. His fingers were firm and penetrating and sent a ripple of feeling across her shoulders. She took a big breath and let it out loudly.

"Hey, what are you doing to her, Vic? You might at least have the decency to go somewheres else," Ray said.

"Jealous, eh?" Vic said. It made Jean giggle. "Relax. I can't do this when you're laughing." She obeyed and her shoulders sagged. It felt exciting and comforting at the same time to have his hands on her. He rubbed until she felt hypnotized by his hands and then he told her, "Stand up and clasp your hands behind your head." He put both his arms through hers, pulled upwards and then down and up again sharply.

"Yeow! What was that?"

"Just cracked your spine."

"Ooh, I have prickles all down my back."

"See? You didn't know how tight you were."

"It feels all tingly." He was right. Tight. She felt suddenly freer.

"That's the oldest trick in the book, Jean. Watch out." Ham chortled.

"I'm watching, but nothing's happening," she said with the confidence of knowing she was lovely to the men who sat around her in the sultry recreation room.

"You'll make Lillian upstairs jealous," Ray said.

Jean smirked. "That'd be something new, somebody jealous of me."

"Naw, that's not Lillian's problem. She's just stuck up," Ray muttered.

"Frigid, probably," Ham added after a pause. "Now Jean here, she'll never have that problem."

"How do *you* know?" Ray teased, echoing Ham's joke.

"She's down here with us, ain't she?" Ham countered.

There was a new pleasure in this give-and-take playfulness with sexual undertones. She stretched and settled back into the chair, into the center of men's attention for the first time in her life. "Do you want to play another hand?"

"Eh? What's that you say? Do I want to play with your hand?"

She laughed. Typical comment for Ham.

"No, too hot." Dale's drawl.

"Too hot to play. Too hot to go to bed. Might as well stay up," said Ray.

"We could tell ghost stories. Or jokes," Jean said.

"What's the funniest thing that ever happened to you?" Ray threw out the question to the group.

"The time I walked into a women's restroom," Ham said. "Some screamy broad didn't believe I couldn't see. Thought it was a trick and that I was about to rape her. 'Lady, I wouldn't touch you if you were built like Mae West,' I said. She had a voice like a hyena."

They all laughed. "Boy, she mighta had a couple of big ones to bump into." Ray snorted through his laugh.

"Lady present," Vic cautioned, but Jean listened intently.

"What was the most embarrassing thing?"

"Going to a job interview with shoes that didn't match."

"Same thing happened to me with socks."

In the oppressive heat, without their instructors there, without their families and friends, without the world, they were finally free to reveal their private selves. Out spilled stories of buttoning shirts wrong and of cutting themselves re-learning to shave. They told of the panic of dropping keys and forgetting phone numbers. Everyone had a story of getting lost. They laughed at the universality of their experiences.

"Just because we can laugh about it now doesn't mean we'll never get lost again, even with our dogs," Ham said. The stark realization quieted them.

"Getting lost is more than a surrender and a lowering of pride." Dale Richardson spoke even more slowly than usual, and his voice sounded hollower. "You've got to admit it. I'm not the only one who feels it. Why not say it? Terror."

Jean swallowed. Yes, that was it. In Munich on the bridge, that was it. In New York when Madame Flagstad grabbed her arm in the crowd. And the countless times she didn't know where she was—at school, at Icy's house, in the riding ring. Terror. No one with sight could possibly know.

The word hung there in the darkness and then it unleashed a flood of talk. "What's worse even than that is to have to admit to my kids when I need help," said Louey. "When panic is private, it ain't so bad, but when you have to ask, then it's public and—"

"Humiliation, that's what you mean. It's humiliating to ask for the privilege of movement." It was the first entirely serious thing she'd ever heard Ray say.

"But our families won't have to help us so much any more," Jean said. She felt the conversation digging itself in and wanted to stop it. "They've got to see that we can do more for ourselves now. And look at what all of you have already done, earning your own living. That makes me feel I haven't accomplished anything." Her voice cracked. "They can't help but see we're even more able now."

She wished she didn't sound like she was trying to convince herself.

"Let's hope so."

"If my wife doesn't, then I'm not sure what will happen," Dale said slowly. His words stretched out as if there were more to come. Everyone waited. "Sometimes I wonder just how long she'll stay. She didn't sign on for this when she married me."

In the long silence, a wicker chair creaked when someone shifted. "Does she baby you?" Ray asked.

"Yes, and then resents doing so much but never admits it."

"Wrong. It's wrong," said Ham. "Treating us like we can't do anything just because we can't do one thing. The world is just plain stupid sometimes. Ever notice how people talk louder to you than they do to anybody else?"

"Or they talk slowly and exaggerate the words like they're speaking English to a foreigner or a kid," said Dale.

"Or an idiot," added Ham.

The remark stopped the conversation. Chiang began to snore. A siren a few blocks away whined its lonesome call through the open window.

"I guess we don't have any right to tell the world in just what way we want it to be kind," Vic said softly, the first thing he said since he'd rubbed her back.

No one could counter Vic's remark, and it hung there in the humid room a long time. The pain in that truth breathed like another presence among them until Jean couldn't stand it any longer. She got up and made her way to the piano. Her hands touched the keys with a gentleness that seemed to ask permission to break the silence. She played a Chopin nocturne. It was something she could offer. Not a sound disturbed the melody. Even the dogs were quiet. When she finished, the men gathered up their dogs and slowly headed for their rooms.

"Thank you, Jean," Vic said in a tender whisper.

In a halting gesture, someone patted her awkwardly three little pats on her shoulder, but said nothing. She recognized Ham by his stomach as she brushed past him while he held the door open for her and Chiang to go out before him. Coming from him, the gesture made her feel like a lady.

When she found her bed that night, she let out a deep lingering sigh. What good people, she thought. She sank into the injustice of it as she lay down absolutely still. What could she do? What could anyone do? Well, she could invite them all to Hickory Hill after graduation.

A silly idea. It wouldn't work. There, they wouldn't have what they had here tonight. Nowhere would she have again what she had here tonight. There would never be another night so honest and intimate. She rolled onto her side and tried to keep it alive by staying awake, but the work of the day descended and the stillness made her fall asleep.

Two days later she wrote:

Dearest Father and Mother,

I won' t be coming home on Monday after all. I
have to stay another week. I failed the big test in
Newark. I couldn' t get Chiang to go in revolving doors.
After I tried to make her do that, she wouldn' t go in
any doors to stores at all. It' s not her fault. I have a
swell, steady pooch. It' s my own. I just have to speak
up and sound like I mean it. Maybe I couldn' t do it
because Miss Weaver wasn' t here saying, " Of course
you can, Jean." It will be awful saying goodbye to
everyone. I' ve become attached to them so. Their last
night is tomorrow. Who knows when I' ll see them
again. If ever. Please don' t worry about me.

I got a wire from Elsa Flagstad. She got married last
Saturday out in Montana. I guess it' s the cowboy. I' m
afraid Madame Flagstad will be sorry she ever took Elsa
on that tour. At least she' s married, though.

Please get a dozen one-pound cans of Pard and a
package of Vita-cubes. I' ll phone soon. You don' t
have to drive down and pick me up. I can take the train
now.

Ever lovingly, Jean and Chiang

The next week was grueling and terribly lonely. She didn't particularly want to put effort into knowing the new class. All she could think about was how the men in her class were doing back with their families. She ate at the end of one table and didn't talk much and didn't stay in the recreation room in the evenings. Instead, she worked alone in the yard with Chiang as long as Lee would let her. When she gave commands it sounded to her as if all of Morristown could hear. After that she worked on quarter turns in the corner of her room. She didn't even write any letters. What if she failed the test again? Did they ever send someone home without a dog? She was afraid to ask. Each night she fell into bed exhausted.

At the end of the week Chiang lay on her side breathing heavily in the heat. Jean moved in jerks, putting everything into her suitcases. The last thing was to put Chiang's harness on.

"Forward," she said. There was new authority in her voice that told Chiang something important was happening. Chiang led her downstairs, her hand firm on the harness. They went into the secretary's office to review her record and sign the release papers.

"Promise me one thing, Jean," Mrs. Campbell said softly. She put her hand on Jean's wrist. "Whatever you do, marry a sighted man.

Chapter Twelve

On her own territory at Hickory Hill and with no trainer in sight, Jean was the only authority. That in itself made her more relaxed. The first day, she gave Chiang a tour of the whole house, even the maids' quarters on the third floor and the wine cellar in the basement. She taught Chiang the way to the pool through the library and verandah. She taught her to go through the living room and out the French doors to the terrace and rose garden.

Jean stopped Chiang when she caught the fragrance of a rosebush in bloom. She leaned down, carefully, and took a deep breath. By its sweetness and by their position in the garden, she decided that it was Peace. She imagined its fluffy whiteness tinged in pale pink. The outdoors held new riches for her now and she felt the same elation as she had at Camp Hanoum.

The next morning they made a complete circuit of the garden. Chiang remembered. Jean thought of the woods beyond the landscaped grounds. "I haven't been there alone since I was a kid," she said. She felt a little foolish, talking out loud, as if Chiang could understand as well as see. But Chiang did understand, sort of. A path led off to the woods from the bottom of the driveway. Surely Chiang could find it. "Forward," Jean said, and they headed around the side of the house to the driveway.

The path through the woods felt dry. They crunched leaves as they walked. She stepped on something hard that twisted her ankle slightly. She bent down and felt along the ground. Acorns. She picked one up and pulled off the cap to smell the dry, woodsy odor of the coming autumn. The deep shade was cool and inviting after the sweltering heat of New Jersey streets. Chiang kept up a steady pace. Jean held out her hand to the side, more to find out what was there and to push away twigs and branches than to help guide her along. Her hand brushed the tough bark of a tree. A hickory, she decided. She began looking for a birch. Its satiny bark would be peeling away. Instead, her arm passed through a spider web. Its filaments clung to her skin. She stopped to brush it off.

The woods were suddenly silent without their footsteps crunching the blanket of leaves. She heard the low, throaty sound of robins interrupted by a blue jay's raucous screech. She listened more carefully for the gurgle of the creek, but couldn't hear it. It had been a dry summer. The scent of wild violets told her she must have stepped on some. There must be a lot of them here, she thought. Too bad I didn't find them first so I could pick some. But I wouldn't have found them unless I smashed the petals enough to let out the scent. "Do you know what forgiveness is, Chiang? It's the fragrance of a violet on the heel of him who crushed it. That's a saying I remember from I don't know when." She let out a satisfied sigh.

"Forward," she said. Her stretched-out arm caught the thin smoothness of a birch trunk. They stopped again and she reached up to find a twig. She bent one back and forth until it weakened and broke off. She peeled away the soft bark and chewed on the stem. It was tender and fibrous and tasted like sarsaparilla, a flavor left over from childhood. She felt like swinging her arms and skipping, but she went on more cautiously, stopping frequently, sometimes stumbling over a root or a rock. She stretched her arm out low to find some undergrowth. Her hand touched a lady's-slipper. Its bulbous bloom hung heavily. She remembered it was a soft lavender pink. Something crawled on her forearm. She didn't move so she could concentrate. Long. Maybe a caterpillar. She brushed it off, stood up and turned around 180 degrees to go back. "Woods remind me of Icy and camp." She felt more comfortable talking to Chiang now, as if she were a companion as well as guide. "I wonder, Chiang. Have you ever been in woods before, or always in some concrete training yard? Have you ever been able to run free?" Chiang was silent. "Well, I can't remember what it was like, either, so I guess we're a pair. Hop up," she said. There was more world to explore beyond Hickory Hill.

They walked back through the woods, down the driveway and onto the streets on the Hill. "We're going to Federal Hill Green, Chiang." She remembered the way; she'd walked there for years to Federal Hill Grammar School. Of course she could find it.

On two sides of the triangular green stood its two most prominent buildings, the First Congregational Church and St. Joseph's Catholic Church, as if confronting each other from a safe distance. They had occupied these plots of ground since the days before the Revolution. Jean felt the shadow of St. Joseph's Parochial School, then the sunlight glancing at a low angle between it and the convent. Shadow and sunlight took turns as she passed the convent, rectory and finally the long shade of the church. She knew that beyond St. Joseph's church was the graveyard. They walked along its edge in the sunlight until she felt another shadow, the grammar school. She hadn't been there alone since the sixth grade. Chiang stopped. That meant Jean needed to make a decision, either to go straight, away from the Green on residential streets, or turn left to walk the perimeter of the common. Jean pivoted what she thought was more than the customary ninety degrees. "Forward." Chiang understood and led her along the edge of the Green. Militia had drilled right here in order to fight for independence. A private similarity occurred to her. She took big strides, her shoulders square. Freedom of movement was as important as freedom of speech or freedom of religion. Her step became more sure. She smiled again even though she was alone, in fact, because she was alone.

On the third day, when her parents were away, she decided to go to Tready's house. It was better to tell them after she had done something. As soon as they left she phoned Tready and asked her to watch for them. Tready's house was a few blocks farther than the Green. She knew the way. She could count the blocks, but Tready lived in the middle of a block. Once on Tready's block, it would be up to Chiang to learn the right walkway to take to the right house. They walked briskly along Oakland Street and at the right block Jean slowed down the pace.

"Congratulations, Jean," Tready called from her porch. Her voice sounded wonderful. It was the first time Jean had visited anyone alone without Vincent to drive her.

Her brother Bill and his wife Ginny would be next. They lived ten blocks away. Jean called and invited herself to dinner for the following day. Father was just coming home from work when she stepped out the front door. Oops. She had left too late. "I'm going to Bill and Ginny's," she said cheerfully.

"Now?"

"Yes, I'm almost late," she said, avoiding the point of his question.

"I don't like the idea of you coming home alone after dark."

"After dark? What do I care about that?" Tactical error. It shouldn't have been a question. This wasn't a time to be cute. "I've got the best bodyguard anybody could have. Lee said Chiang looks meaner than any dog he's ever trained. Don't worry, Father. I'll call when I'm ready to leave and you can watch for me." She knew she had to react as if his concern was just that, concern and not prohibition. "Bye. Forward, Chiang."

In two or three weeks the ten blocks to Bill and Ginny's became easy. It was time to venture all the way downtown. There would be traffic lights and cars. She rehearsed in her mind the streets leading to her hairdresser's, made an appointment and started off. They walked at a hearty pace and found the office building easily enough. It was on a corner. Inside, Jean had to feel along the corridor wall for the third door. After going there a few times Chiang learned it and took her right there. What a marvelous pooch. Jean loved her more and more each day, for the one thing even Father couldn't give her, mobility.

As Jean stretched her radius of travel, her thinking stretched, too. She took on more piano students at the Girls' Club and organized a recital for them. She walked to the Congregational church on the Green to ask if they knew of any shut-ins she could visit downtown. The activities held a double purpose. What helped others helped her. That recognition gave her satisfaction. For the first time in her life, she felt useful.

Fall came and she walked in the rain. It felt refreshing, except for the time she slipped on a leaf or something on the wet pavement and nearly went down. Winter followed and she walked through the first snow. The first Saturday in December, she went around the block in minus-two degree weather, just to write to Dody in California that she'd done it. It was invigorating, but afterwards she felt contrite. It wasn't a kind thing to do to Chiang.

The next morning in the library, Jean and her parents were listening to the Sunday radio broadcast of the New York Philharmonic. Toscanini was directing. An announcer interrupted. Japan had attacked Pearl Harbor. Many lives and ships were lost. At present they didn't know how many. The family was stunned and outraged. "It doesn't seem real," Mother said.

"It does to me." The sick-hearted feeling Jean had had in Germany with Miss Weaver returned. She heard again the pulsing thud of boots, felt again the constriction in her throat at the hated word, "*Heil*." All that was only a build-up to this. And where would it go from here? The war was engulfing the world.

Life changed. Uncle Ed and Uncle Dudley switched the Ingraham Company from making clocks and watches to timers for explosives. Jean's cousins went to work there. Father's factory, Horton Manufacturing Company, formerly making sports equipment—golf clubs and fishing rods—now made antenna shafts for communication systems on tanks. Bill and Mort and Lucy all went to work there. Neither brother could join up. Classification 4F. Poor vision. Jean folded bandages at the Red Cross downtown. She knitted the bulky gray Red Cross sweaters for refugee children and delivered them downtown. She was part of the war effort.

Even though there was a war, there was still good in the world. She felt almost guilty for thinking so, for feeling the exhilaration of freedom. And if that fellow from California ever sent her a letter again, she wrote to Dody, she'd tell him about Chiang. She wrote to Sally Anne about Chiang. She wrote to Elsa. She wrote to Jimmy. And she posted her own letters.

Independence had its price, she learned. While her own activities increased, her dates with Jimmy decreased. Strange. He didn't invite her quite so often to New Jersey, but when he did, she stepped off the train at Grand Central more firmly with Chiang leading her down the steps. Once when she arrived, Jimmy wasn't on the platform as he always was. Jean waited a few moments, listening for his familiar voice. Shoulders brushed by her own. She felt she was an obstruction in the middle of the platform. She turned in the direction they always went. "Forward." In the station she heard him call out to her. He introduced her to two women he had been talking to, a mother and daughter. Their bubbly friendliness gave Jean an uneasy feeling of insincerity. Jimmy didn't say anything more about them as they walked out of the station.

Days passed and Christmas was approaching. She wrote to invite Jimmy to Hickory Hill. He didn't answer. Vincent brought in their nine-foot tree. The two years before, she and

Jimmy had decorated it together. She and Lucy did it this year. The maids hung greens under the chandelier in the stairwell. Jean still didn't hear from Jimmy. She resigned herself to a "family only" Christmas. The whole Ingraham family, nearly twenty of them, came to noon dinner. They started with clam chowder and proceeded to baked scalloped oysters, turkey, ham, and the traditional New England Indian pudding made with corn meal and molasses. It seemed tasteless this year.

A few days later, Japan bombed Manila. Jean wondered what Jimmy felt about it. He'd been born there. She wrote to ask him to a New Year's celebration at Hickory Hill. He didn't respond.

On New Year's Eve Mother and Father had an Ares and Ain'ts party. Years earlier Yale alumni from the Bristol area developed a private bridge group centered around Father, Mr. Yale himself, lifelong treasurer of his class of 1910. The club was called The Ares and The Ain'ts because, as he explained it, "Some of us are married and some of us ain't." Usually Ares and Ain'ts evenings began with a black tie dinner of four or five courses with printed menus. Then they'd adjourn to the living room for bridge and eventually end up in the grill room in the basement, a large room for entertaining fitted up like a British pub with furniture upholstered in deep red velvet. Though the Ares and Ain'ts were conversationally polite at dinner in the dining room, and dead serious about bridge in the living room, they usually raised a storm in the grill room late at night.

Just now, well before the midnight hour, they still occupied the living room. Laughter and music and singing spiraled up the stairway. Champagne corks popped. Glasses tinkled. Jean sat up in bed above the party in a flannel nightgown reading Daphne DuMaurier's *Rebecca*, the wide Braille book spread out on her lap. Mother came upstairs. "Do you want a chicken salad sandwich and some ice cold champagne?"

It tasted good and it was kind of Mother to remember her when so much was going on downstairs, but the interruption made it hard to go back to her book. Her hands were cold, and she tucked them under the covers, giving up reading for a while. She wondered if all of that—the parties, the life with a husband and family, entertaining friends—would ever be for her. Would she always be an Ain't? Was God only going to give her a piece of life? Would she always be an observer of someone else's living? An observer. The irony made her smirk. Why was it so wrong for her to imagine and long for the domestic life of an ordinary woman, a life others took for granted?

She pulled in a deep breath, let it out slowly and ate a bite of her sandwich. Her eyes blinked. If it is to be, it wasn't going to be with Jimmy. That was obvious. She hadn't heard from him for two months. Maybe he was spending New Year's with that girl at the train station. That mother was more than friendly. Overly familiar, she'd call it. Definitely out to nab him for her daughter. If she could tell the designs that woman had on Jimmy just by her voice, then surely Jimmy must be able to tell, too. But men are stupid sometimes.

Maybe he had felt, all along, the silent disapproval of Mother and Father even though they were properly polite. But proper didn't always mean genuine. Maybe he realized that Hickory Hill wasn't for him. Maybe—and this was harder to face—he foresaw that she would become a burden to him. Years might make his extra solicitations grow wearisome. If that could happen, he might eventually resent her. Then she wouldn't want him either. Her eyes narrowed as if she were trying to see into the future. She pursed her lips.

Where was there a person who could share her life without adopting her limitations? A person who would see her as whole? A normal life had been so close with Jimmy, but when it came right down to it, other routes must have looked easier to him. There was no denying it. Life with her would be different. She was different. Oh, yes, she'd had many advantages. She'd been to the capitals of Europe. She'd heard the world's finest musicians, read the world's greatest literature. She never lacked for anything. But she had never eaten a meal cooked with her own hands. Where was normalcy at Hickory Hill?

If Jimmy wasn't going to give her a natural domestic life, she'd have to do it for herself. They had told her that much at The Seeing Eye, loud and clear on the first night. She'd have to cut her own meat or she'd go hungry. Now here was the bigger picture. She'd have to buy it and cook it, too, or she'd go hungry in a far deeper way.

The words she spoke in her mind jangled again, "If Jimmy wasn't going to give her a natural life...." There it was—the deeper flaw that would make her permanently dependent, "give her a natural life," as if Jimmy or any man was going to take the place of Father, providing her with life. Her blindness wasn't making her feel dependent. Father was, unintentionally—she granted him that—and unconsciously, simply by his enormous need to be provider and to have her continue accepting in meekness. It was in that arena she'd have to struggle free. The test wasn't on the streets behind Chiang's harness. It was in her mind. She remembered Miss Weaver's adamant voice, "Of course you can, Jean." Look at Miss Weaver. She never married. Marriage was no guarantee of a normal life. And look at the wide world Miss Weaver claimed as hers. Jean's heartbeat quickened at the possibilities. She reached for the rest of the sandwich and realized she'd eaten it all without noticing.

The first three days of 1942, it snowed continually. Jean opened her bedroom window, leaned out and stuck out her tongue to feel the snowflakes, when she heard Mother call her from downstairs to read her mail. There were two letters. Only one was addressed to her. The other was addressed to Mrs. Treadway, postmarked Summit, New Jersey. She heard Mother open it, but she didn't say anything. "Just read it," Jean said.

Mother cleared her throat. "This one's written to me but it's really for you. It's from Jimmy." Mother's voice sounded odd. "He's asking me to explain to you that it wouldn't work, and that it would be better for both of you if you didn't see each other any more."

It started as a sharp wince, then surged up through her chest. Her throat shrank into a taut line. "He wrote that to you?" Her voice shook. "Why couldn't he tell me himself?" Why did he wait so long, letting me go through the holidays not knowing what happened? All the good times, the laughter and the dancing, Jimmy's funny singing, all this couldn't make up for such a cruel, bungling way to end it.

Jean held on to herself while Mother put into her hand two small items. They were cold. She fingered them for a moment. Her ring from Bristol High and a tie pin she'd given him the Christmas before. Slowly she closed her fist around them. In her other hand Mother put the letter. She crumpled it into a ball.

Mother began to tear open the second letter.

"Later." Jean raced out of the room and ran up the stairs, stumbling at the top one even though she hadn't needed to count them for years. She rushed to her room and pulled the door shut. She flung herself down and hugged her pillow, burying her face in it. She knew she'd been preparing herself for this. On New Year's Eve she'd confronted it, but that had been intellectual then. Now it was really and truly here. She wrapped the pillow around her ears so that Mother wouldn't hear her wail.

After a while she noticed her neck and shoulders, even the muscles in her face, were tense. Where was Vic Gulbransen with his soothing hands now? Jimmy never touched her like Vic had. She imagined again Vic's penetrating fingers loosening her tightness. Then she had felt like a woman. Jimmy only touched her so safely. He didn't treat her with the deep regard she felt Vic had. He didn't even treat her as a human being. Writing a letter to her mother—that denied she was even real, much less a woman. What insight did that show? Only cowardice. Talk about a sighted man! Her face felt tight.

An Ingraham clock ticked. Every other tick seemed to have a higher pitch. She put her hands over her ears. The clock took no notice of the magnitude of this hour. It ticked as it always had. As it always would. Even now, on this winter afternoon, time would already, minutely, begin to diminish the sharpness of the moment, like the snow she remembered rounding the angles of Hickory Hill's roofline. She half recognized this in the part of her mind that was still thinking objectively. Minute by minute her body relaxed. She discovered her fist tight around the crumpled letter and she loosened her grasp. She smoothed it flat and then methodically tore it in two, then in fourths, eighths, and even once more until it was too small and thick to tear again. She stretched across the bed, found the rim of the wastebasket, and let the pieces fall.

What a stereotyped reaction, she thought, throwing myself on the bed as if I were enacting some melodramatic opera role. She found a handkerchief and blew her nose, then lay back down again.

Maybe she was at fault for allowing herself to think she and Jimmy could have a good life together. Maybe she loved him simply because there was no other. Jimmy was always there, gallant and fun but what more? Her imagination had made him into the perfect mate, but how was she to know whether in the years stretching ahead he was the right one?

She lay there a long time without moving. She may have fallen asleep. She wasn't sure. When she drew her face away, she was startled for a moment to feel two wet spots on the embroidered pillow slip. Then she remembered.

The next day Mother reminded her of the other letter. Jean asked to hear it. It was from California. Apparently, Forrest had been having a difficult time, too. His father had died. He told how several years earlier when he came home one day, his mother ran out the front door crying, "Come quick. Daddy's dying." At his father's bedside, in a desperate desire to help, Forrest had poured out his love for his father—how he appreciated him, respected him and needed him then more than ever. His father fell asleep and woke up the next morning nearly recovered.

The letter said he came home from work again recently and his mother ran out to him with the same words the second time. "I talked to him like I did before, but he was too far on his way and didn't hear me." The letter ended with the sentence, "Love alone is Life."

Jean carried the letter to her room. It hardly seemed like it was from the same person. The other one seemed so childish, sheepish, jerky. It was written by a boy. This one showed so fearlessly and innocently a well of feeling, freely displayed. Here was a man. Maybe an unsophisticated man, but a man willing to share. Maybe his whole family loved so openly. What could she say to this person she didn't even know? Strangely, she felt his loss draw her from her own.

A few weeks later she wrote to Dody who was back home in California. Forrest's artless sharing had aroused her curiosity. The morning after she received Dody's reply, Jean made an announcement at breakfast. She'd rehearsed it well the night before. "Chiang and I are going to California to visit Dody and her friends."

She heard Father put down his paper. Jean took a swallow of juice and faced straight ahead. This time, she didn't fear his reaction, but was only amused by her imagination of his face.

"Jean, you've got to be here on Valentine's Day for Mort's wedding," Father said.

"Oh, I will be. I'll leave after that." The feeling that she was finally taking charge of her own life gave her voice new authority.

Mother put down her fork. Her voice was firm and measured. "I think that's lovely, Jean. It will do you good."

Chapter Thirteen

In San Diego, Dody's family lived close to the sea. Her family's Spanish-style house with a tile roof wrapped in a U-shape around a central patio with a fountain, palm trees, and honeysuckle vines so sweet the air was heavy with their scent. Jean felt the tree trunks, rough and different from any tree she'd known, not like a tree at all but pitted like deeply carved cork. So this was California—fragrant blossoms, tropical trees, an ocean breeze, and being outside to enjoy it all even in February.

In the patio with Chiang snoozing, Jean and Dody talked steadily until Dody mentioned Jimmy. Jean braced herself. She knew it would come up sometime. "I have something to tell you and then I don't want to say any more about it. He sent a letter to Mother saying it would be better if we didn't see each other any more." Then she waited for Dody to change the subject. She was determined not to carry that grief across the continent to ruin her trip. This was her first great adventure all by herself with only Chiang to rely on. Leave Jimmy on the east coast, she'd told herself. This is California.

"Did you ever write to Forrest Holly?"

"Once."

"Do you want to meet him?"

"Would it hurt your feelings terribly, Dody, if I told you I didn't come all the way across the country just to visit you?"

Dody gave her a quick hug.

The next morning Dody phoned Forrest who lived thirty miles east in Ramona. "Jean's here. Do you want to come to dinner soon?"

Apparently his answer was enthusiastic; his sister Alice dropped him off that afternoon. Dody led him into the living room and introduced him. Jean stood up and turned toward the direction of "Glad to meet you, Jean."

"Hello." The word caught in her throat. How stupid, she thought. Speak up. She held her hand out as she always did but no other hand grasped it. She moved it to the right and then left. Still nothing. Then she raised it and it touched the back of his. In a momentary scramble, their palms met. She giggled nervously. His hand was large and warm. The skin was rough but his touch was gentle. He smelled like leather.

"Wish I'd heard from you two last week. I just got back from fishing in Guymas. Caught half a gunny sack of halibut. You could've had some." He certainly didn't wait for formalities. Maybe this was the western way.

"Where's Guymas?" Jean asked.

"It's on the gulf, the mainland side."

"Of Mexico?"

"No. Of California, but it's in Mexico." He spoke easily in what she presumed was a western cadence. His voice was rich and mellow.

"Is your ranch near Mexico?"

"No. It's in the foothills northeast of here about an hour and a half. We raise milk cows. Also have twenty head in pens. Some are veal calves, some steers. We feed 'em on corn we grow on rented acreage."

"I thought you raised turkeys."

"My brother Lance does. In fact, he's Turkey Judge."

"What's that?"

"Nothing much. Judges turkeys is all. He rides with my sis in his western duds in Turkey Day parades."

Tready was right. He did sound like a hick.

"I ride, too," he continued, "but not in any parades."

"Where?"

"All over the valley and in the foothills. Mostly with Alice, but sometimes not. Horses know their way and I can remember a lot."

"Do you ride a horse whenever you need to go anywhere?"

"No. Used to. Now I have Shasta."

"What's that?"

"She's my car. Used to drive her myself, but now my Indian buddy drives for me."

"Why do you call it—her—that?"

"B'cause sh' hasta have gas and sh' hasta have oil."

Dody groaned. "I thought Shasta was a mountain."

"I thought it was a horse," Jean said.

"No. That's Snort. Can you ride?"

"I did a little at school in New York."

"Western?"

"No. English."

"Well, then, I think Dody ought to bring you out to the ranch and we can take a little ride. I'll teach you to ride western. Whaddya say?"

"Okay," she said weakly. Her mind flashed to Andrebrook and the controlled riding ring. She hadn't ridden since, but to say no would be to close a door that was being held open for her. Miss Weaver would push her right through it. "Of course," she said more loudly. "I'd like to."

With Dody keeping the conversation moving at a good clip, dinner passed quickly. Jean did not feel unhappy or uncomfortable the whole evening, only curious. Too soon, it seemed, Alice returned to pick him up. "See ya' Tuesday, Jeanie," he said, and then he was gone.

As soon as Jean heard Dody close the door, she asked, "What's he look like?"

"Oh, about six feet tall with dark hair and a high forehead. He always wears sunglasses. He stands differently than most men, with his chest out as if he's ready to do battle with the world. He keeps his head high. I've noticed it more lately. Sometimes he looks like a man fighting against becoming cowed by life's troubles. Other times he looks like a boy just grown into a man's body. He's kind of lanky."

"Is he handsome?"

"Jean, you've never asked that before about any man."

"Quit teasing. Tell me."

"Do you think I'd introduce you to some dud? Apparently before he lost his sight all the Ramona girls were crazy over him. Built up his ego. Too much, Mom says."

It wasn't an easy drive to the little backwater town near an Indian reservation. There was no way to get there without crossing some mountains. On the winding road past the town of Escondido, Jean couldn't anticipate the turns and had to brace herself with both hands on the car seat. Her back was tense and her arms became tired. "My stomach's doing flip flops," she said.

"It's the road," Dody said.

"I'm not so sure." She opened the window to get some fresh air but only smelled diesel from a truck ahead. "It's pretty warm for February."

"This isn't New England, you know."

On the phone Forrest and Dody had stretched the horseback ride to a visit of three days. Jean hadn't counted on that, but she didn't protest. Miss Weaver's famous "life is to be lived" doctrine made her feel ready for whatever the experience would give her. "I don't know what you got me into," she said, more in sport than in trepidation. "What's it like out here?"

"Beautiful. There's manzanita all over. That's a bush with crooked, woody branches. It has a smooth reddish bark that sometimes peels off. It grows in dry places. Ramona is awfully hot in the summer. There's live oak, too, all over these hillsides, and avocado and citrus trees."

"Live oak? As opposed to dead oak?"

"No. It's just a different variety than in New England."

"What kind of a town is Ramona?"

"Tired and kind of ramshackle. The main street is probably only six or eight blocks long. It's picturesque because it's surrounded on all sides by mountains, and sometimes people ride into town on horses, but nothing ever happens in Ramona."

"Everybody probably knows everybody else's business."

"When Forrest lost his sight, it was the subject of gossip all over town. People said things like, 'What a shame about the young Holly boy.' 'He's a proud one, you know. That's what caused it in the first place, going out for a pass that wasn't his.' That was a couple of years ago, before I met him."

"You sure know a lot about him suddenly. Why didn't you tell me any of this before?"

"You didn't seem interested." Jean felt the tease behind the words. Dody waited a minute, then continued. "Apparently the Hollys are well known because they're a little better off than most Ramona people, and Mrs. Holly has done some kindly things for the Indians. They call her Lady Mother."

"Frilly name."

"Or Mother Holly."

"Who told you all this?"

"Mom."

For a moment Jean forgot to keep herself braced. They went around a sharp turn and she swung over toward the door. The road crossed a dry creek, not on a bridge but right on the creek bed. It bounced the car and Jean held her hands out on the seat on each side of her. Then Dody shifted down to climb a hill. At the top she turned in at a long driveway.

"Are we there?"

"Yes. It's a wooden frame house with a screened porch, kind of lonesome. Pepper trees, cactus garden, rail fence. Forrest's waiting outside." Dody stopped the engine and got out. "What do you do, stand out here all day waiting for cars to stop?"

"It's high time you two showed up. Hi ya, Jean."

"Hi."

"It's farther out here than I remembered," said Dody.

"Bring Jean on in so she won't get hung up in the cactus. The cholla can jump right out and get you. Are your bags in the trunk?"

"Yes." Jean got out and let Chiang out and stood by the car door. "Cactus? Are we in the desert?"

"No, but it's pretty dry here in summer, though you couldn't tell that now, and cactus is easier than a lawn." Dody opened the trunk and Forrest felt for her suitcase and lifted it out. "Most of these we brought in. Barrel cactus, prickly pear, ocotillo, century plant and yucca, and they all have thorns sharp enough to skewer a bull's catook, so don't make any wild moves."

Jean laughed. His folksy speech fascinated her. She wanted to remember that one to tell Icy.

Right away Jean met Forrest's mother. "There's a row of field stones around the cactus so if you feel that, Jean, don't go any farther," she explained. That was considerate, Jean thought. Mrs. Holly's voice sounded softly lyrical. The air smelled dusty and it was warmer than when they were crossing the mountains. Inside the house Alice greeted her but Jean hardly had time to say three sentences before both women disappeared. All too soon Dody was ready to leave too. Jean rehearsed her phone number in case—in case of anything. Three days was a long time. There she was, in a strange house, with a near stranger 3000 miles from home. She knew it was a set-up with everybody suddenly gone, but she went along with it. It was the most adventure she'd had since Europe with Miss Weaver.

With his big rough hand making her arm tingle, Forrest guided her to a chair in the living room—she presumed it was the living room—and said, "Now, tell me all about yourself."

What a question, right off. Either there was nothing shy about Forrest or he had no class. She didn't know how to answer.

He filled in the awkward silence. "Just why aren't you so smart? In your letter you said you were a happy family but not so smart."

Suddenly she wished she hadn't written that. "Oh, I don't know what I meant. I guess I thought nothing I could say would be very interesting to you. I guess I meant we were plain."

"How do you mean plain?"

"Well, we don't ride horses and we don't have cows and we don't live on a ranch. We just live in a house and Father goes to work and we just live."

"Sounds pretty breezy."

His words rolled out liquid and smooth and warm. Because he kept the questions coming, she told him about Hickory Hill and school and Miss Weaver's trip and music. At her feet, Chiang breathed deeply and shifted positions. Jean patted her on the neck and told Forrest all about her. "She's a wonderful animal, and a good friend. She's so intelligent and well-trained that people want to come up and pet her. I have to try to sense when that's happening and ask people not to."

"Why not?"

"She's got to be responsive and responsible only to me and not be distracted. The instructors were very firm about that. But I can pet her and love her when she's not working."

Forrest wanted to know how she managed her, so she explained all the commands. When talking got easier, she told of the stumbling closeness between the students at The Seeing Eye and of the ache of saying goodbye, of Lee and how he expected his students to speak up for themselves and live in the real world. Forrest murmured encouragement that made her think he understood. Feeling naïve but going ahead anyway, she told him of Jimmy. She held back nothing. The last part was an effort, but it broke the ice. What did she have to lose?

When she finished, he didn't say anything, but groped for her hand, got her knee instead and then drew back. They both laughed at their nervousness.

"I want to show you around before dinner," he said. "This house started out as just one main room and a kitchen and bathroom, so we called it the cabin then. We still do even though it's bigger now. There's a screened porch you came through to get in." He stood up. "Follow me." They got up. Chiang followed Forrest and Jean followed Chiang, but when they got outside Forrest took Jean's hand. It wasn't necessary, she had Chiang, but it felt comfortable. The grasp of his big hand was firm on hers, swallowing it in tender roughness. Jean changed Chiang from the harness to the leash, which meant "off duty."

"It's warm even though it's February. I can't believe it."

"It gets plenty cold sometimes, and it still may rain tonight. That'll plaster down the dust some. When we were kids, we used to sleep in the screened porch. It was cool in summer, but in winter we'd heat stones about the size of cantaloupes on the oil burner in the living room, wrap them in newspaper and put them in our beds. They kept us dandy warm. But now I have my own little place out here in back. It's a separate room detached from the house. I call it Hermit House. Here it is."

He was careful to scrape his feet at the threshold. That surprised her. It made him seem like a gentleman even though so many things about him were rough. She scraped her feet, too. Inside, he pointed out where things were and guided her hands to feel his table with typewriter and radio, his bed, his dresser. "When I had a Hereford steer slaughtered, I took the hide to an old man, about ninety years old, and he tanned it. Feel it here on the floor, Jean. It's a beauty. I do my push-ups on it."

He led her outside again. They made a circle around the house. The circle seemed small to Jean. Her nostrils flared at the strong scent of horse manure made oppressive by the heat. It didn't smell bad, actually, just earthy. "I smell horses."

"Yup. In the back we have two barns, one for horses and one for cows. I'll take you there tomorrow. Over here on this side of the cabin under the pepper trees are some cages. My father raised peafowl—you know, peacocks and hens—and so we still do. You'll probably hear them before too long."

"I hear them now."

"I don't mean them just walking around pecking. I mean screeching. In mating season they put up an awful racket. Let's go in now. I smell dinner."

The family supper was in the living room, the only other choice besides the kitchen. Forrest introduced his sister Helen and her husband Don. They lived in a tiny house on an adjacent two-acre plot behind the cabin. In a hubbub of commotion and teasing, they all got situated and settled down to say grace together. Jean hadn't said grace for years. Quaint, she thought, and bowed her head. Just after the "amen," Don's voice boomed out, "Forrest, get your hand out of the muffins." The command came like a benediction, without a pause.

"Now, Don, you know I'm going to have to get you back for showing me up as some no 'count in front of Jean here."

The teasing surprised her. So different from Hickory Hill. It continued all through dinner. "All this talk makes me thirsty," Forrest said.

"It's further right, Forrest." Alice's voice was high and tinny.

"Alice, you been drinking my water? If you wanted to share, all you needed to do what to ask. After all, what are brothers for?"

"Oh, Jean, he always does this," Alice said, "misunderstanding on purpose just to make a dumb joke."

A few minutes after they started eating there was a hideous, whining scream. "Help, help," it seemed to say. It came from the front of the house. Everybody kept eating and talking right through it.

"What's that terrible scream?" Jean interrupted.

"Oh, it's just the Indian, Earl Duran, across the highway. Going after his wife again," Don said.

"Sounds like she's just about to be murdered," Forrest said.

Everybody laughed. The screeching continued.

"Tell me," Jean insisted.

"It's just the peacocks, dear. Don't be alarmed." Mother Holly's voice was calming. "Some truck drivers know we have peacocks here, and when they go by on the highway they think it's funny to honk their horn and that sets them off."

"You shouldn't believe everything they say," Alice explained. "Earl doesn't even have a wife."

"But does an Indian really live across the road?"

"Oh, yes, three of them."

Jean felt like she was at the edge of some frontier a world away from Connecticut, or back in time.

After dinner Forrest and Don put on a show of imitating people's walks, apparently a favorite pastime, for they swung into action naturally, describing in exaggerated language what they were doing. The subjects were all local people, women they'd all known for years. One was a slink. Another an old maid teacher who took tiny mincing steps and kept her finger to her mouth. One girl made her bosoms bounce. "That's Gloria. How could I forget her?" Forrest said. Another heaved her hips back and forth so widely she almost tipped over. Jean laughed with the others, her imagination running wild. It was free swinging western humor, not malicious but far from the contained tinkling laughter in the living room at Hickory Hill. But the strange thing was that it was visual. Forrest took part just as if he could see. And Dody had wanted her to write him because she thought *he* was having trouble?

Don and Helen left soon after dinner and Mother Holly and Alice went to bed early. Alone again. Staged. The setup made their being there seem so innocent, so wholly planned by a force apart from them that she felt comfortable accepting the direction events were moving.

She heard some scraping across the room and then a couple of thuds and the crackle of the fire. It dawned on her what was happening but her surprise made the words come anyway. "What in the world are you doing?"

"Putting another log on the fire."

"How?" she blurted. Immediately, she felt foolish.

"Not very well. But I've got a poker here and some big tongs. I just have to poke around to find out what's there." He struggled for a while, and she heard a few thumps as he shifted the logs on the grate and they fell down. "I can tell by the crackling when I get it right. Sometimes."

There were some things she would never tackle, things that probably shouldn't be tackled. But she also knew the frustration of being told "you can't" or "you shouldn't." Even worse than that was disbelief or distrust expressed by silence. One thing was sure. This man had spirit. Where was his despair, the crashing end Dody had said he thought his life had come to?

"Can you feel the heat?"

"Yes." A wave of not only of heat but of feeling engulfed her. Something inside her—was that her heart?—brightened and felt a warmth from within, as an ember below a grate burns from within, making itself luminous, pulsing intermittently with radiance.

She didn't want him to interpret her silence as disapproval. She had to say something. "What's this room look like?"

"Oh, it's a dandy." A couple more thuds, then the crackling increased and she heard the scrape made by pulling the screen closed. "The fireplace is stone with a cougar skin hanging above it. When we were kids, we gathered the stones to make it. There are some crevices between the rocks and one night last winter Alice thought she saw a pair of eyes in a crevice about a foot above the hearth. I thought she was crazy, but everybody looked and, sure enough, a close-set pair of eyes was looking back. A snake, probably from under the house, had slithered through some crack in the cemented pile of rocks and found a tunnel which opened right into the living room. I don't know which was more terrified, the snake or Alice. It was obvious the snake couldn't retrace his path and crawl back out, but we didn't want him coming out into the living room."

"What did you do?"

"Only one thing we could do. Mix up some mortar and pack the varmint in. We felt kinda sorry for him because he didn't mean any harm, but from the looks of his head, he might have been a rattler. I guess his skeleton is still lying there in his tunnel tomb."

Jean gulped. Varmint. That was another one she'd have to tell Icy. But she couldn't imagine telling Tready all this. "What else is in this room?"

"Oh, there's a piano. You can play it if you like."

"Who plays it here?"

"Alice. She rides all over the valley on Pronto to give music lessons in people's homes. There are some Indian baskets and *ollas*, they're water jugs, and an Indian rug in front of the fireplace. There's a pair of elk horns on the wall behind you, so don't get wild and decide to jump up. There's a statue of Lincoln to the left of the fireplace and bookshelves all over. We probably have fifteen years of *National Geographics.*

A log suddenly thudded onto the grate and Forrest poked and pushed at it some more, unleashing a battery of crackles.

Then he came over to sit with her. Her heart sped. He smelled like ashes and the outdoors. "We have two sofas in this room. One's an old leather sofa. The newer one has a big buffalo robe draped over it." He began to talk slower, as if he wanted her to understand more than what he was saying. "The leather sofa is the fighting sofa, for roughhousing when we were kids. The new one is called the sitting sofa. It's for kissing."

Jean's hand went out to feel what she was sitting on. It felt furry. He put his arm around her shoulder. His voice dropped to a whisper. "This is the sitting sofa."

Slowly, his hand traced a path over her shoulder to her neck. It wasn't timid even though it moved with deliberate slowness. She held her breath, suspended in expectancy. His hand moved up her neck and held her head. His weight next to her on the sofa made the cushion dip down so that she was leaning toward him. He drew her head closer and his lips found hers.

She relaxed into his arms and, unguardedly, into his world for perhaps a moment. That was all. Then she drew herself back into her own, imperceptibly, though. She didn't actually move away. Who was he to assume she wanted to kiss him just because they were thrust together and they were both blind? That's too simple. His mouth was gentle, constant, moving over her face, her neck. But false aloofness was stupid, too. She felt part of her move toward him again, toward this man who built fires and rode horses and talked funny. And had sure hands.

Chapter Fourteen

A rooster crowed. From cloudy sleep, she woke but did not move, out of fear of spoiling those first dewy thoughts and the realization of where she was. Embers of the night before still glowed in her mind and made her smile into the blanket she drew up around her face. She often recounted to herself special moments. At honest times she recognized the pure indulgence of experiencing them again—her moments of passionate living were so few. And this morning she indulged herself. Maybe joy was always more penetrating after despair.

She bent her knees and pulled her nightgown down and tucked it under her feet. She thought how she and Forrest had talked late into the night. He had listened so earnestly. He'd never known another person who couldn't see. She could tell he wanted to know about her life and her adjustment. He asked a thousand questions about Chiang, yet he hadn't talked of his own blindness at all, never even used the word "blind," as if it were a subject abhorrent to him. Their similarity drew them to each other as surely as he had drawn her face to his. No one had ever shown such intense interest in all the details of her life, not even Jimmy.

So Forrest was a pole vaulter. Funny. So was Jimmy. Forrest suffered bouts of asthma. So did Jimmy. Forrest said he wasn't "too shabby" on the dance floor. Neither was Jimmy. But that's where the similarities ceased.

Jimmy was an urbanite. Forrest, far from one. He wore cowboy boots. His c.b.'s, he called them, "complete with manure to prove they're used." Jimmy was pretty distant and independent from his family and rarely talked of them. Forrest was unusually close to his, and needed them. But the big difference was that Forrest was a westerner, had hauled hay, milked cows, shoed horses. He did things outdoors, and although he might do them differently now that he couldn't see, he was still doing them. She knew how to value that. But what was she doing comparing? Leave Jimmy out of it! She threw off the blankets and got up.

She dressed and made her way out to the kitchen where voices sounded cheerful. "About time you got up," Forrest teased.

"Is it late?"

"Not for a city girl, I suppose. Just that I've been waiting, doing a tap dance here in the kitchen." His voice dropped. "I didn't sleep much."

Jean tried to think of a way to tease him back—there hadn't been many hours left to sleep—but she stopped herself. She didn't know who else was nearby.

"Now that you and I are going to be friends," he said, "you oughta see what I do all day, and the first thing I do is milk the cows. In fact, I'm late now. You want to come along? I got something special to show you."

"What's that?"

"Just you wait. First, what do you have on your feet?"

"Shoes."

"It rained some last night so that pasture's mighty wet and it'll come near to your waist, you're such a little thing. We got to get you some boots. Come on out to the barn."

Forrest led, then Chiang, then Jean. As Forrest walked, he clapped his hands sharply. Eventually it created a barely perceptible echo. "We're here." He turned left abruptly and

Chiang followed. Clever, he was, to figure that out. Jean wondered if she would have ever thought of that as a way to guide herself. The barn door creaked as Forrest swung it open. Inside, the smell of damp hay and manure engulfed her. Its freshness made it not at all unpleasant. A cat meowed. Forrest fumbled around for a while and found some rope and a pair of black rubber waders.

"Where are you?"

"Over here."

"Do you think these'll fit?"

She reached out and found the heavy boots. "They're huge."

"Well, how abut putting them over your shoes?" He squatted down next to her and held one boot while she tugged at the other. She lost her balance and half fell, half leaned against him. Her arm went to his shoulder to catch herself. It was firm and muscular beneath his flannel shirt.

"Steady, girl," he said.

"Sounds like you're talking to a horse."

"Maybe a filly. Will they work?"

"Yes, I guess so." It must look foolish, she thought, because above the boots she wore a dress. Then she realized it didn't matter.

Forrest headed toward the corral. Chiang and Jean followed.

"How do you know where you are?"

"The rise of the ground. Now, Jeanie, you may have Chiang and she's a seeing eye dog. But you ain't seen nothin' yet. I've got a seeing eye bull."

"There's no such thing."

"Well, the cows are out in the pasture. Eight of them. They could be anywhere in the ten acres. How do you suppose I'm going to find them if they don't come back for milking?"

"I don't know."

"I let my seeing eye bull spot them for me. There's more than one way to skin a cat, ya know."

Jean heard muffled snorting as they moved toward the corral. "I don't want to go in there."

"You don't have to. Put your hand here on the fence so's I know where you are. There's a gate here just to your left, but don't come in. I go in right here and clap a rope around Victor Mature here. That's what I call the moose. Then he leads me out to the pasture to find the ladies."

Jean held onto the corral rail with one hand, to Chiang's harness with the other. She rubbed her hand along the weathered top rail. It felt satiny except where it was pocked by knots. The wood was sinewy, like Forrest's arm was when she stroked it the night before. A breeze made her bare arms tingle. She leaned to the left side and a little forward, her stay-alert-to-perceive-everything stance. She could hardly believe what Forrest was doing. And he was so sure about it. The snorting came again, forceful and low. Forrest announced his presence to the bull just inside the gate. The bull grunted and shuffled a little in response.

"Yeah, big boy. Now I know where you are." Jean heard them scuffle and heard a rope swish. She held her breath. "Hey, hey. Got him, slick as a whistle." Jean heard them come toward her and a little to the left. She slid up closer to the rail in front of her. "He's on his way, Jeanie. Will Chiang follow?"

"I hope so. She's never followed a bull before." Jean moved away from the fence and turned in the direction she heard Forrest. "Forward," she said to Chiang, forcefully, she thought, and the four of them were off, rumbling out across the pasture.

The long grass brushed wet against her knees above the big boots and the ground swelled beneath her feet like ocean billows. She felt just on the edge of danger. What was she thinking of, wandering out in the middle of a pasture with a bull and cows and who knows what else? Still, her awe at what this man could do, what he was in fact doing, every day of his life, was enough to take her out with him to that pasture and to whatever may happen there. She was drawn to him just as if another rope attached to him were pulling her along. Forrest whistled so she could know where he was and sometimes his footsteps splattered in a puddle. That helped her to follow. Air blew up her skirt and felt cool where the wet grass had left moisture. It sent a quick shiver up her back.

"Wet grass smells sweeter than dry grass, or is that my imagination?" she asked.

"No. You're right. Cleaner, too."

"You love it here, don't you?"

"You betcha. It's home. Peaceful even if the rest of the world isn't."

"Are you sorry you're not in the war?"

"No. No one wants to go to war. But I suppose I'd rather go to war than not see, if that was the choice." They walked a while in silence. "I guess I'm fighting my own battles."

There it was again, his fearless sharing. She could grow to love that. Maybe that's what had been missing before. Jean stepped in a gushy spot and the mud sucked at her boot as she lifted her heel. It sounded funny and broke the seriousness of the moment. "How do you know he's leading us to the cows?" she asked.

"Simple. Old Victor Mature, he's always greedy, and where the cows are feeding, he figures they're eating something good and he wants it too. When he stops and I hear the cows bawling because we're close, I sling this other rope around in the air and whoop and holler, and they head for the barn. Slow down. The big guy just stopped. Stand behind me, Jean."

She did as she was told, well behind him. The cows did start to bawl, just as he said. He whooped a wild western sound and his rope cut the quiet morning air. Just like in movies and radio shows, she thought.

"They're moving, Jean. We've got to hightail it back."

"How do you know all of them are moving?"

"Oh, they want to get milked as much as I want to milk them. Sometimes I hardly need to go out to fetch them."

"Why do you call the bull Victor Mature?" She wanted to keep him talking in order to know where he was.

"Because of his broad shoulders. He's heavily stacked and low slung to the ground. And he goes after the ladies."

"Do you do this twice a day?"

"Sure do. Dandy, huh? There's more than one way to skin a cat," he said again. She thought the old saying must be his personal proverb, his battle cry against a world suddenly grown strange. She began to realize that if the need came for him to skin a cat, he'd surely find a way to do it.

The sounds changed as they approached the barn doorway. The cows jostled into position in the darker coolness. She heard a cat again. Forrest spoke to the cows in a soft voice as he moved around the barn. Then he asked, "Are you in here, Jeanie?"

"No," she said from the doorway.

"Well, you got to come in to see what I'm doing. Stand right here next to this stall."

"Forward," she told Chiang. To see what he was doing? He used language just as if they could both see. Most other people were far too sensitive about using the word "see" around her.

"Stay right there so I know where you are."

"Oh, I won't move an inch. I'm not too sure about this milking business." She heard Forrest get a couple of metal pails. "Aren't you afraid one will kick you?"

"No, not if I stand in the right place."

The cat meowed.

"She wants some milk."

"She knows she'll get it, too. She always sits behind and about four feet to the left of the cow I'm milking." The rhythmic squirt, squirt, squirt pinged into the pail. "When she sets up a racket I can hardly stand, I aim a faucet of milk just where she is." The cat begged some more. "Just like this."

"Do you think she got it?"

"Sure she did. Otherwise she'd still be crying. She's busy licking it off her face and chest. When she's ready for some more we'll hear her again."

The milk changed sounds, becoming more muffled as the bucket was filling. Jean heard a tail swish. Forrest moved to another cow. "Do you want to have a go at it?"

"Milking? Oh, no. I'll just let you." She smiled at the sounds and breathed the musty barn odors and cow smells. It was pleasant in there in the coolness with the cat crying and the milk squirting rhythmically and Forrest at work.

"Today I have to work across the valley. We have five acres in alfalfa and we just hired hands to cut it, but I've got to get it loaded. I have a driver and helper, and we take over an empty truck and bring it back loaded. You want to come? We have to ride on top of the hay on the way home."

"Of course I do."

It was so new and free and unlimited, this western life. Bouncing along on top of the loose hay at the end of the day, one hand holding Chiang's leash, the other holding Forrest's hand, she felt supremely happy. *You've got to live a little,* she remembered Sally Anne saying, but she doubted if this was quite what Sally Anne had meant. She talked louder than usual, spilling her words out to the breeze and Forrest. The truck jolted but she didn't brace herself so she was jounced against his chest. One bump was so big she instinctively grabbed hold of his arm. She let her hand linger there. The muscles of his forearm felt ropey and his hair tickled her palm. The hay smelled fresh and pungent, surrounding her with sensations of ranch, work, growing, earth. Life.

Chapter Fifteen

All too soon Dody came to pick her up, and Jean and Forrest had to say goodbye. The next day Forrest came to dinner at Dody's. "I convinced Alice to drive me," he said smugly. Forrest and Jean said goodbye again. Two days later he came again. "Connecticut's on the other side of the world, Jeanie. We got to have a big goodbye."

Dody was thorough. She invited Forrest one last time and then left them alone, protesting she had to make a phone call. Each goodbye was greater than the last.

Jean felt like she was drifting in a dream all the way home. It had been more wonderful than she had dared to hope. Forrest wasn't a pitiful victim needing encouragement like Dody had said, but a proud, vital, active outdoorsman. Although Jean had accused Dody lightheartedly of tricking her just to get her to visit, Dody protested that she only thought Jean could stand a little adventure in her life. On the way home as the significance of her visit settled, she began to recognize that a deeper adventure might have just begun.

Hickory Hill was dull by comparison. It was back to the piano with Mother. Jean resumed her lessons at the Girls' Club once a week. The walk downtown with Chiang was tame now compared to an uncharted pasture.

Icy Eastman was married to an army colonel. Jean played the wedding march. Jean was bridesmaid in Sally Anne's wedding. She was in Louise Barnes' wedding. She was in Tready's sister's wedding. Tready went west to marry an officer.

The men went to war. It was 1942. Some of the women, wives now, still lived with parents. There were plenty of women in Bristol who wanted company. Jean was invited to their homes. They talked of letters from abroad sprinkled with foreign phrases or military jargon. The women took airplane identification classes. They talked of campaigns and marches, of cities all over the world and tiny islands in the Pacific. Jean thought of a pasture.

Miss Weaver closed Andrebrook. She worked for the government as a German translator. Everyone did his bit for the war effort. Jean folded bandages at the Red Cross. Only women came to Hickory Hill to swim that summer. Whenever they wanted a Coke, they put some coins in the Red Cross box on the verandah, and once a week, Jean and Chiang took the money downtown when she went to do bandages.

She haunted the mailbox. Since Forrest didn't have a Brailler, she had Mother read his badly typed letters. They told of milking cows, of trading stock in order to increase his herd, of hoedowns in the nearby mountain town of Julian. Once he wrote, "Victor Mature got some kind of playful notion in his head and led me astray today. Didn't know where I was. I felt like kicking the old moose in the slats, but I wasn't quite sure where they were." She shared that letter with Icy.

Mother began to know Forrest, too. She laughed at his homespun language and what he called P.M. humor, pre-marital jokes, "sanitized for your benefit, Mrs. Treadway," he wrote once. His letters were silly, Jean knew, but that didn't matter. In one letter he announced, "I wrote a book today. I'm going to call it *Mama's Awful Coffee*, or *Grounds for Divorce*." In the next letter he said, "I wrote another book today. This one's called *The Missing Flowers in the White House Rose Garden*, or *Have You Seen Eleanor's Bloomers?*"

Jean timed her day's activities around the mail delivery. Once she grabbed the mail and thrust the letters into Mother's hand just as she was ready to leave for the Red Cross. There was another letter from Forrest. Mother read, "This week I wrote a mystery story. It's called *The Mystery of the Missing Magician: A Houdini Who Dunnit.*" Mother was exasperated. "Honestly, Jean. Do you think the war effort and the Red Cross ought to wait for this?" She rushed out the door. Jean only smiled.

Their letters couldn't be very personal. Forrest's mother read Jean's to him. Jean wondered what they'd be writing if their mothers weren't reading the letters. She longed for a little more privacy. He could at least learn to read Braille better, she thought, so she sat down at her Brailler to give him practice.

"Dear Forrest, Here's a funny story I read when I was little," she punched out. "A guy and a girl got married. The lady had a black ribbon around her neck. On the honeymoon she kept it on all night. 'What's it for?' asked the man.

"'I'll tell you after a year.' All year the man wondered because she never took it off."

The story dragged on and on, the woman not telling him until they were married thirty years. Jean punched out the letters feverishly, feeling a little giddy inside. It took two pages. She hoped he hadn't heard the story before so he'd keep going until the end, just for practice.

"On their thirtieth anniversary he asked again. 'Okay, you promised. Why do you wear that black ribbon?'

"'I'll show you.' She took it off and her head fell off."

With that, Jean ended the letter. It was a dumb joke, but still a little giggle escaped when she sealed the envelope. She pictured him picking out the pinpricks line by laborious line.

Mother read Forrest's next letter. "What the devil were you thinking of sending me a Braille letter? It took me a day and a half to figure the thing out. All for that crummy punch line."

After that she Brailled her letters more frequently. Christmas came and went. On New Year's Eve, there was another Ares and Ain'ts party downstairs. Upstairs in her room Jean sat down at her Brailler again. He had asked about her other boyfriends. What could she possibly say? There weren't any.

"Donald was my first boyfriend," she wrote. "He lived on the corner and went to Federal Hill Grammar School with me. We used to climb trees and play Truth, Dare and Consequences. On lucky days the consequences consisted of a scared little peck on the cheek that lasted half a second. When I was eleven, Donald climbed the tree outside my bathroom window and peeked in. Father caught him. There was a big row. I can't remember what Father said. I was in a panic for what might happen to Don. A few years ago Father lent him money to go to Middlebury College for pre-med. He's a laboratory technician now. He paid Father back and married a woman with a moustache and a low voice. Is that what you wanted to know?"

She loved to play the innocent.

"When can you come out again?" Forrest wrote back.

Jean was bolder in her Braille letters than in her typed ones. She punched out, "If I knew that there might be some future for us, it would be easier to get Mother to make a trip with me."

He wrote back immediately. "There is. There is a future. You know it as well as I do."

In the summer of 1943, Jean and Mother booked a Pullman to Los Angeles.

Forrest began a massive cleanup campaign at Rancho de Los Pimientos. He repaired the barn door. He cleaned Hermit House.

He cleaned the main cabin. He scrubbed the kitchen walls so vigorously that when Alice came in she screamed, "Forrest, stop! You're scraping off the paint."

"I am?"

"Yes, just stop scrubbing and rinse it off. Here. Move out of the way so I can get to the icebox."

"Don't call it an ice box in front of Mrs. Treadway. It's a refrigerator."

"Forrest, she's not the Queen of England," said Alice. "Okay." Her voice softened. "I promise to remember."

Mother Holly was caught up in the frenzy of preparations too. She borrowed an oil stove for the room that the aristocratic eastern lady and her daughter would sleep in. Forrest helped move it in. She borrowed two matching bedspreads, two bedside tables, two lamps.

Forrest made Alice and Mother Holly get to the station in San Diego an hour early, just so they wouldn't be late. The moment Jean and her mother arrived he asked to carry Mrs. Treadway's luggage.

At Ramona, Mother Holly led them into the tiny bedroom with the borrowed spreads and lamps. "All the comforts of home," said Mrs. Treadway.

As before, there was dinner to get through. It seemed interminable to Jean. Forrest was on his best behavior. He moderated his jokes, and he didn't call his mother "mater old pertator" like he did the last time. He talked about his milk cows and his herd. "I have 28 head now." Jean suppressed a smile at his urgency that Mother knew his assets were increasing.

After dinner the door opened and a man lurched into the cabin living room, his boots thumping irregularly on the bare floor. "Thought I'd bring back this busted clock. Darn if I know how to fix it."

Forrest introduced Mrs. Treadway and Jean to Earl Duran, the Indian who lived across the highway. "Ydeño, I call him," he added.

"Pleased t' meet you," Earl said.

He sounded like Gene Autry to Jean. He grinned widely at Jean's mother who told her later what he looked like—a large mouth of uneven yellow teeth, and a Grand Canyon of colored layers on his deeply lined face. The sunburnt chin and overhanging promontory of a nose were a dark reddish brown, the cheeks various shades of tan, moving up to a pasty yellow forehead above the permanent ridge his hatband made. Forrest asked him to stay awhile.

"No, I gotta ride into town to pick up a Sunday *Times*."

"But it's Saturday," said Mrs. Treadway.

"Yup."

"Isn't it unusual to get a Sunday paper a day ahead? In New England the Sunday paper comes out on Sunday morning."

"Well, ma'm, we have a reason for that. Folks out west buy the Sunday paper Saturdays so's when they take it home to read they see the date is Sunday. Then they think they've already had their Saturday bath and don't need to take it again."

Jean was relieved to hear her mother laugh. "I suppose that's as good a reason as any," Mrs. Treadway said. That's Mother. Always cordial. For most of the evening Earl kept them entertained with stories of turkey parades, thunderstorms and Santa Anas.

"Them's the hot, dry winds that blow in from the desert three or four days at a time summer and fall. Dries up the water right off your eyeballs and spreads dust over everything so's all the plants turn that army color. Your throat even tastes brown. Why, them winds can suck milk right out of a cow's tit." Jean gasped, worried about Mother's reaction, but true to her upbringing, Mother kept her response completely internal. Maybe she was loosening up. "Yup," Earl continued. "No other place like it, I reckon." Finally, he left on his gimpy legs. She heard him speak kindly to the peacocks on his way out and wondered if Mother noticed it, too.

Jean could hardly sit still. At last, Forrest said, "Come on, Jean. I've got something to show you out in Hermit House."

They left Mrs. Treadway with Mother Holly and Alice. Jean had waited nearly a year and a half, and now they'd been together for three hours and hadn't even touched yet. The pressure was great. "Hop up," Forrest said to Chiang. Even when Chiang went faster, Forrest tripped over her getting out to the little cabin. Jean noticed he forgot to scrape his feet at the threshold. That made her smile. He closed the door with his foot and they frantically found each other. Chiang was forgotten, her harness dropped.

"Wait, wait, Jean." Forrest pulled away.

"What's the matter?"

"Gotta turn out the light."

She laughed at his romanticism. Gently, Forrest pulled her down to the edge of the bed, and she felt a tightening deep within she'd never felt before. He smelled of shoe polish and soap. Chiang whined. His hand caressed her bobbed hair. He fingered her earlobe, stroked her chin and neck. Their kiss was long and solid and full of yearning.

She discovered his sunglasses and took them off. She kissed him on the warm bridge of his nose right between the eyes. His big hand moved to the back of her head, drawing her toward him. He kissed her right at the hairline and her scalp tingled. He leaned back slowly, her body fitting the contours of his. When he pressed her to him, she let out a long, smooth sigh and didn't dare move.

"We abandoned Mother," she murmured eventually.

"Then I've got to ask you now." He still held her. "Will you marry me?"

She drew away slightly.

"Well, there'll always be everybody around. I don't know when'll be the next time we can be alone together. Will you marry me?"

Her back stiffened. She was not to be had that quickly. It wasn't caution—she knew well enough she wanted him. That movement within when he took hold of her told her that. But he wasn't going to smash her reserve that easily.

"I can't say. It's too soon. We'd better go back."

The next night after dinner Forrest again remembered something he had to show her in Hermit House.

"Will you marry me?" he asked as soon as he closed the door behind them.

Jean moistened her lips. Would saying yes end this once-in-a-lifetime elation? Suddenly, strangely, she didn't want to grab at the happiness offered as though the brass ring would never come around again. She felt giddy as she had years ago bobbing up and sinking down on gaudily painted carousel horses. Not answering just yet might keep the ride going longer.

When he asked again the third night, her hand went around his neck and she drew his head sideways so that it lay on her chest just under her chin. His hair smelled faintly of shampoo. "Yes," she whispered, the sound escaping in a sigh, leaving behind unutterable peace.

He said nothing, only softly kissed her, without passion, as if it were a way to hallow the moment. They passed some time in stillness. It was different, she thought, than how she'd imagined it might be, more tender, reverent, less jubilant.

In the silence she felt him pulling away from her, as if the magnitude of the decision was sinking deep in his thoughts and forming concrete concerns. Unwillingly she yielded her moment of moments, the event that was to assure her of more than the narrow piece of life she had feared God had allotted her. He sat up with a start. It jarred the dreaminess of the moment. He could be excused, she thought a little wistfully. He was so in earnest.

"I don't have a ring for you now, but I've been saving and I can send you one pretty soon. Then you can show all your girlfriends back east. But I do have something for you. Don't move."

Jean heard him open a dresser drawer. He came back to her and found her hand. In it he put something small and cold and hard. She fingered it carefully.

"What is it?"

"A gold track shoe."

A short intake of breath, her fingers tight around the tiny shoe, and then she reached for him. He let her kiss him just once before his words began to tumble out.

"We could live right here in Hermit House. We'd call it something else, though. Anything you like. I know that it's crazy to think of a guy in my situation marrying a sheltered, delicate flower like you, but I'm determined to be worthy of you, Jean. I've got a larger herd now than I did the last time you were here, and I'll work hard and we can buy some more. I get $30 a month from selling milk to people around here. I don't like to tell you this, but I also get $50 a month state aid. That's how I bought my first cow and that was only three years ago.

Someday I'm not going to need it though." He paused. "Do you get any?" His voice was deeper.

"I get $75 a month from a family trust."

This wasn't part of how she imagined it—talking of money ten minutes after she'd said yes. In fact, she'd never talked of money. She never needed to.

Mother was gone for a week on the coast. Days melted together. In the mornings after milking they cut corn for the calves. They went together when he mucked the horses' stalls, the barn smelling warm and fetid. In the late afternoons they sat in Hermit House to talk, trying to see their way into the future, but they told no one.

They visited the related families in the valley—Helen and Don just next door, Forrest's married brother, Lance, and his wife Mary Kay at the turkey ranch on the hill. When Lance took Forrest aside to check on the turkeys, Jean thought she heard him say, "Get a country girl, Forrest." She winced as if she had eaten a grape gone yellow and the bitterness was sudden. How could he say that when she loved it here? She told herself she didn't care what his brother thought, it was Forrest that mattered, but that sourness lingered.

One day Alice drove Jean across the valley to the alfalfa field where Forrest was working. "You're getting used to the ranch more and more now," she said.

"I love it here. It's so—" She searched for a word that didn't sound prissy. "So free." She meant more than that actually. It had something to do with what she imagined was western. Here at the Holly ranch, if you could call it a ranch, she felt under the influence of the free west—an unconfined place where people just were, not where formality and convention ruled every shred of a person's behavior. She'd have to get used to not feeling pinched by propriety.

"You know it's not going to be easy," Alice said.

"Forrest told you?"

"No. He didn't have to. We can see it in his face."

"You mean—?"

"Mother, too."

A sound escaped. That people could know such important things, not with words, but just by looking. Her mouth felt dry and her disadvantage, forgotten temporarily, returned with a sharper sting. Eventually Alice's high-pitched voice brought her back to the present.

"He'll make a fine husband, Jean. And a grateful one. Once he told me, 'what right do I have even to think that such a tender little hot house plant could ever be happy out here in this rough place?' Do you know what I told him?"

"No."

"The right of earnestness." Alice's voice cracked even higher, and it occurred to Jean that whatever gain she felt, Alice felt a loss. "I've seen his determination for years—working to break a horse, working to vault a fraction of an inch higher, working to learn how to walk again. He doesn't know this, but I've seen him whistling in the barn, and I think it's to keep from crying. But he hasn't done that since you came last year. Underneath his silly jokes he's pretty serious." Alice stopped abruptly.

Jean had an unsettling feeling she was taking something from Alice. No matter that Alice was married now and would eventually leave the ranch when her soldier husband came home. Brother and sister felt an uncommonly close bond, and somehow Alice's comment cast her in the role of an interloper. "I'll appreciate him," Jean said quietly after a moment.

When Mrs. Treadway came back from her week of staying out of the way, Jean and Forrest knew it was time. She heard him stand up after dinner. "Mrs. Treadway, will you come to Hermit House with us? Jean and I would like to talk to you." He sounded so formal.

In his cramped room, Forrest stood against the wall. Jean didn't dare sit on the bed with Mother there. She settled on the rawhide rug so Mother could have the only chair. Forrest cleared his throat before he spoke. It made Jean conscious of a violent pulsing in her own throat. "Maybe you can guess, Mrs. Treadway, what I'm going to tell you."

They waited. The wooden floor squeaked. Jean imagined him shifting his weight from one foot to the other, but this was one time not to follow Icy's advice of letting her face show her amusement.

"The fact is, Mrs. Treadway, that I love your daughter." Again he cleared his throat. "And I have reason to believe she loves me. So we'd like to get married. And we'd like to have your approval."

Jean held her breath. She knew Mother would be gracious, but she still held her breath.

"Well, Forrest. That's interesting. We'll see what can work out."

Interesting! What a dumb thing to say. She was surprised at the coolness in her mother's voice, her mother who was always so careful of propriety. Jean lost patience. "We want to be married right away. What I mean is—Mother, I don't want to go home. I want to stay here now."

"That's a little soon, Jean. We should telephone Father to see what he says."

"Right now?"

"Yes. He should know what you're thinking."

Mother and Jean and Chiang and Forrest trooped back into the living room and Forrest showed Jean the telephone. She heard Alice and Mother Holly retreat to the kitchen.

Jean greeted Father nervously, knowing she was at a disadvantage. There was no luxury of waiting for Friday night cocktail hour to loosen him up. She blurted out, "Mother's here and we've been having a good time and Forrest and I want to be married and I want to stay here, Father." It was all she could muster. She began to shrivel up. When Father didn't answer, in one impulsive movement she thrust the phone into Forrest's stomach.

Immediately she knew that was unfair. He cleared his throat and spoke slowly. "Hello, Mr. Treadway. I know this must be a pretty big thing for you to chew on all at once, sir." Silence. Silence from the eastern end of the line, too, she guessed. Her throat throbbed. She knew Father would be trying to appraise him just by the sound of his voice.

More silence. Apparently the conversation ended. She heard him place the receiver down quietly. "What did he say?"

"He just said, 'Tell Jean to come home immediately.'"

The next day was a torture of ambiguity. Jean knew she had no choice. She wanted Father's approval, that was certain. She needed his approval. They both did. There were practical considerations, if nothing else. They said a goodbye greater than all their goodbyes before. "No matter what Father says when I get home, I feel engaged," she whispered close to his temple.

Mother announced they would take the Julian stage, a small rustic bus line that passed through Ramona carrying live poultry and mail to the train station in San Diego.

"Alice and I would be pleased to drive you, Mrs. Treadway," Forrest offered.

"Thank you, no. Let's think of it as an economy measure, for the war effort."

But Jean knew it was to avoid drawing out their goodbye.

Just before they were to leave, Mother Holly put something in Jean's hand. "This is a cactus blossom. It only blooms once a year and it bloomed last night. It's a lovely pale pink. Take it with you."

The bus bounced over the mountains, and chickens squawked under the seats. Jean held the cactus blossom to her lowered face and tried not to cry right out there in public. Her fingers traced the stiff petals, running carefully up one side to the point, lingering there and sliding down the other side back to the base. She twirled the stem slowly in her hand. She realized that Forrest's mother was the last person to say goodbye. Forrest must have deferred to her at the final moment. It was a generous thing to do. There was more gentleness in this man with the rough hands and the western voice than she had guessed from his funny letters. She wondered what his face might have shown at that moment. If only she could have seen it for just a few seconds. It would have told her so much. She could keep it in her mind the months ahead. She wondered if Mother had noticed and she cried into the waxy pink blossom in her lap because she could not ask.

Chapter Sixteen

When they arrived home, Father refused to speak about Forrest or any wedding. "I don't believe it," Jean said to Mother the next day after Father had gone to work.

"He wants you to be happy," Mother offered.

"But not to even talk about it?"

"He just needs time to get used to the idea. He wants to be the one to make decisions."

"But it's my life, not his." She slumped in the wingback chair, hooked her leg over the arm and tapped her heel against the upholstery. The bronze Nathan Hale standing tall by the window would remember this: the day Jean Treadway spoke up to her mother. What was The Seeing Eye all about if her life was still going to be so restricted?

The long wait set in. Jean went back to her piano, hoping that the solace of music might fill the void. She worked on "Moonlight Sonata" all that fall. The expression of yearning in the first movement suited her. The second movement was difficult and she became impatient. She couldn't get it not to sound jumpy. Progress came slowly since Mother was busier than ever with Red Cross and could give her only an hour a day at best. Then for two or three hours more, Jean worked on the new measures, adding them to what she already knew.

She went back to her students at the Girls' Club and saved the little money she earned. She went back to the Visiting Nurse Association and the Junior League. There were always more bandages to fold at the Red Cross. Icy visited Hickory Hill often. Her husband was fighting in North Africa. Jean understood Icy's longings now that she too had someone she loved whom circumstances prevented her from seeing. Whatever she occupied herself with during the great wait, she lived under the guarded hope that Father's innate compassion would win out.

She paced the living room every day when she heard an Ingraham clock strike two. The mail would be coming soon. If Mother were home, she'd be able read her mail right then. If she were gone, Jean would have to wait. Sweet torture. Hearing the letters once was not enough. Sometimes she'd ask Icy or Lucy to read them again. Privacy was sacrificed for the pleasure of hearing again his words, and his plans.

One day after the mail came Jean sat at the piano, hoping the afternoon would go by quickly. "Anybody home?" Mort called from the front door.

"Only me."

"Where's Mother?"

"Downtown. At the Red Cross. What's the matter?"

"I need to borrow some tools from the garage."

"You sound upset. What's really the matter?"

Mort hesitated. "Something happened at work. Again." He sank down on the sofa.

Jean guessed. Other workers had teased him earlier because he didn't enlist. "Were they at it again?"

"Worse. 'Boss's son' stuff. They said I'm not going to war because Father got me out of it." He sounded devastated.

"That's ridiculous."

"Tell that to a bunch of roughnecks."

"Don't they know you're too nearsighted?"

"Doesn't matter to them."

Jean knew he'd been despairing over this for months. "The world isn't always fair, I guess." They sat quietly for a few minutes. She had never been in the habit of sharing so personally with either of her brothers, but now Mort had told her this. The urgency to hear any letter from Forrest was too strong. She asked him to check the mail.

"Letter from California."

"Will you read it?"

Jean missed the first few words because of the odd sensation of hearing Forrest's folksy speech come from Mort.

"'When a fella's going to be married,'" Mort read, "'he's got to earn his bride.'" It was so funny to hear him say bride. Such a formal word for Forrest. "'The whole town knows about you, Jeanie. I tell everybody I'll haul or pitch or muck or load or do any kind of work to earn money because I'm going to marry you, God willing. And they know they'll get their money's worth. I'm strong as a bull moose and I'm not afraid of hard work.'"

That was certain. If only Father knew, if he could see Forrest work, then maybe. But that was impossible. Father would never go there.

The letter explained that after his regular day's work at the ranch, he worked with a friend named Guy hauling hay. "'After dinner we head east with an empty truck into the desert to alfalfa farms to load,'" he wrote. She imagined with awe the sight of Forrest thrusting himself at the bales. He had to dig hay hooks into each bale and, with a great heave, hurl them up on the truck. "'I'm learning about trust, Jeanie. Just got to trust that Guy's up there to catch 'em. Then we head back over Banner Grade in that rickety old truck. By now I know every curve in the road by the sound of Guy grinding the gears. Then we unload at

Whiting's Feed Store in Ramona long about midnight. Earns me $3 each night for more cows and marriage and you, Jeanie.'

"My God, Jean, he's a storm center of energy."

"I know. I know."

"You love him a lot, don't you?"

"How can I help it? Don't you see?"

"He is pretty genuine." Mort chuckled. "He talks like a cowboy."

"Oh, I think he does that just to be cute. He knows I like it."

"What do you think Father will do?"

"I don't know. You know how he is." Her eyes got teary. "I feel so helpless. All I can do is wait like a child for Father to say yes when I've already said it, and meanwhile Forrest is working like a machine."

Mort gave her shoulders a little squeeze. "Maybe I can say something to him. Just trust a little longer."

All her life, it seemed, she had to trust. Trust Chiang, trust the arm of a friend, trust her other senses. Now she had to learn to trust something larger, less knowable, less concrete. The only concrete thing she had, after the cactus flower had wilted, was his gold track shoe. She liked to feel its coolness against her wrist. With her fingers she often traced the tiny raised "R" on the side of the shoe.

She worked on the Beethoven sonata for nearly an hour the next morning after everyone left for the day. Her own movement, her piano, an occasional snore from Chiang and a few rumblings from the kitchen were all the big house contained. A feeling of empty space sat heavily on her.

Her fingers relaxed on the keys and then fell to her lap. She reached for the bracelet, fingered over the charms, but couldn't find the shoe. She went through the charms again. No shoe. She took off the bracelet and laid it out on the keys to count the charms. One short. She felt around the piano. Her hands moved across the keyboard without a sound, exploring the spaces between black keys. She felt in her lap, in the folds of her skirt. She felt along the piano bench. "Chiang, fetch." The dog, lulled to sleep by the piano, was called into action. Seeing Eye dogs were trained to pick up incredibly small items dropped by their masters. Once Jean dropped a pill box and Chiang brought her not only the box and lid, but nuzzled her hand again, and dropped into her palm a tiny pill. She joined Chiang on the floor and they looked together. Her heart beat faster.

This was no time to trust Chiang only, no matter how good a dog she was. She went into the kitchen and asked Delia to help. Delia traced Jean's pathway from her upstairs bedroom to the dining room for breakfast and then to the piano. "I'm sorry, but it's just not here, lamb," she said. "Ask Lucy to help you look when she comes home. I've got to get back to the kitchen."

Jean sank down into a cushioned chair. There's more than one way to skin a cat—Forrest's words echoed in her mind, his voice carrying a hint of smugness, a private pride in accomplishing things simple to others. She moved the piano bench out of the way and kneeled on the floor. Inch by inch she set out to feel the whole carpet, digging her fingers in the nap. It was impossible even to consider writing that she'd lost it. The shoe was too precious to him, too much a symbol of what might have been, for him. Besides, he might think her irresponsible. Chiang fell asleep again. When Lucy came home, she only confirmed the work of the afternoon.

After dinner Jean didn't write him as she had been planning to. The next day she taught at the Girls' Club. The next night she couldn't do it either. Two days later, in the morning, when everyone had left, she couldn't put it off any longer, so she wrote the letter. Now she had to wait for two things—Father's approval, and Forrest's next letter. Jean spent more time at the Red Cross. At least she was doing something there. She went to the mailbox for the next two weeks with dragging footsteps. She wanted a letter but didn't want to read what it might say. When it came, she could tell Forrest was hiding his hurt. "I guess it's stupid to think back on those times in high school. We got more important things to think about now," he'd written. A hollowness settled in her throat. She became restless. She couldn't stick to her practice. She forgot the measure she was working on and her hands dropped to her lap.

A few weeks later a tiny package came. Jean opened it with trembling fingers. The ring he had promised her. All anxiety vanished. She explored it tenderly. It had a large raised diamond encircled by tiny ones. It must sparkle beautifully. He must have borrowed money to buy it, probably from his oldest sister, Elizabeth, the one he felt so close to. Here was proof she could offer Father. If Forrest could buy her such a ring, he surely could support her. Certainly a ring like that would be acceptable in their Bristol circle even if Forrest himself wasn't, at least to Father. At cocktail hour she put it on to show to him.

"I don't want you to wear it," he said flatly.

"No! I don't believe it."

"Don't wear it. The subject is closed."

She felt as if someone had thrown a lead weight right at her chest. Her extended hand dropped slowly, and she cupped her other hand around the ring, covering it and holding it close. What was wrong with her? She was a grown woman. Why couldn't she defy him?

Why couldn't he give his approval willingly? She didn't want to wrench it from him. What would the years ahead be like without his approval? Only tension and alienation. Deeply, she wanted him to want for her what she yearned for, but she didn't even dare to say it. She still lived under his roof.

Every night in her room, she took the ring from its tiny box and put it on while she read a Braille book in bed. Her right hand moved across the line and her left moved down the left margin to keep her place. At the bottom of each page, she allowed her right hand to touch the ring before turning the page.

"Father, I'm engaged whether or not I wear the ring so it's stupid to tell me not to." One night in bed she heard her voice say it, though in her mind the voice was hardly her own. "You just can't let go to let me grow, can you? What are you afraid of? All my life your own precious need to be in control has come first. You don't shelter. You crush. Where is there real love in that? And you expect me to give up love and life because *you're* not sure? No, Father, this is one time you're going to have to adjust."

She sat up straighter in bed and her heart pounded with the thoughts. Never had she allowed herself even to frame such feelings into words. But could she actually say them, right to his face? She conjured up a picture of her father's face, not the mouth or the nose or even the eyes, because she couldn't remember them. All she saw was a scowl, not one of anger but of worry, and after a while it relaxed and she could imagine the eyes—brown and deep and kind. But were they his?

It would be like a dam breaking if she ever actually started to tell him what she felt. That just wasn't her. Yet. A Polly Gillespie or a Sally Anne could do it. She doubted if Icy could. And what would it prove? That she could hurt him back? His obstinacy wasn't malicious, only ignorant, misled. If only he would let go without a confrontation.

To go without restraint, to walk out the door onto the brick porch beneath the hickory trees, like Ibsen's Nora closing the door behind her forever, hearing it latch shut against her placid, sheltered world. The spirit of Nora bore through her chest. She remembered when she'd heard the play at Andrebrook. She smirked. Andrebrook itself was pretty sheltered. She hardly thought Nora could do it, Nora the flittering skylark who seemed at first so contented with being taken care of, Nora whose life centered around new dresses and parties—this same Nora left her safe shelter for what? Nora didn't know for what. Jean let out a faint sound from between closed lips. Neither did she. The room had grown stuffy and she kicked the covers off a little, eased herself down and rolled onto her side.

In the morning she put the ring back into its box and carefully put the box in the left corner of her top dresser drawer.

One afternoon Icy came to pick her up to spend a weekend in Litchfield. Jean took her up to her room. She opened the top drawer, took out the velvet hinged box and opened it. Icy gasped. "Ssh. Don't say a word. Wait till we get out to your car." She closed the box and put it back in the drawer. But what did it matter? She'd already shown it. Quickly, she pulled it out again and stuffed it into her handbag.

Icy and Jean rode with the windows open even though the New England fall was cool. The wind made Jean's eyes water. She reached into her handbag and put on the ring.

"It's magnificent," Icy said. "When did you get it?"

"Last week. Father won't let me wear it, so you must never mention it."

"Mum. Won't say a word." Then, after a pause, "Only that I'm happy for you."

"I know." She felt her throat swell.

"The ash and hickory trees seem like they're on fire today, Jean. Brilliant red and orange and gold. When the breeze blows, some of the leaves blow off and it's like the flames are moving."

"Thirteen years ago, before I knew you, we took this road to Harkness Hospital. It was about this time of year. Mother kept saying, 'Oh Jean, just look at those trees.' I didn't know then that I should have been memorizing a leaf." She could tell when the car reached the outskirts of Bristol and climbed the gentle hills of the farmland. "Just smell that hay, Icy. We're passing a dairy or some cows or a barn, aren't we?"

"Yes, on the right. A dairy. There's a rust-colored barn sitting out there proud as can be."

"Oh, it smells so good and fresh and alive and free." She chuckled sheepishly. "It makes me think of Forrest." Then she told again of going out to the pasture with Forrest's seeing eye bull to find the cows. "Why can't Father understand that I'll just shrivel up and turn into an old maid here? He can't accept that I might want something he can't provide."

"Just like when you got Chiang."

"Exactly. He couldn't accept that a dog could give me something he couldn't. Now he can't accept that Forrest can."

"Is it mainly because Forrest can't see?" Icy's voice was gentle.

"Mostly, though he'd never admit it. Pretty narrow minded, huh? But it's also because Forrest doesn't have any money, and he's so far away. He thinks Ramona is Indian territory."

"Do you have the same doubts he does?"

"Not a shred."

"Can't you just leave anyway?"

"Oh, Icy, you don't have a father, so you don't know." A tear, either from the wind or her anguish, trailed an itchy path down her cheek. "All that growing-up I thought I did at The Seeing Eye, it's gone. I feel like a little kid." She turned her face to the window. She smelled the acrid odor of burning leaves. "Do you see anybody burning leaves?"

"No."

"Must be someone doing it, though, somewhere." She slumped down farther in the seat and rested her head on the window frame. The wind blew her hair back from her forehead. "I don't think he ever really thought I'd get married to anybody." In this she had tapped the underlying fear of her life. It hung out there, naked and true. Only to Icy could she have said it. They rode for a few miles without speaking until the coolness of early evening made her roll up the window.

Fall slipped into the long, white wait of winter. Never could Jean be as honest with Mother as she was with Icy. Mother was, after all, Father's wife. Telling Mother was too close to telling Father just what she thought.

"All you can do is wait and hope," Mother kept saying.

"That's all I have been doing. For months."

Spring came, the season of new beginnings, but no renewed hope welled up in her. There was only a dull ache. Waiting hadn't accomplished anything.

She noticed that one thing Mother never said was, "I know how you must feel." Even that would have been something. But, no, Mother couldn't even bring herself to say that. Maybe because she didn't feel it. How could Mother read Forrest's letters for nearly a year and not know how she was feeling? She could only hope the good in this man would be filtered through Mother to Father. In a sense, each week's letter brought that possibility. Once Forrest let it out that every week he paid back a few dollars to his sister for the ring. Another time he wrote, "Our mothers are reading so much from each of us it's a wonder they don't fall in love and get married." At least that made Mother laugh.

One letter said, "Bought more cattle this week. Now we've got 40 head plus the milk cows. What would the governor think of that?"

"What's that about?" asked Mother.

"Oh, he means Father." She knew Mother missed the most important word in that sentence. We.

Chapter Seventeen

In the spring, Forrest's frustration reached the breaking point. He wrote directly to Mr. Treadway:

I can understand why you are hesitant to let your daughter start a new life out here with me, and I don't want to hold back any truth about who I am or what I have. I don't earn a lot, but I work hard and I aim to continue if and when you allow your daughter to marry me. In great earnestness he detailed to Mr. Treadway his assets, his current jobs and his prospects. *I'll wash windows, I'll muck stalls, I'll do anything to prove to you that I can be a worthy husband, if you would give me that chance.* It was a desperation effort.

Three weeks later, Alice announced, "Mail's here. Letter for you, Forrest, from Mr. Morton Treadway."

Forrest swallowed. "Lemme hear it."

Alice got past brief opening formalities, then stopped abruptly.

"Go on. Isn't there anything else?"

"'I fear she would lead a sedentary life. Marriage doesn't work on love alone. The issue is closed.'"

After a moment of stillness, Forrest asked Alice to look up *sedentary* in the dictionary: "Characterized by or requiring a sitting posture; accustomed to move about little," she read.

He flew into a rage. "The old man has it all wrong." He stormed through the cabin, bumping his shin on the coffee table. "What does he know? He's never met me, and he never saw

Jean out here on the ranch. Come on, Alice. We're going for a ride."

They saddled up quickly and took off at a gallop. The sun was high, and the heat of the day made the horses strain.

"That man doesn't know what he's talking about," Forrest shouted. The two horses ran side by side, and for a while he rode in steamy silence, gripped by the agony of being misjudged, the frustration of not being permitted to do what he knew he could do. The trouble with kindness toward people who can't see, he thought, is that everyone thinks he knows what you can do better than you do. But this man should know. Because of Jean he should know better than the rest of the world. That made his letter hurt all the more.

"Talk about sight. Her father has about as much sight as a mosquito with a blindfold on."

They went to Indian Rock, their usual ride, but Forrest didn't stop there.

"Sedentary, hell." He spurred Snort. "He probably sits at a desk all day in a fancy office."

Alice sneezed in the dust raised by Snort's hooves. She had to spur Pronto to keep up and ahead of Forrest.

"Sits there making money so he can give his family the perfect life."

They crossed the valley and cantered up the hills on the other side, working the horses hard.

"I guess that's not far different from what I'd like to do— work hard to give a family a good life." The thought melted some of his anger. He slowed Snort to a lope, stroked him on the neck and found him wet.

"Let's let 'em walk, Alice."

Alice breathed heavily. "Good." They took another route home and walked the horses in silence for a while.

"What's the old man testing, anyway? Trial by endurance?"

"He probably doesn't trust any love based on only two weeks of time together," Alice said.

"But we aren't kids."

After they crossed the highway and the horses were on the dirt of the Holly property, Forrest dismounted and walked next to Snort back to the barn. By the time they got to the corral, Snort's side wasn't heaving any more and his breath was back to normal.

"I'll take care of the horses, Allego."

"You haven't called me that since we were kids."

"You go on back. Thanks for the ride." Dust coated the inside of his mouth.

The horses walked to the hitching rail. Forrest kept his hand moving over Snort's neck and head as he reached for the bridle. He felt foam. "Oh yeah, you've had a little exercise, haven't ya? And it's mighty hot, too." Forrest spoke softly. He removed the saddles and blankets and slung them over the corral rail to air. One at a time he ran his hands down over the horses' thighs and hamstrings and felt their hocks and fetlocks. He leaned against their haunches and picked up their hind legs to examine the hooves. He discovered a few stones and picked them out, then went to the front legs.

He supposed the old man was just trying to take care of someone he loves. Grudgingly, he allowed him that. He led both horses into the barn, up to the feed trough, and fed them oats and molasses. He reached for the curry comb where he kept it on the shelf and gently curried the sweaty hide. Then, with long strokes, he brushed down the neck, withers, back, shoulders and flanks, then the legs, the mane and forelock and tail, loving the feel of the animals, prolonging the task. This time alone with the horses was always precious to Forrest, a time for communication of love by touch. He did his most serious thinking when tending the horses. Over the years much of his own pain had abated in this healing atmosphere. He did all he could for the horses that had performed for him, and then he let them out to the corral and water trough. He went back into the barn and came out with a flake of hay for each one.

The sun slanted on his face at a low angle, but it was still hot. He stood awhile and then walked back into the coolness of the barn and slumped on a bale of hay. He sat motionless, beaten, until he heard someone come into the darkened barn.

"You in here, Forrest?"

It was his oldest sister, Elizabeth, home for a visit. He'd learned much from her while he was growing up. Once he'd told Jean "I went to school to her." Her very presence soothed him.

He grunted. His forehead felt tight, drawn into a scowl.

She came to him slowly. "Forrest, you know you're going to have to love that man." The words exploded in his ears even though her voice was soft. "Especially if he's going to be your father-in-law."

"But he doesn't have the right—"

"Your willfulness isn't going to make him change his mind, so you'd better stop being so self-righteous and begin to see him as only loving the same woman you love. Maybe he's not loving her the way you think he should, but it's still love."

That was a big idea for him to chew on. He remembered he'd said nearly the same words to him on the phone more than a year ago, a big idea to chew on. He didn't know what to say. He didn't even move.

"Think about it, Forrest. If I were in Jean's place, Dad might have done the same thing." Elizabeth touched him on the arm just above the elbow for a moment. A cat meowed. Then he heard her go back to the house.

He picked out a piece of straw from the bale and bit down on it, but his throat was tight and dry and his mouth tasted sour. He spit it out. He hated to admit she was right. His anger felt better than her calmness. Yet staying angry would be a denial of his private ethic, the affirmation of the power of love. Love had power. He'd seen it before with his own dad. And love could be felt even when it's not said. He knew his horses felt it when he curried them.

Idly, he wondered if he could think something kindly about the governor for five minutes solid without any resentment creeping in. He heard the cat meow every once in a while. He decided to try to think kindly about the governor from one meow to another without thinking anything negative about him. Any shred of anger and he had to start again, he told himself. When the cat meowed, Forrest went over in his mind all the good things Mr. Treadway had done for Jean. How he had given her a good education, how he sent her on wonderful trips, how he provided music lessons. He thought how he had lent that neighbor kid money to go to college even after he'd caught him peeking in the window. A lot of good the old man's generosity did now. Misplaced, it was. And maybe even phoney. Why can't he be as tolerant with me when I have such good intentions?

He felt himself heating up again. Each time he started out with new resolve but each time he spoiled it by frustrated bitterness. His stubbornness wouldn't let him give up. When the cat meowed, he started again. He had no idea how long he sat on the bale of hay wrestling with his resentment. Sedentary, he thought, and chortled. This time he caught himself before he went further. Eventually he did it. He filled the time between two meows with only positive thoughts of this father from the east who thought protection was love. He felt he'd washed himself clean of rebelliousness. He stood up, stretched, and made his way toward the corral to get Victor Mature to help him find the cows. The air was cooler. He thought the sun must be setting low over the mountains to the west. Late again for the cows. That wasn't kind to them. He shuffled along faster.

Summer came and the Treadways ate their breakfast on the screened porch outside the dining room. Early morning on the east side of the house was the nicest time of day. A slight breeze brought gooseflesh on Jean's arms. She heard the leaves brush against each other on the hickory trees in the grove. She heard the cicadas as she had every summer as long as she could remember. She heard the sound of silver on china, and she heard Father put down his newspaper.

"Well, if we're going to have a wedding here, we'd better think about putting up an awning on the terrace just in case it rains."

Jean froze. Mother didn't say a word. Neither did Lucy. The sounds of silver on china stopped. Father folded up his paper and walked into the house. Jean pinched her eyes closed. Let me be awake. Let this be real. She didn't dare say anything until she heard his car leave for work.

"Did I hear him right? Did you hear him Lucy?"

No one said anything.

"Does he mean it?"

"He wouldn't have said it if he didn't mean it," Mother said.

"He's never gone back on anything he ever said that I can remember," Lucy joined in.

"What made him change his mind?"

"I don't know," Mother said, "but it doesn't surprise me. The major things have always had to be his decisions."

The reality began to register. It was as though some wall of suspicion had been penetrated, some mental breakthrough had taken place, some prejudice had dissolved.

"Then why wait any longer. I've waited forever. I've got to tell Forrest. I've got to call him. No, he's still asleep there. Let's plan it right now."

"Right this minute, Jean? You haven't finished your breakfast."

"So what?"

Jean stood up quickly. The wrought iron chair caught on a crack in the cement and tipped over backwards. She left it for Lucy to set right. Mother followed her to the sofa and writing table in the living room. They started making lists. An hour later, Jean phoned Forrest.

"I had a feeling it would happen soon," he said, his voice sounding older, wiser.

Once Father had decided, he was absolutely cooperative. He told her she could have any kind of wedding she wanted. Anywhere. In the days that followed, he asked more questions about Forrest, about Ramona, about the ranch. He asked where they would live.

"Hermit House."

"Not suitable. You have to have a separate house, a real house, not a room. Is there anything else on the property?"

"Yes, Lance and Mary Kay have a big turkey ranch on a hill nearby, but they're all settled. They built it. But Helen and Don live in a little wooden frame house on the ranch just temporarily."

"Temporarily? Until when?"

"Until they get enough money to buy a business. Then they'll move."

"Fine. Ask them if they want to sell it for cash. The money they make could start them off."

More talk. More letters. Jean sent Forrest a telegram. "Please make arrangements to buy Helen and Don's house for $6,000. Father is giving it to us as a wedding present."

Jean told Icy. She wrote to Dody. She wrote to Sally Anne. She wrote to Elsa. She wrote to Miss Weaver. She told Lorraine. She told Tready. Tready said it was a courageous thing for her parents to do. "Oh, yes, you're brave, too, Jean, for wanting to live so far from home, but you're in love. It's even braver for them. That's love of the highest kind."

Chapter Eighteen

Five days before the wedding, Forrest sat on the edge of his seat. In a few minutes he'd be with Jean. That's all he could think about. He didn't know how long a ride it was between Grand Central and Berlin, Connecticut, the stop where Jean, Chiang and Mr. Treadway would meet him. He only knew it was after New Haven. That had been a long stop with lots of people getting on and off.

He'd have to rely on hearing the stops called out, but he couldn't understand the conductor because his words slurred together. To Forrest, the voice spoke of a lifetime of trains and stations. All the stops must be the same to the conductor. Some people got off. Others got on. It was the same yesterday. It would be the same tomorrow. No matter how many syllables they had, the names of the towns all sounded similar. To the conductor, nothing hung in the balance.

To Forrest, everything hung in the balance. If he couldn't demonstrate to Mr. Treadway that he could get off at the right station, how could that man trust him with his daughter? The governor could still call off the wedding. Each time the train came into a station he leaned forward in his seat in the hope that his own alertness would compensate for the conductor's boredom. His hands never left his bags, and his palms gripping the handles began to sweat. "Berlin," he heard, and then the doors into the next compartment opened. There was a loud rumbling and screeching as the train slowed to a stop. His heartbeat quickened. He felt his way off the train and stood on the platform. There was nothing to do but wait for Mr. Treadway to find him among the talking, moving people.

"Meriden," he heard someone say in a snatch of conversation. Meriden? "Meriden? Where am I?" he asked in a loud voice to no one in particular, hoping someone would answer.

"Meriden," a voice said on the run.

Forrest spun around what he thought was 180 degrees and took a few steps. "I need to get back on," he shouted in a panic above the sound of the train whistle. He felt a hand grab his arm and he stumbled as he was pulled up the steps just before the train began to move.

He stood in the aisle the rest of the trip, his heart thumping hard, the skin of his neck and hands sticky. He tried to concentrate on listening to everything for a clue in order not to make a another mistake. "Berlin is next," he heard. He trusted and got off again, stood still and listened.

"Are you Forrest Holly?" It was a man's voice he heard.

He squared his shoulders, raised his head and grinned. "You betcha," he announced, relieved. "Are you—?"

"Mr. Treadway." The voice was businesslike.

"And I'm here too, Forrest, and so's Chiang."

Forrest set down his bag and reached toward her voice, his hug nervous and halting. Jean could wait. Right now the important thing was to take this man's measure. "For a while there I thought I might never meet you," Forrest said and smiled. He held out his hand. Mr. Treadway's palm was smooth—he'd probably never really worked—though the grasp of the fingers was firm.

"Some things take a little time," Mr. Treadway said. His voice had a resonance that conveyed power, but in the first moments of conversation there were a few short silences and a minute stutter, as if this man of money felt uneasy. Christ! He thinks he's got worries? So this was the man who had kept him waiting, had kept his eagerness, his passion, for Jean at white heat for over a year. Yet in the euphoria of arrival and greeting, Forrest found nothing to criticize.

After introductions at Hickory Hill Jean took Forrest through the rooms he'd need to learn. She explained where the furniture was, and they walked around it. In the living room he ran his hand lightly over the curves of the two grand pianos. She walked him across the room to the fireplace. "This is where we'll stand when we take our vows."

"The whole cabin in Ramona can fit into half the living room here." He chuckled. In the library he bumped into the bronze Nathan Hale and nearly knocked him over. Jean took him up the stairs. "The family's bedrooms are on this floor."

"Where's yours?"

"In the middle next to Lucy's," she said, and squeezed his hand. "When Mort and Bill were kids, they had their room at one end and my parents at the other so they wouldn't hear the boys teasing each other." She took him up another flight of stairs. "This is the maids' floor. Their rooms are down the hall to the right. This big room we call the dormitory. When we were kids we played in it, but when we got older we used it for our friends when they stayed overnight. You'll have it all to yourself. Be careful. The ceiling is sloped."

He raised his hands over his head and followed the ceiling as it sloped lower. "Glad you told me or you'd be marrying a guy trying to grow a horn out of his forehead." He stumbled into a bed, sat down on it and said, "Can ya come here, Jeanie?"

"Mmm, no."

"I guess we don't know who's around, do we? Don't want to set off the governor."

Jean came toward him anyway and brushed against his leg. Quickly he drew her to him and she fell onto his chest as he leaned back. He kissed her deeply on her mouth, pressing her lips apart. The time had been too long. Chiang let out a sound halfway between a whine and a growl. "Oops," Forrest whispered. "Any way to keep her quiet?"

"I have an idea." Jean pulled away, then put Chiang on the harness and took Forrest by the arm. "Come on."

"Where're we going, Jeanie baby?"

"To the woods beyond the rose garden."

In the privacy of the thick stand of hickory trees and with the coolness of the little creek nearby, he let go the pent up passions of months. All the fueling of hope though work, the postponement of desire, the anxiety of getting here, that all vanished in how she felt next to him. Chiang could whine all she wanted, he wasn't going to let go.

Until the wedding there was a constant round of parties and luncheons. Forrest met dozens of people. He and Jean were rarely alone. It was the logistics problem all over again, only there was no Hermit House they could go to naturally, without comment, no cool barn for long talks twice a day during milking. The maids were always moving around and might be in a room without talking, so he could never be sure if he was alone with her. He tried to keep his hands to himself, but he didn't try very hard.

The night before the wedding the Treadways gave a small party, and by the end of it he had begun to feel comfortable with the tinkle of crystal and the crisp feel of damask. Mort teased him in a brotherly way, saying, "Here, Forrest, have some olives. They'll make you passionate." Forrest ate 35 of them.

When the guests left, Forrest and Jean and Chiang walked up the stairs together. She paused at the landing. As usual, he didn't know who else was around. Desire pulsed hard in him. His goodnight boomed loudly. He kissed her once and walked up the stairs, his feet landing heavily on each step to announce his departure. Publicly it was an honorable gesture, he thought, but that was all it was, a gesture.

Upstairs even after he slumped down on the bed he felt as if she were drawing him back down to the floor below. To be this close to her and yet to have her remain inaccessible was maddening. He took off his shoes and considered waiting until the sounds of the house had quieted and then working his way down the corridor to the maids' stairway. It was at the opposite end of the hall, farthest from where he thought her parents' room was. He could run his hand along the hallway wall to know where he was. Even though he didn't know that stairway, he could feel along the handrail and then move quietly past the empty boys' room, past Lucy's room to get to Jean. He wasn't quite sure where her parents' room was, but he knew it was somewhere past Jean's. There probably were other doors too, closets and such. If he miscalculated and ended up in a closet, there'd be no harm in that. If he opened a door too soon, it might be Lucy's. If he missed Jean's and went too far, he'd end up in her parents' room. Disaster.

But if he made it—well. He went through the scene in his mind. He would open the door as quietly as he could. He wouldn't knock. Too much noise. He wouldn't say anything, either. He'd just walk in slowly, close the door behind him and reach until he found her. Gently he'd surround her and bend her down with him to the bed. His mind raced until it met one obstacle, the most formidable opponent: Chiang, the one-woman dog trained to protect Jean from all danger. Jean had told him that the relationship of Seeing Eye dog to mistress is indivisible. Chiang probably slept at the foot of her bed, or next to it. But which side? He hadn't asked enough questions. Stationed somewhere by the bedside, Chiang would be sure to raise a ruckus. Even Chiang's movement or Jean's voice quieting her might be heard by Lucy or, worse, the old man.

Logistics ensured her chastity. Forrest lay back in bed, resigned to wait another night. He was torn between feelings of nobility, and tormented frustration at this most recent difficulty that lack of sight—and Chiang—posed. One thing was for sure. Chiang wouldn't stop him the next night.

The next afternoon was warm with the lingering heat of a New England Indian summer. Forrest could hear voices of guests spilling out from the living room below onto the terrace. In the dormitory he was methodical about getting dressed. A rented Prince Albert lay on the bed. His sisters Elizabeth and Mary had arrived and were upstairs to supervise his preparations.

"This place smells like a perfume factory," he said. "Did you see the cop downstairs? Mort said there's a cop down there guarding the second floor landing. Mr. Treadway's wise to thieves masquerading as guests. Isn't that enough to—"

"To what?"

He searched for something familiar. "To make a calf butt his ma?"

They laughed and then Mary helped with the shirt studs.

Forrest's thoughts lurched forward and his words became disconnected. "All week whenever I took a shower, all I found were some skimpy little towels, no bigger than napkins. I thought, what kind of a place is this that the great Treadways of Hickory Hill couldn't have decent towels? But I didn't say anything." He chuckled. "An hour ago I happened to reach under the towel rack for my shoe, and I found a stack of big thick fluffy ones. I can just guess what the maids have been thinking—that that no account cowman hasn't taken a shower all the time he's been here."

Elizabeth laughed again. "I can't believe how calm you are."

"Don't you know me?" He lowered his head toward her. "I realize what I'm entering into. Pretty big stuff. If there was, even today, an absolute message from on high not to go ahead, I'd pack my bags and hightail it home in a flash." He tipped his ear to the ceiling. "But I don't hear any."

He put on the swallowtail coat and Elizabeth adjusted his bow tie. "Check me over good now. How do I look?"

"Dashing."

"Debonair."

He leaned down and aimed a light kiss at Elizabeth's forehead and got her on the nose. Concentrating more, he turned to kiss Mary who put her face up to his. He squared his shoulders, turned toward the door and offered them both an arm. They walked out into the hall and down to the second floor. He paused outside what he thought was Jean's door. "Jeanie?" He knocked on the hallway wall. "Let him in, Lucy," he heard Jean say. A door opened farther down the hall.

"But the bride and groom aren't supposed to see each other before the wedding," Lucy protested.

"We won't. I promise." Forrest walked until he found the doorway. "Where are you?"

"Over here."

He heard Lucy go out in the hall and close the door.

"How's my thirteen-cow woman?"

"What's that supposed to mean?"

"You're my thirteen-cow woman, Jeanie. I sold thirteen cows in order to come here and marry you."

Jean laughed.

"That's nothing. I would have sold 'em all if I had to. Gonna work to earn them back, too." Work at what he wasn't quite sure, but he'd think about that later.

Jean touched him on the arm. "Do you want to see my dress?"

"Can I?"

"You sound like a little kid." She put his hand on her shoulder. He felt down her arm to the sleeve edge and then beyond, down to her hand to touch her ring and then back up to her shoulder and neck. His hand touched the lace that dripped in loose folds from her neckline. He brushed it gently and followed the neckline as it dipped to a deep V. "The lace is from Mother's wedding gown. It came from Belgium."

With both hands he felt the satin smoothness down her bodice to her narrow waist where the cool fabric flowed in gores over her hips. He knelt down to feel the fullness of the gown, as if in supplication at a shrine. His hand stretched around the hemline and he moved to one side to follow the train.

"It's long, Jean."

"You have to watch where you're stepping."

"Oh, I won't be behind you. I'll be next to you. All day. Forever."

He stood up slowly, his hands feeling again the folds of the skirt, up to the waist and the lace. Gently he took her in his arms and turned her face up to his and kissed her delicately, moving moment by moment into passion. Her lips opened to his, but he pulled away and let out a deep breath. This wasn't the time, he told himself.

Downstairs, a string quartet began to play. "It's a Strauss waltz," Jean said. "It must be about time. Do you want to see my veil first?" She reached over to the bed and found the headpiece.

"You have to remember to lift it up when you kiss me." There was a knock at the door.

"Forrest, it's time you went downstairs," said Lucy. "It's almost 4:30. The music's started." There was an urgency in her voice and a bustle of people in the hallway.

"See ya down there, Jeanie baby." His voice was almost a whisper.

Slowly he went downstairs. "You look pretty dapper," he heard Mort say. "And so does Chiang."

"She's got her bow on, does she?"

"Just like Jean's dress." They chuckled. "Chiang's getting married, too," Mort said to some guests.

"Sounds like a crowd here. How many have ya packed in?"

"Oh, maybe 200."

Bill came up to usher Forrest into position in front of the fireplace. "You look splendid," Mrs. Treadway whispered.

"Thank you, ma'm." He grinned. "Likewise, I'm sure." A wave of heat rushed up his throat to his face and despite the crowd, despite Jean just upstairs, he felt unutterably alone.

At precisely half past four, as the invitation had said, the quartet moved into the Mendelssohn march and Jean's heart lurched. Lucy in a mustard yellow gown started down the stairs. Jean followed on Father's arm. Since childhood she had walked these stairs. She didn't have to count. They were in her, part of her, as sure as breathing. She could think about other things— the English ivy she felt entwining the iron railing, the ambrosial scent of lily-of-the-valley in her bouquet, the hush settling over the crowd, the slight dragging feeling her train made on the stairs behind her, the swelling of the wedding march played by the strings, steady but leaping into each new measure. For years she had wondered if it would ever be played for her. Finally here she was, marching to error or to fullness, walking with Father down the childhood stairs for the last time as his unmarried daughter. She squeezed his arm.

He guided her through the crowd, up to the fireplace and stopped her neatly just so her elbow touched Forrest's. She took his arm and dropped Father's. There it goes, she thought, the umbilical cord tying her to Hickory Hill. Everything felt good and right. The room smelled of Chanel Number Five, furniture polish, Forrest's after shave and a breath mint. Reverend Roberts droned on, his dentures clicking so loudly she imagined everyone behind her could hear, too. She couldn't concentrate on what he was saying. Maybe Forrest wasn't listening either because she heard Lucy whisper from somewhere on the left. "Kiss."

And then it came, with all the burning of a too-long wait. A rustle of approval filled the room. So this was it. So this was the moment. She turned to hear her mother's voice. "Congratulations Mrs. Holly." It was too foreign, too unexpected, too wonderful. She couldn't keep back the tears.

Deftly Lucy positioned them in a reception line. An endless stream of people came up to greet them. Icy. Tready. Sally Anne. Miss Weaver, dear Miss Weaver. Lorraine. Louise Barnes. Mrs. Sturdivant. Uncle Ed and Uncle Dudley. People from the Ares and Ain'ts. People from the Red Cross, the DAR, the Congregational Church. Everyone from the Hill. From Farmington Country Club. Some said who they were. Others didn't need to. She wondered if all those people saw a future she couldn't. She leaned forward to receive their hugs. Her dress pulled at the waist. Lying on her train, Chiang had settled into a bored snooze. Jean felt anchored to the floor.

The receiving line was interminable, even when she knew everyone. It must be worse for Forrest, she thought. After cake cutting and champagne punch toasts by the best man, Alice's husband's brother from Ramona, Jean and Forrest chatted with guests on the terrace. Eventually Jean stole a few minutes alone with Icy. They sat on the terrace under the awning and Jean asked her what everyone was wearing. Icy was as meticulous in her descriptions. Lucy came up to tell her it was time.

The new Mr. and Mrs. Holly went upstairs, with Chiang, to change clothes. Afterwards, in the upstairs hallway people moved about hurriedly. Forrest asked, "Am I getting lightheaded or is the air up here actually thinner?" Someone was sniffling. It sounded like Lucy. Forrest put his arms around her and gave her a firm kiss. She stiffened immediately and didn't say anything. He drew away.

A minute later Lucy's voice came from another direction. "You can't get away without giving your sister-in-law a kiss," she said heartily. She rushed at him like a football lineman and Forrest kissed her again. Forrest and Jean and Chiang were whisked off to the car in a shower of rice and rose petals.

Jean had arranged that they should spend the first few nights at a guest farm in Bridgewater, Connecticut. "It's not the kind of place most people would think of as a honeymoon spot," she admitted. "It's more for New Yorkers to get a taste of rural atmosphere and to watch a farm in action. They have sheep and cows, a vegetable garden and a hay crop. I had to think of a place that could accommodate Chiang. Besides, I thought it would make you feel comfortable."

"Sort of like a postman taking a walk," he said.

Bill and Ginny delivered them there late at night, ushered them into their room and promptly left. As soon as the door closed they were in each other's arms. Together the three explored their new surroundings. Chiang walked Jean around the room and Forrest followed, his hand on her shoulder. They felt the bed and learned where the bathroom and closet were.

They opened the luggage and pulled out the top layer of clothes. A shower of rice rained down at their feet.

"This isn't a farm," said Forrest. "It's a rice patch." Every piece of clothing they lifted from the suitcase brought a new trickle of rice. They walked on it, crunching it and sliding where it had fallen on the bare floor.

"I bet Chiang will try to eat it," Jean said.

"Nope. I don't think she wants any part of this wedding."

For a time Jean busied herself with changing, with hanging up clothes, with tending to Chiang. Part of her wanted to prolong the tender anticipation.

Forrest asked, "When we were upstairs after the wedding and after we changed our clothes, who else was in that upstairs hallway?"

"Lucy and Mort, I think. Maybe Bill."

"Who else?"

"Mother, for a minute."

"Is that all?"

"No. Alexina was helping me."

"Who's that?"

"The upstairs maid."

"Was she standing near you?"

"Yes. I think she was crying a little, the poor dear."

"Well, I'll be the son of a pig stealer. I thought she was Lucy. I planted a big one on her and she tensed up like a stone cold statue."

Jean laughed. "It probably did her a world of good. I don't think she's ever let a man kiss her."

She imagined Alexina's anguish at receiving the misappropriated kiss. "I'm going to miss the maids," she said softly. She'd known Mary since childhood, and Delia, too. There had been a steady stream of upstairs girls. She had shared some part of her life with each of them. Vincent, too, she'd miss. He'd always been so accommodating. And of course Icy. No more long evening talks huddled around the furnace grating. She grew quiet and was glad Forrest wasn't saying anything just now. Chiang gave a little whine. Jean tied the leash to a chair and felt for the small pocket in her suitcase, the same suitcase she'd taken to Europe with Miss Weaver, the same one she'd taken to The Seeing Eye, the one she used on her first, bold trip West.

"What are you doing?" Forrest's voice had a velvety softness that reminded her of a child's voice asking, "Do you want to come out and play?" She realized she had grown distant for a moment and he was reaching out to her with his voice alone. She loved the voice—its mellow humility, its simplicity. She wanted it more.

"Hmm?"

"What are you doing, Jeanie?"

"Oh, nothing." She opened Chiang's mouth wide and carefully dropped two sleeping tablets far down her throat.

"Do you want to come over here?" His voice was tentative.

She wiped her hands on the bedspread and moved toward his voice.

"What do you have on?" he asked.

"A black ribbon."

"No. Really?" From the edge of the bed, he reached forward and his hand brushed her knee. He moved up her thigh and hip, and explored the distance to her neck. He drew her onto the bed. There was no black ribbon. Anywhere.

Chapter Nineteen

At 6:00 in the morning, Jean awoke with a start and threw back the covers.

"What in tarnation are you doing?" Forrest asked in a daze.

"I have to take Chiang out to the garden."

"Now? You've got to be kidding."

"I have to, Forrest. It's the first thing we learned at Seeing Eye. Take care of your dog first."

"Even today?"

"It's ritual," she said as she flung on a robe. "You didn't think Chiang was smart enough to do everything by herself, did you?"

"I don't know. I just feel kind of funny lazing in bed alone."

"I won't be gone long."

Breakfast was a communal affair, eaten in the dining room with other guests. Chiang led Jean into the room and Forrest followed, his hand resting lightly on her shoulder.

"Chiang's doing double duty," Forrest said.

"I think she knows it already. But that doesn't mean we're going to feed her twice as much."

"Did you wake up at all during the night?" Forrest asked once they were seated.

"Not for a minute."

"Then you didn't hear anything unusual?"

"Like what?"

"Well, like snoring."

"Forrest, you didn't tell me you—."

"Hold on. I mean I heard it. I didn't do it. When I moved over toward you, it stopped. That worried me a minute or two, but I fell asleep, and then I heard it again. That time I sat up and leaned over toward the end of the bed and it came again, from her. Thank the Lord for that, I thought."

"I didn't want to tell you."

"Can't she sleep somewhere else?"

"She isn't supposed to."

"Holy petunias, Jean, she won't even let me get close to you half the time."

"She'll learn."

"She may have to be taught. But I don't even want to touch her. She's like to devour me in one gulp."

"If Father can get used to her, you will too."

After a while Forrest asked, "Are you finished eating?"

"Yes."

"Let's go back to the rice patch." It wasn't his soft, childlike voice. Jean heard some muffled laughter from people in the dining room and her face flushed. Chiang led them back.

They didn't emerge again until afternoon when they took a slow walk around the farm. The sun slanted low, and Jean felt it warm her face weakly. "The hay smells so sweet and clean and earthy. I love it."

"It's alfalfa, probably, and maybe ragweed. It's tickling my nose something fierce."

"But Forrest, that's the smell that reminded me of you all last year."

They walked arm in arm with Chiang leading them. Forrest offered to do the evening milking for the farmer. Jean smiled when the man relinquished a cow with some hesitation. "By George, you got more milk than I ever get out of her," the farmer said, his voice an octave higher than before. With Forrest's hand on her shoulder afterward, Jean could feel him stand up straighter.

After dinner Jean played "Moonlight Sonata" on the upright piano in the living room. She heard doors open all down the hallway. People came back into the living room from their rooms to listen. When she finished, Forrest said, "You know, I think this is the first time I've relaxed since I've been on the east coast."

During the second night Forrest had an attack of asthma and had to sit upright in a chair until morning. When Jean came back from taking Chiang out, he said, "I'm in no shape to go down to breakfast. You'll have to go alone." Jean sat by herself at the same table for two with Chiang lying at her feet. She listened to other guests in the dining room and imagined them staring at her wondering why a bride on only the second morning was eating breakfast alone. She ate quickly and went back upstairs.

Forrest continued to wheeze the two remaining days at Bridgewater Farm. Jean tried to make light of it, but privately she thought it an inauspicious beginning to married life. He rallied, though, as soon as they were installed on the train south for New York.

They spent one night at the Roosevelt Hotel with Mother and Father in the adjoining room. Jean felt suddenly shy and embarrassed to tell her parents goodnight at the doorway. In just a few days, everything had changed. Father's arm had been replaced by Forrest's hand on her shoulder. Mother wouldn't be

there to put her buttered toast on the plate just so. Father and
what he could provide would be a childhood, a continent away.

When she climbed into bed that night, she felt her wedding
ring on her hand. So this is how it feels to be a married woman.
They were to succeed or fail, the two of them together. They
were to shape their lives jointly, either empty, sedentary, limited
lives, halting in their movement through the years, or confident,
adventurous lives, finding a way to experience what other
couples do naturally. She put these thoughts behind her the
moment Forrest reached for her.

In the morning Forrest checked his wallet. "I'm low on
cash," he said. "Got to cash this last check from the cows. Three
hundred. That's about six and a half cows." After breakfast he
asked Mr. Treadway to take him to a bank on the way to the
airport.

"Oh no, we don't need to do that, Forrest." Father's voice
had a distant quality in it, Jean thought, as though it didn't even
belong to the same man anymore. He was no longer law to her.
Even his voice carried the difference. It sounded less firm. He
had relinquished her.

"I need to cash a check," Forrest said.

She knew what Father was thinking—that he'd like to just
give Forrest the money and not take the check in return. Father
was like that—generous with people he thought worthy. She
could feel the decision working in him. He could give Forrest
the money easily. It would make little difference to his bank
account. But she knew it would make all the difference to
Forrest, the difference between trust that he could support her on
his own, and doubt, the difference between pity and love. She
held her breath and prayed Father would understand and
suppress what he'd like to do. Surely, he must know the
significance to Forrest.

"I can change it for you."

Bless you, Father. You knew.

Forrest let go of her hand to do the business. It had probably taken him nearly a year to save enough for six cows. She waited, wondering what his face showed. He was probably unaware of Father's agony of having to relinquish the role of provider. It took a long time, but then she heard him. "There's two hundreds, then four twenties and two tens, with the tens on top."

At the airport Jean hugged Father with more enthusiasm than usual. "Thanks, Father." He just cradled her without speaking, holding her to him longer than he'd ever done before. She turned her face sideways so she wouldn't get his tie wet.

Forrest and Jean stayed a few days at the Los Angeles Biltmore. Dody and other friends met them for dinner, for afternoon excursions, for evenings out. In between, there was the getting used to.

"Jeanie, I think I have to teach Chiang that she doesn't have to protect you from me."

"That's a pretty big task. She's trained to be wary."

"How should I do it?"

"It might be a good idea for you and Chiang to be alone together," Jean said.

"No, you've got it backwards. All I want is to be alone together with you, without Chiang."

"At The Seeing Eye when we first got our dogs, we had to be alone with them in our rooms for 24 hours."

"Too long."

"I could go shopping with Dody."

"And you'd forget about me here with this critter. No telling what she'd do. She hasn't been without you for years."

"I won't forget you. We'll only go for a couple of hours."

"Why stay away so long? It'd only take a couple of minutes for her to make a mince pie out of me."

That afternoon, the moment Jean left with Dody, Chiang leapt to her feet and bounded across the room for the closed door. Then she was still for half a minute, panting from the force of collision. She whined unhappily and repeated the attempt, determined to escape and find Jean. He imagined her eyeing the open transom above the door. He heard her jump. She couldn't possibly. Too high. Then she tried running up the door. Scratches, pants and thuds. Too vertical.

He stood still listening to the commotion race from one side of the room to another. He was at a loss. Even his bull was easier to handle than this varmint suffering pangs of withdrawal. At least with Victor he had a lasso and plenty of space. The manager was sure to hear this ruckus. The door was probably scratched already. What in tarnation do I do now? he wondered. Shut her in the bathroom, that's what.

He felt like a mouse trying to coax a cat into a cage. There was only one way to keep that animal from attacking the door. Pull up a chair right in front of it and sit there like a man. That would protect the door and keep the dog well below the transom and show that he was plucky and daring.

It was a bold stroke.

Chiang backed up to the opposite wall. Her whine took on a tone of desperation. Without warning, she charged for the door, the chair and Forrest, gathered momentum in flight, leaped on his lap and shoulders and made for the transom four feet above his head. The sudden impact thrust him backwards and the chair tipped over. This ain't exactly the marital bliss I've been imagining all year, he thought as he picked himself up.

"The leash," he muttered. "Get the leash and tie her up." He rummaged among Jean's things, found it, snapped it on Chiang's collar and lassoed an overstuffed chair opposite the door with the free end. He let out a deep breath and sat on the bed. Then he pulled his legs up just in case.

Chiang still wanted Jean. Her voice alone told him that. It had reached a whimpering falsetto, the epitome of canine grief. Then he heard her lunge into her collar and haul the chair towards the door. "A-ha! Now you did it. Bad judgment, eh?" The two chairs and the narrow passageway between the bed and the dresser boxed her in. She couldn't go forward or backward. Forrest guessed as much but was content not to explore. Instead he waited it out on the bed. The whines continued, but the commotion ceased. Forrest's breathing returned to normal just as Jean and Dody edged their way back into the congested room.

"Boy, am I glad to see you! I was beginning to wonder if you'd ever come back," he said.

"What happened?"

"The critter was heartbroken. She went crazy. Shamed me to my face."

"How?"

"I can't jump around and whine like that to prove how much I love you. When I proposed to you, I didn't bargain that I'd be a stepping stone for some varmint."

"Varmint! I do believe you're jealous."

"Well, I didn't think I'd have to fight a dog for you. A father, yes, months of separation, 3000 miles, our mothers reading our mail, yes, even poverty, all that I could take—but a bloody mongrel?"

A few nights later Forrest's cousin, Chester Henry Brown, and his wife arrived to take them to dinner and dancing at the Coconut Grove. Forrest followed Jean and Chiang out into the hotel hallway. "Forrest, what the hell are you doing?" Chester asked. "They're not going to allow a dog in the Coconut Grove."

"But this is a Seeing Eye dog," Jean explained.

"And he's a smelly nose dog, too."

"You haven't seen any guide dogs for the blind on the west coast?"

"Haven't smelled any either. Until tonight."

"Chiang goes everywhere with me," Jean said flatly.

"But what do you do with her B.M.'s?"

"Take her outside. Obviously." Forrest was surprised at the force in her voice. "Forward," she told Chiang. Forrest hurried to follow, hand on her shoulder. Why couldn't Chester be a little more delicate?

"I bet we look pretty swish," he whispered to Jean at the doorway to the restaurant. "What color is your dress?"

"Amethyst."

"Is that anything like ammonia?"

"It's violet."

"Sure feels silky."

"Maybe because it is, silly."

"Shall we tell them a party of five?" he said.

The maitre d' was taken off guard. "No dog, not even a Seeing Eye dog, has ever been admitted to the—"

Chester slipped him a twenty.

The maitre d' looked north as the five moved south to a table adjacent to the small dance floor. They sat down, four in chairs, the dog beneath the table.

"Pretty well trained animal," Chester said with chagrin.

Jean snapped her leash to the table leg. "Of course she is." Forrest straightened in his chair and grinned.

The music was the Freddy Martin Band. In between courses, Chester and his wife guided Forrest and Jean the few steps to the dance floor. With Jean in his arms, Forrest glided around in a small circle in rhythm with the crooning sax. "You're an angel and a pretty smooth dancer, too," he breathed in her ear.

Then he heard a loud scraping noise back at the table. "Oh, no. I don't think we're out here alone," he said. "Betcha our table's dancing too. Old lonesome Chiang's hot on your scent, Jeanie."

The table scraped across the dance floor and he felt Chiang come between his legs and Jean's. The head waiter swooped down on them in a flash, directing them to a more secluded table in a corner, a booth in fact.

Forrest put his hands on the edge of the table and tried to wiggle it. "Feels like the table's fastened to the floor," he said.

"And it has a three foot mahogany fence around it, too," Chester said.

The rest of the evening Forrest and Jean bungled their way through the crowd, bumping into other couples from time to time. "Bet Chiang thinks she can do better, but she doesn't have the chance," he said.

"Is that a little note of triumph I hear?"

He kissed her on the cheek and led her into a turn.

The next few days were less eventful. Forrest bashed his head on a storage door left open in the hotel hallway. After that he established the habit of walking down the hall with his hand out to the side along the wall, his other hand on Jean's shoulder. This worked well until one day, walking this way, he reached out to the side and felt something soft and round.

"Hop up," he said to Chiang and squeezed Jean's shoulder tightly.

"Ouch!" Jean said. "What's wrong?"

"Tell her to hurry."

"Hop up," Jean directed. They reached the haven of the elevator and scrambled inside. "What happened?"

"I had my hand out to the side and felt some woman's catook."

"No! How do you know for sure?"

"Unmistakable. I know one when I feel one. Must have been some chambermaid bent over with her nether end protruding."

At the end of the week, friends drove them back to Ramona. With luggage and packages and gifts, there was not an inch to spare. The only place for Chiang was the window ledge behind the back seat where, of course, she fell asleep, snoring right behind their ears.

When they arrived in Ramona at the vacated frame house, Forrest said, "Jeanie, I want to do things just right, like any normal groom would do, including carrying the bride over the threshold. But we're a different sort of couple—or triple. Should I carry Chiang, too?" he teased. "I feel like I married her when I married you."

"I don't think there are any rules."

"What do you think Emily Post would suggest?"

"This is the West. Emily Post doesn't live out here."

"But I've got to be careful. I know the order of things—Chiang won your affection before I ever had a chance. Maybe I should carry you together over the threshold. No. That would be too much."

"Physically or emotionally?"

"Maybe I could carry Chiang first, deposit her and then be free to do the act with more romantic stuff with you?"

His concern solidified into resolve. With a proud flourish, he gallantly whisked Jean off her feet, kissed her, and left Chiang whining on the doorstep. "For the first time I feel kinda equal. No matter where Chiang can lead you, she can't lift you."

Chapter Twenty

"When I'm finished, Jeanie, I'll come back to get you and we'll have breakfast at Mother's," Forrest said the first morning in Ramona. "I'll teach you the way. It's only a hundred yards past the barn." He gave her a vaguely placed kiss on her temple and held her head in his big hands a moment before he turned to go out the door.

The screen door squeaked and then closed. His whistle got fainter as he walked away. For some moments, she stood still, a sense of separation engulfing her. She thought she heard the barn door creak open. Turkeys squawked. She'd have to get used to that. Chiang's claws tapped on the bare floor of the empty house. It was the one sound familiar to her. There would be only one morning like this in all her life, she thought. Only one first morning as wife in a new house.

In the early quietness with the air still, she walked from room to room, her hands out to learn her way. The tiny frame structure was little more than a cabin. She measured the living room. Only eight steps across. An oil stove stood in the corner. She wondered if that was the only heat. A pair of rickety wicker chairs faced the wall, apparently the only furniture. Strange the way they were positioned. She felt the wall and found a window. That must be the reason. She wondered what the view was. She followed the wall until it led into the narrow hall to the second bedroom. She walked its perimeter, smaller than the other bedroom, then crossed it twice, her arms out widely. As far as she could tell, it was entirely empty. There were no lamps in the entire house. No matter. She breathed the stale air of the naked house closed up too long against the rural freshness on the outside. She looked for the window again, tried to open it, tugged, but it raised at a slant and then stuck.

At one end of the kitchen was a redwood picnic table with two benches. One of them wobbled. She felt the uneven surface of the table to see how large it was. A splinter of wood along one edge jabbed at her. Instinctively she sucked her finger. Tablecloths would be pretty important, but she'd have to wait six weeks before any of her things would arrive. There was no stove and no refrigerator. The used, three-burner stove Father had bought her in Connecticut and the old refrigerator from the basement at Hickory Hill were being shipped by freight train. It was war time. New goods were scarce. She was glad to have the ones from home. Her piano would arrive then, too. It would take up most of the remaining space in the living room.

She felt her way back into their bedroom and bumped her shin on the bed. She started to empty their suitcases into the dresser, but the drawers kept sticking and she had to wrestle with them. When she lifted the clothes, a few grains of rice fell to the wooden floor. It made her smile.

She yanked hard on the first drawer and something slid off the top into her arms—the one present that had been waiting for them at their new home. More thoughtful than all the silver and crystal and china from her New England friends was this practical gift from her new mother-in-law, a Braille cookbook. It was a humble present. She'd never read a cookbook before. She carried it to the wicker chair in the living room and settled herself to learn something of this enigma of making meals. She had memorized lists of German verbs, had remembered sonatas note by note. Now she turned her attention to memorizing the steps in making meatloaf. It didn't seem too hard, she thought, once she could buy some measuring cups and spoons, and once she could decide how to organize a kitchen so she'd know where things were. But how would she get the things? How would she shop? A grocery store was as foreign as an Arabian bazaar. She didn't want to be dependent on Mother Holly to take her. She slumped back into the chair. The wicker creaked. There must be a way.

For the first six weeks, they ate at Mother Holly's. Before breakfast, sometimes, Alice read a Bible lesson to Forrest. Jean didn't know what to do when this went on. After she learned the way, she walked by herself a little later each morning so she'd arrive after they finished. While they ate, Forrest and Mrs. Holly and Alice talked about people they'd known for years. The threesome was as tight as a new acorn. After meals Jean wanted to help clean up instead of acting like a guest. The first time she tried to dry the dishes, Alice said, "Oh, Jean, just let me."

"But a member of the family would naturally help."

"Oh, yes, but I know where everything is. Then we can get it done faster."

Jean was left standing in the middle of the kitchen not knowing where to put the plate in her hand. She felt like a newcomer they could do without. She knew she could do it, though. Washing dishes couldn't be that difficult. There was no mystery about it. It would be different in her own kitchen, but in the meantime, she felt in the way.

"Why don't we eat breakfast, at least, in our own house?" she said to Forrest one day.

"What would we eat?"

"Oh, dry stuff. Crackers and such. And I can make tea on the oil stove."

"It'd smell like oil, Jean."

"But it would be ours."

Eventually they did.

Until her kitchen wares arrived, there was little for her to do, so she often went with Forrest to check on the cattle and the young calves in the rented acreage of Ramona's back country. Usually Alice would drive, but when she was busy, Mrs. Holly would have to. Roads were rutted dirt and she tasted dust the whole way. The truck cab was an inferno of heat. The crook of her elbows, under her arms, her palms and the back of her knees were moist, so the dust stuck. Alice loved the adventure of careening around the back country, but Jean saw that it was a ruggedness Mrs. Holly could do without. She was a timid driver so she bumped over gullies, braked too late and hesitated around curves. Jean had to keep her hands braced firmly on the seat on both sides of her. When the truck jerked and Forrest felt his mother hesitate, he'd growl, "Just step on the gas and let her go!"

"Forrest, just because you don't see it, you think there's no danger. I do what I have to do." Sometimes that would send Forrest into a pout. She'd never seen this side of him before, and it gave her a hollow feeling in the pit of her stomach. What would prevent his impatience and gruffness from being directed at her?

The second week in October the Bischer Truck Line arrived with barrels and crates and her piano from home. It was a great day. Forrest hired two boys on leave from the war to help unload. Jean unwrapped each piece with affection, putting an Ingraham clock on the piano, folding satin slips in her dresser drawer, arranging crystal on an upper kitchen shelf, plates and cups and saucers on lower ones. The nesting instinct was strong, and she sang as she fused the things of her Hickory Hill past with the containing structure of her new life. She thought her things brought a grace to the bare cabin, though their elegance was probably out of place in this western cow town. Still, it made her feel like a bride.

The next day she asked Alice to take her to a grocery store in town. She was to be a real wife after this. After studying Mother Holly's cookbook, she Brailled a list of foodstuffs and, arm in arm, Alice and Jean walked the aisles of Willard Butters' Ramona Cash Grocery. It took forever to gather all the food. She tried to hurry but Alice didn't seem impatient. When they were through, Alice guided her to the counter. "Mr. Butters, this is my brother's new wife, Jean," Alice said.

"Well, hello, Mrs. Holly."

The words caught her by surprise. That was her, she told herself. "Hello."

"I heard Forrest went east to pick out a bride. Pretty big doings for Ramona folk."

After he totaled the bill, Jean fumbled in her handbag and held out some money. Nothing happened. She was used to the instant of hesitation in conversations with store clerks as they noticed her blindness. That was common. But this wait was longer. What was so astounding? Only that they both were?

His hand was gentle when he took her money. "If you'd like, ma'm, you can just phone in your order and I can have my boy deliver it to you each week, that is, if you'd like. It'd be an honor for us, ma'm."

"Why thank you, Mr. Butters." She turned her head in his direction and smiled. She wanted her face to show she was grateful.

In the afternoon she studied the cookbook again and that evening she cooked a meal for the first time in her life.

"What did you make?" Forrest asked as he sat down, his child voice full of admiration.

"Fish and mashed potatoes and spinach," she announced in triumph.

After a few moments of silent eating, she discovered all. The spinach was burnt, the fish was too dry and the mashed potatoes watery. "It isn't your fault," Forrest said softly. "You shouldn't take it on yourself." She managed to eat it, and heard his fork against his plate from time to time, but when she rose to take the dishes to the sink, she found his plate heavy with food. Her face flushed hot with anger and embarrassment. Even though he hadn't complained, leaving her brave efforts untouched was the same thing as being cranky about it. Probably just as well that he couldn't see her face.

"How much did the groceries cost?" he asked.

He had to ask, didn't he. "Forty-five dollars."

His silence rankled as much as his refusal to eat. She knew that was nearly the amount the state gave as his monthly support, but she couldn't help what things cost. "I had to get lots of staples to start us out. It won't be so much the next time."

"Still, we've got to eat by ourselves and be a normal married couple." He said it as if to himself and then was quiet while she made her way back and forth from the table to the sink. "I'm going to sell another calf. Food for food. Maybe I'll have to sell one every month for a while until—No." In that one word his voice fell as if a heavy idea had descended. "Sell Snort instead. Snort's for pleasure. The calves are for business." The counter was closer than she expected and she bumped into it, clattering a teacup into the sink. Her concentration had been broken.

She learned many things in the next weeks—that Forrest refused to eat what wasn't to his liking and that he told her so, that ovens burn arms and elbows, potatoes in potato bins should be counted because forgotten ones begin to smell, pans and spoons get lost because unseen, heads get smashed on open cupboards, relatives come uninvited and announce that ants have invaded kitchen counters, dinners get cold waiting for husbands still outdoors, and forty-five dollars' worth of food doesn't last forever. But she also learned that Forrest's velvety voice meant "come here, honey", that his whistling as he moved around outside gave her a warm reassurance of his presence, that snuggling in bed at night made the troubles of the day recede. *We're living on burnt hamburger and hope*, she typed in a letter to Icy.

And so this was life, the Ramona version of Hickory Hill's damask dining room of tinkling crystal and Ares and Ain'ts conversation. She could entertain here too, she thought one day not long after her initiation into cooking. It would be like fresh air to have someone other than Forrest's family. She invited Dody and her current naval officer boyfriend to dinner, and she called Willard Butters to order a flank steak. She wasn't quite sure what one was, but she remembered Mother telling Delia to order one once. She had no idea what it would cost, either, but this was to be her coming out, so to speak, and she wanted it to be special. After all, Dody had been instrumental in putting her where she was. Her fingers searched the cookbook to find what to do with this thing called a flank steak.

By midmorning the sucking dry October winds from the desert to the east had begun. Dust settled over everything so she closed the windows. She thought this must be a Santa Ana, like that Indian Earl Duran had said. What had he said? "Suck milk right out of a cow's tit." She chuckled to herself. The house became stifling so she had to open the windows again. She would dust right at the last moment before Dody came. Other cleaning could come first. She started with the bathroom, wiping up the floor and sink and toilet and bathtub, but how was she to know if they were really clean? It would be an embarrassment if they weren't. She could go ask Alice to look at it for her.

With Chiang leading, she stepped out of the house into the dry mountain heat. She squinted in the brightness and her eyes watered a little. Chiang sneezed from the dust. They passed the tom turkey pen right by the house. It was her responsibility to fetch Lance or Forrest immediately if she ever heard the toms fighting, but how was she to know what turkey fighting sounded like? They were always squawking. She didn't want to alarm the men and then be embarrassed by calling them for nothing. Forrest said that if a rattlesnake got into the pen, the toms got around it in a circle and mesmerized it by a low clucking until someone would get rid of it. Right now the sounds were just squawks and flapping wings, no clucking as far as she could tell, so she and Chiang walked on by. She wondered what Chiang would do if she saw a rattlesnake. No matter how thorough Lee had been at The Seeing Eye, she doubted that he'd trained Chiang for that. All she could do was walk and listen.

The route along the one lane dirt track to Mother Holly's was familiar to her by now. Nearly every day she thought of some reason to walk the pathway. It was the only time she got out, and Mother Holly and Alice were the only people she knew. She could tell by weeds brushing her legs if she aimed too far to the left or right. The heat baked right through the soles of her shoes. Fine grit blew against her face. She kept her eyes closed as she walked. Dust blew in under her eyelids anyway, and she still felt the glare. The wind caught a newspaper in a tumbleweed and it crackled across her path. "Alice?" she called when she thought she was close. Chiang led her to the door and Alice came out, cheerful as she always was. On the way back, they stopped at the barn to pick up empty milk bottles and money from the box where neighbors had left it after taking fresh milk that morning. Jean's job was to sterilize the bottles each day.

In the house Jean showed Alice the bathroom. "Is the bathtub clean?"

Alice hesitated. When she spoke, her voice was a threadlike vibrato. "No, Jean. There's a horrid ring."

"Oh, I thought I got it clean." She felt her shoulders slump.

"I'll do it, if you like."

"No, I've got to learn."

"Here, put your hand here." Alice stretched Jean's hand over the ring. "You can feel the dirt. It's not as smooth as the clean area."

She felt a gummy line. Mother had never told her how to clean. In fact, she doubted if Mother had ever cleaned a bathtub. She couldn't tell Alice that, though. There was much to learn, and Alice could help, but she shouldn't depend on her, or on Mother Holly or on anyone too much.

Jean had no time for her piano that day. She made a peanut butter sandwich for lunch and sank down on the picnic bench. A fine covering of dust skinned over her lemonade. By the time she bit into the second half of her sandwich, the peanut butter had glued together two boards of dry, stiff, tasteless bread.

In the late afternoon, Jean was cutting turnips in the kitchen when Mother Holly came in.

"Who who?" It was her usual greeting, like a mockingbird, lyrical and loving. "Jean, I just got some tomatoes from Heddy's garden. They're big luscious ones, ripe today. I thought you could use them tonight." She put them in Jean's wet hands. "Oh, Jean, Forrest doesn't like turnips."

"Yes he does."

"But he's never eaten them."

"He's going to eat these."

"You should just cook what he likes. He used to say to me to find something he liked and cook it for him every night."

"I'd eat whatever was put in front of me if that was what had been prepared. Even if it was scorched spinach."

"He likes things that go down easily, puddings and smooth things."

"Last night I made mashed potatoes for him. Again. He took two bites and said 'I won't eat this.'"

"You shouldn't take it to heart. He's always been a finicky eater."

"Because he was allowed to be. Before dinner he eats handfuls of peanuts and then he won't eat what I fix. I can't tell him not to eat peanuts. He's a grown man, not a boy. But he's going to eat these turnips or go hungry."

Mother Holly said nothing more. Jean felt her gaze. Maybe she's realizing I'm right, Jean thought. Maybe she's recognizing that her indulgence of him has made it harder for me.

"Things will get easier, dear."

"Thanks for the tomatoes."

Anticipating the meal with Dody brought back the feeling of closeness they had shared years ago. But how could she achieve even a semblance of Andrebrook style on a redwood picnic table in the kitchen? At least she could move it into the living room for the evening and serve the meal in courses. She began to drag it across the floor, then had to turn it on its side to get it through the doorway. As soon as Forrest came in the door she'd have to tell him she moved it.

Dody's presence when she arrived that night with her new man brought a touch of the old life back, but it also made Jean aware of the tremendous breach she had crossed in coming west. Dody seemed so much more polished than anyone out here. The salad course went smoothly except for Chiang snoring.

"When I first heard that snore on our honeymoon, I got worried," Forrest said. "Then I leaned down over the foot of the bed, and when I learned it was coming from there, I was relieved."

Here he goes again, Jean thought. She got up to get the next course from the oven.

"That varmint wouldn't let me get close to her for weeks with all that whining and howling and carrying on. She wanted to be in bed with Jeanie and have me sleep on the floor."

That might have been funny the first time he said it, but he was so pleased with himself for thinking it up, that he'd said it to everyone by now. She leaned down to get the steak out of the oven where it was warming. He had no right to tease me about Chiang who's been so good to me. She pursed her lips, stabbed the meat with a fork and plopped it on a serving plate. It landed off center and, unbalanced, it flipped off onto the floor. Jean gasped.

"In fact I want you to take a picture of us like that, Dody. Chiang and Jean in bed, me on the floor."

He's still talking. Good. They hadn't heard the meat flop. She bent down and reached out along the floor. Nothing. She had to find it. She had nothing else to serve. Good thing Chiang was asleep or she'd find it first. Her throat constricted and she put the serving plate on the floor, lifted her skirt above her knees, kneeled down and patted around on the floor with her hands. She felt a fine grit on the linoleum. The refrigerator hummed, rattled, and then stopped. Dear Lord, don't let anyone get curious and open the swinging door. Eventually she found the steak, but what shape was it in? Just how dirty was it? She couldn't be sure. The floor was covered with Santa Ana dust. The day had raced by and she had no time for floor cleaning. Gingerly, she tried exploring the hunk of meat with her fingers to detect any disaster, but it was too hot to touch. There was only one thing to do. She stabbed the meat again, flopped it back on the serving plate, stood up, rinsed her hands quickly and delivered it to the table.

If Dody noticed, she had the courtesy not to mention it. Now *that* was friendship.

Chapter Twenty-one

"She could really make it come on hot. War or no war, give me a Jap woman any day."

Jean raised her head. Earl Duran's words coming through the open window shocked her, incongruous in his colorless, off-key voice. Forrest laughed roughly, in a way she hadn't heard before, but when he came inside, his voice was velvet.

"Jeanie, where are you?"

"Here. You were gone a long time."

"That crazy old Indian still can't drive. He doesn't know first gear from reverse."

"I thought you said he was a teamster?"

"Did. But he drove a team and wagon."

"Then how does he manage a truck?"

"We do it together. I work the gears and pedals and he steers and talks to me." Forrest let out a smug little grunt. "There's more than one way—"

"Forrest, you never told me you did that!"

"Earned ten big ones today at the Bradley place. I can't have the governor think I married you just for your money. I've got to earn you new every day, Jeanie." Smelling of hay and sweat, he kissed her just below the left eye.

"Forrest, what were you and Earl talking about just now?"

"I guess my letters about a job worked."

When Forrest didn't want to talk about something, he didn't, and that was that.

"After we came back from putting up Bradley's hay, we stopped at the feed store. Whiting found out about a job loading grain at the depot. Work for three. Shoveling grain from a rail car into gunny sacks and sewing 'em up. Earl and I grabbed at it and the Bradley kid did, too."

"That's good, I suppose, but when are you going to do it?"

"At night. Seven to eleven or so."

He was a tornado of energy, rarely home, always hiring out to other ranchers for odd jobs, and now this. Meanwhile Jean contributed to the new Holly economy in the only way she knew, with scant dollars collected each month from giving music lessons.

The first Ramona Christmas was meager, differing from other days of the week only in the big breakfast gathering at Mother Holly's with Helen and Don, and Lance and Mary Kay there, too. Forrest had said he wanted to spend the day at home, just the two of them, like a normal married couple. Jean made a ham. A little dry, but adequate. She gave him a sweater she'd knit. He gave her Evening in Paris perfume. That was all. Then came the restless quiet of a long, uneventful afternoon. It was wild, cold, and blowy outside. The wind sliced through clapboard joints and curled under doorsills, but there was no snow. There was no tree, no big family dinner, no gathering of cheering voices, no piney fragrance or smell of molasses and cinnamon from the Indian pudding. She tried to remember some Christmas carols to play on the piano, but without voices to accompany them, the melody sounded thin.

She thought of how, as children, she and Lucy would race over to Tready's after the formal, slow-paced opening of presents, how itchy she would be to see what Tready got, and how Tready would always come back to Hickory Hill. She'd go through the presents one by one, taking things out of boxes and putting them carefully back in. But telling Forrest about it all would only underscore the sparseness here.

A long, newsy letter from her parents wished them a happy day and said they'd come to visit in February to see what they needed and have Christmas then. Mother Holly had read it to her the day before. She wished she could hear it again. Besides a letter from Icy a week earlier, only one other piece of mail had arrived.

Forrest paced around the house. "Do you want to open Dudley's present?" His voice sounded tentative, almost shy. He handed her a box still wrapped in heavy paper and twine, from Uncle Dudley in Connecticut. The two sat side by side on the picnic bench in the kitchen. She explored the package, feeling the bow and ripping the paper slowly, as if to prolong the experience.

"What is it?" Forrest asked. It was his child voice, all soft and wondrous.

"Stockings. Silk stockings." She counted. "Twelve pairs. Poor dear Uncle Dudley. He doesn't know. What am I ever going to do with twelve pairs of silk stockings out here? They run if you even look at them wrong." Her voice rose to a squeak. The inappropriateness of her only gift from home struck wide the chasm of difference, and she cried with a suddenness that unleashed weeks of tiny, unspoken aches. Opera and black velvet capes and dinners in the Village and taxis on Madison Avenue and the hush before the first chord at the Hartford Symphony and Farmington Country Club parties—where was all that now? That's the world silk stockings belonged to, not the world of turkeys and pastures and Indians and dirty stories.

She knew Forrest guessed what she was thinking when he enfolded her in his arms. For a long time he cradled her, letting her cry, not trying to stop it, just holding her, quiet and still. She drew in her breath in a series of little inward gasps. "But, Forrest, I want to be here. I chose this and I don't want what I had. I want you and us and life. Here."

But the great gulf in her life and the pain it created was no longer private, and she wept for the sorrow the revelation caused him. She thought it probably was a relief for him, too, when the Ingraham clock struck ten and they could go to bed.

The next day dawned cold and damp. The air felt wet, smelled wet, even tasted wet. "It feels like New England," Jean said.

"Weather for a jacket," Forrest said, "or a bear." He opened the door, ready to do the milking. "Must be foggy." He stood at the door for some moments letting cold air seep into the house. Jean shivered. Then he closed the door and turned back inside. Jean felt his arms go around her, drawing her to him carefully, slowly. "You're a treasure, Jeanie, maybe a little too delicate for out here, but you'll grow. We both will."

She pressed her face into his chest.

"Maybe that's what marriage will do," he said softly, "stiffen you into manhood and gentle me into a softer womanhood." He kissed her, lightly at first, but then firmly, opening her mouth, welding the two together, seeking some union, seeking the assurance that in spite of yesterday she was his. She knew she was, but maybe he didn't. "How about if I quit early today so we can take a walk?" He spoke his offering softly. "You can learn what's here around you. We can walk up the road and you can meet Karl and Heddy at the chicken ranch. They're nice folks and you could stand to have a few friends here. Or we can go over and sit at Indian Rock. Or anything you want to do." He kissed her again on her forehead and went out the door.

Jean waited longer than other days for him to come back from milking. The fog muffled the usual morning noises and left her utterly alone. It was a striking thing he'd said—stiffen her into manhood and gentle him into womanhood. At first she wasn't sure she'd heard him right. This was a different side to him, more introspective. It wasn't the funny, exaggerated western speech he liked to imitate, but something much deeper. He'd never shown it before, and it gave her hope. She shivered and put on a sweater.

She made the bed and got breakfast ready. Not a sound from him. She fed Chiang. Still no Forrest. What if something happened? He was accustomed to walk the property by himself—their two acres, the ten-acre pasture, the barn, Mother Holly's, Lance's turkey ranch—all without help, yet he'd always come back before this. She could call Lance or Mother Holly, but if he were just talking to someone, she'd feel silly for causing an alarm. Or if he just wanted to be alone, that would be worse. She'd wither from embarrassment. Nothing to do but wait. She sorted the laundry. She turned up the oil stove in the living room and pulled up the wicker chair to read, but her fingers halted over the same line again and again.

A distant, hollow whistling came through the fog. She jumped up. When the door opened, she smelled a foul odor like sewage or rotting meat.

"Forrest?"

"Boy, am I glad to see you, Jeanie baby."

"What happened?"

"Fell in a well." His voice had none of the velvety smoothness of earlier that morning.

"You what?"

"I fell into a pit I dug once." He sounded agitated that he had to repeat it.

"Are you okay?"

"Yeah. Just let me get out of these clothes. I smell like a cow's catook." She heard him yanking off his clothes right on the porch. "A couple of years ago Lance and I dug a well in the pasture about 300 yards from here, dug it 25 feet deep, but it never gave any water so we put barbed wire around it and used it for a trash dump. Threw in tin cans and tree branches and a dead calf once and turkeys whenever they died. I forgot it was there, I guess." His voice trembled, like a phonograph record going too slow.

"How could you fall in if you had barbed wire around it?

"I thought it was the wire at the other end of the pasture." His voice cracked. "Wasn't concentrating, I guess." She understood only too well. Disorientation. "It was partly broken down, and I thought the cattle had broken over it and had gotten into the next field. All I thought of was what a hard job it would be to find 'em now and drive 'em back. I guess I spit a few words at 'em when I climbed over the fence. Next thing I knew, I was in the bottom."

"Are you hurt?"

"No. Maybe scratched up some. It was a good thing we'd thrown a lot of junk in there. I don't think I fell more than 15 feet."

"How did you get out? Who helped you?"

"Nobody. If I yelled, nobody could hear me, so I began feeling my way around in there. There were a lot of branches over me I'd fallen through. I felt some things I wish I hadn't, too. When I cleared the branches above me, a lot of stuff fell down on me. I don't what to guess what. The top six or seven feet of the well is square, faced with boards. Where the square part joins the round part there's a little corner ledge." His voice cracked again, this time to a falsetto. "I don't know how, but I pulled myself up on that and then found the edges of those boards and dug my hands in to pull me the rest of the way."

Jean wanted to hug him but was afraid to. He smelled awful. "I'm glad you're okay." Unnecessary to say, but she said it anyway. She felt his panic. She relived it with him as he bathed, as they took a walk to Indian Rock and to the neighbors' chicken ranch. It made her feel ashamed for crying the day before. After all, he was struggling, too, working until eleven every night, getting up early every morning, facing a world no easier than hers. And still he whistled on his way back from the well. Perhaps there had been a tone of desperation in that whistle, but it was whistling nonetheless. Alice was right when she said he must do it to keep from crying.

Chapter Twenty-two

Father's presence shrank the house. Everything Forrest and Jean did, all they had accomplished, just living actually, seemed inconsequential and provincial when they showed it to him. Not that he said anything critical. And certainly Forrest didn't seem to feel that way. Maybe it was just her.

The first afternoon Forrest took them around the ranch, to the barn, to Mother Holly's, even up to visit Heddy and Karl. "Yeesus Christ, Forrest," Karl said in front of everybody. "You didn't tell me you was bringing the governor. We might have swept out the place first." Jean forced a little laugh.

On the way back she whispered to Forrest not to take them to Lance and Mary Kay's turkey ranch.

"Why not? That's part of the family."

"But it's—well, not very nice. You said so yourself."

He did anyway. "It's too cold. I'm not going," Jean said loudly. She turned what she thought was vaguely the direction of the house. "Forward," she told Chiang.

They got through dinner without any greater disaster than Mother telling her she took too much off when she peeled the potatoes. When was the last time Mother peeled potatoes? And of course Father missed his cocktail. At least he had his pipe. Still, she knew her wedding damask didn't hide the rough redwood picnic table underneath.

When Earl stopped by after dinner to talk about digging a well, Forrest invited him in and introduced him. "Oh, I remember you, ma'm. Evening to you." Even with the piano bench, Jean knew there weren't enough places to sit, so she began to drag one of the picnic benches from the kitchen into the living room. Earl saw what she was doing and hurried to help.

"Father, you sit in the wicker chair," Jean said. "Hardly like your green leather one, but it'll have to do."

"This is just fine, Jean," Mother said quickly.

"We're going to get you some furniture," Father said. "This trip. For Christmas. A nice sofa and maybe even a leather chair. And anything else you need."

"Nothing else can fit in," Jean said. She was tempted to give him a quick hug, but he wasn't the hugging sort. And she didn't want to fumble for him. She went back into the kitchen to finish the dishes. Mother followed. "I don't want you to do anything, Mother. Just visit." Jean tried to listen above the dishwashing sounds and Mother's news of Lucy and home to the conversation in the living room. She could tell Father was trying to be cordial, asking conventional, get-acquainted questions about home and family.

"Does your sister live in Ramona, too?" he asked.

"Nope. She's peddlin' her ass somewheres else, don't know where for sure."

Jean turned the water on fast. Maybe Mother didn't hear. Why doesn't Forrest change the subject? It was Father who did. "Are most of the homes in the valley served by well water?"

"Yup. That's the only way. No public water service. We have to find it ourselves."

"How do you know where to dig?"

"A witchin' stick," Earl said.

"No! That's so primitive. I can't believe that's still used."

"Works fine."

Jean shifted her weight at the sink and smiled. The visit would be broadening to Father, if nothing else.

"I'll show you how, tomorrow, if you'd like. Forrest and I are going to sight one at the Bradley place. Except you'd do better to wear some boots or other pants."

"He's got some," Forrest said.

"Boots?"

"No, I bought some Levi's today. First pair I've ever owned. Where'd we get them, Forrest?"

"Ransom Brothers Hardware. You don't have them on now?"

"No. I was afraid I wouldn't be able to bend enough to sit down at the dinner table."

"So Forrest showed you the town, eh?"

"More than that. He was a big spender today," Father said. Jean could hear Forrest laugh with chagrin as Father warmed to his story. "He thought he'd take us out to lunch. Where was it?"

"Warner's Hot Springs. But they were closed for the winter." Forrest chuckled again.

"So we went to—."

"Lake Henshaw."

"But they were closed, too, so we ended up eating at some fish house on a rickety old dock. A little smelly, but great cuisine, though. We had our choice of codfish sandwich or fried egg sandwich."

"I only spent $3.48 for all of us," Forrest announced with bravado.

She could imagine Father telling this at the Ares and Aint's. Well, it was probably good he felt he could tease Forrest. "Tomorrow night we're going somewhere else. I had a roommate at Yale, George Richardson, who owns an inn near a golf course west of here. Rancho Santa Fe Inn, I think it's called."

"Yup, I've heard of it," Earl said. "Pretty slick place, I'm told."

"Well, he'll give me a manhattan, even if Forrest won't."

"I don't hardly know what one is," Forrest said.

That night was the coldest one all winter. Why this week, of all weeks? It wasn't that Jean had never been cold in Bristol, but never in the house. She walked into the tiny second bedroom, practically filled by the borrowed bed. The heat from the oil stove in the living room didn't penetrate that far and she shivered. "You'd better wear your robe to bed," she warned Mother.

In the morning Forrest got up early to heat up the oil stove before he left to do the milking. It crackled as the metal expanded in the heat and made the house smell like oil or diesel. Jean got up early, too. She knew Father and Mother were used to having their own bathroom. Father would die when he realized he'd have to sit in a bathtub instead of take a shower. They weren't used to making their own bed, either. She would have to try to get in there to do that when he was in the bathroom. She could orchestrate the visit as smoothly as things allowed, but she couldn't cushion Father from the reality of her life here. The week ahead seemed long.

As soon as Mother got up, she came out to stand by the oil stove.

"Do you want another robe, Mother?"

"No, dear, I'm fine. But I think we'll spend the rest of the week at the inn."

It surprised her, relieved her, too, and she spoke up. "I think that would be very nice."

"We're perfectly comfortable here, but I think your father would like to see George."

Jean knew it wasn't true. That was her mother—always tactful, even loving in her diplomacy, but tact wasn't closeness, or even openness. Underlying her parents' decision to stay at the inn was an unwillingness to be temporarily uncomfortable for the sake of sharing and of closeness. Staying here would have shown a different kind of love than her mother's which was, perhaps, just sweetness.

It wasn't resentment Jean felt. She just grew aware of an abyss which separated her from Mother, a difference in temperament. She could not, would not, be an echo of her mother out here in Ramona. The separation had been noiseless, the sundering merely a relaxation of ties. Probably Mother hadn't even noticed.

Father came out and pulled the wicker chair up to the oil stove. "Kind of like camping out," he said.

Forrest stomped dirt from his boots at the doorstep and came in. A gust of cold air killed whatever heat the oil burner had struggled to create. "You missed the first milking, but you can help on the next. I'll show you my seeing eye bull. After breakfast, do you want to come with Earl and me? We've got to check on the cattle in the rented pasture before we go to Bradley's."

"No, Forrest, I think I'll just supervise the view from the porch."

When Earl came to pick up Forrest, Father cornered him when Forrest was washing up. "Do you think it's safe for Forrest to follow that bull out there?"

"I'd worry about the bull if I was you, Mr. Treadway. Forrest can sling one mean rope."

After Mother and Father left that afternoon, Jean discovered Father's stiff new Levi's, folded and laid carefully on the corner of the bed, with the price tag still on.

Chapter Twenty-three

It shouldn't have happened, she thought. Icy deserved better. She was always the one to help me live. She always wanted a fuller life for me.

Jean blinked back tears and brushed away a fly that landed on her nose. Her hand dropped to the pile of damp balls of rolled up pillowcases, shirts and slips. She counted. Only eight more to go. The tired, old ironing board creaked as she worked. At each pass of the iron, a wave of dryness rose as vacant and sterile, she thought, as this dry, forgotten town. A crow cawed. Its scolding hung in the air.

It was a horrid way to find out—turning on the radio to listen to Amos 'n Andy and hearing instead the news announcement: "A military transport en route for Frankfurt carrying 321 wives and children of American servicemen visiting their husbands on leave went down over Newfoundland. There were no survivors." The canned voice had echoed in her mind for days while part of her didn't believe it until Mother's telegram confirmed that Icy had been among the passengers.

Her throat felt stuffed with cotton wadding, dry and bursting for Icy's death—so wrong, so undeserved—and for their girlhood gone. Up to now, the war had threatened, exploded and died and had hardly touched her. Lucy had joined the Red Cross Club Service and was sent to India at the base of the Burma Road, but she was safe, and was helping those servicemen pouring down from the mountains now that the war was over. Tready lost her husband in the South Pacific, but Alice's husband came back safe, and Alice had left Ramona to join him at the Army base in Hattiesburg, Mississippi. The war had affected others much more directly than it had her. She had lived in relative domestic peace, hampered only by lack of household goods—a washing machine and, for a time, a telephone—and the war had played out its distant drama of numbers, names and places, all without direct personal loss.

Until Icy. For years she had confided in Icy her fears that her life wouldn't be full, and Icy had helped to fill it. Now it was Icy who had been cheated. What a dirty trick. She ached for Mrs. Eastman.

She put aside the iron and, with both hands, lifted the sheet and spread out a new section. She stretched her arms above and behind her shoulders and raised her hair to let in some coolness where a few wet strands were plastered to the nape of her neck. A cicada buzzed its tight, dry squeak. Icy. Icy. She reached for the iron without thinking. The hot triangle caught the knuckle of her little finger. Instinctively she put her hand to her mouth and sucked the burn. A tear crept down her cheek. She wiped it with the back of her hand, reached more gingerly for the iron and worked it back and forth across the sheet. A new tear made a wet, tickling path down her cheek and sizzled when it hit the iron. The sound startled her and made her smile a tight, quick smile. Icy's lesson, even now: show on your face what you're thinking. Another raced down the same trail and sizzled again. She imagined it bursting into tiny bouncing droplets like the ones she had seen as a little girl when Mary spit on the iron to see if it was hot. She worked more intensely, in order not to think, but one after another the drops fell and sizzled. Hearing them only unleashed more.

What would she do if Forrest came in? She'd already cried in front of him about Icy twice, and that was enough. He had little tolerance for tears. He'd want to know what was wrong now, and then she'd have to explain. It wasn't just Icy, anyway. It was a dozen chronic aches that her mind played over during the brooding afternoons at the ironing board when Chiang, the cicadas and the whirring arms of some windmill were her only company. She couldn't say she felt homesick, cramped up in this tiny cottage stuck out away from any real culture. That sounded snobby and would injure Forrest who was so contented here. Besides, she had chosen it. She couldn't say he wasn't good to her, even though he teased her too much. But telling him would be an admission that she was frail in character, a thing contemptible to him.

She heard him whistling outside. She sniffled quickly and wiped her face with the back of her hand. The door opened.

"Hey, Jeanie baby. Where are ya?"

She swallowed before she spoke. "Right here. Ironing."

"Here's the mail. Looks like another record from your folks."

Good. He hadn't detected, from her voice at least, but she was still afraid a leftover tear might fall to a sizzling exposure. She moved toward him, away from the iron.

"The fence in the south pasture's busted. Cows could be anywhere. Earl's here and we're going over in the truck. We have to find 'em and fix it before we load." She turned away from the door in case Earl was standing there looking in and would tell Forrest she'd been crying. "It'll be after midnight before we're done tonight." His voice sounded agitated. He walked toward her and handed her the mail. "Just thought I ought to warn you."

A new tear fell on her hand. Day and night were the same to him, she knew. She dipped her head so his kiss would land on her forehead or hair instead of her wet cheek. He turned, his boots struck the bare floor, the door closed, and the truck was off. Dust blew in the open window and she closed her eyes momentarily.

She always seemed to be waiting for him. Time alone inched forward. Self-reliant, that's what marriage was making her, she thought. Self-contained, so that whatever happened she'd go on. Whatever Ramona would say about Forrest's "high falutin' eastern bride," whatever Alice would do that cut her out of that cramped sisterly tightness she had with him, whatever Mother Holly would say about how she wasn't washing her son's precious wool socks right, whatever Forrest would say teasing her about Chiang and even about Jimmy—calling him an African because he'd lived in Morocco—whatever anyone would say, she'd stiffen up under it. Forrest had said that. Okay, maybe he was right, but it still hurt.

She blew out a puff of breath, lifting the hair on her forehead and thought back to the time she'd dreamt of marriage, marriage to anybody, before she met Forrest, when Tready tried teaching her how to iron and it was fun and new. She hadn't known then that marriage could hurt. Even after she met him she didn't think it would be like this. Maybe you don't ever really know a man until you live with him, until you wake up tired and brush your teeth with him and wait for him while the dinner gets cold and wait for him to love you at night—maybe you just don't ever know him before you marry him. And maybe that's good, because otherwise no one would ever marry.

She pushed the iron. At least she had books to read. The Braille Institute sent new ones each month. And there was always her piano and now the children who rode their bicycles out from town for weekly lessons. And Heddy and Karl at the chicken ranch were good company. She and Chiang knew the way and walked by themselves now. Heddy and Karl took a midafternoon break for tea and cookies around 3:00 every day. Visiting them broke up the long afternoons. She liked it when Karl told her stories of his nomadic life as a lumberjack, of how he had emigrated to work on the railroads in Canada, and of how he tried to learn English from the gang boss. Jean smiled when she remembered him saying, "Yeesus Christ, Yeanie, after a year I discovered it was Russian."

Once Heddy invited Jean and Forrest for a pork chop dinner. "Yeesus Christ, Forrest," Karl bellowed, "let me cut that up so I can eat my own meal in peace." When they came to visit Forrest and Jean, Karl said, "Yeesus Christ, Forrest, can't you turn on some lights in here or haven't you paid your bill?" She was surprised at his bluntness. In Bristol he would have been a factory worker and Heddy a serving woman, but in Ramona, things were different. Although she couldn't talk to them about music or books, they slipped into each other's lives naturally. Heddy was like Mary, the downstairs maid back home, genuine and earthy. She felt she'd known them for a long time.

Two months after Icy died, Jean and Chiang walked up the hill in time for afternoon cookies. "No tea for me today, Heddy. Do you have any milk?" Jean asked.

"Yeesus Christ," Karl said. "You have something you want to tell us?"

Jean giggled. "Maybe."

She felt him looking her up and down and it made her smile. He cleared his throat. "Does Forrest know?"

"Of course he does, Karl. And we're going to name him Forrest, Junior, if he's a boy."

Heddy rushed over to her and smothered her in a hug.

"Yeesus Christ, Yeanie. Have some more cookies." Karl put four more on her plate. "But how you going to manage? I know Forrest works hard, but, well, you can't feed a kid on music lessons."

In that, Karl touched the only apprehension Jean and Forrest had about the new baby. Right when he needed it most, his evening grain loading job dried up. After the war, Commodity

Credit Corporation resumed shipping grain in gunny sacks instead of open bins. Forrest wrote more letters. He asked relatives for ideas. Nothing was too humble. He knew he had abilities and talents. He just needed opportunity, yet opportunity always seemed so dependent on others, just what he didn't want to be. He hated the thought that he wasn't being given a chance by a skeptical world.

One night, with the baby only weeks away, he walked outside. He lifted his arms up over his head, grabbed hold of the lowest branch of the Chinese elm in the front yard, and took a deep breath. His senses were keen on listening. He heard crickets, the distant bark of a dog when a lone car went by on the highway, Jean running the water at the kitchen sink, but he heard no new ideas. Still, he felt in close touch with the ranch and the world. Somewhere, here in Ramona, must be the answer, he told himself. He wasn't the only man in the world ever in this situation of need. Others had been guided. He remembered Alice reading to him from the Old Testament the story of the poor widow asking Elisha for help to pay creditors. "What hast thou in the house?" the prophet asked her, turning her thought to what she already had. And she poured out oil into all the vessels she had and paid the debt. But what did Forrest already have to pay for the baby, and to continue to pay? Two arms, a strong back, endurance—and hope. That's gotta be enough, he said to himself, and prayed that it was true.

His brother Lance came by the next afternoon out of breath. "Forrest, you remember the McDonald boys on the other side of the valley?"

"Yeah, big red-headed guys."

"I just saw them, back from the war. They're making some kind of Indian bricks, adobe maybe. Digging the ground right up and putting it in wooden frames. Maybe you could do that. If we could find out how, what to mix with it to make it solid, I'd pay you to make some for me for a new turkey brooder."

What did Forrest have at his house? Dirt, plenty of clay dirt, and shovels. And an Indian buddy who could build the wooden forms. He knew he couldn't do it alone. He reached for his jacket and headed out to the highway. He stopped when his feet felt the pavement. "Hey, Ydeño," he called, and he heard the Indian come out of his house and cross the road.

In the next few days they learned the formula—dirt, sand and bitumen, an emulsified asphalt or tar suspended in oil. When it dried, it would solidify the dirt. With Forrest shoveling and combining the mixture and with Earl pouring into the wooden frames, they made 48 bricks the first day. The next day a few more. When they dried, Forrest leaned them on end and shaved off the rough edges with a trowel. It was filthy work. Wherever the bitumen fell on their clothes, it stuck and solidified. Their shoes hardened until they couldn't bend. By the end of the second week, they began taking off their pants in the brickyard at the end of the day and leaning them up against the barn until morning. Earl would turn the hose on Forrest before he went in the house. But it was work, using the land, using his strength, using what he had, and what he could do.

Chapter Twenty-four

Forrest Merton Holly, Junior, came early, on April Fool's Day, a squirming, scrawny jumble of arms and legs. In the hospital, as soon as they'd let her, Jean stroked every crevice, every curve of smooth flesh. Jean's mother came out for two weeks. "He doesn't look like any other baby I've seen," she said.

"What's that mean?" Jean asked.

"He looks like a little man already. The fuzz on his head is so light he looks like he has white hair."

"What else?"

"The fuzz is curly."

"And?"

"He's got a tiny little mouth, perfectly symmetrical, and translucent skin. He's looking up at you like a little dumpling."

Jean tried to hold onto the vision.

After Mother left, Jean used her family trust money to hire a practical nurse. She didn't know a thing about handling a baby. Miss Andrews was an English old maid who talked as if she had false teeth that didn't fit. Jean had mixed feelings about this woman who took over so completely. The first time Jean tried to diaper Forrie with Miss Andrews' brusque instructions coming over her shoulder, Forrie wiggled so much that she dropped the open pin. Her hand fumbled for it on the towel under him. Miss Andrews moved her aside. "I don't know how you're ever going to take care of this baby by yourself," she sputtered.

"That's just what I don't need to hear."

Miss Andrews was so capable, so utterly in charge, that Jean had to fight her way to Forrie whenever he needed changing so she could do it herself. With Miss Andrews' critical eyes on her, Jean's hands shook whenever she struggled to pin his diaper without jabbing him. One day she was heating milk for Forrie and got confused about where she'd put things. The saucepan in her hands touched something on the counter and she jerked. The warm milk splashed on Forrie. Above his cries Miss Andrews said, "I hope that teaches you that you shouldn't have another."

"Miss Andrews, you're dismissed!"

"You don't mean that, so don't say foolish things."

"I do indeed." She wiped off Forrie with a wet wash cloth.

"You're missing some spots. How are you going to keep him clean? Not just now, but always?"

"You mean when he poops? Why don't you say it? I'll, I'll fill up the sink and give him a seat bath."

"That's not the proper way."

"If it works, it's proper enough."

"But how are you going to know when he has a rash?"

"I'll feel it."

"My dear, sometimes you can't."

"Then he'll tell me. He's got a voice."

"Yes, just listen to him now."

"You telling me I can't is all the more reason I will. I'll give you your money and then please go."

The next day was trying. Jean didn't have a moment's rest. It seemed like she wrestled for fifteen minutes just to stuff his feet into his pajamas. When she finally got Forrie to sleep after dinner, she dropped into bed herself in absolute fatigue. The next morning she discovered she hadn't done the last night's dishes. It started the day off wrong.

Three days later she hired Lupe, a humble creature with a soft voice who seemed to love little Forrie. "*Callate, niñito, duermete, niñito,*" she crooned as she walked the baby to sleep. It calmed Jean, too. But she was either going to be a mother herself or she wasn't—ever. The second alternative was unthinkable. A month later, Lupe left for a better job and Jean ordered a washing machine. Washing diapers with a scrub board in the bathtub had gotten old fast. She just couldn't keep up with Forrie by washing diapers by hand. "We can afford it on time, can't we?"

"By the time it gets here, we'll probably have enough in cash," he said. "But by then, Forrie will be old enough to wash his own diapers." Forrest's adobes, selling now to builders in the valley, were bringing in a little more money each week. In fact, he and Earl fixed up living quarters in the barn for two Mexican laborers and hired Luis and Ezequiel.

"One hundred, Jeanie. One hundred bricks already today!" he shouted one afternoon and scraped dirt from his feet at the doorway. Jean was crying in the second bedroom. She heard him hurrying through the hall, and she tried to get control of herself. She always seemed to be trying his patience with tears.

"What's the matter?"

She only sobbed louder and crushed little Forrie to her.

"Is he okay?"

"Uh-huh."

"Jean, tell me." His voice was smooth as warm honey, all concern. She felt his big hands laid gently on her shoulders as he came up to her from behind.

She sniffled and drew in her breath in quick gasps. She had to tell him, now that he'd discovered her, but she knew it would only frustrate him, too. "I just want so badly to see him, just once."

Forrest turned her toward him and wrapped her and the baby in his arms.

Mealtime became a battle that often ended in disaster. Finding Forrie's mouth to feed him mashed fruit or vegetables was like chasing a goldfish in a pool with only your hand. Jean strapped him in a highchair, but that didn't prevent him from turning his head and backing away from the oncoming spoon. She tried holding his head with one hand, aiming the spoon with the other, her little finger stretched out searching for his mouth, but she could never be sure of what actually stayed in his mouth and went down his throat. She suspected that most of it went down his front, on his hands, on the highchair, and on her. She touched inside the little jar of baby food to find out how much was left and brushed her hand along his bib and on the highchair table to see how much had spilled. "This baby is fed by guess and by hope," she typed to Mother in a few stolen moments.

Each little victory over feeding the baby made Jean realize that it was not the first. Surely throughout history and throughout the world, mothers without sight lifted babies' spoons upward, hunting for the mouth, hoping the baby would help, impatient for the time the child could pick up a piece of food by himself. Perhaps, in some primitive culture, a sightless woman in a reed hut scooped a handful of mush, held it in her right hand while her left reached for the baby's head, the two hands coming together at the baby's chin. Or by the shore of the Galilean Sea a woman knelt, her head held straight ahead, her babe in the folds of her wrap, her hand guiding his head to her breast. Or near an Asian river, a woman with unseeing eyes chewed a piece of fish, felt for the child's mouth, took the fish from hers and put it in his.

There was no immutable law, she told herself, which decreed that no woman without sight shall be given a child—the task is far too difficult. No, there was no such law. She could march forward, her life a continuation of the triumph and heartache of all the sightless mothers before her, strong in the thought that some force had helped these women. They didn't give up, didn't stop having children, didn't say the world and life were too hard, too foreign, too frightening to have a child.

There must be ways to do things, and she had to learn them. When Forrie began to crawl, she asked Forrest to build a playpen in the shade of the Chinese elm. Putting him there gave her a little time to catch up. One day while she was washing dishes with Chiang at her feet, she heard the screen door open.

"Forrest?" she said.

"No, ma'm." Earl's out-of-tune voice contrasted to Forrie's gurgles. "Here's the baby." He put Forrie in her arms. "I found him in the bull pen. He must have climbed out. I just happened to look up from the brickyard and saw his round, white bottom crawling along in the dirt."

"In the bull pen? Is he all right?

"Yes'm, but it scared the hell out of the bull. He shot out of there in a hurry."

As the months passed, Jean felt Forrie's body grow sturdier. Measured against her extended arm, he was inches longer—and pounds heavier. When Forrie began to walk, Jean definitely needed some help. Lupe's cousin Celerina came to do housework, and some days after school a girl named Hilda Baker came for a couple of hours to tend to Forrie while Jean made dinner. But what did a fourteen-year-old girl know of babies? She did her best. The job was important. Hilda's mother was an Indian, her father a screaming red-headed Irish Bolshevik out of work. The family had no money. Hilda worked for dimes and quarters. And she learned. Hilda, Celerina, Mother Holly, neighbors, Forrest, everyone helped out at odd moments.

Forrest's help was often mixed with playfulness, but he had a short fuse whenever Forrie cried or fussed. In a mix of sportiveness and exasperation, Forrest would brandish a slipper, shake it at the crying Forrie and threaten him with something silly, trying to sound fierce. It had little effect on the baby and only made Jean laugh. But when the baby's sounds became serious, she also knew that Forrest explored with his hands all the possible problems with utmost gentleness.

Life became a game to see who would be one step ahead of whom. When Jean walked into the living room one morning, her foot kicked something out of place on the floor. She reached down to see what it was. The opened box of Vel laundry soap. She had bought it only the week before. Now it hardly weighed an ounce. She touched the floor, then the furniture. Soft, flaky powder everywhere. It was time to put bells on Forrie's shoes.

In bed at night in the minutes of conversation before exhaustion took over, Jean and Forrest shared the events of the day. One night Forrest told her, "I had a scare a coupla hours ago because of that crying kid."

"What happened?"

"I didn't know Hilda was here when you were in the kitchen, and when I went in the bathroom to shower, I heard Forrie bawling like he wanted Heddy and Karl up the road to know it. He kept crawling back and forth in the hallway right in front of the bathroom door. By the time I was stark naked, I couldn't stand it any more. I grabbed my slipper, flung the door open and shouted, 'D'ya see that slipper?' Only Hilda was carrying him, I guess because she squeaked at me, 'Yes, sir,' in a quavery voice."

Jean laughed. "You sure gave her an eyeful." Back home, Jean thought, that would have been horrors, but here, under the circumstances, it was a normal part of life.

Eventually, as Forrie grew more active, what they shared at night became more worrisome. "Forrie pets Chiang, and I don't know what to do about it," Jean said one night.

"That's natural."

"But it's not good for Chiang. She's less effective as a guide then. That's one of the first things we learned at The Seeing Eye. I think he teases her, too. I hear him run after her more and more lately, but today when I yanked his arm to stop him, I found that little Mexican chair in his hands. He's been rushing at her with that.

"And I noticed something else, too." Her voice lowered. "Chiang's claws tapping the floor when she walks don't sound rhythmic any more."

Chapter Twenty-five

Diapers flapped in Jean's face. She pushed the basket along the dirt with her foot and guided her own movement by touching the clothesline above her. She reached down to the damp pile, pulled out a shirt and hung it. A breeze gathered momentum, not the dry desert winds of a Santa Ana, but a humid, skittish wind. It made the windmill across Ash Street thrum and then rattle. At least the air's moving, she thought. She had an odd sensation that her face could slide right off her if she stayed out there long, so she hurried to get the laundry hung and go back into the cooler house. She bent and stretched, bent and felt the inner sides of the basket. Nothing more. She picked it up, hesitated and turned what she thought was 180 degrees, back toward the house. Accuracy about direction was more important now that Chiang was gone. Slowly she put one foot in front of the other. She still thought of Chiang nearly every time she walked outside and had to get her bearings by herself. But it wasn't just Chiang's help she missed. It was her constant presence near her as well, her companionship.

She sometimes thought she had traded Chiang for another child. Months earlier, when she wrote to The Seeing Eye that Chiang was petted, teased, and played with by a toddler and that another child was due, they advised her that perhaps Chiang's purpose had been served. A Seeing Eye dog could not be treated as a family pet. Yes, a guide dog should be loved and petted by his master, but not played with by a child. Furthermore, if Chiang's movements suggested lameness and a vet confirmed that, prolonging her life when a child's teasing could not always be detected and stopped was not a kindness. Even though she half expected their response, her hands traced the line of Braille over and over until she'd memorized it. Still, she had sat there. The washing machine stopped but she didn't get up. In the new quiet she recognized with a start the sound beneath it, Chiang's snoring. It had grown comforting, a part of her life. Not hearing it would leave a void.

Chiang's vet recommended the same awful solution. In the next several weeks Jean leaned down often to stroke Chiang's bristly coat, and stood so close she could feel Chiang breathing against her leg. One night when she put Forrie to bed, Chiang nuzzled against her as she stood by the crib. Her heart pounded. It was as though Chiang knew. She sunk to the floor and buried her face in Chiang's thick neck, her arms around the sturdy body. Chiang wiggled her hind end, and her coat above the stub of a tail wrinkled in a way that always told Jean Chiang was happy. "Thank you, Chiang," she said. "For being unselfish. I love you." She wondered if Vic and Ham and the others still had their dogs. She'd probably never know. She stayed on the floor with Chiang for several minutes, her tears wetting Chiang's coat.

When she stood up, she found that Forrest was right there beside her. "I know," he whispered.

She swallowed to try to stop her throat from throbbing. "When I go to the hospital, will you and Earl take her?" Of all the commands she'd ever given, all the thousands of times she'd said "hop up" or "forward" or "fetch," that was the hardest to give.

"Yes." Forrest drew her head close to his chest. "I guess you'll just have me to pet."

So now she had to be even more alert to know her position around the property. She headed slowly back to the house, her basket in front of her. Each step she planted firmly, squeezing her toes down in her shoes to feel through the soles for any clues about where she was. A big part of life was still learning how to move. But she had done fine back in Bristol when she was maid of honor in Lucy's wedding and had to walk down the aisle without Chiang. Publicly it may have been Lucy's moment, but privately it was Jean's personal triumph. Now every day she had to repeat it.

"Come in house, Señora." Celerina's voice directing her from the kitchen sounded alarmed. The wind whipped Jean's skirt and threw dust in her eyes. Needs of the day always prevented her from grieving. Just as well. Besides, there was Faith to attend to now, round baby Faith. "*La niñita roja*," Celerina called her because of her wispy reddish curls. Jean set down the empty basket in the hall and made her way toward the new baby sounds, little growls actually, cross and aggressive. She picked up Faith to try to quiet her. Faith felt sturdier than Forrie had and her face was rounder. She fussed almost all the time, it seemed.

"Where's Forrie?" Jean asked.

"Here. He eats." The wind threw grit against the window. "Oh, no, Señora. It comes." Outside a wild funnel of leaves and dirt and twigs twisted and whooshed through the yard, spraying the flapping laundry.

"What happened? Is it a dust devil?"

"Oh, Señora, I sorry. It come to the clothes."

The sound retreated. Jean sighed, put Faith down, picked up the empty basket and went outside again. She squinted into the glare, the heat making her dizzy. She felt for the laundry. Grit clung to the damp diapers. "Dammit," she muttered. They'd have to be done again. She groaned and began taking them down again. At least she had a washing machine now.

A washing machine, yes, and a house of her own, and soon a larger adobe one, thanks to Father's generosity and Forrest's

willingness to accept. In fact, Forrest's enthusiasm about
building a house turned out to be stronger than his pride. And
there were other things too, a perfect son who could walk and
talk and finally feed himself—whoopee! A healthy baby girl
with firm arms and legs, and a husband who had a business of
his own—she often rehearsed these steps in the progress of their
lives. Gratitude, Forrest sometimes said, equips us to receive
more. Gratitude for everything was sometimes hard to squeeze
out.

Perhaps for Forrest it worked; his adobe business was
prospering. He made nearly two hundred bricks a day, and more
orders came in all the time. One man ordered four truckloads a
day for three months. Forrest told her, "We'll make more on the
hauling than on brick making." And now five people worked for
him, including his old friend Ed Nelson, their nearest neighbor
who had just moved back to town.

Jean smiled in remembrance as she brought the soiled
laundry back inside. When she was in the hospital with Faith,
Forrest had come every evening. "We made a hundred and
twenty-four bricks today," he had reported. "A hundred-thirty-
six," he had said the next day. When he and Mother Holly
brought her home with Faith, he had planned a celebration. All
day, in anticipation of her coming, his workers wore ties. No
shirts, but ties. With their dark-skinned bodies caked with a
plaster of dusty sweat and bitumen, they worked with ties
hanging in their way. Ed's wife, Franny, described them, and
Jean smelled their tar grime. It was hard work, but Jean knew
Forrest was proud of his little brick empire, for it was real, and
his, and it was growing.

Every week Ed drove Forrest in the truck west over the
rugged grade, through Escondido to the coast and then north
toward Los Angeles for their supply of bitumen. Each trip
Forrest loaded empty barrels into the truck, and at the depot he
held the spout for the liquid asphalt to be poured into them.

Late that afternoon, just as Jean was hanging the laundry again, she heard the truck grind up the dirt road. Forrest headed right for the house instead of the brickyard.

"Jean, help me get this stuff out of my hair."

She followed him inside to the kitchen sink. "What stuff?"

"Bitumen. Hurry. Wash it out with this." He lifted a can to the sink ledge.

"What is it?"

"Gasoline." She gasped. "Just do it."

She dug her hands into the gooey, wadded-up mess of his hair that had been hardening for the hour trip home, and felt the gasoline begin to dissolve the tar. She felt him wince more than once, but all he said was, "Can't you get it out any faster?" She tried not to breathe deeply, but her eyes still watered and she felt nauseous. It must be worse for him, she thought, stinging him terribly, but saying anything more would be admitting defeat or forsaking his credo of gratitude.

"How did it happen?"

"I just bent down over a barrel at the wrong time and got rained on is all."

She struggled with the matted hair. "I can't get it all out."

"Then cut it. Get the scissors and cut it off." He sounded impatient.

She did as he asked. "I hope I don't make you look lopsided."

"Just hurry. I got to get back to work." She was hardly through when he left abruptly to help unload the truck. After dinner he loaded it up again with an order of adobes to deliver with Ed that night. Jean was with him for only twenty minutes at dinner, a wilted, warmed-over dinner.

After Jean got Forrie and Faith to bed, she heard someone come down the dirt path. Franny Nelson. She often came when the two men had a long night delivery.

"You still doing dishes, Jean?"

"Yes. Celerina left again. She just took off without saying anything. I thought she was in the kitchen, but when I said something to her, she didn't answer and Forrie said he saw some man outside with a bag and a blanket in his hand. I guess it was Ezequiel."

"Maybe they're wetbacks. They hear about border authorities coming over the mountains, so they hide somewhere."

"Mother would absolutely die if she knew. They come back a week or so later, but in the meantime, all the socks get mixed up and the ants attack the kitchen."

The evening dragged on longer than usual. Jean dumped a mountain of laundry on the double bed to sort it while she had some help. Franny matched the socks and wrapped them so they'd stay together. Then they lay down on the bed with the windows open and talked of their own families back home and marriage and getting by.

"What time is it?" Jean asked.

"Quarter after eleven and it's hardly cooled off at all."

"They're late."

They shifted positions, they jumped at a noise outside, they sighed, they repeated news of the day, the bitumen in his hair, the dust devil, but neither of them spoke their worry. "I'm glad you're here," Jean said. "It's nice to have somebody besides family. Mother Holly is good to me, but it's different to have someone who doesn't have to be a friend, but is."

"I know."

"Have you met any other women in this town, someone that maybe we could play bridge with, or talk about something other than diapers and family? I have Braille cards, and they could call out their plays."

"You need something more out here, don't you?"

"Don't *you*?

Franny grunted agreement. "Will you play something on the piano?"

"What do you want to hear?"

"Play 'Night and Day'."

Jean went through all the popular music she could remember and was starting on "Moonlight Sonata" when they heard the old truck clatter to a stop.

"Any ladies here?" Forrest asked when he came in.

"Yes. Two. Why are you so late?"

"Just be glad we're here at all."

"Why?"

"Big ole buddy here, he didn't know how long the hill was. Wore out the brakes on Banner Grade, so when we headed down Cigarette Hill afterwards, we didn't have any."

"The pedal fell clean to the floor," Ed said. "So Forrest tells me it's all right, not to worry. 'Just kick it out of gear and coast. The road's a straight arrow for two miles,' he says. But he didn't see those trees up ahead."

"So, big buddy, he starts weaving back and forth to try to slow down. He takes it up the left side, up a bank, swoops down and then up the right side. Bounced me from here to kingdom come."

"I had to. There was a bunch of cattle up ahead. I wish you could have seen that last steer take a flying leap over the bank. Yee-up."

"Jumped over the moon, did he?" Forrest laughed, too.

"But why did that make you late?" Franny asked.

"The bricks," Ed said, his voice fallen. "They slid off the truck bed and spread all over the road behind us."

"We only found 30 good ones out of the 280," Forrest reported.

"Do you know how hard it is to find bricks spread out over a half mile in the middle of the desert? In the dark?"

In the days that followed, Jean thought more about starting a bridge group. Of course, it would not have the ordered calm of Mother's bridge groups in the living room at Hickory Hill, but it would be what she could offer, a card table in the cramped living room with brick workers talking in Spanish outside, hired men working on the new house Forrest was building for them only twenty feet away, and a whiff of bitumen whenever the breeze chose to contribute it. Her need for companionship beyond family had become stronger than embarrassment. Besides, this was Ramona, not Bristol. Franny suggested some women, and Jean invited them the next week.

If she timed it right, Faith would take a long afternoon nap and Forrie, well, she could tie him to a tree. She'd done it before when alone and hard pressed, a long rope knotted intricately to his belt loop. He was too old for the playpen. The Chinese elm was the solution. That would give her enough retreat from mothering for a few hours to do something other women did. She had lovely china and could make an almond cake. Cooking was not so threatening to her now that she'd learned to identify spices and flavorings by smell and had become accustomed to cooking by taste rather than by measuring.

Interruptions piled up that morning so she had to hurry to get the cake done on time. When she poured the almond extract into the batter, she couldn't seem to get enough flavoring from it so she kept adding more. Finally she gave up and shoved it into the oven.

Franny arrived a few minutes early. "What in the world did you get into, Jean?" she squealed. "You've got green stuff all over your face." Jean scowled in puzzlement. Gradually the truth dawned.

"Oh, Franny, I think I made a mistake." She uncovered the cake. "Is it—?"

"Green! A greener cake I've never seen. Kelly green."

"No wonder I didn't smell the almond." Jean laughed until her eyes were wet. "Well, too bad it isn't St. Patrick's Day."

Before the other women arrived, she found Forrie and tied him by his belt loop with a long horse rope to the Chinese elm and put his toys around him. He could swing on the swings or play with his trucks. He seemed contented enough. He didn't cry, maybe didn't even notice.

Midway through the afternoon, with much of the green cake still uneaten on Jean's wedding china, one woman said, "Would you look at that?"

"At what?" Jean heard the women laugh—not the easy sound of delight, but forced and phoney, as if indulgence could hide judgment.

"It's Forrie." Franny's voice was protective. She opened the screen door, gathered him up and gave him to Jean. He was naked from the waist down. The little devil, getting off the leash like that. Jean hustled him off to the bedroom. Dressing him there, she smelled something on his shirt. The same smell as washing out Forrest's hair. Gasoline. She breathed in and then choked. She could smell it on his hands and face, too.

"Did you drink anything?"

"No."

She hoped it wasn't fear that made him say that. "Where have you been?"

Forrie only made whining sounds. Was it from the pump by the barn or from the can she'd used to clean Forrest's head? She didn't even know where it was any more.

"Do you feel all right?"

"Uh-huh."

In the bathroom she made him drink three glasses of water, yanked off his shirt and washed him until she could no longer smell the gasoline.

She wouldn't dare tell the others, except for Franny, later. Though not expressed in words, the criticism in their laughter sounded real. Let them try to do what I'm doing the way I have to do it, she said to herself and jabbed Forrie's left leg into a clean pair of pants. I do what I have to do.

When she finally got Forrie and Faith to sleep that night, she came back into the living room and dropped down on the sofa, jostling Forrest at the other end. Her movements showed that the day had almost been too much for her. He reached over and drew her to him, resting her head on his chest. He hummed a simple melody as he stroked her temple.

"Do you think he'll get sick if he drank any?" she asked.

"No. Even if he tried it, it would taste so awful he'd spit it out."

"I thought he'd be okay out there," she said, her voice small against his chest. "He's usually pretty content by himself. He had his toys and he could swing."

"He probably just saw something out of reach he wanted to play with. He's no dummy." Forrest chuckled. "When he wants to do something, he does it. About halfway up to the window at the bank yesterday with Ed he tugged at me and said, 'Pop, I need to go.' I told him to hold it, but he was serious. Pretty soon Ed whispered that Forrie dropped a little brown one about two inches right on the floor next to the railing." Jean gasped. "When Ed asked what he should do, I told him he should kick it under the railing."

"Oh no!"

"What else were we going to do? When we got outside, he told me it rolled right under the manager's desk." Forrest howled. "Isn't that a garter-snapper? Just picture the old man's face when he found it."

Jean laughed in spite of being weary and in spite of being exasperated with Forrie. She shouldn't laugh at a thing like that—Mother or Miss Weaver would be shocked to hear her—but she was a world away from anything they knew.

"I want to do something," Forrest said. He stood up abruptly and took her hands, pulling her up off the couch. "You got any shoes on?"

"Yes."

"I got something to show you." He hummed the same little tune as he took her outside into the cricket night, holding her hand.

She took a deep breath. "Even the air feels tired."

"Lazy, sort of. Cool, too."

They walked out to where the new house was being built. "Look at this, Jean. The walls are almost four feet high now." They felt along the walls and walked inside, their hands out guiding them through the new rooms, measuring them with footsteps, imagining where windows would be, what views they would look out on.

"It's big. And it feels so solid."

"See here, this is the beginning of the fireplace." Their hands brushed the adobes protruding into the room. "And out here'll be a screened porch and we can have roses outside and smell 'em sitting right here."

It felt odd to be inside a house, touching solid walls about waist level and still feel the slight movement of the night air and hear crickets and the gentle rush of leaf against leaf in the Chinese elm.

"Let's stay out here for a while. The air's so silky. It's too hot in the house." They listened for baby sounds but heard none.

"Follow me." Forrest took her hand again and walked toward the breeze. Out there in the leafy night he found the swings under the Chinese elm. He turned her around. "Sit down." It was his velvet voice. She hadn't heard it for a while. Its smoothness carried reassurance.

"Hold on." He pulled her back. "Ready? You holding on?"

"Yes."

The chains creaked when he let go. She swung forward and back again, and she felt him push again gently.

She giggled. "I feel like a little girl."

Forrest started humming again, the sound becoming louder and softer as she swung. His voice across the night was a caress, melting away the trials of the day.

She began pumping herself higher, a little bit at a time. Forrest moved to the other swing and began, too. She could feel the movement of his swing affecting her own.

They swung for a long time, Forrest adjusting until his swing was in rhythm with hers. The cool air moving through her hair felt free.

"Oh, my stomach." She groaned and then laughed.

"Gives you the collywobbles? Then one more and we'll stop together." At the next peak they both relaxed and let the movement carry them slowly to stillness.

"Can you smell the mint?" she asked.

"Yeah. We must have stepped on it. There's a lot of it here under the elm."

"It smells like it painted the air." That sounds like Icy, she thought. The ache stabbed again. "What's that song you were humming?" she asked. "I've never heard it before."

"It's about a swing." He put words to the melody.

"Swing-ing, swing-ing,

We look all around

And hear the sweet sound

Of swing-ing, swing-ing." Forrest's child voice singing had a new softness, it seemed to her, an innocent wonder at what the world had to offer.

"All around us there below

Birdies sing and flowers grow,

Ponies prance and breezes blow.

Life is joyous, this we know;

Love's around us where we go.

There's nothing quite so gladdening

As summer in a swing."

"Oh, that's precious. Teach it to the children." She turned her face toward him with a new admiration, this man who could do heavy work outside, who made bricks, raised cattle, but who, in the privacy of the night, could sing a child's song and make it eloquent. "Where did you learn it?"

"In third grade. But I sang it at a talent show in high school. After about three or four lines people started to laugh, but I finished it anyway." He chuckled. "Then I sang it again."

That's Forrest, even then unwilling to succumb. She felt enfolded in peace.

"Forrest?"

"Hmm?"

"I love you."

She felt him pull on her swing chain until they were close together. He found her face with his other hand and kissed her, a fine big kiss sufficient in itself. They sat, their swings drawn together, each one waiting for the other to move first.

"Do you think there's a moon tonight?" She wanted there to be one.

"Yup."

"How can you tell for sure?"

"I can feel it."

She thought of the moon smiling down at them through the vast, empty air, amused by two children playing in the darkness.

"Me, too."

Chapter Twenty-six

The next morning Jean sat at the picnic table in the kitchen with a cup of tea and toast. Faith made baby sounds from the playpen and Forrie moved around near her, doing just what, she wasn't quite sure. She sang dreamily, "Life is joyous, this we know. Love's around us where we go. There's nothing quite so gladdening as summer in a swing." She took a sip of tea but drew the cup away. Something tickled her mouth and gave her a queer, repulsive feeling. She dipped her spoon in, brought it up and gingerly touched the bowl of the spoon. Something was in it. Two flies. Ugh. Disgusting. She dipped in again and brought out some more. She threw down the spoon and pushed back from the table. Her throat tightened and she swallowed and grimaced, squinting her eyes.

A muffled little-boy sound came from behind her, a mixture of glee and fear accompanied by an intake of breath. The realization struck. She knew there probably were dead flies on all the windowsills. With horses and turkeys nearby, flies were always in the air. But Forrie using them as a way to tease her—that was too much, too cruel. She winced at the imaginary hyena laughter of the gods. In one flash, the source of her happiness in motherhood had become a vehicle for the world's taunt, reminding her of her limits, snatching back the settled happiness of the night before. It seemed an unexpected swipe taken at her by the universe and it flattened her.

She knew she should discipline him. "Forrie," she said, but she didn't trust her voice. It wavered and lacked authority. The old problem. "That's an awful thing to do." Forrie slunk away out of her hearing. The cup rattled in the saucer when she stood up to pour the tea down the sink. The morning was soured irrevocably.

A week passed before she could tell Forrest about the episode. After dinner and children's bedtime, she took his hand. "Got your shoes on?" She took him outside to the Chinese elm and they sat in the swings again. With a steady voice she explained what Forrie had done. His silence told her he knew the significance—deceit and exploitation by their children, as well as by the world. The swings hung motionless. The off-key sound of crickets filled in the empty time. Jean knew he would chafe at the incident, but she hadn't expected it to silence him.

The swing chain creaked as Forrest shifted his weight. "Tell me something good about Forrie." His voice was a monotone, flat and tired.

She trailed her feet in the earth and walked her swing seat back and forth slightly. She knew what he wanted, to turn around her thinking. And she wanted it, too. She thought a moment. "Yesterday when I went over to Heddy and Karl's, Forrie was leading me, and I guess he looked up at the sky or clouds and he said, 'There's Mr. and Mrs. Wind.'"

"Yeah?" His swing moved some. "Mr. and Mrs. Wind," he repeated.

"And on the way to Franny's once, I think he led me around a puddle in the path."

"He's done that for me, too, with a rut or something."

"When do you think he learned we couldn't see?"

"Early. Real early. As soon as he could walk. When I used to roll a ball across the floor to him, he'd bring it back and put it in my hand, but Ed said that when he did it with him, Forrie just rolled the ball back. He knew the difference."

They thought of as many positive things about Forrie as they could to reduce the injury of the flies. The coolness bathed

Jean's face and neck. She felt refreshed by the slight dampness in the night air. Or maybe it was because she had told Forrest and, once the mistreatment was shared, it had diminished. She reached for his swing chain, found his arm and followed it where it rested on his thigh. He put his hand on top of hers.

Eventually, Forrest stood up. "I want to show you how far they've gotten on the house. They put the rafters up today, and I want you to see the dandy way they're put together."

"I'm not tall enough," she said as they made their way over to the adobe.

"You can climb up there. I found a way. I did it this afternoon. It's real easy."

"Easy! Easy to fall through!"

"No, you won't. I'll hold you."

"I stopped climbing on roofs when I was twelve."

"Just put your feet where I tell you."

So here it was again, Forrest getting her to ride western, to walk out into the open pasture, to do things, sometimes absurd things, that she would never attempt on her own. It made her think of Miss Weaver's, "Of course you can, Jean." Not too willingly, she climbed up a ladder and put her knees and feet just where he told her, tightly grasping the beams where he put her hands. She reached for the next rafter, stretched, and felt only space. She screamed.

"You okay?"

Her stomach contracted and she regained balance in an instant. "I guess so, but my stomach flipped."

"Your stomach flipped because you looked down. Don't look down."

"I didn't look down, but my stomach flipped anyway. I'm out of my mind to be up here on an unfinished roof." She barely breathed as Forrest explained how the joints in the rafters were designed. Feet on the ground moments later, she took a deep, relaxed breath. "This is one I'll never tell Mother."

Two months later, Father sent her a plane ticket for a trip back to Bristol. She told them only of the lovely new house that was taking shape with money Father had sent. She told them of the rough texture of adobe walls and the spaciousness of the rooms, of the brick hearth and the Mexican tile flooring. She thanked Father for his help. And she told them she was pregnant again.

When Jean was in the hospital for the third child, Forrest and his crew worked late into each night to finish the new house and move everything in. William Treadway Holly, skinnier than Forrie had been, and quieter than Faith, came home to the new adobe. "He's purple," Forrie said the first thing. At three years and four months, Forrie had just learned his colors from Franny. Faith was 17 months and feeding herself—halleluiah—but still too young to help. The feeding battles began again. With Billy so scrawny, Jean knew she had to be victorious. He didn't fuss or cry or even spit. He just turned his head away. She couldn't find him, but imagined his skinny purple arms and legs backing away, his wrinkled face retreating from the loaded spoon.

Days were triply tiring with three to keep track of. Faith was at the bells-on-shoes stage and Forrie's radius of operation was widening day by day. Jean had to get used to not quite knowing where each one was every moment, even with Celerina's help.

One day Celerina's husband, Ezequiel, approached Jean at the clothesline. "Señora, Celerina work only eight hours a day." She didn't know if that was a request or a statement of fact about some new regime. It turned out to be a statement of fact. Celerina began to come and leave according to her own clock, whose hours, Jean thought, must be shorter than the rest of the world's. Jean adjusted, fuming at first when Celerina left in the middle of feeding. But she didn't want to lose Celerina altogether. Her crooning to the baby soothed everyone. "*Callate niño, duermete niño,*" she'd half sing, half say, when it was time for afternoon naps. "*Que tengo que hacer—lavar los panales y ponerme a coser.*" By the time Celerina finished, Billy would be asleep, Faith would be calmed, and Jean could breathe normally for a few moments before she'd have to find Forrie.

It seemed like she was always looking for him. Once she couldn't find him for a couple of hours. She walked through each room of the new house, called him, stood still to listen for any movement, heard none and went on. Was this a game, his new way to taunt her? The thought stirred ugly memories of the fly episode. She walked outside onto the patio. "Forrie?" No answer. She went to the garage across the gravel breezeway and called louder. No response. She didn't know whether to be angry or alarmed. Neither felt very good. She called Mother Holly. He wasn't there. She called Lance and Mary Kay. They hadn't seen him. She called Franny Nelson. Not there either, but neither was Franny's daughter, Judy.

Franny came over and looked, too. "Well, you haven't missed him in any of the usual places," Franny said. Then she checked the barn and corral, the brickyard, the pepper trees along the dirt road, the swings under the Chinese elm. She went into the old wooden house, empty and waiting to be moved off the property. The two children, barefoot, wearing sunglasses and talking gaily, sat on blankets and held open umbrellas.

"What are you doing in here?"

"Playing beach," Forrie said, and giggled. Franny corralled them back into the house.

"From now on, Forrest Holly, you're going to tell me where you're going when you leave this house," Jean announced.

"Do you actually think he will?" Franny asked when they went into the kitchen.

"No. But maybe he will sometimes." She tried not to think of the potential disasters that lay in wait for unaccompanied little boys on a ranch—a fall from a tree or barn loft, an angry horse, even a rattlesnake. "I can't keep him within reach or even within hearing range. You can't do that to a little kid. I have to trust."

"Last week when you couldn't find him when Marge Baker brought her girl to piano lesson, she must have been shocked," Franny said.

"Why? How do you know?"

"She talked about it and it got back to me." Franny's voice was apologetic.

A fly buzzed close to Jean's face, hovering near her temple. She scowled and waved it off fiercely. "They just have to find something to occupy their minds in this forsaken town."

Meanwhile she had dishes to do. She always had dishes to do. Willard Butters' boy made more frequent deliveries. Trailings of jam left by Forrie on the sink drew ants, marching with undisturbed freedom through breakfast, sometimes through lunch, until spotted by Celerina—if she was there. If not, Mother Holly found them. Faith cried out for attention. As if aware of the chaos he was born into, Billy retreated into the shadows. In cluttered mornings his quietness made him disappear. He seemed to wait to be noticed; sometimes he wasn't.

Jean stumbled over toys left in odd places where small hands had dropped them. She discovered a truck in the toilet when she went to clean it one day. Another day it was a child's wooden block, swollen with water and stuck in the same toilet. Forrest tried to get it out with a brace and bit. Finally Ed had to remove the whole toilet.

Laundry stacked up. Diapers stacked up. Training pants stacked up. Sheets stacked up.

Jean walked outside to the clothesline one day, her loaded basket in front of her. Celerina was gone again and had been for several days. Someone banged on the piano. The noise didn't bother her though she realized it would probably drive others crazy. To her it meant life, activity, family. It meant that Faith must be up from her nap. Billy would probably be next. Forrie was somewhere. Outside, maybe. More often now, he'd tell her where he was going when he went out, but often things distracted him and he'd wander off. He could be anywhere—and Ramona would be sure to notice. She could hear their criticism even though Franny tried to act as a buffer. Neglectful mother, neglectful mother—the dreaded accusation pounded in her head. She raised her hand above her head to find the clothesline. "There ought to be a law against people like that having babies." She could imagine them saying it. People like what? she thought. People who, after years of being afraid they'd always be alone, love their children all the more? People who feed and bathe and clothe and teach them with more intensity and concentration than others could ever imagine?

She shoved the laundry basket along the packed dirt with her foot, pulled out a sheet and searched for the corners. Just let them try to do what I'm doing. She stretched it up to the clothesline with one hand, reached for a clothespin with the other. The damp sheet slipped and fell to the dirt. "Dammit." She bent down.

A soft scraping sound came from behind and to the left.

"Forrie?"

"Yeah."

She winced, involuntarily raising her shoulders. He must have heard her. "That wasn't a nice thing for me to say. I shouldn't have said it," she snapped. She heard him scraping again. "What are you doing?"

"Digging."

"Making a hole? It's not a safe place for holes, not here near the clothesline." She could twist her ankle in one. She'd done it before.

"No. I'm just scraping. I need some dirt."

"What for?"

"Pop said I could build a dam near the pepper tree."

They were so important to him, his dams and moats and forts. The precious urgency of Forrie's make-believe world touched her and dissolved her annoyance. In such moments she felt included in a universe of trucks and caves and tunnels, the fluid world of a normal boy at play.

"A flood's coming so I got to build it fast."

"Really?"

"Aw, Mom, you know what I mean."

She knew he didn't want to admit it was only play. In his earnest absorption, he had unconsciously granted her a disclosure of the workings of his imagination. One comment by Forrie could lift her out of tiredness into the realm of fantasy where dams are always built in time to hold back the flood and caves invariably lead to adventure.

But for the most part, she was tired, too tired to do her own playing, too interrupted to read or play piano, too distracted to invite the women for bridge, too weary to make love or even concentrate on moving. When she was tired, she was less alert and she didn't sense doors left open in her path. And now there were more little people around to leave cupboard doors ajar. She wore a constantly changing pattern of bruises and scrapes.

Forrest probably did, too. She only guessed that. They never spoke of those things. Their evening talks out at the swings after the children were asleep did not consist of bashes and dropped sheets. Only when blindness led them into humor was it ever alluded to.

"Poor, dumb old Mort," Forrest told her one night, referring to his new horse. "What a numbskull. He's as slow as a slug."

"Is that why you named him after Father?"

"No. But it sure takes him just as long to catch on. Today I rode out past Lance's, between the fields out to the oak trees. Thought I knew where I was going—done it a hundred times, but somehow I went further east than I meant to and ended up tangled in someone's clothesline."

"Whose?" Jean stood behind him as he sat on the swing, her fingers trailing through his cropped hair.

"The Bradley's. I felt brassieres and panties flapping in my face. Big ones. I never knew she was so hefty." They both laughed. "Had to wait there with Mort twitching under me like a nervous kid seeing a naked woman for the first time. Finally Mrs. Bradley came out to set me right."

"Maybe Lance was right about Mort." She traced the outline of his ear with her fingertips and giggled. "Maybe you paid too much for him." She kissed him on the ear. She knew such episodes amused him, threw fuel onto his fire of life.

"Today in the brickyard some fella bought an order for a whole house," he said. "He asked me if I knew someone who could build it for him."

"Who did you tell him?"

"I told him I would."

She nearly choked. "But you don't know anything about building a house."

"I can ask questions, can't I? And Ed and the men can do the work, and I can do the planning and ordering materials and supervising. Ed's due to get his contractor's license next month. It'll make more money than brickmaking and hauling."

She thought he had the nerve of the ages, but she didn't want to darken his hopes. He'd probably learned a lot from the crews building this house—he was always asking them questions—and he had built a garage for Mother Holly. Let him. That was his arena. Hers was children.

And soon there would be another. By the time Billy was potty trained, she was pregnant again. She couldn't contain what she had to recognize as despair. Alone during the children's afternoon naps, she collapsed on the sofa. How was she going to tell Mother? There had been a note of disapproval in Mother's voice when she had told her of Billy, even her own mother implying that full blown motherhood would be too much for her. Now she had a couple more years of diapers and the nightmare of feeding all over again.

Maybe Mother was right. Three were enough. They were pushing their luck. But the pregnancy was undeniable. She buried her face in the sofa pillows, overcome with tears and self-reproach. There was something unseemly, maybe even inhuman, about not wanting another baby, the natural consequence of lovemaking. Shame at her tears made her sob more. Her stomach cramped and she contracted into a ball. If she had to let it out she'd better let it out now while Forrest was at work. This was one time she couldn't bear to have him discover her. Her breath came in jerky, wet gasps and her hand pressed against a hard center of regret hurting in her stomach.

Chapter Twenty-seven

"Take him home, Mrs. Holly. I can't do anything for him, but you can." Dr. Lipe's words lanced the wound she had tried to ignore. She knew something was different with this baby. Alanson Perry Holly felt different, like a bowl of jelly. He could bend back as easily as forward and seemed to slide through her grasp.

She slipped back into town quietly and tried to learn how to tend this difficult infant who would not eat and whose movements had an erratic discontinuity, as if he were spastic. More than the other children, his little neck lacked the strength to hold up his wobbly head. Gravely she thought somehow it must have been her fault in the birth, or in having a fourth child. In despair, she chased his mouth with a bottle, then with a spoon, sometimes with determination, sometimes in desperation. As much as she had with the other three, perhaps even more, she bathed him with love, exploring his limbs, his receding chin and slightly drooping lids, brushing the gossamer eyelashes with a lingering tenderness, yet in her loving there was a note of self-torture.

How had she come to this state of affairs? she asked herself one day. From opera in black velvet capes and tea served by a butler at a boarding school to this, force-feeding a limp, unwilling child in some remote town with turkeys squawking in the background and three other children moving around her, she wasn't quite sure where until they tugged at her sleeve? Where was the calm order of her youth, the placidness that Harkness thought remarkable in a young girl? How had it eluded her?

For weeks she walked from room to room with a constant lump in her throat. So what would Miss Weaver have done, given this situation? She didn't need to wonder. That woman was unsinkable. Oh, yes, Mother would coddle, Dody would understand, Icy would have suffered with her, but LCW would be adamant. "Of course you can do something about the condition of that child. It's foolish to accept as permanent what you see. Now blow your nose and get busy." Jean could hear her throaty voice conveying absolute control. "Of course you can." It wasn't the words themselves. They were simple enough, even superficial in themselves. It was the attitude they conveyed— that our frame of mind determines our experience, that it was absurd to accept obstacles as law. Instead, it was natural to go beyond limitations. Furthermore, not to be stalwart was shameful and might even transmit character weakness to the child.

Others voiced their worry. "How's he ever going to sit up and eat by himself?" Franny shook her head. "I don't think he'll ever—"

"Oh yes, he will. He's going to sit up and he's going to walk. In fact, he's going to walk me to your house every day. He can outgrow this. He was put here on earth to do some good, and I'm going to see that he can." Declaring it might bring it to pass. She held his head firmly from behind and, using two fingers to open his mouth, thrust the spoon home.

To his own strange incompleteness the child was oblivious, Jean discovered with gratitude. His sounds had none of the crossness of Faith's nor the sullenness of Billy's. He gurgled through babyhood with a glee that spoke of his willingness to be in the world, on whatever terms. "He's happy," she said to Forrest one night, almost in wonder. And his name became Hap.

Other than feeding, he was easy to tend to. He stayed put on a blanket spread out on the floor. While Jean gave piano lessons to local children, Hap was content to be held and played with by accompanying mothers or older sisters who circulated the gossip—the Hollys had another child, one too many. Jean choked at their censure.

Once a girl was brought to her lesson by her aunt, a Mrs. Betty Kenworthy. Jean steeled herself against potential criticism from a new voice, but let the visitor in anyway. "Mrs. Holly, something must have happened to your son," the woman stammered. "He's got blood all over his face." Her voice didn't have the daggered edge of superiority that Jean had grown to expect, but only concern. It reminded her of a mourning dove.

"Well, he hasn't cried. I can't imagine what. Oh, I bet I know. I fed him tomato juice at lunch." Her hands reached for the child, and they both laughed in relief.

"Here, let me."

Jean relinquished Hap to arms that seemed to take him with love. "I ought to know by now he'll be messy whenever I feed him."

"It must be hard to remember when you don't see it. But he's not the only one who looks injured. What about you? Whatever happened to your forehead?"

"Do you know what it feels like to bump into an adobe wall?"

"No, but I can see what it did to you. You're swollen into a purple knot."

It wasn't criticism, but compassion in her voice. Jean's relief unleashed a flood of talk, and Betty stayed after the lesson was over. In fact, she came again, even without her niece. A welcome friendship developed quickly, focusing on Hap as he grew through infancy. Without children herself, Betty and her husband Warren became part of the fabric of Ramona life. They took drives in the mountains and had picnics in the desert. And

Betty was thrilled to take care of Hap when the rest of the family
went to Bristol for Jean's parents' fortieth wedding anniversary
at Christmas, 1951.

Trips to Bristol were common for Jean—she went
practically every other year—but they were rare for the entire
family. This was the first time five Hollys would make the trip.
Knowing the children would be so excited they'd be
unmanageable days before, Jean took Forrest's suggestion that
they keep it a secret until the last minute.

They were to take a late night flight so the children might
sleep on the way. It would take 15 hours, with five refueling
stops. Jean packed bags of new toys to keep them occupied—
puppets, dolls, crayons and coloring books—and hid them until
that night.

Faith was the first to notice anything unusual. Scuffling
down the hall in pajamas with the feet too big, she stood by the
bathroom door. "Pop, why are you shaving now? It's bedtime."

"Oh, thought I'd try to look good in my dreams."

Faith didn't say anything for a moment, apparently intent on
evaluating his answer. Jean waited. Forrest whistled a children's
tune. "No, Pop, why are you really?"

"Do you want to know the truth?"

"Yes. You say we should always tell the truth."

"Oh, I just thought I'd go to Connecticut tonight to see
Grandma and Grandpa. Want to come along?"

"Wow! Yeah! Is it true, Mommy, is it true?" She squealed so
loud it drew the boys from the living room. In a moment all
three were jumping on the sofa, chanting in chorus, "We're
going to Grandma's. We're going to Grandpa's. We're going to
Connecticut. We're going on an airplane."

Right on schedule, the Kenworthys arrived to take Hap, and the Nelsons arrived to drive them across the mountains to the airport in San Diego. The toy planning worked. Whenever a child got restless on the plane, out came a new toy. Fortunately, the children slept easily, but had to be awakened around dawn in Chicago for a change of plane and even a change of airport. Billy was in charge of getting all the toys back into the bags, Faith of counting and distributing the bags for carrying, Forrie of leading them behind an agent through the airport to the right bus to get from O'Hare to Chicago Midway Airport on the South Side. Big responsibilities for children so young. During the hour-long bus ride Forrest asked "Is it light yet?"

"A little."

"What do you see?"

"Snow!" Faith said. It brought an awed murmur from the others.

"We'll see a lot more of that in Bristol," Jean said. "And you can play in it and make a snowman."

"Can we make a snow cow, too?"

"You betcha."

"Hey, Pop," Forrie said. "All the trees are dead."

"Pee-you. What's that stink?" Faith let go of Jean's arm in order to hold her nose. "Smells like the barn only worse."

"Probably the stockyards," Forrest said.

In the airport, Forrest kept up his questions in order to get to the right gate. The little troop stopped often and Forrest made his oldest son read every sign he could, which wasn't much. Forrie was only in first grade. He did fine with "men" and "women" and "gate" but struggled with anything more complicated. "I can't read big words yet," Forrie whined, nearly in tears, the weight of responsibility heavy.

"Spell them then."

Forrie gave tedious renditions of "b-a-g-g-a-g-e-c-l-a-i-m" and "p-a-s-s-e-n-g-e-r-s-o-n-l-y."

Jean had Billy on one hand and Faith on the other, with bags hanging from her forearms. Her wrists ached, but they all made it to the next plane. It swelled her heart to hear the children's wide-eyed commentary on the big world.

Father and Mother and a new Packard limousine met them in jovial spirits at La Guardia. The roads were icy, and they crept along, spinning sideways once. Awed by what they saw, the children were quiet. Soon they fell asleep again. Like limp sacks of laundry, all three had to be carried into the big house and up two flights of stairs to bed in the dormitory.

The next morning was too stormy to go out so Mother and Father let the grandchildren have free run of the house, and they explored every room, closet and cupboard, talking about everything. Billy's "lookie, lookie," echoed through the halls. Faith found the dinner gong in the hallway to the kitchen and, boosted by Delia, played an inharmonious melody. Billy spied the wall sconces and asked, "Are those really candles?"

"Don't be a dumbhead," Forrie said. "You think this place doesn't have electricity?"

The children took over the third floor and discovered the row of cedar chests where costumes were kept. They played dress-up with abandon, and clomped up and down the stairway in high heels, tall black pirate boots, velvet capes, wooden shoes. Jean's father took pictures. Eventually he led them downstairs to the basement where he had an extensive electric train layout. "Don't touch anything unless Grandpa tells you it's okay," Jean cautioned. For the children, the world was bursting with novelty. For Jean and Forrest, it was a triumph just to get there, and they relaxed into the large home with ease.

It continued to snow all night, dropping eight inches by morning. For such an eventuality, Mother had borrowed from Lucy and Mort and Bill a supply of children's snowsuits, mittens, scarves, boots and caps—clothing the children had never needed before. Morning dawned cold but clear. The children peered out the tall living room windows across the terrace and couldn't believe their eyes. "Everything's pillowy," Faith said. "Looks like a Christmas card." It was hard to get them to finish their breakfasts before they went outside.

Jean and Forrest aimed wiggly arms into armholes of bulky sweaters, and bent unwilling knees into layers of pant legs. Then came snowsuit stuffing, with sweaters caught in zippers, the children roasting.

"Too much to wear," Faith whined.

"You're going to wear it anyway. Here, give me a foot. You have to wear shoes today, that's for sure." Forrest tugged on boots, and Jean and Mother tugged on mittens.

Father went out the front door to find a sled in the garage. A whoosh of cold air that ruffled the doilies and tinkled the chandelier gave the children a preview of what was to come. "Here, use these," Mother offered. Mufflers two yards long. Jean and Forrest started winding, two, three, four times around necks and heads. Out came a distant, muffled voice. "I can't see."

"I can't talk," said another.

"That's what muffler means." Forrest chuckled.

"I can't move my arms," whined a third.

"Doesn't matter. You'll be warm."

The door opened again, another whoosh of cold air, and they were gone. Forrest and Mother and Jean collapsed on the sofa. Before Jean caught her breath, the door opened again. She shivered. The chandelier tinkled. "I have to go bathroom," Billy announced.

"I'll take care of him," Mother said, and ushered him down the hall.

Jean and Forrest had the moment to themselves. "Come here, Jeanie," Forrest said. "I need a smooch." He kissed her with the easy affection that comes when two have accomplished something together. "There was a time once when I would no more have done that here than spit in church." He stretched, leaned back and sighed. "It's good just to be with family and not be working."

The next days were full of visits. At Lucy's, the two sets of children got acquainted through play. At Bill and Ginny's, Bill and Forrest developed a teasing camaraderie. Jean telephoned Mrs. Eastman and had a long talk weighted with pauses and melancholy. Jean was mildly curious about the Hill crowd and asked Mother to bring her up to date, but she didn't visit any of them. Instead, she telephoned Lorraine to invite her to Hickory Hill but Lorraine was too busy with Christmas in her own household of four children. "I do have some wonderful news, though," Lorraine said. "I've opened a piano studio in Hartford and it's going well. I already have eleven students."

"You know something, Lorraine. Our lives are coming closer together. I mean, we live now more like each other than we ever have."

The world seemed whole and rich and full of joy. Christmas Eve at Hickory Hill was radiant. Mother brought out Christmas stockings and they all hung them on the mantle. Delia and Alexina had festooned the chandeliers with holly, and carols played in the library at cocktail hour. Jean couldn't keep the children from eating up the cocktail nibbles, but Father's annoyance even took on a gentle tone. "Don't you think we'll feed you tonight, Faithy?" Jean sat in the rocking chair where

Mother had read novels to her as a young girl, her hands in her lap, relishing the utter peace. Life was good. She felt something placed in her hands, Faith's big stuffed doll. "What's this for?"

"You don't look right," Forrie said. "You don't have a baby on your lap."

She thought of Hap at home. Love for her whole family welled up, and Father stood behind her and laid his hand on her shoulder.

The next morning all three children padded down from the third floor and climbed into bed with Forrest and Jean to hear the marvelous events of the day. Christmas dinner was to be a festive event.

Mort and Bill and Lucy and their families were all there, and the long stretch of damasked dining table displayed the Treadway's most formal service, complete with crystal stemware and silver candlesticks.

"The whole room sparkles," Faith said, and then added, "I can't move my chair." The tall, heavy dining chairs were a bit much for the children, and being served by maids in formal black and white uniforms was a thing of fairytales. "We have a maid, too, only she speaks Mexican," Faith said.

"She's probably with Ezequiel in Tijuana for Christmas," Forrie added.

It was good to be with her brothers and their wives, Anne and Ginny. Talk touched on the events of the year—Joe McCarthy and the Communist threat, MacArthur's unexpected turnaround in Korea. Father held to his traditional stance. "This is just a little police action," he said. "We've had all the big wars we're going to have. Let's not let it worry us. Forrest's doing well with his adobe building, Mort. He's got some fine prospects."

"What's the cost of an adobe house compared to a frame house?" Mort asked.

"Somewhat more expensive but it will last longer and there's no danger of fires."

"What about an earthquake?"

Mort was always the serious one, Jean thought.

"The walls have reinforced steel." Here was something Forrest was an authority on, and it was kind of Father to steer the conversation in his direction.

"I suppose you have a thatched roof out there in the West to go with your Indian bricks," Bill teased.

"Thicker thatch than what's on your head, as I've heard tell." The easy give and take told her that her family had accepted Forrest, and that Forrest was beginning to feel valued by Father.

When the flaming plum pudding was served, the children all chorused their approval. "Aw, it went out," Lucy's daughter said.

"Why don't you put more kerosene on it and start it again?" Forrie's offer of a helpful suggestion was meant in earnest and he didn't understand why everyone was laughing.

"Don't you know what's good for you? It's brandy that flames, not kerosene," Mr. Treadway explained.

"Is that the kind of thing you feed your son out west, Forrest?" Lucy's husband teased.

"Yup." Forrest reveled in the attention. "That's how come us cowboys have tough guts."

Two nights later the fortieth anniversary party was a gala affair. There were nearly eighty guests—family and Ares and Ain'ts, Father's business associates and Mother's DAR and Red

Cross friends. Jean was sure Faith was getting an eyeful of gowns and jewelry she'd never even imagined before. Hickory Hill was alive with spangles and music and laughter. "Every light in the house is on," Forrie said.

One of mother's long-time DAR friends asked Jean about her life out west. "And what does your husband do?" The tone of judgmental curiosity, akin to asking what *can* he do, scraped a raw place on her heart. When Jean told her about the adobe brick business developing into a building firm, the woman said, "Well, I'm sure that's lovely dear." Jean's mind flashed to Sally Anne saying, "You look lovely, Jean," the first time she tried to pin up her hair without help. She was glad to hear Forrest and Bill walk by so she could excuse herself.

On their way to the Grill Room, Forrest drew her aside in the library. "Wouldn't you rather be living here where there are lots of fancy parties?" It was his velvet voice.

"Not a chance! I love our life." She squeezed his hand to show she meant it.

Chapter Twenty-eight

Celerina had left for good. That discovery made the return to Bristol an even greater contrast. Faith did what she could to help, playing house for real. Circumstances forced her to grow up quickly. "Okay, here comes the train into the tunnel. Toot, toot," she would say when in good humor, and, little more than four herself, she aimed the spoon for Hap's mouth. Usually she forgot to clean up. To her it was a game, playing mother to baby brother, but like any game, it could be discarded at whim. When Jean asked her to do something, she never knew if it would get done civilly, or at all. She realized that, for any little girl, sorting cans week after week for mother to put in order on the shelf was dull. Sorting socks was worse, but often Faith had to do it rather than escape down the dirt road to Judy's, Franny Nelson's daughter.

"I wanna go play with Judy," Faith proclaimed one day.

Jean winced at Faith's brassy voice. "You can after lunch. Right now we have to feed Hap."

"I wanna go now. Naaoow. Naaoow." Her whine stretched out the word. It was a horrid sound.

"Be quiet."

"Naaow." Jean thought she had probably brought on the sound herself, or her condition had. Her unresponsiveness to facial expressions taught Faith early that a pout to show displeasure wasn't going to get any action. Either she might as well forget it and do as she was told, or she had to resort to stronger measures: Faith learned the tantrum.

"Here. Feed your brother."

"No." The word exploded with finality. Jean walked toward her, fuming, but before she got there, Faith threw herself on the kitchen floor, kicking and screaming.

"Faith Ingraham Holly, stand up."

"Naaoow."

Jean pursed her lips. How did Faith learn to do that when she'd never seen it and it must feel terrible?

"Sit up." Jean's voice rose higher.

"Naaow." More kicking and crying. Jean went for her to pull her up. Faith bit. Jean bit back. Faith screamed louder and wiggled out of Jean's grasp. Jean's anger flushed hot. Here was a perfect child with nothing to cry about, acting like a wild animal. And Hap, with everything to cry about, strapped into his highchair gurgling, dear Hap, content with the world. Faith was going to stand up. Jean grabbed what she could find—it happened to be Faith's hair—and yanked her upright. The shock silenced her.

"You're going to stand up and help me. Then you're going to eat your own lunch at the table like a lady. Then you can go to Judy's."

Faith was sullen for the rest of the day, and Jean was rigid and shaken. She didn't want to admit she didn't know how to handle her own child. By bedtime, remorse had tarnished victory, and Jean felt a need to reestablish closeness with this fireball. She sat down on the edge of Faith's bed. To talk about the incident would be to dilute the lesson she wanted to remain firmly planted, yet she didn't want to dislodge a love essential to both of them. Jean stroked Faith's head and played with her curls, twirling them over her forefinger, using her hand as a comb. The curls stretched through her fingers until they sprang free. It was soothing to both.

"Maybe you'll have a nice dream tonight."

"I'm going to dream the same dream I did last night."

"What was that?"

"I dreamed about a whole box of hand-me-downs from cousin Lancey." Her voice was a drowsy murmur.

"You did? What was in the box?"

"Dresses. Pinky ones." There was a long pause between slow words. Jean sensed the misty region between sleep and wakefulness which put the close on the little one's day. She wished she could drift off to sleep so early and without worries.

Faith rolled over onto her side and her arm fell across Jean's hand. Jean stroked the little hand. "I love you," she whispered.

"I love you too, Mommy." Carefully, trying not to move the bed, Jean stood up to go to the next child.

She had survived one more day, but the problem of needing to do things faster would still be there tomorrow. Eventually, it came to an impasse; she needed help. She wanted to run her own house, but she had to face it. For the present anyway, it was too much for her. She took on more piano pupils in order to hire Mamie—monstrous, tobacco-chewing, bellowing and black.

Mamie sidled her way into the family fabric, watched the wrestling matches in the evenings on the family's television, slapped her leg whenever something delighted her, spit in a pot under the most comfortable chair which she claimed as her own, and commandeered all domestic chores. When Franny and Ed dropped in one night, Mamie, sitting in her chair directly in front of the television, let out a whoop. "Lawdy, I knew if I took my teeth out, we'd get company." Mamie cornered Franny in the kitchen, leaned over her and in a breathy whisper asked, "Are you sure they can't see? Saturday morning, sure as I'm standing here, I saw Mr. Holly back that truck down the drive." A week later, Mamie ambushed Franny outside and announced, "You're right, Miz Nelson. Yesterday at breakfast I flapped my arms in front of their faces an' they didn't even blink." Franny, ever faithful, told Jean everything.

Week by week Jean felt Mamie become more autocratic, and it made her uneasy. Because she was desperate for help, she permitted Mamie's encroachments, each one a small thing if taken singly, but together, they made Jean feel she had lost control of her own house. She walked around looking for something to do. She set herself the simple chores of spraying for flies and watering the plants in the window boxes. "Ma'm, you're gonna drown them violas," came Mamie's booming voice. Jean retreated into quietness.

Forrie did just the opposite. Once Jean overheard Forrie backtalk an order from Mamie with "I don't have to. You're not my mother."

Mamie retorted, "You say somethin' like that again, I'm gonna chop your tongue out, chop your tongue out, chop your tongue out." Her voice raised an octave with each repetition so that she sounded fearsome, even to Jean. She suspected that Mamie's towering figure convinced him, quivering and wide-eyed, that she could. It was just one more wedge driven in to separate her not just from housework but now from raising her own children as well. Jean ached with the conflict of needing Mamie and hating her dominance.

Forrie and Mamie's little war escalated. Jean heard about it only after the fact, in the darkened privacy of bedtime tucking-in weeks later. Apparently Mamie had taken a saw without asking from Forrie's tool kit to cut a bone for Rusty, their new dog. "So I kicked her in the shin," Forrie said simply. "But I told her I was just swinging my foot and it hit her leg." Evidently, Mamie didn't buy it. In somber, seven-year-old tones appropriate to the gravity of the incident, Forrie related how she picked him up by the shoulders and cracked his head a few cracks on the kitchen window sill.

Two furrows deepened in Jean's forehead and she took a long, ponderous breath. It was courageous of him to tell her, but wrong for him to kick her. It was also wrong of Mamie to punish so viciously. "You shouldn't have kicked her," she said softly. Beyond that, the problem was too knotty. She never spoke to Mamie about it. She didn't want the confrontation. She never told Forrest, either. He'd only smoulder at her inaction.

Nevertheless, she needed Mamie's help. Mamie kept a close watch on Hap and ushered him into the more advanced world of potty training. "Hap, go pawt pawt," she shouted several times a day, interspersed with "Hap, close mout'." One thing about Mamie was undeniable; she had standards. She stomped through the house one afternoon and announced, "This house is terrible, Miz Holly. Everything's filthy."

Jean couldn't believe her ears. She felt sure Mamie's hands were on her hips. That was the limit. Seething, she put hers on her hips, too. She wished she knew exactly what direction to glare. "Did it ever occur to you that if my house weren't dirty, you wouldn't have a job?"

Jean could hardly wait until Hap could go "pawt pawt" by himself. The first time he did, Jean was bursting with triumph. "Look what Hap did," she announced to Mamie. But it might only be a fluke. She waited. Then he did it by himself the second time. When he did it the third, Jean was resolute. She grabbed her checkbook, strode across the breezeway to where Forrie now had a separate room, and found him amid the jumble of his erector set. "I know you can print nicely if you're careful. It's time you learned how to write a check." She spelled out Mamie's name, told him the amount and signed where Forrie told her to. "Mamie, where are you?" she called, turning back to the door.

"Right here, Miz Holly." Mamie's voice came from only a few feet away.

Jean held out the check. "I don't need you any longer, Mamie. You can go." The words sounded glorious.

Mamie was outraged. She snatched the check out of Jean's hand and stomped back into the house. It only made Jean smile. Firing Miss Andrews had never felt as good as this. The next time she cleaned, she discovered Mamie's tobacco pot on the floor under her chair. With gusto, she hurled it in the trash. The sound of smashing pottery had all the grandeur of a Beethoven crescendo. In that act, she reclaimed full command of domestic operations—with Faith's help.

Plump and aproned, no more than three feet tall, Faith played house with a vengeance. Soon she seemed to take Mamie's place, ordering Hap to close his mouth and commanding Forrie and Billy to put away their toys. It sounded cute at first, and it was certainly preferable to Mamie's bellows, but Jean sensed that trouble lay ahead.

When Faith was nearly five, the family could finally have pancakes on Saturday mornings. Although Jean could cook many things, she couldn't turn pancakes. She loved them, but hadn't had any for years. So when Faith begged to make them, Jean set her on a stool so she could reach the stove. It might inflate her already queenly ego, but that was a risk she was prepared to take; the rewards would taste divine. Stirring up muddies with Judy Nelson in the dirt of Pop's brickyard was sure to become a thing of the past, a childhood cut short by need. Pancake batter was real.

Betty Kenworthy and her husband Warren came one Saturday morning and found curly-haired Faith nearly hidden by a massive apron. Her chubby cheeks were flushed and she was bent down over the stove.

"Oh, Mrs. Kenworthy," she said, and let out a monstrous sigh. "I'm so tired. I wish they'd quit eating."

"Are there any more ready?" Jean asked and held her plate out with a smile, enjoying the turnabout.

"She's cute as a button," Betty said in a low voice, leaning into Jean's ear. "A pink-cheeked darling."

"Not always. She's no angel," Jean muttered. She knew that behind those bright button eyes that friends always cooed about lurked a mischievousness that, like the other children, exploited her situation. Faith scraped her peas onto the floor just as her brothers did, a practice which soon taught Hap the same. But when Faith didn't do it with corn, her favorite, and the others did, she was sure to tattle on them. Often Jean caught them if she remembered to feel their plates just before the end of a meal, but she suspected they frequently got away with it, dropping spoonful by spoonful during the course of a meal. Jean wondered if Faith made faces at her or stuck her tongue out when she made her do something disagreeable. Franny had seen Forrie and Billy do it, so Faith probably followed suit. They had all learned how to lift the glass cover off the candy dish in the living room without making a sound; she could never keep it stocked.

The same with peanut butter. Faith and Judy could climb soundlessly onto the kitchen cupboard to steal spoonfuls of it. If Jean walked into the kitchen soon after, she could smell it on the spoon they usually left in the sink. Short-sighted kids, she thought. Then she remembered with chagrin how simple-minded she and Tready had been when they forgot to flush their cigarette butts down the toilet and how Father had known even before they came downstairs. Maybe someday she'd have to tackle that problem, too. But for now, the problem was smelling peanut butter before mealtime, not cigarette smoke.

"You've been into the peanut butter again," she said at least once a week.

"How do *you* know?" That had become Faith's standard taunt, whatever the issue.

"George tells me," she said, naming the parrot who was the newest addition to their household. "He's a watchful pair of eyes, and he's very loyal. To me."

"Mo-om, parrots can't do that."

"How do *you* know?" she challenged her back. "Are you a parrot?"

When Faith eventually figured out that she'd have to brush her teeth afterward to escape being caught, Jean still won. Toothpaste smelled too, and toothbrushes remained wet for a while. And what kid would voluntarily brush her teeth in the middle of the day?

The ultimate skullduggery occurred in the enclosed patio. Just inside the three-foot adobe wall by the row of rose bushes was forbidden fruit, a kumquat tree that produced its miniature fruit from May to August. Jean loved the piquant fruit and its infinitesimal sting that numbed her lips momentarily, but one person loved it more: Faith. The rule was that you did not take any kumquats without asking. When the edible rind achieved its maximum sweetness, the fruit still packed a load of puckering power, and Jean knew to be wary. She had to enlist Franny's detective resources, too. Faith and Judy had matching shorts with oversized pockets and when Franny noticed both girls wearing them on the same day during kumquat season, she phoned Jean from her kitchen. By craning her neck, she could see across the field to the kumquat tree and keep Jean apprised of the escapade.

"They're doing an army low-crawl around the house under Forrest's office window. Can you believe it?"

"It's their game," Jean answered. "They pretend they won't be seen that way."

Franny described how the girls awkwardly picked each kumquat—from the back of the tree, of course, so missing fruit wouldn't be noticed. They were careful not to yank the fruit or do anything to disturb branches or make noise. If the take were particularly grand, Jean would be able to smell the sweet orange odor on their breaths and the jig would be up. The old apple tree in the garden of Eden was nothing compared to the forbidden fruit of the kumquat tree in the south patio. Like its more ancient cousin, it became the center of many a moral lesson.

"How many did you eat?" Jean asked casually, later in the day, to try to catch her off guard.

"How many what?" Faith shot back.

"You know. Kumquats."

"None. I didn't eat any."

Dishonesty was becoming a big problem. She had to recognize it. Forrest already had. He'd come home snarling about his workers. "They just slap up a crooked wall and think, 'good enough for the boss; he'll never know.'" When he fumed at the general tendency many people had to lie or withhold information from the blind, Jean shrank with helplessness.

He became fierce in his lectures to the children about absolute honesty. When he'd catch Billy or Forrie sneaking away from him, he'd call them back in a thunderous voice. "Listen you guys, if you two don't start acting right and telling me the truth, I'm gonna cloud up and rain. Sell you back to the Indians, that's what I'll do. Now look me in the eye, you couple of hamburgers." It wasn't the words, silly in themselves, but the intensity of their delivery which sent the children whimpering. Sometimes he sounded so ridiculous Jean had to leave the room and muffle her laughter. Yet *he* got results. They knew it was too serious for comfort when he'd threaten them with any mention of Indians. She imagined Forrie's spindly body quivering, and Faith's gaze riveted to the ground, when Forrest lit into them.

Wearily, she recognized that taking advantage of her was easier. She wouldn't lecture. Instead, she was saddened and hurt. She couldn't put on a show like Forrest did. That just wasn't in her. On Saturdays when the bakery truck came around, she often bought six cinnamon rolls for Sunday morning breakfast—one for each, round and full and puffy, a definite treat. Sometimes, on Sunday morning Jean found only five. Usually she blamed Billy who loved them most, but she couldn't ever be sure. Dishonesty wasn't in his nature. It was Faith who could lie with bravado. Rather than push the issue, Jean went without.

"You shouldn't do that," Forrest said.

"It's too tiresome to force the truth out of them. What's to be gained?"

"It's what we're losing. We're breeding a bunch of fibbers."

She sighed. "Let's just have peace in the house today."

But when the truth about a deception was incontrovertible, she had to act.

"Faith Ingraham Holly, I'm disappointed in you," she said one day.

"But Mr. Butters didn't see me."

"That's not the point. Why did you do it?"

"I wanted the comics. There's a comic wrapped around each one."

"How many did you take?"

"I don't know."

"Yes you do. The first thing you'd do would be to count them. Tell me."

A sniffle, then, "Six."

"How many do you have left?"

A pudgy hand opened slowly, uncovering two cubes of bubble gum.

"How many?"

"Two."

"Any others? Tell me the truth."

"Yes. One."

"Where?"

"My mouth." Another sniffle.

"Put it in my hand. The others, too. I'm going to call Mother Holly and we're going back, and you're going to tell Mr. Butters and give him what you have left. Get your piggy bank."

Faith's cuteness worked against her character. "Too many people tell her how darling she is," Jean said to Forrest that night. "They're always talking about her pink cheeks and red curls. Tell your mother not to do it any more. And I bet strangers are always chucking her under her chin. Just because she's cute she thinks she's treading the path of the elite. The world exists to please her, and she thinks she's princess of it all."

When Faith got feisty, force didn't work on her. At least not Jean's version of force, which probably seemed all too forceless to that scamp. Jean was in a quandary. She tried gentle talks in the evening at Faith's tucking-in time. Jean's fingers ran through her curls. "You have to be beautiful on the inside. It doesn't matter what you look like on the outside, or how many people say you're cute, you've got to be good on the inside, too. What if you had a big present that was wrapped up in the most gorgeous, shiny silver paper and a huge pink bow and you could hardly stand it, it was so pretty, and you opened it up and there was nothing in the box? Wouldn't be worth much, would it?"

The analogy had no effect. The next several days Faith was still show-offy to Judy and self-righteous to Billy. She had tiptoed away when Jean was talking to her, and she was bossy toward Forrie, ordering him to clean up his room. When Jean asked her about her own room, a notorious arena of catastrophe, Faith said, "Just you come in and see." Jean did. She knew it was a horrid mess—she'd just tripped over some clothes on the floor an hour earlier—but when she got there now, she couldn't find much out of place. Stashed somewhere. Infuriating. "See? Clean. I told you so." It was a snotty taunt.

"Faith!"

"Besides, when I grow up, I'll be a beautiful movie star, or somebody important like Annie Oakley, and I won't have to clean my room. I'll have servants. Like you did."

The next day Jean discovered mounds of Faith's clothes around the laundry basket. She couldn't tell what was clean or dirty. She slumped down on a stool in a heap. If only I could take a break, she thought, not a break from family, but just a break from not seeing. Proving her capacities hourly sapped her energy. She wondered if Forrest ever thought that. No, probably not. She sighed. And Dody had pleaded with her to write to some stranger because *he* needed encouragement?

Well, she supposed there were times he did. Two days earlier she was sure he did. It was that thing with Forrie and the new horse. He always tried so hard to do for the children what other fathers did for theirs. And the latest was riding horses.

Forrest just bought Honeybunch, a Welsh pony with black and white spots and a black roached mane, apparently quite a beauty. The weekend before, after Forrest had installed Forrie on Honeybunch, she broke into a run. Forrie pulled at the reins with all his puny might, but the bit had no effect. Out of control, Honeybunch ran under some pepper trees along the fence. Forrie's bare foot ripped on the top strand of barbed wire, causing a bloody gash.

It nearly crushed Forrest. Away from the children, he stalked back and forth in the bedroom, seething at his own carelessness in not asking Forrie what he had on his feet. Abruptly, he walked out into the living room. "You kids are going to have proper riding boots, and Jean, too, no matter what the cost," he had said, "and you're going to wear them."

As soon as Forrie's foot had healed, Mother Holly drove the whole family to Buster Brown's Shoe Store in Escondido, the larger town on the other side of the mountains. "Wow! We're going to have real cowboy boots. Yippee!" Faith squealed out the window going around a curve. "I'm going to be a real cowgirl, like Annie Oakley. I don't have to pretend anymore. I have a real horse, and Judy doesn't. Now I'm going to have real cowboy boots, and Judy doesn't have those, either. And I can ride better than she can, too." Jean only saw Faith riding farther down the path of conceit. Her impudence had to be put to an end.

Buster Brown's had an X-ray machine.

"Wow! That's spooky, looking right at the insides of our feet!" Faith said.

"Aw, it's just modern, that's all," Forrie retorted.

"Have you ever seen it before?" Faith challenged.

"Nope."

It was easy for Jean and Mother Holly to slip off to another store. They came back with a huge bag.

"What's that?" Faith and Forrie chorused.

"Nothing. Just something for Mother Holly."

The next morning Jean woke Faith before the others. She laid on Faith's bed what she knew was the most gorgeous package Faith's five-year-old eyes had ever seen. Jean imagined her sleepy child squinting against the brightness of the silver paper. Faith sucked in her breath.

"Ohhh, it's bee-utiful. What is it, Mommy? Is it cowgirl clothes?"

Jean said nothing.

"I'm afraid to touch it. The paper's so shiny I can see myself."

Jean just waited.

"Can I open it?"

"Yes."

With all the sweet anguish of childish anticipation, her plump hands reached out to unwrap the marvel and lift the lid. Jean heard an intake of breath and then stunned silence. Empty.

Without a word Jean walked out into the hall. Another day lay ahead.

Chapter Twenty-nine

"Faith, I don't want you to go to the cemetery."

"Why not?"

Jean wasn't actually sure why not. "It's not a nice place for little girls to play."

"But I like it. It's spooky."

"It's still not a play place. Just don't go."

"Okay." Her voice fell on the last syllable. Faith was six now, old enough to have a bored-and-exasperated-with-Mom tone. She used it often. Jean knew Faith would go there anyway. And, what's more, she would hear about it later, just as if she hadn't told her not to go. That was one thing about Faith. She shared everything.

Actually, Jean loved it when any of the children chose to offer her some of their child world. From bits of conversation and her own constant encouragements to describe things, she could piece together what the children did when they weren't in the house. Sometimes she could even imagine what was going on in their heads.

Right now she knew Faith had figured out what all those cars were doing at the cemetery on the other side of the Nelson's pasture. She also knew Faith was impatient for them to leave so she could inspect the new grave. Even though they had Honeybunch now, Faith still rode the headstones at Nuevo Cemetery, pretending they were horses. Faith wasn't so old that imagination had been supplanted by cool reality.

Over the last year, Faith had described the place many times. Wild purple everlasting grew in the cemetery, even on the graves. Some of the stones were rounded, some pointy, some block-like. The rounded ones at the oldest part of the cemetery made the best horses, just tall enough so that straddling them kept their feet off the ground. Faith and Judy picked switches from the brush in the pasture to use as whips. They named their play horses after the names on the headstones—Angela and Sam and Bella. Some of the stones had a lot of writing. One had only one word, Esteban, and the single year, 1917. Once Faith had told her, "There's a headstone that looks just like the front of a church in the *National Geographic* at Lady Mother's. But that's not my favorite." Jean didn't want to encourage her by asking which one was. Faith told her anyway, and told it again at dinner that night. It was a short, narrow grave and the headstone had an oval picture of a little boy's face. "He's so sad-looking and lonely," Faith said.

"Probably the MacIntosh boy," Forrest said. "Drowned in Mataguay Pond."

"I'm never going to ride that one," she said. "Judy and I put a bow right under the picture."

"A bow? Where did you get a bow?"

"From off some flowers at a grave."

"Faith!"

"But that grave had a lot of stuff already and this one didn't have any. That old man who takes care of the graves, he let us."

Faith slipped away. When Jean called her, no one answered. She had to be more stern with Faith, but the constant effort wore her down. And who could she tell that to? Not Forrest. How would that help him?

Icy. If only Icy—Icy didn't have a grave. Not a marker anywhere on the earth to show she'd been here. Did it matter?

To her husband, wherever he was. And probably to her mother. Not to Jean. Markers didn't mean much. The only important marks people leave are in each other. Invisible.

An hour later Faith came back, trying to whistle. She shoved a bouquet of flowers in Jean's hand.

"Faith, you shouldn't do this."

"It's okay, Mom. I didn't take them all from one place."

"Faith!"

"Guess what? One of the old men there asked us if we wanted to help dig. I bet Forrie's never done that."

"And you won't either, Faith."

"Too late. We already did."

Jean was perplexed. It seemed as though she was always saying no. No, don't do this. No, you can't do that. She was afraid if she always scolded, the children wouldn't share their private world with her. Their heads teemed with adventure, fancies comprehensible only to them, and Jean wanted to feel their wonder, too. She loved the secrets they shared and their close, personal events—a quarrel with a playmate, a lost truck, a master plan for a new fort, the nagging guilt of a chore undone, the anticipation of a loose tooth. In these she might see some marks, however transparent, of her life, her thinking, on theirs.

"Pop, how does the tooth fairy know when to come?" Faith asked one night at dinner. To her, it must have been a mystifying consideration.

"Just knows," Forrest answered.

"How?"

"He has a big book and keeps records."

"Of all girls and boys in the whole world?"

"Well, no. There's more than one tooth fairy, so that each one takes care of a place."

Faith stirred her soup, clanking her spoon against the side of the bowl, thinking. "Like senators?"

"Yeah. Like senators."

Jean wasn't so sure Forrest should tell her such tales, but it was fun to listen. Faith must have mulled that over for hours because after dinner she asked, "How do they know where to go?"

"Who?"

"You know. The tooth fairies." Her voice had the impatience of one who couldn't understand why someone else didn't know what she was thinking.

"They have maps." His storytelling thrived on the children's curiosity. He did it as much for his own entertainment as for hers.

"Of streets and houses?"

"Of streets and houses. And even insides of houses, to know where the children's bedrooms are."

"Who lets them in?"

"Nobody. They just find a way in, a little place or something. Come here, Faithy, let's have a look at that tooth."

Faith shuffled over and stood between his knees while he wiggled the tooth gingerly. "Looks like it'll be ready in a few days."

"In a few days?" Her voice was a high squeak. She struggled free and raced down the hall to her room.

Jean didn't understand why she ran off, but then there were a lot of things about that child she didn't understand.

Several nights later she heard a strange noise down the hall. Every time she walked toward it, it stopped. Late the next afternoon she heard it again, a sound in the wall or on the floor, like mice scuttling or scratching against something. She stood still to listen. It was near Faith's room.

"Faith, is that you?"

No answer. The noise stopped. Jean went back to the kitchen, but after a while she heard it again. Quietly, she walked down the hall. The noise continued. She came into Faith's room and the noise kept on. It was down by the floor on the other side of Faith's bed. After a moment it stopped. Jean went toward it and stumbled over a child on the floor.

"Faith, what are you doing?"

"Nothing."

"You must be doing something." Jean crouched down, felt for Faith's shoulders, then reached out to her hands. "What's this?"

"Popsicle stick."

"What for?"

"I'm making a hole in the wall so the tooth fairy can come in. Pop said it needs a little hole or something."

Jean couldn't help but laugh. Sitting there on the floor with Faith, she explored the wall. Down by the floor there was a hole in the adobe about the width of her finger.

"Don't tell Pop," Faith pleaded. "He'll get mad. Please don't tell Pop."

No, he wouldn't get mad. He'd think it was cute and would imagine Faith's curly head down close to the floor as she earnestly worked that Popsicle stick around in the hole until it was worn down to the nub. But here was a chance to establish some good will. "Okay, I won't. How will you ever get it through?"

"I've been making one outside, too."

Jean stifled a laugh, gave her a quick hug and left her alone to her task. The next day when the children were at school, Jean went outside and felt along the wall between the bushes under Faith's bedroom window. Yes, there was a little hole there, too. Forrest's adobes were twelve inches thick, though, and the tooth fairy assigned to Ramona made his call long before the two holes met.

"How'd he get in?" Faith asked at breakfast the next morning, breathless.

"Just found a secret way, I guess," Jean said.

"I still don't understand," she said wistfully.

It was a precious moment. Jean wished she could prolong it. "Understanding some mysteries will just have to wait, maybe until second grade," she said.

Forrie wasn't one to share quite so openly, but Jean still learned about him through a variety of sources. He had his problems, too, and in the third grade a major one was school. Specifically, handwriting, and, at times, self-control. One day Jean got a phone call she didn't expect. It was Mrs. Kelly, Forrie's teacher, notorious among Ramona children for her motto, "Self-discipline secures success; dishonesty determines defeat." They constantly imitated her prissy voice. When Jean met her once at PTA, she discovered the children's impersonation was remarkably accurate. And here was this same voice on the phone, testy and high-pitched.

"I simply had to speak to you, Mrs. Holly."

Jean could just imagine what that stereotype of a stern old schoolmarm looked like. She probably wore faded cotton print dresses that fit poorly and buttoned up the front. "Why? Did something happen?"

"Your son, Mrs. Holly, did something no child has done in the 27 years I've been teaching at Ramona Elementary. I simply cannot believe it. You know, of course, how difficult it is to read his handwriting."

"No, I wasn't aware—"

"Yesterday afternoon I kept him after school to practice. For a time he was alone in the room, and your son, Mrs. Holly, relieved himself in my thermos."

The conversation was brief. What could Jean say? She stammered out an apology and a promise to reprimand and tried to get off the phone quickly. Then she slumped down in a chair, numb. She tried to imagine Forrie doing that. Surely it couldn't have been vindictiveness. It was kind of funny, she had to admit. Maybe Forrie had to practice with one of those boring handwriting books with solid blue lines equally divided by a dotted line. The fat letters always looked so impossibly neat. Jean remembered seeing them herself. She had hunkered down over them, too, her round glasses perched on her nose, trying to imitate the masters. "Make your e's look just like these, round and wide," Mrs. Kelly probably said.

Fat chance, lady, Forrie probably thought. It was his latest expression. He was getting pretty independent, maybe even a little mouthy.

The door slammed closed. "Who's that?"

"Me," Forrie said.

It would have to be now. She sat Forrie down in the bedroom with the door closed. "What did you do after school yesterday?"

"Played in the fort with Chuckie."

"No. Before you came home."

He groaned and his voice fell. "That old Mrs. Kellybelly made me stay after school."

"What for?"

"Handwriting."

"Tell me about it."

Forrie didn't say anything for a few seconds. "She made me do one page over and over again. It was boring. It was "E's." You know, "b-e," "c-e," "d-e," "f-e.""

She could tell Forrie was trying to deflect the conversation from the critical point. "It doesn't matter what the letters were."

"Yes, it does, Mom."

"I had a call from Mrs. Kelly this afternoon." The words must have exploded in Forrie's mind. He didn't say anything. Apparently, he didn't even move. A mockingbird outside filled in the silence. "I'm not angry, Forrie. Just tell me what happened."

"I had to pee, Mom. I couldn't help it. She didn't even let me go outside after school was over, and she told me not to leave the room and to keep practicing until she came back." He paused a moment and then began talking faster and faster. "I looked for a plant first, honest I did. But there wasn't any. And her wastebasket was that wire kind. I was scared to leave. 'Don't leave the room, Forrest Holly,' she said in a real screechy voice. She stayed away a long time. I bet she was peeing, wherever teachers go to pee. I tried to keep writing that dumb stuff, and then I got to the p's and had to write 'p-e.' I couldn't help it, Mom. It was the only thing. I looked out the window first and no one was there and I didn't hear her clumpy feet, so I—I just did it." Forrie sounded as though he was about to burst into tears.

Despite herself, Jean began to laugh and grabbed him in her arms and nuzzled him by his neck. "It's okay."

"I thought maybe she'd just pour it out and not notice. I stayed until the z's and she came back and let me go. Are you going to tell Pop?"

"Of course I am."

Forrest laughed that night when she told him. "He was probably dancing on the walls, terrorized by that biddy. It might have even taught him to pray," he said, and laughed some more.

Jean felt closer to her children for these glimpses into their private lives.

She felt further from them when they didn't obey. And that usually centered around chores. Animal feeding was a chore. And with two horses, chickens, Roosty the rooster, Rusty the dog, Jean's parrot, ducks, Angelina the cat, and Hap's array of guinea pigs, there were plenty of animals in the Holly menagerie to feed. When Faith was seven, Angelina was her responsibility, which meant that Angelina was frequently hungry, and would eat anything, particularly human food.

March was often a rainy month, and Easter vacation that year was near the end of March. Rain drummed monotonously on the roof for a week and kept everyone indoors. When it rained a lot, the adobe soil around the house became slicker than ice. Feet slid out from under running children, and even Jean fell once just walking. So, for the whole week, the children were inside. The house seemed as small as the old frame cottage.

"When'll it stop, Mom?"

"I don't know, Forrie. When it gets ready to, I guess."

"I'm ready for it to now. I gotta go see my fort."

"It's probably all washed away," Faith chimed in.

"What do you know, dumbbell?"

"Mo-om. Forrie called me a name."

"And you've never called him one?"

"Your fort's probably a big pile of mess, all caved in."

"What do you know about forts, stupid?"

"I know you're not supposed to have 'boys only' forts. That's what I know."

"Who says?"

"President Eisenhower."

Their bickering had started earlier and earlier every morning this week. Probably more than they did, Jean hoped the rain would stop so they'd go outside. "When it lets up some, you can go feed the animals."

The next day it let up. Jean opened the windows in the stuffy house. Peacock and turkey droppings smelled foul and pungent in the wetness. In a steady stream of hallway clatter and doors slamming, the children headed outside.

"Ugh, it's all slippery gush," Billy said.

"Then stay inside."

"No. I'm going to the barn."

"Close the door, Billy."

"Me, too," Faith said and headed out the door followed by Hap.

"Not me, I'm not going where she's going," Forrie said. "I got to go see my fort."

"Wear a jacket. Not your new one, Forrie."

He came back inside, raced through the kitchen and down the hall, then back outside again. "Close the door," she said again.

All day, in and out. But it was better than having them cooped up. By midmorning she wondered what her floor looked like. She couldn't keep track of who was in and who was out. "Close the door," she kept repeating, like a stuck record. They'd have to get a spring-loaded closer. Why they hadn't before this, she didn't know.

When Forrie came in for lunch, Faith squealed. "Mo-om, Forrie's got mud all over his jacket."

"Quit it."

"And it's his new one, too."

"Keep your mouth shut, dumbbell."

"Forrie, didn't I tell you not to wear it?"

"I couldn't find my old one."

She took the tomato soup off the burner and started in on a lecture about school clothes and play clothes. It was tiresome, even to her, so she stopped abruptly. She went back to the stove. Feeling for the pan of soup, she found the cat on the counter, her head in the pan. "Dammit! Stay out of our lunch!" she yelled. She grabbed her by the scruff so roughly that Angelina squeaked. Jean headed for the door and felt with her foot. Open, of course. She pitched the cat as hard as she could outside. Angelina's jangling two-note shriek as she hit the adobe wall across the breezeway was the stuff of nightmares. Four children sucked in their breath in unison.

"Mom!" Faith cried.

"If you'd keep the door closed, and that means you, too, Billy, the cat wouldn't come in. And Faith, if you fed her when you were supposed to, she wouldn't be so hungry that she eats our food. You didn't feed her yet, today, did you?"

A meek little, "No."

"If you don't start doing what you're supposed to, that cat's going to the Humane Society, do you hear?"

"Yes." Even softer.

The rest of the day the children walked on tiptoe, quiet as mice, closing the door without a slam.

But the effect of Jean's outrage didn't last. Before long, Faith again began forgetting to feed Angelina. After four days in a row of that and another discovery of Angelina on the kitchen counter indulging in the family's dinner, Jean was determined. On Monday when the children were in school, she asked Ed Nelson to take the poor, neglected cat to the Humane Society.

Nothing happened the rest of the week. Just as Jean suspected, Faith didn't even notice. On Saturday they had pancakes for breakfast. Faith cooked them. After the meal, Faith took the remnants outside on a plastic plate. "Here, ki—" Suddenly, truth dawned. She turned on her heel, flung the plate in the sink and raced through the house, bawling. The door to her room slammed. She didn't come out all day.

By late afternoon, Jean wondered if she'd done more harm than good.

Chapter Thirty

The 1928 pickup was a rusted hulk, skeletal and barren. It had no distinct color, no windshield, no fenders, no sides, no division between cab and bed. A wooden bench served as a seat for driver and passenger. Forrest sat behind the wheel, shoulders squared to the task ahead, unaware of any discomfort as they bounced over the deeply rutted dirt road. By gum, he thought, I'm taking my family out to dinner just like any other father, risks be damned. Excitement pumped hard in him, and his muscles were tense, though his feet worked the pedals slowly and accurately. On his lap sat eight-year-old Forrie.

"Stretch up tall now so you can see everything ahead of us." Forrest rested his hands gently on Forrie's skinny arms, tight with the responsibility of holding onto the man-sized steering wheel.

"Have we passed the three big pepper trees on the right yet?" Forrest asked.

"Yup," said the boy.

"Then we're right by Lance's."

"Yup."

"Do you see that bad place in the road yet?"

"Nope. Slow down."

Forrest let off on the gas pedal.

"Oh, yeah. Now I see it."

Forrest felt the muscles in Forrie's arms grab on tighter as he prepared to steer around the ruts in the road. He let off on the gas a little more and the jalopy inched along. When it hit the ruts, it lurched and Hap grunted.

"Those were some nasty ones," Jean said. She sat bracing herself on the seat with one arm, holding Hap in her other.

"No cars up ahead?" Forrest asked.

"Nope."

"Po-op. Of course there's no cars. This is private property," Faith said from behind. "And this is our own private road." The smugness in her voice coat the dry air.

"What's that mean, private?" Hap asked.

"That means we have to pay to have it smoothed out." Forrest chuckled. "That's why it isn't."

The end-of-day sun slanting at a low angle made Forrest's face warm. He tasted dust. Hap squirmed next to him and leaned down to look between the wooden slats that served as a floor.

"Mommy, you can see the road go by."

"Tell me what it looks like," she said.

"Just dirt."

The truck jolted again and Forrest grunted. "As if we didn't know." After a pause he asked, "Do you have shoes on, Forrie?"

"Yes."

"Do you, Hap?"

"Uh-huh."

"Do you know if the others do, Jean? I don't want them looking like a bunch of moth-eaten ragamuffins."

"I think so."

Hap wiggled out of Jean's grasp to look behind. "Yeah, they do."

"Are they holding on?" Jean asked.

"Yup."

"What's up ahead now, Forrie, the big gully?" Forrest asked.

"Pretty soon."

Forrest loved the closeness of driving with his son. He would do it with each of them, when they got old enough. He knew Forrie was hardly old enough now, but need made him grow up fast. Forrest felt the truck head down the incline. "We're just about there, aren't we?"

"Yeah."

"This is good enough. Pull off to the right." Forrie steered off the road and Forrest put on the brake. "Now, set it in reverse so we won't slide down." He guided Forrie's hand on the gear shift and together they set the handbrake.

When they got out, Forrest tussled with Forrie a bit, ruffling his hair. "Pretty good job, buckaroo," he said. "Billy, can ya find a rock to put under a wheel?"

The children walked half a step before their parents and guided them the surest way down the gully and up the other side. Forrest held Forrie's hand and Jean held Faith's. A furrow in the hardened dirt threw Jean sideways into Forrest. "Careful. Pull her back on course, Faithy." He was feeling exultant, just like he used to as a teenager after a track meet when he'd vaulted well. He talked heartily while they made their way slowly up the half mile of dried-up Santa Maria Creek to town. He liked the way the heels of his boots dug into baked silt, crunching at every step.

Ramona was a one-street town, less than ten blocks long. Forrest knew it well. Main Street was lined by grayish green eucalyptus trees whose branches drooped from the heat. Toward the end of the day everything in Ramona was tired. Even though the street was paved, dust rose when a car went by and it made him swallow as they walked along the sidewalk. The shade of a row of eucalyptus trees gave only slight relief from the heat. Forrest felt whole and proud walking with his family down Main Street.

"Pop, there's weeds growing right out of the sidewalk," Hap said. "They're scratchy."

"What else do you see?"

"A dog."

"What's he look like?"

"Dead."

They laughed. "He's probably just hot. Have we passed Johnny's drugstore yet?" Forrest asked.

"Just now," Faith said.

"Did I ever tell you I worked there in high school?"

"Yes, Pop, at the soda fountain. We already know," Forrie said with a sigh.

Ransom Brother's Hardware was next, after the big crack in the sidewalk. Across the street was Whiting's Feed Store.

"Is the feed store painted yet?"

"Nope. It's still all peely."

The roof of Riley's Cafe, warped by years of sun and rain, sagged a little to the right, leaning toward the Ramona Four-Square Church. The screen door squeaked its customary high-pitched welcome. Inside, a ceiling fan with one paddle missing stirred up the air and the flies. It was just as hot inside, but at least the air was moving.

"Forrest Holly, where you been keeping yourself?" Pat Riley hollered from the kitchen like he always did.

"Jean didn't give me any money this week. Can't come in unless Jean gives me my 'lowance."

"Then why don't you get out and work, heh?"

"Don't have to. Got Jean."

Several voices in the restaurant laughed.

"Jean, Forrest. Come on over here." Warren Kenworthy's voice came from somewhere in the rear of the narrow cafe.

"Hey, hey. Sounds like my itty bitty buddy. Is your girlfriend here, too?"

"Sure am," Betty said.

"Got room?"

"We can make room."

The children led them onward and Warren slid two tables together. Often they'd meet a friend at Riley's. Ramona had only one other restaurant. Forrest thrived on chance meetings with friends. This one felt especially good, a cap to his driving victory.

"I want a cheese sandwich and—"

"Grape soda. We know, Billy," said Faith.

"Mommy, do you think Mr. Riley would make gingerbread man pancakes?" Forrie asked. "They're my favorites."

"I'm sure he would if you asked him nicely."

Talk ranged over domestic events and local affairs, the move from turkeys to chickens in the valley, wells going dry, efforts to join the Colorado River Authority.

"I tell you, we've got to get into that or the whole town'll dry up like a raisin," Forrest said, keen on organizing.

"I know, but for right now, here she comes with your plate," Warren said.

"Did you get your Nehi, Billy?" asked Forrest. He marched his first two fingers across the table until they bumped into Faith's arm. He grabbed hold. Faith giggled at the attention. Then he did the same in Billy's direction, but he couldn't find him. He was sure he had the direction right. In others ways too, he couldn't find him. Instead, Forrest's fingers ran into Billy's plate.

"Do you mind if I take the toothpick out of your dill pickle, Forrest?" Betty's voice was solicitous.

"If you need a toothpick, Betty, for heaven's sake, help yourself." He explored his plate a moment, then said, "Hey itty bitty, would ya cut up my meat for me?"

Warren took the plate and cleared his throat. "How did you come tonight?" He spoke the question softly.

"Drove." Forrest sat up straighter in his chair, ready to draw off the conversation from the one subject odious to him. "Forrie and I did together, didn't we? He can manage that steering wheel just like a trucker. Show Warren your muscles, Forrie." Talking about blindness would erode the vigor he needed to deal with it daily. Let others gain mileage out of their limitation, or use it as an identity. Not for him the tame shelter of some suffocating institution, some limited world apart. Instead, he competed in the construction business with people who could see. Forrest took another bite.

He heard Warren shift positions in the rickety wooden chair. Knives and forks clanked for a moment against plates, and then Warren spoke softly. "I think I ought to tell you, I've heard some talk around town that people think you shouldn't do that."

Forrest kept eating.

"He doesn't do it on the streets, only private roads," Jean said.

Warren put his knife down against his plate. "You know, anytime you want to come to dinner here or go anywhere, Betty and I'd like to come along."

Forrest lifted some peas on his fork, but when he reached his mouth, nothing was there. "Thanks, buddy." He tried for a jovial tone, but the words sounded flat.

The next morning the house was a flurry of activity. "Bring your shoes here." Forrest stood in the service porch, ready for the Sunday morning ritual of shoe polishing. It was essential to Holly respectability as well as to making the shoes last, at least until the children's feet outgrew them. Discarding shoes that still had some sole left was against his doctrine of gratitude for present riches, so it was important that their tops be preserved as long as their bottoms lasted. He spit in the tin of shoe polish and scrubbed his rag in little circles in order to make just the right moist mix. The sweet, musky odor had always meant Sunday to him, even in his youth when his father did the polishing. He counted four little pairs and two adult pairs lined up on the washing machine top, and hummed intermittently as he worked.

While Jean cooked breakfast, Forrest got the children ready for Sunday School. He soaped the little-boy body of Hap, feeling the smoothness of the slippery skin under the soap film. Week by week, Forrest found the limbs growing stronger and more stable. He scrubbed the head, playing with the lather. He wormed his finger behind the ears, into the ears, making a funny slurping noise until Hap giggled. Forrest felt the toddler's arm twine around his leg below the knee, infinitely precious at that moment, dependent in its wet nakedness. With tenderness he wrapped him in a towel and patted dry his round stomach, the plump bottom, the wiggly fingers. Preparations for Sunday church were among his most cherished hours in the week. It was time for a fatherhood of touch.

One by one, he called the children to him to cut their fingernails. Billy hung back. Hap squeezed his hand into a tight fist. Forrest had to pry it open. After three fingernails, Hap's giggles turned into wails.

"What are you crying for?"

"They're going to bleed," Hap whined.

"Does a tree bleed when you cut it? Nails are just like trees." When Forrest had finished three pairs of hands, he called out, "Billy, where are you?"

He heard him down the hall. "Mommy, I don't want Pop to cut my fingernails."

"Why?" Jean asked.

"He always cuts them too close and they bleed."

"Billy, come in here," he bellowed. Letting one child go without would set a precedent. "Billy."

Shoes shuffled toward him in the hall. "Here I am." The voice was low and grumpy. Forrest reached forward, found a fist, and the struggle began again.

After breakfast they assembled outside when they heard Mother Holly's car come up the driveway.

"Everybody here? Sound off," said Forrest.

"One."

"Two."

"Four."

"Where's Billy?"

Forrie, the organizer, went off to look.

"Faith, check to see if Hap has underpants on," Jean said. "I can never be too sure."

After a while, Forrie came out with Billy in tow.

"Uh-oh." Mother Holly's voice sounded concerned. "I think Billy's got the mumps. His cheek's swollen out like a golf ball."

"Guess I have to stay home." Billy's voice was bursting with triumph.

"That doesn't impress me," Jean said. "Come here." She poked her finger into Billy's puffed up jaw. "You packrat."

"What are you doing?" Forrest asked.

"He had a soggy piece of sausage stashed in his jaw."

"How did you know?"

"I knew I'd cooked enough, but the plate was empty in two minutes."

Forrest laughed in amazement. "You just can't fool your mom, Billy, so you might as well give up."

After church the children had their shoes off before they got out of the car. "Change out of your good clothes before you go play," Jean said.

"What are you going to do, Billy?" Forrest asked.

"Go to the barn."

"You want to take a ride?"

"Nope. Gonna climb on the roof."

A few door slams and a little shuffling in the hallway and they were gone—except for Hap who hunkered down and stuck his nose into a coloring book.

It was Faith and Forrie, not Billy, who were crazy about horses. Forrest knew that, so it was Forrie he looked for after lunch. He thought he'd give him a tough decision. "Hey, Forrie, do you want to try out the new mower or take a ride?"

Forrie didn't answer right away, just what Forrest expected. He knew Forrie's fascination with mechanisms had to battle a moment with the lure of adventure. Whenever Forrest took the children on a ride, they went farther or to some new place the children weren't allowed to go on their own. "Try out the new mower," Forrie said.

"Aw, let's take a ride. Go get your sister. You can trade off on Honeybunch. Meetcha at the corral."

This fine, breezy Sunday was too good to waste staying home. He loved to have a child ride with him on Mort, his hefty paint who could easily handle two riders. It gave Forrest a chance for physical closeness, and he could tell how they were growing when their bodies nestled against his chest. Lance often teased him about these rides, saying that the reason Forrest wanted a kid with him on Mort was because Mort was too dumb to pick out a decent path and a child could do better. Forrest knew that in the horse world, Mort was a plug, but he loved him anyway. Now Honeybunch, there was a horse with promise. So gentle with the children, Honeybunch could offer them a widened sphere of activity and companionship as well as play. Forrest saddled her first, simply because she was the first one he found. "We're going for a little ride, Honey," he crooned.

When Forrest was teaching the children, their usual ride was to Indian Rock, just across the Ramona-Escondido highway past Earl Duran's and the pomegranate bushes up the hill. Indian Rock was a flat granite promontory shaded by a tree and edged by sagebrush that had purple stringy blossoms from late spring to fall. When they went to Indian Rock, they brought back the deserty sage smell on their clothes. If Rusty went with them, his coat carried the smell of sage the rest of the day. The children called it Indian Rock because of the *metates*, hollowed-out places in the rock where the Indian women used to grind their corn. Once in a while, if they were particularly purposeful, they could find an arrowhead. When riding to Indian Rock became tame, Forrest took them farther, out to what he called The Eighty Acres. They'd have to jump a wide ditch at a gallop in order to get there. This Sunday, though, he felt like going far beyond that. "No. On second thought, Honey, I think we'll take a long ride." He stroked her on the neck and then went on to saddle Mort.

On the ride out, the children were in high spirits. "How far we going, Pop?" Forrie yelled from behind when they passed right by Indian Rock.

"How far do you want to go?"

"I want to go all the way to the ocean," Faith said, the bounces making her speech sound funny.

"The ride's kinda lumpy bumpy, eh?"

Forrest heard Honeybunch stop behind him. He reined in his horse and called back. "What happened?"

"He fell off," Faith said. When they got back to where Honeybunch waited, Forrie was dusting himself off, but crying.

"You all right?"

"Yes."

"You standing up?"

"Yes."

"You're not hurt?"

More crying. "No."

"Then what are you crying for?"

"I don't know."

Forrest waited, but only heard more sobs. Crying like that was like wallowing in a mud puddle of self - pity. He could stand it for only a few seconds more. He shifted in his saddle. "I'll give you one minute to quit bawling. If you can't do it, then

you're going to have to walk home. Faith'll ride Honey both
ways."

Sniffles.

"And we're going up the mountains on the other side of
Eighty Acres." Forrest knew that would get him.

"You are?" Forrie sniffled one more time, picked up the
reins and hoisted himself on. They headed off through brush and
live oak, Mort and Faith picking out a safe path, Honeybunch
following. Along the way, Forrest asked his usual, "What do
you see?"

"Hills," said Faith.

"Come on, you can do better than that. What's growing on
them?

"Oak trees."

"Anything else?"

"Big boulders."

"I smell orange trees. Why didn't you tell me about them?"

"Dunno."

"What's right ahead of us?"

"Just sagebrush. And some trees."

"What kind?"

"I don't know. Tall ones with skinny leaves."

"Are the leaves kind of gray green, and do they curve to a
point in one direction?

"Yes."

"Then they're eucalyptus. If you crunch some of the leaves
in your hand, they have a musky smell. Not as strong as
sagebrush, though. Alice used to string the pods together to
make garlands for our Christmas tree. What's on the left?"

"A rail fence around a ranch."

"Let's go left after the end of it up into those mountains." He trusted his memory about the shape of the valley, and he knew the children trusted him.

They rode a long way, talking of what they saw—a big, frog-shaped rock, a dead sycamore—singing Gene Autry songs when they walked their horses, galloping where they could, climbing higher and higher up the valley wall, filling themselves with the liberty of a long spring day. The afternoon cooled pleasantly in the higher foothills and a breeze gathered momentum.

"Okay, time to switch." The children jumped down, tussled a little as they changed places, scrambled on again, and they headed back. Forrie's narrow shoulders were higher than Faith's. "You're getting taller every time we ride," Forrest said. "Pretty soon I won't be able to see over your shoulder."

"Aw, Pop, quit teasing." Forrie became quieter and quieter as they rode. A little whimper escaped.

"Pop?"

"Yup."

"I don't know where we are."

Forrest reined in Mort. "Faithy, do you?" He waited.

"No."

The realization descended with quiet force. "Look around you. Look behind you. Do you see anything we passed?"

"Nope."

"Look where the sun is. Feel where the breeze is coming from."

"It's coming from all around," Faith whined.

"Do you see any trees you saw before? Any fences?"

"We're lost," Forrie said, and slumped against Forrest's chest.

"Then, we're going to just sit here on our horses and pray until we know the way."

He said it with finality so that the children wouldn't question. They didn't say a word. Honeybunch sneezed. A crow cawed somewhere off to the left. Mort changed his weight and the saddle creaked. Forrest kept his head straight, his chin slightly upward, his shoulders back. They mustn't see him afraid. If they so much as wondered if he was, they'd crumble into whimpers. He stiffened against the naked judgment calling out from the mountains that he who pushed against the reins that bound him had stepped beyond his limits. Limits were for limited minds, for people who clutched their limitations to them like coats of arms on a shield. He blinked away a fly.

Okay, so pray, he told himself. It was good just to be there, to smell the sage, feel his children against him, and have the freedom of movement that horses allowed him. In accordance with his credo of gratitude, he went over in his mind all the good things in their life, and felt thankful for their source. Forrie began tracing the stitching on the leather pommel with his fingers. It was distracting. Forrest gently put his big hand on top of the smaller one.

They sat on their horses on the side of the mountain for a long time with the sun glancing lower. No one said anything. All right, he thought. I'll go through it again. It's good to be here. I'm thankful for sun on my neck. I'm thankful for family. I'm thankful God gave them good minds, good eyes, good memories. I'm thankful for—

"I think it's this way." Faith's voice was a tiny squeak. He had to trust her. They headed off slowly, Faith leading.

"There's the frog rock," Faith yelled back. Forrest felt his son sit up straighter, sign of a hairline crack in the wall of anxiety that surrounded them.

"And the dead tree," Forrie added after a while.

The crack grew. "You know where you are now?"

"Yeah. Those are the fence posts we followed." Against his chest Forrest felt Forrie take a big breath and let it out in a gush. The wall collapsed. Forrest clucked at Mort, and he moved into a trot. The children began to talk and laugh.

"I think I'm going to have Honeybunch bred," Forrest said after they had gotten to more familiar ground. "Then we can have a colt."

"Yippee! Another horse to ride."

"Yup. Won't that be dandy?" When they got to The Eighty Acres, Forrest said, "Come on, let's let 'em loose." He spurred Mort, then Faith did the same to Honeybunch. Both horses took off at a gallop. "Faith, is that you I hear flapping against the saddle? You must be bigger than I thought."

"Po-op," she wailed in protest, the word bouncing into two syllables. He knew that even this teasing was permissible now that they knew their way.

"Flapsaddle, that's what we'll call you. Mrs. Flapsaddle."

Forrie squealed. "Flappy. Flappy."

"Pop, make him sto-op." Faith spurred Honeybunch again in an effort to get ahead, out of range of hearing, but Mort, knowing well his rider's habit, kept close, and they galloped back to the ranch in a wild burst of energy.

Maybe they won't tell Jean, Forrest thought.

Chapter Thirty-one

Honeybunch foaled the following spring. She had a sprightly paint filly, healthy and perky. They named her Skippy. When she was old enough, Forrest gentled her, and the children curried, brushed and petted her. More and more, Faith and Forrie spent their time in and around the corral, the barn, Indian Rock and sometimes Eighty Acres.

"Watch out for Hap," Jean would always say when the older ones went to ride. She couldn't keep a four-year-old from going around the ranch, but at least they could have rules—Forrest saw to that—rules like closing the barn door so Hap couldn't get in, and the corral gate so the horses couldn't get out, always putting curry combs in the same place so Forrest could find them, and keeping up the water level in the corral trough.

One Saturday in late September, Forrie went into the barn and came out, his arms loaded with a shovel, pick, hammer, some warped old boards and two-by-fours, his pocket bulging with nails, items of play for his project, to expand his fort under the pepper trees. He dragged his feet in the dirt. It was one of those glaring hot days when searing Santa Ana winds swooped down the valley from the east and enlivened the tumbleweeds. Forrie busied himself for hours, studying the lengths and shapes of the available boards, engineering and then erecting a new roofline to give maximum shade so that the flat, broad roof of his fort could double as a raft if he pretended the dry ditch surrounding it was a muddy river.

The day lazed on, quieted by the dry heat. Billy wandered aimlessly, picked up some gravel from the breezeway between the kitchen and garage, and ambled out to the pasture to throw the pebbles at tin cans placed on fence posts. Hap played in the cooler dirt in the shade of the water trough. The faucet dripped so that the motion of the water rippled the moss clinging to the edges and the plopping sound of water drops lessened the oppressive heat. He poked his head down close to the water level and watched the bugs landing on the moss.

When the first hints of a cooling-off came in the afternoon and the air lost some of its heat, Faith went into the corral to saddle up for a ride. Honeybunch hung her head listlessly. She stood without moving when Faith climbed the rail fence and slung the child-sized saddle on her back, but when Faith jumped down again to cinch in the strap, Honey balked.

"Come on, Honey," Faith crooned the way her father had taught her. "Let's try it again." The second time, Honeybunch permitted the cinching of the strap. Faith climbed the rail fence again and got on. Honey's legs faltered a little under the child's weight.

"Let's go." Faith clucked at her in the usual way, but Honey just stood there, blinking away flies, her head lowered. Faith flicked the reins. "Come on. Come on," she urged. She dug in her heels. Honey shifted weight. Faith kicked harder. "Get going." Honey didn't move. Faith waited. A dry gust blew some grit in her eye and she blinked away tears.

"Come on, Honeybunch." Her voice had the irritation of childhood impatience. She kicked three or four times, hard. Honeybunch staggered, going down on her front legs, then twitched violently so that she righted herself. Faith slid out of the saddle in a panic, flung the gate closed and raced toward the house.

"Pop, Pop, something's wrong with Honeybunch," she screamed.

"He's out in the pasture," Jean said, alarmed.

The door slammed and Faith ran out, yelling. Forrest heard her and came toward her cries, his strides longer than normal. He stumbled, then held out his hand to feel the periodic fence posts.

"Pop, Honeybunch won't go and she kind of fell down a little."

Forrest shuffled across the dry grass and onto the dirt area surrounding the house and barn. Faith's agitated voice was ahead of him, talking fast. He clapped his hands sharply to hear the echo off the barn to guide him. Jean came out to the corral, and Faith's yelling brought the others.

Mort whinnied. There was a scrambling sound in the corral. Honeybunch jerked in convulsions and made guttural moans. Behind her, Skippy thrashed around in grotesque movements, her legs splayed widely, out of control. She jumped as if her legs were foreign to her, extensions she wanted to shake off. Her jaw opened and shut, opened and shut. Faith stood paralyzed at the corral fence, her hand clutching Jean's skirt. Forrest opened the gate and went in toward the noise, his hands in front of him. Skippy, maddened and wild, bolted for the open gate, scraping her flank along the fence post. Her spastic movements carried her down the road past the barn toward Mother Holly's.

"Mom!" Forrie screamed. "Skippy's going crazy." He leaned up against her, his body rigid.

In an uncontrolled contraction, Honey collapsed, her legs paddling the air. Mort reared up, then backed toward Honeybunch.

"Mom, Mort's going to kick Honey," Forrie screamed. Jean held Forrie's shoulders tight in front of her. Then came the solid thud of hooves against belly, like a baseball bat against a bed pillow. She held Forrie tighter.

Mort's hard breathing and snorting told Forrest which end of the big animal was which. "Hoa, Mort," he said in a low, commanding voice. He slapped Mort on the rump, found his tail and twisted it to try to get him away from Honey. "Hoa, Mort. Hoa, Mort." Mort kicked again, inches away from Forrest. Honey lay on her side, unable to protect herself from oncoming hooves.

"Let me go," Forrie screamed. Jean tussled with thin arms and kicking legs trying to wrench themselves free. "I'm going in there."

"No, you're not."

"He needs help," Forrie screamed. "He'll get hurt."

Jean heard snorts and belches and whinnies, Faith's cries, Hap's whimpers and above it all, Forrest's breathy voice, "Hoa, Mort." Dirt sprayed her face. Rusty barked and jumped around the perimeter of the corral, as if afraid to get too close. Forrie struggled and jerked. "Let me go."

Jean held on tighter, squeezing his arms. His elbow knocked her under the chin. He fought harder to get loose. "Forrie. Go in the house!" Jean thundered, her commanding voice as foreign to her as it was to Forrie. His limbs went limp and Jean stood up straight. "The rest of you, too."

"But—"

"Go."

She felt Forrie move backwards and heard the sound of dragging feet recede. In the midst of confusion she felt, for a fraction of a second, a strange buoyancy: they were obeying. All four probably walked backwards, watching the fierce spectacle in horror as long as they dared, but they still obeyed. The door closed. She stood at the corral fence, her fingers tight around the top rail, listening for indications of what was going on.

Forrest slapped and shoved Mort away from Honey, pushing him into a separate enclosure. He turned back and headed toward where he thought he'd been, but was too far off to the right. He clapped his hands again to learn where the barn was and adjusted his course. Guttural rumbles drew him to Honeybunch. He felt for the mauled belly, half afraid to stroke it but needing to find out. Bloated. He loosened the cinch. He felt her nose. Cold. Her mouth. Cold. Abnormally cold. A sick feeling erupted in his stomach, it was so cold. Her head moved aimlessly, raising up, then flopping down again. He crouched in the dirt with her and smoothed her coat. Her head raised up again, and he put his knee under it. The skin of her neck twitched beneath his stroking hands.

"Easy, easy Honey." Honey's contractions subsided. She ceased trying to raise her head. Instead, she let it lie on Forrest's knee. "That's a good girl." His voice reached for that velvet quality, but trembled. Forrest stroked Honey's big bony head.

He couldn't hear Honey's breathing. In fact, he heard nothing but the hot wind, calmer now than earlier in the day. Honey's skin shivered once more under his touch and then was still. "Easy, Honeybunch," he murmured. After a while he got up and walked toward the fence.

"Forrest?" Jean asked. He went toward her.

"She's dead."

Forrest and Jean stood facing each other, the fence between them. Forrest put his hand on the top rail and discovered hers. "Where's Skippy?" he asked in a low voice.

"I think I heard her go out of the corral."

Forrest called for Faith to go look for her, and Faith shot out of the house toward Mother Holly's. She raced back to the corral. "Skippy's tangled in the wire fence by the highway. She isn't moving and she looks horrible." Her voice cracked.

"Go back inside."

Shock mixed with confusion. Forrest went back into the corral and felt for Honeybunch again to confirm what he thought. Her skin was motionless when he touched her. She didn't breathe. He stood up in numb incomprehension and wandered slowly around the corral, trying to piece together what had happened, listening to see if maybe there was another animal in there. He walked over to the small enclosure where he heard Mort moving around, checked his pulse and his breathing. "You okay, buddy?" he asked. Then he followed the rail to the water trough. He smelled a chemical odor and stretched out his hands to feel around the ground at the base of the trough. His hand touched a metal container. It was empty. He picked it up and went back toward the gate.

"Jean, you still here?"

"Yes."

"You'd better call the slaughterhouse." The word stabbed the truth home. Together they started back toward the house and the waiting children. "Wait a minute." Forrest turned back, clapped once and walked toward the barn. He felt for the weathered wood of the door. It wasn't where he thought it should be. He felt further to the left. The door was wide open. "Go be with the kids, Jean. I'm going to find Skippy."

He called to his mother when he got near her house, and she came out.

"I saw," she said flatly.

"Honeybunch too?"

"No, just Skippy."

"Where?"

"By the fence." They walked together to the fence by the highway. Forrest felt for Skippy's bloated belly, found a barbed wire across her neck. Her legs were angled abnormally, one on the opposite side of the fence. She didn't respond to his touch.

"What do you think happened?" Mother Holly's voice was soft.

Forrest turned to her. "What do I have in my hand?" He held up the can.

"DDT," she said softly.

He picked his way back to the house, his shoulders slumped. The incline of the dirt road seemed steeper. He heard wails and sobbing coming from the house, a chorus of hysterical voices. Jean must have told them. He walked past the house back to the corral, felt for the water trough and pulled the plug.

He took a deep breath when he approached the house. "It's the wrong time to cry," Forrest said when he entered. His flat comment changed the children's cries to sniffling whimpers.

"Who's here?"

"Everybody." Faith's voice was low.

"What's printed on this can?" He held it out.

"DDT," said Forrie. "What's that mean?"

"Insect poison." His voice sounded defeated, not angry.

In that moment, everyone knew all. The realization struck like a hatchet into green wood. Forrie, sitting on the floor by Jean's feet, buried his face in her lap. Numbness silenced the whole household. "Was anybody playing with it by the water trough?" Hap scraped his feet on the Mexican tile floor and sniffled. Forrest let the question go unanswered. Too much at one time. "I found the barn door open, too." Forrie shrank in Jean's arms, even though the words came without accusation, just as fact. "Everybody, go wash. With soap. Don't touch anything, don't eat or drink anything until you do." Forrest took the can into the kitchen, wrapped it in a grocery sack, put it deep in the trash container and washed his hands up to the elbows. In near silence Jean bathed Hap. A pall settled like a fog blanket, muffling all movement except his. For more than an hour, nobody said anything. The Santa Ana wind had stopped and, by contrast, the air seemed lifeless. Rusty hung around close to the family, his tail down, his head drooping.

Just before twilight a truck clattered up the dirt driveway and stopped by the corral gate, too narrow for the truck to go farther. Forrest went outside alone. Billy crept off to his bedroom, but Faith and Forrie pressed their noses against the window. The sign on the door of the big truck said, "Ramona Slaughterhouse, Maurie Schneider, Proprietor." They couldn't hear what Pop was saying. The two children slipped out another door and came round to watch. In the leaden end-of-day gloom, they could see the man strap ropes around Honey's stiff legs and tie the other ends to the truck. Forrest tugged at the saddle to get it free from the body, then undid the bridle and worked the bit out of Honey's mouth. The man got in the truck and drove slowly. Honey's body made a heavy rasping noise as it scraped the dirt. At the corral gate her back leg caught on the fence post, stiff enough to slow the truck momentarily until the body twisted. The truck dragged Honeybunch past the two children. Her tongue hung stiffly out of her gaping mouth so that it bounced slightly when Honey was dragged over the earth. Her eyes were open. Then the man turned a heavy crank on the back of the truck to hoist Honey onto the flat bed. It creaked with her weight.

The two children slipped back inside the house without Forrest or Jean knowing what they'd seen.

Chapter Thirty-two

Eventually, Jean roused herself to cook an ordinary supper. No one ate much. Only the parrot talked. "O-oh, say can you see" he screeched again and again, high and jarring. Jean had an uneasy feeling the children had seen too much.

What was left of the evening passed in restlessness. "No one's to blame," Jean said to break the oppressive silence, even though no one accused anyone else. They had all fallen.

Billy clanked a spoon against a half-filled glass of milk. When he moved the spoon up and down, the pitch changed. He kept it up for a long time. In the silent house, it was the only noise. "Cut that out," Faith snapped. The spoon clanked two more times and then clattered on the table. He went into his bedroom.

Tucking-in ritual would demand all Jean could muster. She knew that Hap was too young to know the part he had played in the disaster. When he found the open can of powder, he was probably curious to see what patterns it would make sprinkled over the water in the trough. Any four-year-old might have done the same. Billy asked no questions, said little. Jean was relieved that at least on the surface, he could take care of his own grief. That left only two.

When she went into Faith's bedroom, Faith finally let go the aborted tears of earlier in the day. "I kicked her. I kicked Honeybunch." She sobbed without restraint. Jean sat down on the edge of the bed, letting her cry. Faith's heavy-hearted remorse was probably a new experience for her. Obviously it didn't feel good.

"You didn't know," Jean said. "When you know someone's hurt and you hurt him more, then that's wrong, but you didn't know. The rules change when you don't know." She held the chubby hand gently, tracing the dimpled knuckles. "We can love them even though they're gone because they're still in our thoughts." She stroked Faith's head, separating her fingers so that her hair slid through. The short curls were wet at her temples. Jean continued, moving her hand more and more slowly, until her breathing became regular.

Down the hall she heard Forrie's sounds of crying slightly lower than those she'd just quieted.

"I killed them," Forrie wailed. "I killed Honeybunch and Skippy." Forrie's voice didn't seem to disturb Faith, lost in her own thoughts, but the words made Jean wince.

"No, you didn't," she heard Forrest say.

"I left the barn door open."

"I know." Forrest's voice sounded tired. Jean took her hand away from Faith who moved slightly but said nothing. Sobs from the next room subsided some. "There are reasons why we have rules, Forrie. Rules aren't made just to be mean." That velvet tone of Forrest's voice could calm anyone, she thought, but she worried that the words would set off Forrie's tears again. She stood up slowly, trying not to jostle the bed. Faith didn't make a sound, so she made her way quietly down the hall.

Forrie sniffled one big sniffle after another and then let out his breath in a squeaky sigh. "Why did Mort kick Honeybunch?" Jean stopped outside Forrie's door and listened.

"He was frightened. I guess Honey wasn't moving normally. Sometimes it happens with animals that the strong, healthy ones destroy the weak ones."

"But they were friends."

"It's different with animals, Forrie. They don't think like we do. There's something primitive or wild in animals that makes them shun the imperfect ones. They don't like to have them around. Well, maybe people are a little that way, too, only they try to hide it and animals don't."

"Why didn't Mort—?" Apparently the word stuck in his throat.

"I guess he was too dumb to take a drink on a day like today."

"I was dumb, too."

"No. We all—we've just got to be more careful from now on. Actually, dumb old Mort might have been smartest after all."

Jean went into the room and sat down on the bed next to Forrest. She reached over and found him slumped, his arms resting on his spread knees, his hands hanging down between. Wearily he hauled himself upright and left the room, giving over Forrie to her.

She knew Forrie felt the weight of responsibility too heavy for his years. He turned on his side, curving his body around hers, and cried some more. She caressed him gently. "We should remember them for the good times and for the happy horses that they were."

"All I can remember is Honeybunch jerking around and crumpling up, and then it was like she exploded or something."

"Try not to think about that."

"I can't help it. I'll probably remember it forever." Jean felt helpless to try to make him forget a sight so vivid. She knew she'd remember the thud of hooves against belly for a long time herself.

"Why did they have to die?" he asked. "Why couldn't they just be sick for a while?"

"Sometimes we can't understand everything right at the time, but maybe later we can."

She could see Forrie clearly in her mind, a narrow form covered only by a sheet, hurt and confused, with the drawn forehead of an old man who wants to sleep but whose thoughts are too active. He never had a chance to be a kid. He was forced to grow up early, and it made him too serious sometimes. He had to be their leader in public places as soon as he could walk in front of them. Even when he was six, he had to read airline tickets, guide the whole family through airports. She knew things like that were hard on him, especially with Forrest's too-demanding expectations. Always Forrie shouldered the burden that circumstances laid at his feet. She wished she could lift some of the responsibility he felt, not only for the horses, not only for watching out for the others, but even the responsibility he probably felt for her.

A half hour later Jean and Forrest sat at opposite edges of the bed in their room. Jean drew in her breath wearily and let it out in one long sigh. She felt Forrest sink down under the covers and draw her to him. She nestled his head under her chin and stroked the back of his neck. She searched for an attitude that wouldn't hurt so badly. "At least it wasn't a child." Her voice was a near whisper. He pressed his face against her, and his arms around her tightened. In a moment she felt his tears trail across her breast.

The days that followed were difficult. Forrie remained inconsolable. Often, in the middle of play with cousin Lancey at the turkey ranch or with Billy, he'd drift off by himself. Lancey told Jean, "He's always scowling, like he's mad at me or like he's doing arithmetic. He just sits in his fort and scrapes a dumb old stick on the ground."

Judy complained, too, about Faith. "She won't play with me anymore. She just goes up to the cemetery, but if I catch up with her, she turns around and goes home. I watched her there, walking around moping. She won't even ride none of the headstones. She just sits in front of her favorite grave, the one we put the bow on, but she won't talk."

The solid gloom became impenetrable, mesmerizing the family into heavy melancholy. Jean knew that four woebegone little people dragging around the house would eventually wear on Forrest, but she didn't know how to combat it.

Eventually Forrest blurted out, "All you long-faced, sad-eyed, sorry-voiced, sick-hearted, gloomy-Gus little critters are so droopy I don't know what I'm gonna do or where I'm gonna sleep tonight."

His efforts to cheer up the others by being momentarily playful were transparent to her. Better that than anger or more depression. With overzealous attention he tried all his usual methods to get a rise out of the children. While walking with Forrie, he swung his left leg out behind him and across to the right side, trying to get Forrie just behind the knee to make him collapse. He put his fingertip in Faith's ear, made a noise pretending he'd found wax or dirt, and wiped it on her shoulder. He marched his fingers across the table to Hap and Billy. One night too hot for clothes, he did a little dance down the hallway in his underwear and cowboy boots. It was the first time the children laughed. That encouraged him. He continued into the kitchen by the screen door, kicking his feet and singing a silly song until a knock and a frail voice at the screen door interrupted.

"Excuse me, but may I use your telephone, please, sir?"

The children howled, especially Forrie. "You should have seen her. Her eyes bugged out, and then she ran away."

"Who was it?"

"I don't know. Never seen her before."

There was bravery in Forrest's attempts to cheer the children—he would miss the horses no less than the children would. Jean wanted to support him in his efforts to ease the gloom. She had to do something, too, but what? She announced that she'd make their favorite Sunday dinner, roast lamb with mint jelly. "And you can swish all the jelly you want all over it."

"Can we have mashed potatoes?"

"Yes."

"And lots of gravy?"

"Yes."

"And corn?"

"Of course."

"And candles?" That was Forrie's idea of a special event, used only when they had company.

"Mmm, we'll see."

"Aw, Mom."

It hurt her to deny him something that children of other families would have as a matter of course.

"Okay, you can have candles, if you light them with your father. And we'll eat in the dining room and learn how to pass things in bowls and we'll say grace."

When the time came, Faith set the table without being asked. "Can we have a tablecloth and real napkins and everything?"

"Yes. Use the blue one with fringe. And why don't we have some music going, too." Without urging, everyone worked to buoy up everyone else.

Just as Jean was finishing, she asked Forrest to call in the others. When he passed behind her at the sink, he asked, "Where are ya? I want to plant a smooch." He put his arms around her waist from behind, tickled her below her ribs, squeezed, and then kissed her on the neck, a loud, wet kiss that made her smile. They were one in this effort—the dinner, the cheering. Even in happier times, she had never felt closer. "The dinner smells great," he said. Then he stepped out the back door by the gravel breezeway to do his characteristic whistle, an eerie sound like a mourning dove that the children could hear as far away as Indian Rock. Forrie came immediately.

"Pop, Mom said I can light the candles if you help."

"Okay. We can do it together."

That sounded nice, Jean thought. "Faith, will you take these in to the table?" She motioned to the platter of lamb already sliced, the gravy bowl and mashed potatoes.

Faith made several trips and then asked, "Where's the mint jelly?"

"Look left."

Faith picked it up. "It wiggles when I walk."

Father and son crouched on the Mexican tile floor just beside the table, Forrie sitting cross-legged.

"Got the candles?"

"Yup."

Forrest pulled out two wooden utility matches from a box with a sliding cover. "I'm going to strike the match and when it's lit, you take it and light a candle. I'll do one match for each candle."

With his little finger he felt for the rough grout between tiles, struck the match on it and held it aloft. "D'I get it?"

"Yup." Forrie took it from him at the base and lit the candle in front of him on the floor, then blew out the match. "Okay."

They did it again. Forrie took hold of both candles at their silver bases at the same time as he uncrossed his legs to stand up and put the candles on the table. He lost his balance and tipped to one side, not noticing a flame touch the fringe on the tablecloth. He centered both candles evenly on the oval table, studying to get them just right. Faith came in with a bowl of corn. "That's where I was going to put this."

"But we have to have the candles even."

"Move it, Forrie."

"No. Put that somewhere else."

"Just move everything closer so there's room," Jean said. She heard them adjust the bowls. The candles smelled funny. "Everything okay, Forrie?"

"Yup." Then she heard a gasp. "Mom, Pop, the tablecloth's burning."

"Where? How much?" Forrest asked.

The children could only stammer vague replies.

"Forrie. Take the candles," Forrest ordered. "And the bowls. Got 'em?"

A hesitant "yes" came from both children. Forrest didn't wait. He grabbed the cloth and whisked it away with a magician's gesture, only most of the dinner was still on the table. Dishes and lamb and gravy and mint jelly clattered to the floor. Instantly Forrest rolled up the flaming tablecloth, raced through the kitchen, out the utility room door and dropped it on the gravel.

Four children stood immobile, looking at their special dinner spread in a devastation of broken plates and splashed gravy over the tiles. There was a shocked silence; then all four exploded into tears. "It's my fault," Forrie wailed. "Again." He rushed at Jean and buried his face in her waist.

After a lengthy cleanup with everyone helping, Jean opened three cans of spaghetti. They sat in the kitchenette, all the gloom descending again. Jean slid in beside Forrest. He reached out to each side for someone's hand, signal for grace. Jean squeezed his hand but he shifted and pulled back, then offered it again. He must have gotten burned. She touched his hand more gingerly. "Start us off, Billy."

"God is great and God is good

And we thank him for this food.

By his hand we all are fed.

Give us, Lord, our daily bread."

For a while all Jean heard was the clink of silver against plate, Billy gulping his milk and George screeching, "O-oh, say can you see."

Perhaps Forrest had acted too quickly, but it was true— neither of them could tell how fast it was spreading. After a while she said, "It could have been much worse. Your father did the right thing."

Jean and Forrest struggled through the next week, trying to rouse the children's spirits, encouraged by the touch of each other's hand or a quiet word whispered in passing. Mutual loss bound them tighter. On Friday Forrest asked, "Anybody want to go to Mexico with Betty and Warren tomorrow?"

"Yeah, me!"

"Me, too. Yippee!" All four chorused their approval.

The route to the U.S. border town of Calexico went across mountains studded with huge rocks, then down into the low desert where population was sparse. The American Canal outlined the edge of the desert, and fields of cantaloupes, lettuce and flax grew in irrigated rows.

"Lookie, lookie," Billy said, sitting on Forrest's lap in the back seat of Warren's crowded Dodge.

"What d'ya see?" There was Forrest at it again. He never missed an opportunity to get someone to describe things, especially non-communicative Billy.

"A big machine."

"What's it doing?"

"Smoking," said Billy.

"It smells like a cotton gin," said Jean. "We found one here the last time we came."

After a while the smell changed. "We passing some alfalfa now?" asked Forrest.

"I love it," Jean said, breathing in. "It smells so fresh."

Then there came pungent animal smells.

"I can tell what this is." Forrest chuckled.

"Cows, hundreds of 'em, all bunched up together." Billy was unusually talkative.

"Must be feed lots where they fatten them up just before slaughtering them. What kind of cows?"

"Dunno."

"What color?"

"Reddish brown with white spots."

"They're probably Herefords. Are they Herefords, Warren?"

"No, more like Durhams. They've got more roan."

"What else d'ya see, Billy?"

"Horses."

The word clanged against the windshield. Forrest's effort backfired. Jean felt sure all the children had their noses glued to the windows looking, saddened and wistful, at every horse they had passed. They'd have to begin saving money to replace them.

Honeybunch and Skippy had brought too much joy. The vacancy they left carved too deeply not to have horses again. Jean tried to redirect their thought.

"Faith, read me every sign you see. That'll be your job."

"For sale. Fresh eggs."

"What else?"

"Roder—Roderigo's Garage."

"It's bright orange," said Betty from the front seat.

"U.S.-Mexico border, 3 miles."

The group of eight stayed at the De Anza Hotel where, from the wrought iron railing on the balcony, the children could see the medley of red, turquoise and passionate pink plaster buildings which was Mexico. After they got settled, they made their way across the line to Mexicali, really only across a raggedy street, to the incongruous Shangri-La Chinese Restaurant where George Wong remembered them from times before. "Missa Holly, Missy Holly, good to see you. Come in, come in. I fix barbeque pork, your favorite. Sit here." After lunch George Wong gave them change in centavos. Forrest gave a handful to each child, a fortune in 1955 Mexican buying power.

They walked along the uneven sidewalk, raised two or three steps from the street, and ate the sweet, finger-sized Mexican red bananas. Out of one doorway came the rich musty smell of rawhide. "Must be a leather shop," said Jean.

"Forrie, what's in there?" Forrest asked.

"Boots, saddles, belts, whips."

He asked at practically every doorway where there were voices or Mexican music blaring from a radio. When a child hesitated or just said, "Stuff," that would set Forrest off. The next store was a "just stuff" store.

"Let's go in." The whole family trooped in, Forrest and Jean careful to follow right behind the child leading them through the narrow aisles piled with all sorts of items, some hand-made in Mexico, some from Japan. Forrie found a mechanized charging bull that won his heart. Once outside the store, Forrest stopped on the sidewalk. "Tell me everything you saw, Forrie," he said.

"Tubes to catch your fingers in."

"Made of what?"

"Straw."

"What else?"

"Bull banks with flowers painted on. Puppets."

"Is that all?"

"Mmm." Forrie faltered.

"Not enough. Let's go back. Look more carefully this time." Jean waited with Betty while the others made the route through the store the second time and came back to the street. "Turn around," Forrest said. "Now tell me everything."

"Watches, little cameras, baskets, big paper flowers."

"What else?"

"Lanterns, wooden clacky things for your hands and those round things you shake to make music, turquoise jewelry, radios, big hats."

"Much better. Let's trade. Faithy, where are you?"

"Here."

They walked on and did another store. At the next doorway mariachis with guitars wailed a soulful love song on a scratchy radio. Forrest stopped. "What's here?"

Faith whined, but said no words. Behind them Forrie let out a quick, naughty, little boy laugh.

"Tell me. What's in that door?"

Faith still didn't answer.

"Is it a bar?" Jean whispered to Betty.

"Yes," Betty whispered back.

"Po-op."

"Tell me."

Faith pulled at her father's arm to draw his face toward hers. "I think it's a bad place."

From the rear, Forrie and Billy screamed their laughter. "Oops," Forrest said and walked on, humming the Mexican song.

Jean felt more relaxed and happy than she had all week. Forrie bought a rubber dagger, Faith a Mexican doll, Billy a bamboo rattlesnake, Hap a rubber tarantula—wondrous treasures that filled their minds and broke their somberness. Temporarily.

Chapter Thirty-three

Billy came through the gate into the patio, scraping a stick along the adobe wall. He felt restless. There was nothing to do.

"Hi, Pop." Identifying himself was automatic.

"Hey, hey, Billy. Where ya been?"

"Walking around. T'the cemetery."

"What have ya' been doing?"

"Watching a celebration." He traced the mortar between the adobes with his stick.

"Pretty soon you can take a real ride."

"Ride what?"

"Horses, of course."

"Only Faith does that. What a turtlebrain—pretending a hunk of stone's a horse."

"I don't mean a hunk of stone."

Billy stopped scraping the stick and looked at his father. It was nearly two years since Honeybunch and Skippy died. He thought Pop had forgotten about horses.

"Next week we're getting two new horses and a pony."

"All at once?" It was hard to believe.

"We got to have that many. Otherwise, how would we all go into town together to Riley's?"

"Do you mean it, Pop?"

"Course I mean it. And the pony is just your size."

The next weekend the horses were delivered in a big truck. Faith and Forrie jumped around like crazy but Billy watched from the top rail of the corral fence. When the driver led the first one out of the truck, Forrest felt him all over in order to get acquainted. "This one's Macginty, a thoroughbred," he told them. The horse was a palomino with a golden coat and white mane. "You can run like the wind, can't ya, big guy?" Forrest turned to stroke Macginty's neck. "Remember our little ride last week?" Jody was a chestnut quarter horse and Tony was a black Shetland pony. Forrest explored them, too, talking to them and stroking them. Then he led them into the corral with Mort. Billy didn't say anything, just watched from the fence, but Forrie and Faith petted each one, jabbering like parrots.

When spring came, the whole family rode the four horses into town to Riley's Cafe. Forrest rode with Hap on Mac, and Faith and Forrie rode together on Jody. That left Mort for Mom and Tony Pony for Billy.

On the way back Billy trailed along behind, unable to manage the feisty Shetland. "I only hear two of you. Who's missing?" Forrest asked.

"Billy," Faith said. "As usual."

"Get Tony on up here. He's holding us all up," Forrest called back.

"I can't."

"You can, too. Just set your mind to it."

Tony had stopped to eat grass. Billy kicked him, but he kept on eating. "I can't make him move."

"Yes, you can. You do what you got to do, just like anyone else in this world."

When Tony finally got going, it was off to the side, not following the others. Billy yanked on the reins, trying to steer the horse's head right, but it didn't work. "He won't do anything I want him to," Billy grumbled. It was hot and Billy was sweaty. Tony lurched forward from time to time, always when Billy was unready for it. "Dumb horse," he muttered and kicked Tony again, harder. He didn't want Pop to get any madder. It didn't make any difference. It was just like kicking a log you were straddling. Everybody knows you can't get a log to move.

"Maybe you're not kicking him hard enough. Show him who's boss, Billy."

That's just it, he thought. Tony is.

Billy yanked and kicked and waited. He couldn't help what Tony did. He hated it when Pop yelled, but he hated riding Tony even more. He pulled on the reins and held them in and kicked again, his eyes blurry with frustration all the way home. Just inside the fence, he slid off Tony and let him go into the pasture, saddle and all. Then he wandered out to the highway. He kicked a pebble around but that wasn't any fun, so he kept walking out toward Indian Rock. Looking for arrowheads there was boring—he never found any, only Faith and Forrie did—so he just sat down on the rock and stared, a sick feeling rumbling in his stomach.

He knew he'd done wrong by just leaving Tony without even letting Pop know. Or leaving Pop too, for that matter. When Pop would talk to him or ask him something, and he wouldn't be there to answer, Pop would get mad. And now, when Pop would find out he just let Tony go, he'd get mad all over again, only worse. Billy picked up a twig and bent it back and forth until it broke. He did it again with the pieces, then threw them into the greasewood bushes. Pop would be waiting for him when he got back, standing there like he always did, his head facing straight ahead, his eyes blinking. Putting it off would only make it worse. He stood up and squinted into the sun.

When he got back, Pop was standing by the corral gate, right where he knew he would be, just as if Pop knew exactly when he'd be coming home. He could try to be quiet, but what was the use? It'd happen eventually. He scuffed and dragged his boots in the dirt even though he knew Pop didn't like dust raised on purpose.

"What were you thinking of, going off by yourself and letting Tony go? What's got into you?"

"Nothing."

"Don't you sass me. Why'd you do it?" Billy didn't even want to talk. "Look at me."

Dumb thing for him to say, Billy thought, but he did as he was told anyway. Pop was scowling.

"Why'd you do it?"

"Didn't want to."

"Didn't want to?" Pop bellowed. "What do you mean, didn't want to?"

"To do anything with Tony."

"That's part of the ride."

"I couldn't. He won't ever do what I want him to. I can't ever—"

"Don't go crawfishin' around making excuses. Now you go out into that pasture and bring him in and tend to him like you ought to. I don't want you in the house until you finish, you hear?"

Billy turned. He couldn't stand it when Pop looked that way. "Don't ever want to ride a horse again," he muttered. He dragged his feet through the tall grass, yanked some out and flung it into the air. "Everybody's always yelling at me, and the stupid horse does just what he wants."

Out in the pasture Billy saw that the reins had fallen between Tony's two front legs. A hard, hurting place formed high up under Billy's rib cage. He knew he'd have to reach down there between Tony's legs and get the reins. When he approached, Tony backed away. Billy snatched the reins and pulled them tight, but Tony didn't budge. They struggled. "Stupid horse," Billy said. "Can't you do anything I want?" Tony didn't come in until he was good and ready, and when they finally headed toward the corral, Billy knew that he wasn't actually bringing the horse in. Tony was bringing him in.

Pop wasn't outside anymore. Good. In the corral, Billy unsaddled Tony easily enough, but when it came to getting the bit out of his mouth, Tony went after his hand. Billy pulled back, but not in time. Tony bit. "Damn you," Billy yelled. He grabbed for the bit again and yanked it clean.

"Never going to ride you again," he cried. "Never ever." His tears made it hard to see what he was doing, but still he slung the bridle on the hook, did only what he had to do and pushed the corral gate closed with an angry shove. It swung all the way through and creaked open again. He kicked dirt up on his way to the house, and it made his eyes water even more. If any of the horses got out, he'd catch it again, only worse. He turned on his heel, ran back to the gate and latched it, then ran for the house. Inside the door, he made a beeline for his room.

"Well? Did you do it?" Forrest's voice thundered.

Billy grunted, afraid to talk.

"Answer me straight. Did you finish?"

"I said yes." His voice cracked, and he shot through the living room to the bathroom to clean his hand. He wrapped it in gauze, then bolted down the hall. His bedroom door slammed closed.

A while later someone tapped at his door. "May I come in?"

It was Mom. "Yeah."

"Where are you?"

"Bed."

She sat down next to him, took him in her arms and rubbed his head. It made him cry again, but he tried hard not to make any noise.

"I know it's not easy to bring in your pony, but finishing off is an important thing to do."

"Nothing ever goes right for me," he said, half a sob and half a mumble. "I can't do anything right."

She rubbed the back of his neck. Her hand felt cool. "I know how you feel." She didn't say anything for a long time, just rubbed his neck. "I wish you didn't feel that way, Billy, but do you know something? I feel that way sometimes, too."

"You?"

"Sure I do. I felt that way every day right after I married your father and I didn't know how to cook. I burned or spilled or ruined practically everything I made. And he was harsh with me, too. But that didn't mean he didn't love me."

Billy grunted.

"It took me a long time, and tears too, to learn that. Slowly it got better." Billy let her hold him for a while and he relaxed. "And I'll tell you something else. I'm not all that excited about riding horses either."

"You aren't? I never knew that." He lay back on the pillow and looked at her. Her eyes were kind of misty, as though she had been the one crying. A bruise on her forehead was almost gone now, only a green shadow. She always had bruises. As soon as one was gone, another one came. A brown curl turned the wrong way.

"You know when we have to jump the horses to get across the gully at Santa Maria Creek?"

"Yeah."

"I always get scared there. I don't think Mort will know where to put his feet. When Forrie or Faith yell 'get ready, Mom,' I always feel a hard knot in my chest and I can't breathe."

"You never told anybody."

"Except you." Her voice was a near whisper. Her hand stroked his arm, but when she got near the gauze, he drew his hand away. "I haven't really been comfortable riding a horse since I was in boarding school."

"Then why do you?"

"Because it means a lot to your father."

She said it facing forward, the way she often said things, not looking down at him, but just out. He turned on his side, and she reached to stroke his arm again. Her hand felt soft on his skin. He wondered about her, how she could ride a horse. He hadn't thought about it, or other things she did, before. She seemed strange to him, like he didn't know her. "Mom?"

"Yes?"

"What can you really see?"

It looked like the question shocked her a little. She didn't move her head, just blinked and kept facing straight ahead. It took her a while to answer. She moistened her lips first, as if she had to do that to speak.

"Nothing, Billy. Sometimes it's just a little lighter than other times. That's all."

She did a funny thing with her mouth, squeezing her lips together just for a second. Then she reached for him and began to rub his arm. When her hand got close to the bandage he jerked slightly, but didn't move away. She touched it.

"What's this?"

"Nothing."

Her fingers moved gently over the gauze where the dried blood had made it crusty. "What happened?"

"Nothing." She didn't need to know. What would she do about it? Probably nothing.

"Billy."

Her voice was pleading and it made his throat swell. "Tony kind of bit me." He pulled his hand back. "It's okay. I don't want to talk about it." He rolled over on his side, away from her.

Jean left the room feeling hollow. He was so untouchable. This was one child with whom she feared failing. He was an enigma to her, only a shadowy presence. Like an iceberg three-quarters hidden, he glided about in mistiness, just out of reach. He was not inarticulate, yet he talked so rarely. If she could only see to read his face. He gave her so little to go on, and then sometimes, like this, he shut her out.

She walked into the kitchen and stood at the sink. There was a separateness about him, not one of space merely, but of time. He was so different from Faith or Forrie. He seemed to be waiting to live, not living now. He didn't enter into the boisterous cowboy games Forrie played. Instead, he would climb into the barrels of horse candy in the barn and eat it. Or he'd climb into the fireplace or sit up on the roof for hours. Often when Betty and Warren or Heddy and Karl came in the evening, Billy wordlessly snuggled up to them on the sofa with a winsomeness that demanded nothing, only the pleasure of being there.

Once, she couldn't find him all afternoon. She walked through each room, called his name and listened. She asked Faith to look in the barn. She called the logical places—Franny Nelson's, Lance's, and Mother Holly's. Franny walked in an hour later and discovered him right there in the living room all the time, curled up on the sofa facing the fireplace.

"What have you been doing?" she asked.

"Sleeping."

"When did you wake up?"

"I don't know."

She wasn't sure she believed him. It had annoyed her at the time because she thought he enjoyed playing possum, underscoring her disadvantage. It made her feel watched and tricked. Continually, he withdrew from interaction, and now again today he pulled away from her. She felt inadequate, not knowing whether to draw him out or just let him retreat to his own dreamy world. A world far different from what Forrest would have for him, that's for sure. Billy retreated from Forrest too. It was wearisome always softening Forrest's sternness. A father couldn't always be so demanding; he'd drive his children away. She'd have to confront him. Billy would wither, otherwise. Even though Billy had turned away from her, maybe she had reached him with something that bound them closer. Maybe. And maybe not. She knew Forrest hadn't felt anything like that with Billy, and she wanted it for him, too.

That night in their bedroom, they were quiet as they got ready for bed. Forrest was often uncommunicative when mulling something over. Under the cool sheet she reached out, felt the ropey muscles of his back toward her and moved closer. In bed at night certain things could be said that couldn't be said in the day.

"Go easy on him, Forrest. He's just a little boy. Hardly eight years old." She spoke slowly, pausing.

"Well, it's time he grew up."

"But he can grow up in his own way. He doesn't have to grow up in yours."

She could tell he was holding tight onto his opinion and his anger. Even though she stroked his back and neck, it was a long time before he relaxed. When she told him about Billy's hand, he tightened up again. "That might not have happened if you'd let him be."

He didn't answer, but his body was rigid against hers. He had heard her. That she knew. Maybe that was all she needed to say. She tried to stay awake trailing her fingers along his neck and shoulders from behind. After a while, her hand slowed and then stopped and she slept.

Forrest was quiet in the morning, unusual for him who always woke up robust and ready for a new day. In fact, he was subdued most of the week, and he worked late each night. The next Saturday he went out to do some gardening. She passed by a window and heard him talking in the patio, heard the snap of pruning shears.

"See any roses?" she heard him say.

"Uh-huh. Two." It was Billy's voice. She stood still to listen.

"What do they look like?"

"Fat red ones."

"Only two?"

"Nope. One more. But it's only a bud. It doesn't count."

"Sure it does. Didn't you know that inside that bud, wrapped tight around each other, are all the parts that the big opened ones have? There are just as many petals and a center, only it's not time for it yet."

"When'll it open?"

"When it's ready."

"How does it know?"

"It just knows, all by itself." She heard two more snips of the pruning shears. "Just like you."

Billy didn't respond, but at least she didn't hear him walking away. Her eyes teared a little, not for Billy this time, but for what Forrest must have undergone this week.

Chapter Thirty-four

A rooster crowed.

"And God saw everything that he had made, and behold, it was very good." Jean felt Forrest shift positions. Her voice was soft so as not to disturb the children when she read the Brailled Bible lesson to him in the morning sitting up in the big bed, covers still wrapped up to their middles.

Two feet padded down the hallway and a small form climbed into the bed and settled himself between them. It was six-year-old Hap. Soon his breathing became heavier, more regular. When Jean finished and got up, the motion of the bed woke him.

She walked out to the kitchen and filled the tea kettle. His footsteps followed her.

"Mommy, it's foggy out. Can't see anything," Hap said.

"What's it look like?" she blurted, her question pouncing on his stray comment. She held her breath and heard him climb into the breakfast booth by the kitchen window.

"Gray. Trees are gray. Barn's gray. We're trapped in here. Can't go out."

"You can. Later. It'll go away when the sun comes out."

She relaxed. If it was color he was responding to, that was okay. She opened the kitchen door and stood outside for a moment. The air did feel damp. She heard the shower water and the hum of Forrest's electric shaver. A mourning dove gave a distant who-whoo. The tea water boiled and the kettle began to screech. She took it off the burner and stirred the oatmeal. The pull on her spoon told her it was almost ready. "Hap, go get the others. Time for breakfast."

"*Sacca la puerta, Cocareeto.*" George was waking up too. She reached into his cage to refill his water cup. "*Cocareeeto.*" He stretched out the third sound of the greeting learned from Celerina. She wondered what it meant.

A knock on a door, then, "Hurry up, Flappy." Forrie's voice down the hallway sounded impatient. A toilet flushed and a door opened. "About time, two-ton."

"Mom," Faith wailed as she came into the kitchen. "Forrie called me Two Ton."

"Well?"

The single word silenced her.

A hand placed on the upper register of the piano scraped all the way down to the last base note. It set off George.

"Mommy, George's been chewing his perch again," Hap said.

All four scrambled into the kitchen booth.

"Can I have syrup on my cereal?" Faith asked.

"A little."

"What day is today?" Billy asked.

"Monday."

"But no school. Summer. Yippee!"

She smiled. Though summer stretched long ahead of her, this first day of liberation always brought high spirits.

Someone opened the refrigerator door, letting out coolness into the room. It stayed open for a long time.

"Close the door."

"I can't find the syrup."

"It's there. Just look."

"But I can't find it," she whined.

Jean walked over to the refrigerator, stretched both hands in, felt the tops of a row of bottles along one side, and pulled out the syrup. "Having eyes, see ye not?"

Forrest's hard shoes echoed down the hallway.

"This cereal's lumpy," Hap grunted.

"Eat it anyway," Forrest said, coming into the kitchen.

"Can't. Lumps as big as marbles."

"Just got to take the lumps as they come. They're good for you, too. Why, I like lumps better than the smooth stuff."

"You can have mine."

A crash in George's cage sent a shower of seeds onto the table. Piercing squawks and a flutter of wings followed.

"What happened?" Jean asked.

Caught in a fit of laughing, no one could answer. She heard Forrest chuckling, and she began to laugh, too.

"He fell down, right through his perch," Faith explained between gasps.

"He looks so funny, like he doesn't know what happened. What a seed brain," Forrie said.

"Rubbed his beak on that old stick one too many times, did he?" Forrest said.

"Hey, there's seeds in my cereal," Billy grumbled.

All mornings weren't like this, but when they were, the day seemed to zing by, and before Jean was ready, Forrest would be home from work. Now that he had his contractor's license, he had an office in town. It was different not having him nearby, but all right, too. In fact, some days it was a relief.

She put a load in the washing machine and then opened the windows to let in some air while it was still cool. The windmill across Ash Street began to thrum as the midmorning breeze picked up. She could hear it squeak when it turned its tail away from the wind and the blades twirled. The change in the direction of the wind brought a rumble of cackling and cawing from Heddy and Karl's chicken ranch. The sound of 40,000 chickens was almost like a waterfall. Karl's doing well, she thought. That's good. They deserve some prosperity. She thought she smelled warm feathers. Too early to smell the droppings. They hadn't heated up to a pungent odor yet because of the fog. When the wind changed again, and the windmill slowed and squeaked to a stop, like a train pulling in to a station, the chicken noises diminished and she became conscious of a low engine roar. Airplanes never fly over Ramona, but it couldn't be anything else. It grew louder and more ominous. The children ran outside.

"Wow, look at him," Forrie squealed and made engine sounds. It made Jean smile.

"Look at how high he is," said Faith.

"Look at what?" Hap's voice sounded bewildered.

"Over there."

"I can't see anything."

"Right there, right where I'm pointing."

"Oh," Hap muttered. Then the horn on his trike sounded three times. "Move it."

The air became drier as morning progressed, and she could smell the eucalyptus trees on the road edge. Mockingbirds in the pepper trees sang an infinite variety of notes. Japanese glass wind chimes at Franny's tinkled faintly.

"Got any string, Mom?"

"Have. Do you have any string," she corrected. Forrie was eleven now, old enough to say it right. "Bottom drawer in the service porch. What are you going to do?"

"Fly kites. Chucky doesn't ever have any string. We wanna send messages to the graves."

"How?"

"See, we make these little notes and send them up on our kite strings with a paper clip. Then we yank on 'em and they fall down over by the cemetery."

She heard him rustling in the drawer. Then the door slammed. The motor on the well hummed, high and whining, when the breeze brought it to her. A truck on the highway shifted gears near the crest of the hill and set Mother Holly's peacocks to screeching. She heard footsteps on the roof. Must be Billy. She headed outside to the clothesline with her laundry basket. Already there was the constant, high, raspy hum of cicadas. One of the horses whiffled. A lone meadowlark pierced the morning with its liquid song. It chilled her with its beauty. She fed on the sounds. They spoke of continuity and order. The temperature felt a few degrees hotter than the last time she was outside. She walked back to the house, let the basket fall to the floor of the service porch and puffed out a sigh.

"Why do you always sigh like that?" Faith asked.

She listened again for the meadowlark.

"Mom, why do you always do that?"

"Hm? Do what?"

"Why do you always sigh?"

Kids can ask a question a dozen times, she thought. "Oh, I guess it feels good. It just feels good to sigh sometimes."

"Are you sad, Mom?"

"Not a bit."

"Me either."

Faith's sandals scraped against the floor on her way into the living room. She pulled the piano bench out and drummed her fingers on the base notes. She began the first three measures of her lesson. Long ago she had graduated from *Teaching Little Fingers to Play* and was now on *Thompson's Book II*. She pounded out a simple arpeggio.

The telephone rang. It was someone from the Junior Women's Club asking if Jean would help again with the father-and-son banquet. Yes, of course she would. It had been fun the year before. Together they baked twenty turkeys. Jean was given the job of grinding onion in a meat grinder for dressing because she could do it with her eyes closed. She had felt part of the community. The women were genuine and she enjoyed being with them.

Another truck came barreling down the highway, its brakes screeching on the down side before it climbed up to the crest at Mother Holly's.

"Will you play 'Kentucky Babe,' Mom?"

The truck sound made Jean wonder.

"Mom, will you play 'Kentucky Babe?'"

"Now?"

"Yeah."

"Just a minute." She finished loading the washing machine again and sat down at the piano. "Watch my right hand."

Before she finished, the doorbell rang. Nobody in Ramona rang doorbells. They just you-whooed or knocked. Jean and Faith both went to the door.

"Is this your boy, ma'm?" came a husky male voice.

"Hap!" Faith cried. "Where've you been?"

"Yes, I guess he is," Jean said.

"I found him on his bike, going down the middle of the highway, right down the center line. You'd be right smart to keep an eye on this kid, ma'm. We have to get rolling pretty fast to make it up the hill when we're loaded."

Jean stammered out her thanks and apologies and then scolded Hap.

After lunch the air hung heavy. Humidity always made her neck sticky, but this day there was a restlessness in the air that made her slightly nervous. She heard Rusty chasing the hens, his barks competing with their cackles. Thunder rumbled low. It sounds a long way away, she thought, remembering her sheets on the line.

"Faith, what color's the sky?"

"Kind of gray."

"You let me know, won't you, if it looks like it's going to rain."

A door slammed. "Mommy, here's the mail."

"Bring it to me, Hap."

She felt through the stack. One envelope had the bottom left corner clipped off. For years that had been Lorraine's method of letting her know a Braille letter was inside. She opened it and read. Lorraine's husband's union was still on strike. "We're getting by, though," Lorraine had written, "and a settlement is promised any day now. I have three more piano students so that helps." Typical of Lorraine always to be cheerful. Then, in Lorraine's characteristic fashion, she commented on every bit of news Jean had told her of the children. It was good to have a friend so interested in the details of her life.

"But I have to tell you one sad thing," the letter said. "Last week I saw in the newspaper that Miss Jennings died. It got me to thinking of all the kind things she did and how she brought us together. I felt badly that she may not have known what she really did for us, our friendship." Dear Lorraine. Her heart was so good. If they had lived closer to each other, she might have loved Lorraine as a sister.

Jean felt through the rest of the mail and found a stiff, square envelope, the kind that always contained Sound Scriber records from Mother. She opened it and put it on the machine. "Hello all. Today is Wednesday, so I'm headed for the reading club soon. Yesterday Lucy came to swim with the children. The twins are growing up so nicely. Sam was voted most valuable player of his hockey team....We're going to the club at Farmington tonight.... The Barnes are on another cruise, to the Bahamas again....The Ingrahams just got back from London with lots of stories." News hadn't changed much. Mother's voice sounded as it always had, gentle but this time a little tired.

"Mommy, how do they tell what day it is at Grandma's?"

She smiled. Certain things always puzzled Hap. "The same way we do here."

"But it's different. Forrie said today is Monday and they're on Wednesday there."

Jean laughed and then explained. "When the others come in, we can make a record for her and, Faith, you can play 'Dance of the Hours' on the piano."

She heard sheets flapping outside on the clothesline. She opened the back door and stepped outside. The sultry air felt solid, as if it hung low over the house. "It feels like rain for sure. Is the sky darker, Faith?"

"Yeah."

"Don't say 'yeah.' Say 'yes.'"

"Yes. I can see it raining."

"Where?"

"Over the mountains. I can't even see Mt. Palomar. It's all gray."

Thunder cracked and seemed to shake the earth. She picked up the basket, went out to the clothesline and walked right into a sheet. Thunder clapped again, louder, as if struggling to free itself. It made her lift her shoulders involuntarily. A drop of water plopped on her cheek. She hurried to get the sheets in. A few flaps of wings and an angry squawk came from over near the corral.

"Get away, you," she heard Hap say. "You meanie."

Rain plopped faster, but she made it back in with the dampened sheets while it was still in the threatening stage. The screen door banged a second time behind her.

"Mommy, Roosty's a mean old bird. I don't like him anymore."

"Why? What happened?"

"He jumped off the fence and flew at me."

"Were you bothering him, Hap?"

"Nope. He's just mean, that's all. He pecked at me for no reason."

"Where?"

"Right in my face."

"You have to leave him alone. He didn't hurt you, did he?"

"Naw."

The rain came in big, splats, not the steady, day-long rain of winter, but the short, spontaneous outburst of a fast-moving summer storm. It smelled muddy. She heard more doors slam as the others came inside. A sharp breeze caught Franny's wind chimes and made them jangle. The rain interrupted play, and the children, impatient to be outside again, bickered in whiny voices. She heard one child following her around, not saying anything.

"Can I have some ice cream?" Faith called from the kitchen.

"What time is it?" Jean asked.

"Two-thirty."

That seemed about right. She didn't recall hearing a clock chime three times. "Yes."

"She eats too much," Forrie muttered. "That's why she's so fat."

"Oh, Forrie, don't say that." The rain stopped as suddenly as it began. Jean stepped outside to the patio. After-rain air was always so still. The dust that had hung suspended was settled now, tramped down by the gift of water drops. She reveled in the coolness and tried to think of something that needed doing outside.

"What are you going to do next?"

A funny question for Forrie to ask, she thought. "Oh, fold the laundry, I guess."

"When's Pop coming home?"

"The usual time." Another odd question. "Betty and Warren are coming to dinner tonight."

"Can you fold the laundry in your room?"

"I suppose so."

They walked down the hallway, Forrie carrying the laundry basket. Once inside, he closed the door.

"Mom, I got to tell you something." His voice quavered with urgency.

She chuckled softly. "I could tell." They sat on the edge of the bed.

"No, something real big. You're not going to like it." He paused for that to sink in and when he began again, his voice was strangely off key. "'Member when Chucky was here this morning?"

"Yes."

"We went out to the clubhouse." He came to a dead stop, his usual way of making her guess so he wouldn't have to say it outright. She just waited. "Nobody was around. I don't know where he got it, but Chucky, he had a real cigarette."

Ah, so that was it. Jean still didn't say anything, forcing him to go on.

"And he lit it. And smoked it." His voice rose a half register. "And I did, too. Oh, Mom, I'm sorry. I knew you wouldn't like it." The words tumbled out between sobs. "And Pop. He'll whomp me if he knows." He flung himself at her and buried his face in her lap. "I know I did wrong." The words were muffled.

Her heart ached for him. She had felt the same fascination when she was his age. Still, she knew that remorse was necessary to bring the lesson home. His shoulders shook, and he made funny gasping sounds reaching for air. She stroked his shoulders and they shook some more.

She let him cry in tortured suspense for a while. "I'm glad you told me. You did the right thing by telling me, even though it was wrong to do it just because Chucky did."

"I know," he wailed with all the pain of hearing what he already knew.

"You don't need to do it anymore, do you?"

"No." His voice was hardly more than breath. He sniffled. She let him keep his head on her lap until no more sounds came.

Forrie stayed in the bedroom with her and sorted the socks while she folded the rest of the laundry. When they were through, she opened the door and heard the television. She walked across the living room up close to the TV so as not to trip over a child on the rug. Briskly she felt her way, an arm's length from the wall, but even there, within two feet of the television, she stumbled into someone and had to catch her balance quickly. "Who's that up so close?"

"Me," Hap said.

The one muttered syllable clutched at her heart.

The afternoon wore on with clucking of chickens, an occasional sneeze of a horse, doors constantly opening and swinging shut, child talk. In a way, she felt privileged to hear Forrie's agonized confession. It meant he trusted her and that was precious to her. The motor on the well hummed a high whine. A cow mooed its hunger, and a killdeer repeated its thin, three-note whistle. She loved the sound, all the sounds—cows, dogs, footsteps, birds, even Forrie's sobs. They were sufficient. Children and animals and breezes moved around her, but did not penetrate completely. Maybe not seeing was a way to be alone, to experience a semi-solitude, peaceful and reflective. A million things could be going on around her, she realized, but none of them as significant as her own thinking. Perhaps she had, after all, a filtering process that eliminated the trivial in order to embrace something truer.

She stirred the spaghetti sauce on the stove. The oregano smelled rich and musty and the steam made her eyes water. The day had passed so quickly she hardly had a chance to value it. Living was good today. Bursting with love for everything around her, she felt close to the Creator of it all. *Forgive me for not appreciating it enough,* she thought.

A car drove up, a door opened and closed, and the car drove off. Rusty barked and Forrest's whistle came up the dirt road. The sounds—animals, children and now Forrest—and the thoughts alive in her mind, *they're all so good and real,* she thought. *Maybe those who can see the ants in the cupboards and the sullen pout on a child's face are more distracted and see less of the good things.* It was a dear, not-to-be-repeated day, and when it was all over she would share it with Forrest.

She positioned herself in the doorway so that he'd find her. "Hi," she said.

"Hey, Jeanie, baby. We had some rain, huh?" He walked right into her and kissed her on the side of her face, right by her ear. They stood together, arms around each other, loving their closeness. It was good to feel that he anticipated this moment every day too.

After dinner they sat on the patio, the sounds of sunset full of harmony—coffee cups in saucers, quiet talk with Betty and Warren, a radio in Faith's room playing "Love Letters in the Sand." Jean smelled the fecund odor of the damp earth. Warren's mellow guitar joined the crickets to usher in the night.

"Hey, itty bitty buddy, how about a little horseback ride?"

"Forrest, it's black dark out here."

"So?" The one flat syllable came quietly.

Warren didn't respond. Jean guessed that he didn't want to refuse him. She sympathized. There was no refusing Forrest once he got an idea in his head. Warren continued playing while Forrest headed for the barn. She heard him clap twice.

After a while he brought the horses up to the house. The music stopped and horse sounds started.

"You take Mort and I'll ride Mac."

"Be careful, Warren," Betty said.

The clomp of hooves on the earth retreated until they heard only crickets, coyotes yapping their haunting, high-pitched chorus, as if there were a hundred of them out in the darkness, and close by, a boy's voice.

"Mrs. Kenworthy, please may I play Mr. Kenworthy's guitar?" Forrie sounded so serious.

"If you hold it carefully and sit in that chair, you can."

Soon Forrie was making vague, dreamy strums on the guitar while Betty and Jean talked.

Even a sheet was too much that hot night. Forrest kicked the covers off the end of the bed. "It was beautiful riding out there, Jeanie." His voice echoed the sable softness of the night.

"You knew Warren didn't really want to go, didn't you?"

"Well, yeah, I guess so, but he did all right." Forrest chuckled, then turned toward her.

Lying there on the cool sheet with the cricket music and Forrest's presence surrounding her, she knew that the logical consequence of coming to know someone so nakedly was embracing him with all his faults—his continual stretching of others, his refusal to see the obvious, his too-quick judgments and too-demanding expectations. She had to see with love, and what love sees, however imperfect, is whole and beautiful.

Chapter Thirty-five

"Oh, you're so stupid," Forrie said. "Don't you know how dumb you look?"

"We do not. What's it to you?" Faith returned.

They probably did look pretty silly, Jean thought. She had given Faith some worn-out high-heeled shoes, an old fur coat from Hickory Hill and a lipstick Franny had told her looked too dark and gaudy. Faith pranced around the living room, clomping in the too-big pumps, Billy escorting her in a black Zorro costume.

"You're too fat," Forrie said. "Hundred and plenty, that's what you are." He had latched onto that when she weighed in at 120 on their new scale.

"Mind your own business, dodo."

"Hush up the fussing, you hear?" Forrest snapped. "It's Sunday afternoon. Let's have a little peace around here. Go outside."

"You two look so stupid I can't stand to look at you," Forrie said.

"Forrie!" Jean chided, but got no response. She winced when the door slammed after him.

"Come on, Billy. Let's go," Faith said. "It isn't any fun in here anyway." The door banged again.

"I can't stand it, hearing them at it all the time. It's getting worse," Forrest said.

"Forrie always has to have the last word," Jean said.

"It's not just him. It's all of them."

Quiet settled deliciously when the children were outside, but after a while, Faith's stubborn voice rose to a high pitch from beyond the patio wall. "We can be here if we want to. It's a free country."

"Fatty." Forrie's tease shot back. He came inside again. "Mom, Faith and Billy are bothering me."

"Well, just leave them alone."

"I been trying to." The door slammed again. Jean heard her high heels scraping on the tile floor. "Give me back my Zorro cape." Forrie's voice was pouty. "You didn't ask."

"He doesn't have to," Faith chimed in. "I told you already, it's a free country. Can't you even hear?"

"That's it. I'm fed up with this nonsense," Forrest muttered, and stormed outside.

She knew Faith's last comment got to him—impairment too close to his own. "Hold it down," she warned. "Your father's getting upset."

"She thinks she's the boss," Forrie retorted. "Well, I'll tell you one thing, Two Ton. You're a big, fat boss."

"Cut it out, dumbbell."

"You think you can tell everybody what to do. Acting like a mother. But you're a messy slob."

"I'm warning you, Forrie."

"And I'm warning both of you," Jean interjected. "Drop it."

"Your room looks so sloppy, you ought to be ashamed," Forrie said. "What if President Eisenhower came here and saw that? Then you'd be sorry."

That's one for Forrie, Jean thought. He's right about that.

"Just wait till I tell Mom what it looks like."

"Shut up."

"Or I'll tell Pop. I'll tell him right now."

Forrie started for the door. Jean heard the solid thud of fist against flesh. "Stop it," she said. "Go to your rooms."

Forrie slugged Faith back and pushed. "Can't even knock you down, you're so fat."

"Stop it right now, before your father comes back." She wondered where Billy was. Lost in the middle, probably, not quite sure where his loyalties lay. Another smack.

"Cut it out," Faith wailed.

"Make me."

"Shut up." They fell to tussling on the floor.

"Hold it." Forrest's voice thundered as he came back into the house. "I've had enough from you hamburgers." For years that word, incongruous though it was, meant that the jig was up. Forrie and Faith were suddenly silent. "Come over here, all three of you, and stand face to face."

"He started it," Faith whined.

"I did not. Billy took my Zorro cape and you—"

"Quiet," Forrest bellowed. Jean jumped at the sound. "I don't—*ever*—want to hear another quarreling, self-justifying word from any of you." It was his tone of voice that told them he was serious, that and the long pause before the expected word "ever," as if it were hard to get out. Even Jean always waited for the word. It was bound to come. "Now stand still and belly up. Closer."

He took the rope he'd brought back with him from the barn and wound it around all three meek, silent children four or five times so they were bunched in a tight bundle, their arms strapped to their sides, their legs tied so that they couldn't walk. "Just like a roped steer," Forrest muttered. The loop that got Forrie across the chest, got Billy around the back. "Not another word until you're untied. By me." Forrest left the room. The shock made them all speechless.

Jean was as surprised as the children. She had to smile, imagining them standing there in a triangle, brothers and sister actually touching each other. She guessed that eye contact was nil even though three sets of eyes must be only inches apart. The only sounds were belabored breathing, air puffing out of dilated nostrils, and the tick of the Ingraham clock. Maybe Forrest was being too harsh, but if it worked, it was worth it. The quiet was heavenly, and she sat down with a Braille book. Her hands moved regularly across the pages.

Hap came into the living room, let out a quick derisive laugh, but cut it off abruptly. The glare from six eyes must have silenced him. As if to accentuate his freedom of movement, his bare feet slapped the tile floor as he went through the dining room to the kitchen. He opened and closed the refrigerator twice, banged several cupboards and finally settled on some noisy potato chips. Jean practically laughed. Hap rarely ate potato chips, but they were Faith's favorite.

He came back into the living room. "Mom, there's nothing to do."

"Well, let's see. Why don't you find Eddie and play with your airplanes?" Franny's boy, Eddie, was Hap's eternal shadow. Jean listened to their play enough to know that Eddie would throw his little balsawood airplane and go get it himself, but when Hap threw his, he'd tell Eddie to go get it.

"He had to go visit his grandma," Hap said. "Guess what."

"I don't know. What?"

"This morning me and Eddie took this magnifying glass and—"

"Eddie and I."

"Yeah, and we held it over an ant." Hap giggled. "He stopped walking."

"Then what?"

"He started smoking." Hap's giggle turned into a laugh.

Jean imagined the poor, unfortunate bug incinerated in his tracks. "That's not kind, Hap. You shouldn't do that."

"Aw, Mom, it's only a bug."

"What if you were a bug?"

She knew his actions had been motivated by a wish to know, to discover the secret of those little lives, rather than by cruelty, but it still bothered her. "Are you still tying strings to moths?" He had told her once how he and Eddie tied thread to the bodies of flying insects, but didn't kill them. Then the insect could only fly around in circles while the boys held the thread.

"Naw."

"Good."

"I want to. I just can't do it no more."

"Anymore. Why not?"

"Just can't."

Jean pulled in her breath. It was coming. Three years earlier she'd been told. Inherited myopia.

Outside, Rusty barked at something which caught Hap's attention. He ran out the front door.

A half hour later Forrest came back into the living room.

"Now do you think you can be friends without squabbling?"

"Yes," Faith and Forrie chorused, their voices sounding droopy.

"Billy?"

"Yup."

"From now on, every morning I want each one of you to greet each other pleasantly, and say good night to each other kindly. Every night. Not grumpy, either, but with common courtesy. You know the hymn says to 'speak kindly when we meet and part' and we're going to do it. And Hap, too."

"Dumb idea."

"Faith." His voice rose threateningly.

"Okay."

Faith's phoney bass tone showed that she was beaten, at least temporarily.

The next morning as each one came out to the breakfast nook, she heard a litany of greetings. "Good morning, Mom, good morning, Pop, g'morning, Forrie, morning, Billy, morning, Hap." Faith's voice started strong and ran out of breath midway, but at least she got through them. In the weeks that followed, Jean thought they dropped their ritualistic monotony and began to sound more natural.

Hap wasn't usually involved in the wrangling of the others. As the youngest, he was left out of their quarrels. He spent a lot of time with Betty Kenworthy. Ever since he was a baby, they had a special affection for one another. In fact, some days it seemed like Betty was a heaven- sent help. With no children of her own, Betty poured out her love in gentle, wise doses to Hap. Sometimes he spent the night or the weekend with Betty and Warren. She taught him poems, made Christmas nativity scenes with him, taught him about trees and birds. She let him pick the geraniums in her yard. At six years old, he was beginning to read, his nose buried in his book, and Betty helped him to learn.

When Betty and Warren brought him back one rainy afternoon, Warren lifted Hap up onto his shoulders in one great swoosh. It was something Forrest never did. Hap squealed his delight. "The world is spinning," he said.

"He's probably never been that high before," Jean said.

As soon as Warren set him down, Hap wanted him to do it again.

Betty took Jean aside into the laundry room. "Hap and I had a picnic in the lemon grove." Her voice was low and serious. "I asked him to bring me all the lemons on the ground. He brought about half a dozen. I rolled them out like balls and asked him to bring them back to me. When I rolled them about eight or ten feet, he'd trot out and bring them back. But I kept increasing the distance." Betty paused. "Jean, he can't see a lemon beyond fifteen feet."

Jean's forehead knotted together. "I suspected as much." Her throat closed. "I thought he'd have more time." It became hard to talk, but she wanted to, now that it was obvious to others. "Several years ago, I found him watching TV through a toy telescope. It worried me, so we took him to a specialist." Her voice cracked to a falsetto. "Inherited weakness, he said. Nothing can be done." She felt her upper lip quiver and she stood there awkwardly, not knowing what to do with her hands. Suddenly she felt Betty's arms around her.

A week later Hap padded into Jean's bedroom after dinner. "Mommy, I see green shadows, kind of ripply ones out to the side. When I move my head they go away, but then they come back."

At that moment, something inside her ruptured. "Don't move your head. Don't turn it from side to side." With her hands on both of his temples, she marched him off to bed.

"It looks like I'm looking through an insect wing, shiny colors like a fly has." he said. "Why?"

"I'm not sure. Hold your head still." She helped him get into his pajamas. She propped pillows on either side of his head in bed and stayed with him quietly until he became muddled by sleepiness.

"Mommy, where are you?"

She bent down and kissed him with tenderness, her love graver. "I'm right here." When he fell asleep, she left to tell Forrest and phone for help. Advised just to keep him still through the night, she came back and sat at the edge of his bed.

The next morning she found Hap sleeping soundly. A little later in the kitchen, Forrie went through his greetings. "Morning, Mom, morning, Pop, morning, Billy, hi, Faith." When Billy returned the same, they heard the crash of someone bumping into a door.

"Help! Mom!" It came as a raw cry. "I don't know where I am." All sounds and movement in the kitchen stopped instantly. Terror in Hap's voice funneled through the hallway. "I don't know where the kitchen is. It's dark." He stumbled down the hall, scraping his shoulder along the wall, his hands groping out in front of him.

Faith gasped. Forrie's fork clattered on his plate. Forrest's hand shot out and grabbed Jean's forearm, as if to forestall her reaction. Time stopped for a moment of utter blackness, shared.

A moment only, then Jean mobilized. She called Franny to be with the other children while she, Forrest and Mother Holly took Hap to San Diego. Most of the day, Hap was stunned. He answered questions, cried, then answered more questions, and constantly held onto Jean's hand. When she drew it away once to get a handkerchief from her purse, he grabbed for her. Even when they came home, Hap still didn't seem to understand. "It's still dark," he cried.

The truth hit Forrie first. He fled the house and ran across the gravel breezeway to his separate room. Jean heard the headboard bang against the wall when he flung himself on his bed. His bawling triggered others and one by one their shock turned to wails. Forrest would have to comfort them. She had Hap to attend to.

She told everyone to go to bed early that night. She had no energy for tucking-in. Except for Hap, they'd have to do it themselves. After he fell asleep under her touch, she wandered from room to room, her mind a kaleidoscope of sharp, painful images. Hap tomorrow. Hap next week. Hap as a young man. Her life again. She picked her way out to the Chinese elm, walking in a daze, her throat choked tight, her eyes burning. She plopped herself in one of the swing seats and wept, trying to be quiet, her fingers cramped around the swing chain.

She had already paid, she told herself. It wasn't fair.

What made her think that they could do it all? Why, after all, was she so special that the manager of the universe would grant her not one or two or even three normal, perfect children, but four? They had gambled too much. Like a tightrope walker overconfident, she had set her line too high.

How would she tell Mother? How could she? She remembered Mother's calm acceptance the day Dr. Wheeler told Mother and Father by her bedside that nothing more could be done. "Well, we'll just go on," Mother had said. If Mother had felt any outrage at the cruelty of Jean's own loss, she kept it to herself. She didn't remember Mother being a blubbering fountain of emotionalism.

Then she mustn't be either.

But it was too much, too much to ask of her. She knew. Better than Mother had known, she knew what this would mean for Hap—isolation, confusion, frustration, an anger which always had to be held in check, and always the question, What can I do? Mother hadn't known that, still didn't know it. No wonder Mother could be calm. She didn't want to know.

Growing up, she had always submitted so easily—to teachers, to Father, even to blindness. Only recently had she felt strong enough to stand up to things, but how could she stand up to the universe? How could she do anything but submit to this? She sank into a hump on the swing.

Crickets, always there were crickets by the swings. Their urgent chirp penetrated her thoughts, and for a moment she listened absently to their syncopated melody. Occasionally, they left an unusually long pause, their note suspended. Each time she thought they had forgotten to chirp, they resumed their uneven rhythm. Usually she loved cricket sounds, but now their irregularity irritated her. It was jangling. Why couldn't it just stop? The continuity hurt.

So that was to be the way. Another person in the world who must walk by faith, not by sight. Another person whose vision must develop alternatively. Another person for whom just living is an achievement.

Suppose that all this time—through her years with Miss Weaver and her inexorable "of course you can," through finding her voice at The Seeing Eye, and through each battle to stuff food down a child's mouth—suppose she was being led to this, to Hap. Yes, that was it. All that for the real test, the life out of hers. Hap's.

Hap would have to enter their own queer shapeless world. He'd have to learn as they had. She gripped the swing chain fiercely and held tight to Miss Weaver's principle that life wouldn't give people what they couldn't handle. Maybe as our capacity for endurance grows, she thought, it is no longer endurance, but just plain life. She wiped her eyes on her skirt and stretched her shoulders back. Her mouth tasted sour. Forrest was somewhere, maybe out with the horses, working through his despair in his own way. Tonight, she thought, he's got to hold me until I fall asleep.

She took a long, slow breath. Hesitant footsteps came from the direction of the barn. "Jeanie, are you out here?" He nearly choked when he spoke.

"Yes."

He came closer. "Are you okay?" His voice was hollow, hardly sounding like him.

"Yes," she said, but it wasn't true. She couldn't say anything else when she knew Forrest felt things, even small things, so intensely. Forrest's highs were always higher than hers, and his lows lower. Despite her own black pain, she felt a need to soften his. She felt older. Stronger. Older than this tree she smelled, this town, older even than words was some impulse that makes woman want to shelter her man.

"We'll work it out together," she said. "With God and with Hap."

"Yes." Uncertainty quavered in his voice thin as a thread. She felt him reaching for her, and she stood up and put her hands on both sides of his head.

"We know what it's like. So we know what he has to do," she said. "He has us. And he has God. And we can teach and trust."

"You're right." The words barely came. "We can. We can."

She brought his head down onto her shoulder. She wanted to articulate what he couldn't, what needed to be said. "God is still good. We've got to know it."

After a moment he nodded, his face buried. They stood by the elm for a long time holding each other, exchanging need for strength by their touch until Jean took him by the hand and they walked back slowly into the house.

Chapter Thirty-six

"Mommy, Mommy!" The panic in Hap's voice knifed through her. "I don't know how to get in." He had gotten outside the three-foot adobe wall surrounding the patio. Though Jean tried to stay right with him for the first few days, he had wandered away when she answered the phone. "I can't find the way in," he called, his voice tremulous.

Inside, Jean came to the doorway. "Yes, you can." She tried to sound calm. "Your father and I found the way in. You can, too." She kept talking to him, knowing her voice would be his only anchor in a swimming world.

His first days passed in the confusion she expected. "I don't know where I am," he whined continually. It was because he tried to do things the same way he always had. He forgot where he set down his toys and lost them, then became angry.

Jean understood. She tried to give him what she knew he needed, moment-by-moment instruction so the frustrations wouldn't swallow him. "Creep up on your milk glass like you're creeping up on a bug," she said. It was a skill he needed immediately. Wiping up his spilled milk was, at best, guesswork. Jean fought against inadequacy all over again.

There were some things she knew she couldn't do. She couldn't teach him how to cut his meat. Mother Holly or Faith or cousin Lancey would have to do that. At every meal he needed a sighted person to guide his hand to the food, to get him sensitive to the weight of food on his fork, to tell him when his fork was level and when it wasn't. Soup was one of those things no one can teach. He'd have to learn how to eat it himself, eventually. She just wouldn't make soup for a long time. She couldn't tell him his mashed potatoes were at six o'clock on his plate and his peas at nine because he couldn't tell time. Before he learned that in first grade, he had probably lost sight of the clock on the schoolroom wall.

Jean drew a clock on his hand with her fingers. "Twelve is at the top. To the right we start at one and then two." She traced the hours around the circle of his palm. Then she did it again. It was tedious and he became fidgety. She touched his hand to a plate. "Pretend this plate is a clock. There's nothing on it. Point with a finger." She guided his chubby index finger in a circle, stopping at each hour. Then she put his hand in the middle of the plate. "Point to twelve o'clock," she said. After a moment she felt for his hand. The method wasn't very accurate, but they had to start somewhere.

Then there was the problem of keeping track of his things. Once she heard him wailing in his bedroom. "What's the matter?" she asked.

"I can't find my shoes."

"Where did you take them off?"

"I can't remember."

"Look in the closet first. Feel around on the floor."

"I did already."

"Did you look by the bed?"

"Yeah."

"Maybe you kicked them under the bed. Look there."

He did. They both did, padding around on hands and knees, bumping into each other.

"Did you have them on when you went to the bathroom before you went to bed?"

"Can't remember."

She understood. So many times she'd forgotten, too, before she had developed a system. "Well, honey, you have to learn to remember where you take them off. And always put your socks in them, too. It's more important now to wear shoes all the time." She reached for him, bent down and kissed his tousled hair.

Yes, she could tell him these things, but it was only talk until he learned for himself. The lessons all came in a rush of immediacy. He needed his clothes now. He needed to eat now. He needed to walk now. And, like any seven year old boy, he needed to play.

"There's nothing to do," he grumbled one day.

So many of the things he used to do were impossible now—riding freely all around the ranch, drawing, flying his airplanes. Instead, he spent time in Billy's room playing his drum set until one day his too-enthusiastic lead foot sent the plunger right through the bass drum. That had been her suggestion, and was good while it lasted, but every day she had to think of a new one.

"What can I do?" He was insistent.

She thought of Forrie's electric train set. It made great engine sounds. "You could probably play with Forrie's train. I think he'd let you if you were careful." It was in Forrie's room, attached to the garage and separated from the house by the breezeway, nearly fifteen feet across the gravel. That would mean another challenge. She heard the screen door close.

"Forrie, where are you?" Hap called.

"Inside. Just come," Forrie said. Echoing the attitude he'd heard, he added, "Mom and Dad can find the way here. You can find it, too."

Good for him, Jean thought. A flood of love welled up for this son whose childhood was tempered by premature responsibility. She heard the train going around the track, but she didn't hear shoes crunching on the gravel. Maybe Hap hadn't started yet. It seemed a long time. Then she heard him bump into the wood pile too far to the left. Pieces slid down. "Ow," he wailed. "Dumb logs." She forgot to ask him if he had shoes on. He'd just have to learn.

"You made it!" Forrie said seconds later, the pride in his voice swelling Jean's heart.

"Yeah."

During the first weeks, Mother Holly did a lot of the cooking to give Jean time to instruct Hap. But Betty was a savior. Life had always been good like that, providing someone just when she needed help. Lucy. Lorraine. Celerina. Even in the hard times, life had a continuity of good to sustain her. She couldn't forget that.

Betty took slow walks with Hap, first along the roads on the Holly property, then more broadly, and reported back to Jean how Hap was doing. Once Jean went with them to Heddy and Karl's, the three walking hand in hand with Hap in the middle.

"The road's a little wet right here," Betty said. "Can you hear it?"

"Nope."

"Walk backwards a few steps. Can you hear the difference?"

"Oh, yeah," he said, and learned something new.

"Can you feel the road go uphill?" Jean asked.

"Yeah." They passed into a cooler area. "Where are we now? What trees are making the shade?" he asked.

"No trees. It's the water tower," Betty explained. "But there are some trees up ahead. Tell me when you think we're there."

Betty made it a game in a way Jean couldn't always do, not just because she couldn't see to do some things, but because she was weary with it. She had lived with it herself long enough. They walked into the sun again and, after a while, they entered shade.

"Here they are," he said. "What kind are they?"

"Hmm, I'm not sure, Hap. Some kind of piney tree with needles nearly as long as your fingers."

"Can't you smell them?" Jean asked. "It reminds me of New England."

Betty walked him over to the tree trunks and had him feel the bark. She was so good with him. She taught him poems and songs, and described what particular birds looked like when they heard them. It occurred to Jean that she leaned on Betty to make the world beautiful for Hap in the same way she'd leaned on Icy. Her grief about Icy's death had dulled now. The sharp wince whenever she thought of her had been replaced by a wistful recollection of carefree days. She wondered if she could ever reach that point with Hap.

She knew he must be full of feelings for which he didn't have words. His questions were usually "What's happening?" or "Where am I?" And still, he seemed basically happy. Was it that a very young child can adjust more easily, she wondered, because he doesn't know the future? Every day when she heard the killdeer and meadowlark whose songs penetrated right to her bones, she tried to convince herself that the same birds she heard sang for Hap as well. A person with perfect vision may not see life at all. She knew this to be true, but that didn't take the pain away.

After the shock lessened, the children became almost too casual around Hap. They went on with their play, because, what else was there to do? The final weeks of summer brought a pressure to squeeze in whatever play they could. Billy drifted in the shadows, probably watching one more, now, who couldn't reach him. Faith listened to Rickie Nelson and covered her bedroom walls with posters. She and Jean still tussled over her messy room and her clothes and laundry excesses until Jean decided that it was time Faith did her own laundry. It resolved some of the tension. Forrie discarded his homemade toy banjo for a real guitar, expanded his train operation and raised three bantam chickens. When one hatched a baby chick, Forrie kept it in a carton in his bathroom.

One day Jean heard him race towards her, yelling in panic. "Mom, Mom, Chickie fell in the john."

"Oh, no, Forrie. Where is he?"

"Right here." Forrie put the limp, dripping chick in her hands.

"Get a towel." Carefully she felt the wet feathers. "He's still breathing." She dried him as best she could, and they laid him in dry towels in a small box. "We have to keep him warm." They took him back to Forrie's room and put the box in front of an electric heater. "Stay with him," she said. "Your father will be home soon, and I've got to get dinner started."

When he came in to eat he told her he had rigged up a light bulb suspended over the box to keep him warm.

"What else can I do, Mom?"

"Sing."

"Sing?"

"If you love him, that's what you do."

When he went back to his room after dinner, she heard his shaky voice singing a few hymns and then "America The Beautiful." She went out to his room at bedtime.

"I don't think he's any better," Forrie said. "Isn't there anything else I can do?"

"Just love him, all night long." Jean sat on the bed. "Don't touch him, but just love him with your heart. It doesn't matter if you get sleepy. You stay with what you love as long as it takes."

"You mean to stay up all night?"

"Yes, if you need to. Don't ever stop loving him, even for a minute. Chickie has to feel your love. You can't discard him just because he's hurt. Feel like you're wrapping your arms around him to keep him warm."

Jean aimed a kiss at his forehead and went back in the house, weary. She went into the big bathroom to run the bath water for a soak. It was one luxury she allowed herself. The air was steamy now, and she nearly tripped over the rumpled rug. "It's clammy. Anybody in here?"

"Me," Faith said. "I just washed my hair, but I'm done now."

"Hap, come on in," Jean said out the doorway. "I've got your Braille, and we can practice a little."

He picked his way down the hall and suddenly cried out in terror and lurched ahead, slamming himself against the wall.

"Geez, it's only a brush, Hap," Faith said. "You don't have to panic."

"It felt like a snake. I thought it was a snake on my back," he said, his voice a tremulous quaver.

"Faith, think before you do something," Jean snapped.

"I just touched his back. How was I to know he'd jump like a grasshopper?" She brushed her teeth, spit with a vehemence into the sink, flung the toothpaste across the tile and left.

"Faith!"

Nothing happened. Jean closed the door, undressed and climbed into the tub. She started Hap on his lessons. A few moments later, there was a knock at the door.

"Yes?"

"It's me." Faith's voice carried the slight grumpiness common when she felt remorse. She moved something at the sink. "Hap, the toothpaste is right behind the cold water knob. I'll try to remember to put it there all the time."

The door closed. Jean felt her eyes puddle up, and she soaked her face with the hot washcloth.

In the morning, Forrie burst through the door into the kitchen. "Mom, Chickie's still alive."

"That's good." She sighed. Actually she was glad, but it seemed inconsequential. Bigger things demanded attention.

In the next few weeks, the chick became Forrie's constant companion. It rode on his shoulder as he walked about the ranch, and sat there content while he practiced guitar.

One afternoon Jean heard Forrie's horrified voice outside. "Mom, help!" He kicked open the screen door. "Mom, I ran over Chickie with my bicycle," he blurted out when the door slammed.

"Oh, no." Jean took a deep breath and held out her cupped hands. Again he gave her the sad little bundle. She explored the fluff delicately and put a finger on his neck under his beak.

"Is he still—?"

"No, Forrie. I don't think so." She steeled herself for his sobs, but they didn't come. "I'm sorry," she said and handed it back. Her own grief was still swollen and she could think of nothing more comforting to say.

Chapter Thirty-seven

Franny brought over some mending she had done for Jean. Every September there were knees to be patched and torn seams to be rejoined. Their midafternoon cup of tea in the kitchen booth stretched to two. They heard the piano in the living room.

"'The Old Gray Mare,'" Franny said. "Faith's at it again."

"That's not Faith. She went up to Heddy's for some cookies."

"Who is it then?"

"Wouldn't be Forrie. He won't touch the piano now that he has his guitar. Could be Billy."

They walked out into the living room.

"It's Hap," whispered Franny in amazement.

"Ssh." They stood there listening while he went through the entire song twice.

"Let him be," Jean whispered and walked back to the kitchen. Franny followed.

"Has he ever done that before?"

"Not that I know of."

"He looked so cute. He was sitting on two pillows. His hand was in a fist and he was punching out the song with his knuckles. He only used the black keys."

"I could tell."

Then Hap went on to other melodies, familiar children's tunes and songs Faith had been practicing. Jean and Franny listened for a long time.

"You didn't know he could do that?" Franny asked.

"No, not at all. When he was three, Mother Holly gave him a toy xylophone for Christmas. You know, one with only an octave of metal plates and a wooden hammer. As soon as he unwrapped it, he started to play 'Silent Night,' just as if he'd been doing it forever, but he needed another note and hit the floor with the hammer. 'I can't do it. Not enough notes,' he said, and put it aside and went on to another present."

"You may have something here you didn't realize, Jean."

"Just at the right time."

"He had his eyes closed."

"That doesn't surprise me. The kids say he does it all the time. We've got to break him of it because it doesn't look normal. Just like not smiling or not facing you. He's got to learn to do that too. Otherwise, anybody who's talking to him feels cut off."

"Eddie doesn't seem to feel that way. Only curious. The other day I found him walking through the house with a blindfold on, just to see what it was like."

"What a pun'kin. How do they play together?"

"Hap hangs onto his belt loop. I don't know how they started that. Sometimes they walk with their arms slung over each other's shoulders. I've even seen them both climbing the tree in our backyard."

"He probably remembers that well enough."

"Sometimes he grabs the long hair on the back of Rusty's neck and follows where Rusty goes."

"Yes, Faith told me that. It seems to work, except that Rusty smacks him with his tail like a whip and sometimes goes off and leaves him. It's not like he was a trained guide dog."

"Listen," Franny said. The sounds from the piano changed to 'Silent Night.'

Jean began working with him on the piano every day, in addition to teaching him Braille. Time was short. She got up an hour earlier to get her things done so she'd have more time with him each afternoon. Her first task was to get him to unfold his hands and use the tips of his fingers on the keys. But he had ability. There was no question about that. He picked up simple melodies she played for him only once or twice. She was elated and wished she could pour into him all that she knew, all the ways she had learned how to live.

The Ramona schools were not equipped to handle unsighted children, and his special teacher wasn't particularly effectual.

"Mrs. Holly," she said one day in a puffed up voice. "You made a serious mistake by starting Hap reading Braille with his right hand. It's caused me a lot of extra work. That child's left handed."

"So?"

"We must allow him to follow his natural inclination."

Jean thought she sounded as if she were reading out of a manual. "He may be left handed, but Braille books aren't. If he traces the line with his left hand, he'll loose the next line and have to search for it. Anyone can figure that out. He's going to read with his right and keep place with his left, regardless of what you say."

"But it's not his natural inclination."

"But it works. Faster and better. I know." She could feel the woman fuming, but she didn't care. What did that woman know?

Hap was caught in the middle. It slowed his progress. His afternoons in the regular second grade classroom were a muddle of confusion. He got further and further behind and was labeled "slow learner" on his report card. It incensed Jean.

She started making phone calls. The larger town across the mountains, Escondido, had ample programs for the unsighted, but it was nearly an hour away on the narrow highway the children called Throw-uppy Road. Still, they enrolled him, and after Christmas vacation they hired a driver.

When Hap arrived home after his first day in the Escondido school, his words tumbled out in excitement. "Mommy, my teacher lets me read however I want to."

"Good."

"And I started to learn to type today. There are four rows and we learned the second from the bottom."

"That's called the home row. What are the letters?"

"ASDFJKL and something else I don't know. Tomorrow we learn some others. And we already started to write Braille. They've got machines like yours to punch it out. And we're going to learn arithmetic on a thing with beads on sticks."

"That's an abacus."

"Yeah, and they've got a big round thing of the world where I can feel the edges of the countries. It's 'chin."

"What?"

"'Chin."

"What's that mean?"

"Oh, you know, good or something."

Every day he had new reports of the 'chin things he was learning or doing. Through his bubbly stories, Jean saw that he loved his teacher, and that apparently other children in the class were friendly. But the ride was long. Sometimes after a rain, huge boulders which had fallen on the road closed it for several days. Often there were mudslides. On those days, he had to be driven the long way around the mountains. It made him two hours late. Sometimes the driver couldn't make it through at all.

"He can't afford to miss school so often," Jean said to Forrest late one night after it had rained all day. "Besides, what kind of school life is he going to have in the years ahead if he can't play with his school friends? He'll always have to leave immediately to come back here."

"You're right. But he can't go to school here. I know every schoolteacher in Ramona. I can just hear them saying the same things they said to me." His voice went up an octave in mimicry. "'It's a shame about the youngest Holly boy. I can't see how he'll ever learn.' That's only because *they* don't have any notion of how to teach him."

"Then I think we'll have to move." Her voice was even. She spoke with as much assurance as if she were saying, "We're having spaghetti for dinner tonight."

"Huh?"

She knew it would catch him by surprise. "I think we'll have to follow him to Escondido." She waited a few moments for it to sink in.

"You're way ahead of me, Jeanie."

"The schools provide free transportation in that district. It'll be better for all of us. Then none of the children have to deal with people who knew Hap before. You know we're a curiosity here. Ramona is too much of a fishbowl. You've said so yourself."

"I know. I know."

"The children will be better off if they see they have to make it on their own, developing their own identities where the Holly name doesn't mean anything in the community. Everybody knows everything about us here, so the kids are expected to be certain things."

"Well, I'll be a bull moose's uncle. You surprise me."

She pressed her advantage. "This is too small a pond for you too, Forrest. Ramona's not growing. Escondido is. You could run your business there, and probably expand it, couldn't you?"

That took longer to settle. Rain drummed dully on the roof. "Yes, I guess I could," he said finally. "After I got established it might grow more there than here. Ed says the city's taking off."

"We can learn a new city. I want some new streets and shops and businesses. And there are cleaners and delivery services and theaters in Escondido that we don't have here. And we could find a good music teacher for Hap. And taxis. We wouldn't have to depend on your mother or Earl or anybody. We could go where we wanted, whenever we wanted. It would be new for all of us."

"You remind me of a female goose leading her gaggle off to new territory."

"Instead of just enduring, we've got to challenge life back. All of us. What you do think?"

"I think, I think you're getting pretty adventuresome."

"No. Not getting. You forget. I have been all along. Only you haven't noticed. If I weren't, I'd still be back in Connecticut."

He let out an astonished, sheepish laugh. "I love you, Jeanie."

He came closer, and she felt his arms enfold her. "What do you think the kids will think about it?" she asked.

"Faith'd like it. It would give her a new bunch of friends to boss around."

She kissed him first on the jaw, then moved to his lips, until a thought interrupted her. "Remember from the Bible where it says 'and a little child shall lead them?'" His arms pressed her tight to him. "It'd be 'chin." She snickered.

"What?"

"'Chin. Hap told me that word. It means good or great or something like that. You haven't heard it?"

"No, but I'll make a wager we're not hearing the whole thing."

In bed, Forrest tossed restlessly. "It's not going to be easy," he said.

"That's not the point. It's necessary."

This private time swelled with the bigness of an idea only they knew. She loved all their private times, their world apart from children, apart from work or houses or bricks or families, apart from his public, guarded self, the moments when their souls were naked and when she knew, though she'd never say, that he was greater by reason of her being there, that she, too, was greater than if she were alone.

Water dribbled from the rain gutter outside their bedroom window. She stretched between the sheets made warm by their bodies, settled in, and, full of love, she fell asleep.

Three months later, moving day came. It was crisp and the morning air felt pure and clean. They ate their last breakfast in Ramona at Franny and Ed's.

"Mom, Hap's got his eyes closed again." Faith's voice wavered between tattling and helping.

"Peeps, Hap," Jean said, her abbreviated reminder to keep his eyes open. Hap grunted.

"Boy, you'd better be glad your water pistol's packed," Forrest said, "or I'd pop you one, right between the eyes."

"And you know he can do it, too," Faith chimed in. "Pop does it all the time, Franny, whenever we tell him."

"I'm going to throw it away," Hap grumbled.

The Mayflower moving van arrived and the family trooped back across the dirt road between the two houses for the last time. Jean wrapped her sweater tighter.

Faith held Jean's hand as they walked. "I'm going to miss Judy, Mom."

"Oh, she can visit weekends any time. And we'll learn places in Escondido you two can ride."

"But I won't have any friends."

"That won't last two days, I bet. We've all got to keep growing. Old friends are sometimes too comfortable. Sometimes old places, too."

"I don't want to say goodbye."

"When you say goodbye to one thing, you usually say hello to something else."

"Can we have a kumquat tree at our new house?"

"Sure."

One by one, the pieces of their Ramona life were carried off and disappeared into the depths of the moving van. The older boys stood staring.

"Mom, one of the Mayflower men has lots of muscles," Billy whispered.

"I'm sure he does."

"How's he going to move the piano?"

"How do you think it got here? Grew? They have a way."

The two men guided it on rollers and hoisted it neatly on pulleys into the van.

"Wow. Look at that," said Forrie, his voice breathy and full of admiration.

"That's 'chin," Billy said.

"What's 'chin?" Jean asked. "Suddenly I hear it all the time."

"Aw, Mom, it's only a word," said Billy, wandering off.

"Is it short for something else, Forrie?"

"Yeah."

"What?"

"Just a word."

"What word?"

"Bitchin'."

"Forrie. That's a barn word. I won't allow that in the house."

"I won't say it in the house. Anyways, we're between houses. We don't have a house today. Besides, we don't say the whole word."

His logic amused her. Maybe she'd just have to grow up with the kids. She went back in the house to find what was left.

Midmorning, Mother Holly brought a pot of coffee for the moving men, and they took a break in the patio. Jean could hear her outside.

"Do you know these people well?" one of the Mayflower men asked Mother Holly.

"Pretty well."

He spoke more softly. "Neither one of them can see?"

"No."

"And the littlest kid, too?"

She heard Mother Holly clear her throat. "Do you remember that old saying about the Lord putting burdens on backs that can bear them? More coffee?"

The six-note melody of a meadowlark trilled through the air and Jean came outside again. "Doesn't that just chill you it's so beautiful?"

"What, ma'm?"

"You mean you didn't hear that, the meadowlark?"

"No, I guess I didn't."

"We hear a couple every day," said Mother Holly.

"I sure hope there are meadowlarks in Escondido. Do you live there?"

"Yes."

"I don't suppose you know?"

"No, ma'm, I guess I don't listen much to birds."

"What a shame. Just think what you're missing. Well, are we nearly loaded?" Jean asked.

"Just about."

Jean asked Mother Holly to write out the check. Then she felt for the lower right corner of the checkbook, edged her hand up a half inch and three inches to the left, signed it slowly and held it out. After a momentary hesitation, the man took it. "Where's your husband, ma'm?"

"Probably out loading his horses. A friend's going to move them."

"He rides horses?"

"All his life he has."

He cleared his throat. "Do you have family where you're going?"

"No. The only family we have is here, and back east. We don't know anyone in Escondido." She sensed what was coming next, but she didn't harden herself against it. She just stood naturally, without the old tense, stay-alert, forward leaning posture. She faced him directly and let a slight smile play over her mouth.

"Excuse me for this, but lady, I don't see how you're going to get by, seeing as how three of you—"

"Your job is to move us. Ours is to keep on moving once we get there." She smiled at him with what she meant as kindness, turned back into the house, and paused in the dining room when her heels tapped against the Mexican tile floor. Right about here was where Forrest lit the matches for candlelight that day. Slowly, she walked through every room and trailed her fingers along the adobe bricks. In Faith's room, she bent down low and felt along the first row of adobes until she found the tooth fairy hole. She smiled. It would be a curiosity to the family that bought the house.

After a while she walked outside again toward the Chinese elm. Her feet felt the scooped-out dips of packed earth where the swings had hung. A warm breeze brought the rumble of Heddy and Karl's chickens. The mint smelled fresh and sweet and green. Her arm went around the trunk of the Chinese elm.

"You look silly, Mom." Forrie laughed. "Looks like you're saying goodbye to a tree."

"I am, Forrie." By themselves, echoing in the darkness, the words struck her with the authority of a private, solid declaration. "I am."

CPSIA information can be obtained
at www.ICGtesting.com
Printed in the USA
LVOW03s1444150817
545102LV00002B/257/P

9 780795 324536